Katharine Noel is a Jones Lecturer at Stanford University, where she formerly held a Stegner Fellowship. Her writing has won grants from the Henfield-Transatlantic, Barbara Deming, and Rona Jaffe foundations, and was included in *Best New American Voices 2003*. She currently lives in San Francisco, where she is at work on her second novel.

Halfway House

Katharine Noel

PIATKUS

Copyright © 2006 by Katharine Noel

First published in Great Britain in 2006 by
Piatkus Books Ltd.,
5 Windmill Street, London W1T 2JA
email: info@piatkus.co.uk

First published in the United States in 2006 by
Atlantic Monthly Press, an imprint of Grove/Atlantic, Inc., USA

The moral right of the author has been asserted

A catalogue record for this book is available from the British Library

ISBN 0 7499 3703 3

Data manipulation by
Action Publishing Technology Ltd, Gloucester

Printed and bound in Great Britain by
William Clowes Ltd, Beccles, Suffolk

For Eric

Nights, the girl came and stood at the edge of the yard. From inside his unlit kitchen Pieter Voorster could just make out her dark shape, bulky in a parka, beneath the oak. A car passed, a sweep of headlights. Hoarfrost covered the grass, and for a moment the girl flared into relief, dark against the silver lawn like the negative of a photograph. She didn't lean against the tree but stood, serious and attentive, looking up at Pieter's son's bedroom. Posture achingly straight.

It was nearly midnight. Pieter pulled the carton of milk from the refrigerator. He turned on the overhead light, then turned it off, self-conscious about being so visible to the girl outside. From overhead came the faint noises of his daughter moving around. She was seventeen and had begun to show signs of the night restlessness that afflicted Pieter.

He lit the stove burner, a blue ruffle of flame. By its light he poured milk into an enameled pan, added cinnamon and nutmeg and a tablespoon of brandy. Small scales of ice puckered the milk's surface: the refrigerator thermostat hadn't been working and couldn't be turned down. His wife, Jordana, sometimes said they lived at fifty-one percent, things working just well enough, or just enough of the time, that they didn't seem worth replacing. There was the CD player whose left-hand side needed to be propped up on magazines, the shower they turned on and off with pliers, the basement that flooded every year in the spring rains. They'd gotten used to eggs that rattled in their shells and half-frozen tomatoes, slushy and bland.

He poured milk into his mug and checked the yard once again. The girl was still there. It was December; they lived in New Hampshire; didn't she get cold?

1

She was still there at one, when he came down and made himself another cup of milk. He managed to sleep then until four, by which time she'd vanished.

At six, he brewed coffee and climbed the stairs to wake the kids for their swim meet. At his knock, Angie yanked the door open. 'Dad!' she cried, sounding delighted.

'Shh. I brought you some coffee.'

'You're wonderful, wonderful, wonderful.' She took the mug, which sloshed dangerously, drops spattering her shirt. His daughter had always been passionate, but lately her enthusiasms were fiercer and could collapse unpredictably into irritability. It reminded Pieter – who was a cellist – of some of the musicians he knew. He had the sense, though, that Angie would grow out of this stage, as she'd grown out of sullen listlessness last spring.

Angie moved a pile of clothes with her foot, clearing a space on the floor so that she could put the cup down. 'Let me read this to you.'

She rushed over to the desk. He bent down carefully to pick up her mug from the floor's welter of clothing, splayed textbooks, and plates of hard toast. 'When did you get up?'

'I've been up. Let me read my paper to you.'

'Are you nervous about the meet? You need sleep—'

'I'm going to win my races anyway.' She searched through the drifts of paper covering her desk. A few sheets fell to the floor. 'Here it is. Listen: "Environmental concerns in Alaska should be the first national priority. In solving the problem of Arctic warming, we also address unemployment and many, if not all, forms of addiction ..."'

Her face shone. Pieter found a space to perch on the edge of her bed. He was tired and not really following. He listened to the rise and fall of her voice, occasionally saying, 'Quieter.'

Angie had her mother's dark, straight eyebrows. Otherwise she looked like Pieter's side of the family: high cheekbones, narrow blue eyes, blond hair. Her shoulders were broad as a man's. This season she'd won nearly every race she'd been in, and she'd broken the state record for girls' hundred-meter butterfly. Then she broke her own record. Even this last month's insomnia didn't seem to affect her power in the water. Since her freshman year, colleges had been courting her, sending catalogs with pictures of multi-

2

racial students studying on the lawn. Now, as application deadlines approached, there were dinnertime phone calls, handwritten notes from administrators and coaches. Her jumpiness and exuberance made sense, given all the attention and pressure.

'What class is this for?'

'It's extra credit. Shh. "The problem of homelessness can be solved by the same means as we repair environmental damage: if every family donates one car. Air-conditioning rips up the ozone layer, which leads to global warming and more air-conditioning. When people die—"'

'Angie. *Angie.*'

'What?' she said, irritated, not looking up.

'You need to get ready. You can work on your paper this afternoon. Or Sunday. Come have some—'

'I'm right in the middle of this.'

'When do you think you'll—'

'*Soon.* As soon as I'm done with this.'

He put the mug down on the desk. 'After the meet, I want you to get the food out of here.'

There was a noise from the side of the room, faint enough he wasn't sure he'd heard anything until it came again, a soft scrabbling. Mice lived in the house's walls. He said, 'I want you to get the food out *tonight*' – just as a nose poked out of the closet. Long whiskers, and then the brown and cream face of a Siamese cat.

'Bean!' Angie cried. She rushed across the room; the cat retreated backward into the closet. Angie fell to her knees and reached inside. Pulling out the cat, she held it under the front legs, its cream-colored body stretching down like taffy. She kissed its nose. 'Did you wake up from your nap?' Kiss. 'Are you hungry?' Kiss kiss kiss.

'There's a cat living in your closet?'

Kiss, kiss. 'They were about to put her to sleep. She has this mark here, like a coffee bean. *Don't* you, Bean? Yes, you do.'

His daughter had a cat in her closet. He knew he should be angry. That his wife would be angry.

'Bean was in a breeding factory, and when her uterus gave out, they dumped her at the pound.'

'What were you doing at the pound?'

'Isn't she beautiful? Can you believe someone would do that?' Angie rubbed her face on the cat's flank. Bean had the crossed eyes

3

and look of sour displeasure that all Siamese cats seemed to have, but she was purring loudly. 'Oh, God, I just thought of something else.'

Shifting her arm so it was under the cat, she rushed over to the desk, found a pencil, and, without sitting, bent to write. 'The hole in the ozone layer's connected to pounds,' she said. 'If we paid more attention to animalsthenwewouldn't—'

'Slow down. I can hardly understand you.'

'No one understands it's all interrelated. *I need to get this down.*'

'Your mother's not going to be happy about the cat.'

Angie whirled around to face him. 'Don't tell her. Tell her it's okay with you.'

'Will you get ready?'

She nodded. 'Will you tell Mom it's okay? Please?'

'We'll see.'

'Thank you, darling, thank you.' She blew kisses off the tips of her fingers. Then she turned and began scribbling on her essay.

It was a relief to let himself back out into the hall, to close the door on his daughter's fervid activity.

Squatting, Angie dunked her goggles in the pool. She ran her thumb around the foam eye sockets. Once she had the goggles on, Angie was almost unrecognizable to Pieter, long blond hair hidden under a swim cap, her arms massive as she shook them out. Most of Cort's teenagers went to Cort High, but the southeast corner of town – where his family lived – belonged to the school district of Applefield, the next town over. Angie's black racing suit had a red *A* on the chest and another smaller *A* on the cap.

Winter sunlight shone through the high dirty windows of the community college gym. The room was warm. The chlorine smell, so much like bleach, and the way sound echoed against tile, always made Pieter think of high school, when he used to take his cello from Queens into Manhattan and play for money in the subway there. If he let himself, he could get lost in memory for half the meet.

Instead, he put his arm around Jordana's shoulders and focused on the swimmers. Clumps of them stood talking; others stretched on the cement floor. The address system crackled, and a man read the names and high schools of girls swimming the Individual

4

Medley. When he said *Angela Voorster,* there were cheers from the Applefield team. Pieter searched their faces, picking out his son. Luke wore a team sweatshirt, hands in the front pocket, the hood covering his short hair. He was sixteen, a year and a half younger than Angie. On another team, Luke might have been a star, but Angie eclipsed the other Applefield swimmers. Angie stretched her arms behind her back. With her oversized shoulders and yellow goggles, she looked like a praying mantis.

'What time did you come to bed last night?' Jordana asked. 'Was the girl still there?'

'There's something kind of heroic about her, isn't there?'

'I was that way about you,' Jordana said. 'Teenage girls are just like that.'

'Angie isn't like that.'

She did her one-shouldered shrug. He was being too literal. 'Angie's Angie.'

Jordana's dark curly hair was frizzy in the humid pool room. She had a thin sharp nose, and her chin – also thin and sharp – pointed up. Today she wore a pilled black sweater she'd had at least since high school, tucked into a pair of boy's jeans Luke had outgrown. Pieter never tired of looking at her face, its angularity and intelligence. To him she was achingly beautiful, even as he was able to see how someone else might find her ordinary, even ugly. She pushed her sleeves up her forearms, which were smooth and olive, the gesture oddly arousing. He needed to tell her about the cat. Later, after the meet.

Kneeling, their daughter splashed water up on her arms and legs. Then she climbed onto the starting block and began to position herself. Up and down the line, other girls were doing the same, their toes over their block's edge, legs slightly bent, hands between their feet. Someone adjusted her cap. Girls pulled backward, testing their positions, then relaxed forward again.

The starter drew an air horn from the pocket of his red sport coat. The girls quieted, making quick last-minute adjustments, reaching a hand up to snap goggles into better position, curling their hands around the edges of the blocks.

'On your mark—'

The swimmers tensed. A little boy near Pieter covered his ears. There was a blare and then immediately a second: someone had false-started.

Pieter and Jordana both groaned. He hadn't realized he was holding his breath until he let it go. The starter had to sound his horn twice more, for the girls who hadn't heard it during the long underwater pullout. Some of the girls took practice strokes before turning and swimming, heads above water, back to the edge.

'Was that Angie?' he asked Jordana, though he knew it was.

'Shit!'

Among the neatly chinoed-and-sweatshirted parents, Jordana stood out with her height and wild dark hair and old clothes. And none of the other mothers yelled *shit* – though they might mutter it – when their kids messed up. Pieter turned away so she wouldn't see him grinning; sometimes his affection made her feel patronized.

'Will the swimmers please take position?'

Raggedly, the swimmers were lining up. A girl in the green-on-green suit of Whitman High School said something to Angie. She laughed, throwing her head back. The laugh echoed in the steamy room. The other girl frowned.

'Will the swimmers *please* take position.'

Angie was the only swimmer not in position. Still laughing, she placed her feet, then bent to hold on to the starting block's edge. When the starter said, 'On your marks,' her body tensed with the others, though their faces were set and grim while hers held the ghost of a smirk. The horn went off and five of the girls shot forward, Angie a beat behind.

The butterfly looked nothing like its name. It was lacerating. Angie tore down the lane, pulling even with the fifth-place swimmer, then ahead, not interrupting the power of her stroke to breathe, passing the fourth-place girl, then the third-place girl just as they hit the first turn. It was as though she and the other swimmers were attached to a pulley; as Angie was pulled up, the others were pulled slowly back. She drew even with the girl in second place. When finally Angie raised her head to breathe – yellow goggles covering her eyes, mouth nearly square – she looked extraordinary, alien, arms rising up together from behind like gigantic wings.

She slammed both hands into the wall, bringing her knees up and pushing with her legs to launch backward. The IM required that swimmers switch from butterfly to backstroke to breast to freestyle. She moved into second place in the first lap of back-

6

stroke, slowly gaining on the girl in the green suit. For two laps they stayed even. When they turned for the second lap of breast-stroke, the other girl's face was long with exhaustion.

'She's pulling ahead!' He had to shout so that Jordana would hear him. He was laughing: breaststroke was Angie's worst. Across the pool, the Applefield team was on their feet. Pieter could see Angie's friend Jess jumping up and down and screaming. Luke cupped his hands around his mouth. Angie hit the turn, shifting into freestyle. The girl in the green suit had fallen back, overtaken by two more swimmers. Angie twisted under for the flip turn and came slashing down the last lap. Around Pieter and inside him was a wave of sound: *Angie, Angie, Angie, Angie.*

Angie slapped the wall. She raised her head and looked around herself, then shouted, pumping her arms in the air, teeth bared. She used her hands to gesture to her team, a gathering motion to mean *cheer, cheer.* The noise dropped back. Angie had won this race against these competitors many times. She continued to roar, pounding the water. Her mouth was jagged, like a bottle broken off at the neck. The pool grew quiet save for her voice.

Pieter and Jordana made their way over to Applefield's area. On land, Angie was graceless. Her height embarrassed her so she slouched. Shoulders rounded, cap still hiding her hair, she talked emphatically to a giggling boy, his neck splotched red with razor burn and pimples. Angie was saying, 'I swam *my* race. If you swim someone else's race, you're fucked up the ass—'

'*Angie!*' Jordana said.

'Up the *ass.* Not that their team doesn't suck. I think I could have swum that race with one arm. I should next time, I should with one arm. The coaches from Yale are watching, though. Not them themselves, they send people to watch. You see that guy? No, don't – Jesus. He saw you look. He's been at every meet.'

Embarrassed – what was she doing? – Pieter stepped between them to hug his daughter. 'You swam a great race.'

'Hi. Hi! I'm just telling him something.' She moved around Pieter and told the kid forcefully how much the rest of the swim team sucked, how all the swim teams in New Hampshire sucked, how stupid people at Applefield High were. The boy, still giggling, tried once or twice to interrupt – *I need to go* – but Angie talked over him. Finally she gave him a bear hug and he escaped. 'Swim

7

your own race!' she called.

'You shouldn't say things like that,' Jordana said. 'God, Angie, that was rude.'

Angie, glowing, seemed not to hear. 'No advice is going to matter for him anyway. This whole team sucks. All's they're interested in is sex.'

Pieter gave his wife a warning glance, not wanting to ruin Angie's happiness. He said, 'You swam a wonderful race.'

'You noticed my breath. You saw that? I was trying not to let on too much. If everyone knew, they'd learn how. So *be wewy, wewy quiet.*'

Angie's best friend Jess came up behind her. She was almost as tall as Angie, with the same broad shoulders and bad posture. Around her waist she'd wrapped a maroon-colored towel that trailed the ground behind her. Jess didn't acknowledge Pieter or Jordana except by a small dip of the head, not quite a nod. She was shy with adults; Pieter had learned that every time he saw Jess their relationship had to start again almost from zero. To Angie, she said, 'We need to see the Clerk of Course.'

'We have plenty of time. Anyways, they'll wait for me.' To her parents, in a pinched, chirruping voice, like a kindergarten teacher's: 'Jess is *such a good girl!*'

Jess bounced on her toes, looking around. 'They won't wait. Come *on.*'

'You should go,' Jordana said to Angie.

'Maybe *you* should go.'

'What has gotten into you?'

Angie laughed.

'You'd better go register,' Pieter said.

Angie gave him an odd, long, serious look. She cocked her head as if trying to figure something out. Then she nodded and followed Jess.

Jordana looked at Pieter. He noticed her hands were trembling slightly.

'She was trying to be funny,' he said.

'I don't think she could swim like that if she was on drugs. Could she?'

Recently, Jordana had been returning to this worry often. Over at the Clerk of Course, Angie was talking loudly and laughing. He said, 'She was up most of the night. The pressure's hard on her.'

8

Jordana shrugged her shoulder, turning away. 'I suppose we're lucky. Beth's daughter has been difficult since she was thirteen.'

A whistle blew and boys lined up for the hundred-meter freestyle. He and Jordana made their way back over to the bleachers. This was Luke's best race, after the hundred breaststroke. Like most of the swimmers, he wore shorts, only stripping down to his Speedo at the last moment. Luke had rusty-brown hair, crew-cut so short it dried almost instantly, and a heavy, jutting forehead. Pulling off his shorts and kicking them aside, he climbed to the block.

Just as the air horn sounded and the swimmers launched themselves into the air, Angie cried out from the side of the pool.

She was running across the wet concrete toward the racing lanes. Still a yard from the water, she threw herself into a high, arching dive that made an almost imperceptible splash.

His wife's hand flew to her mouth. There was a moment of stillness, then race officials scuttled toward the pool edge and Jordana pushed through the suddenly chattering crowd of parents. Pieter followed behind. The starter sounded a painful blast on the air horn; some of the swimmers lifted their heads, confused, looking around. Luke hadn't heard the horn yet; he moved doggedly forward.

'What is she playing at?' one lane judge asked another. 'Is she from Applefield?'

The starting horn blared again; people clapped their hands over their ears.

Angie was swimming along the bottom of the pool. Chlorine clouded the water. The blurriness made her slow strokes seem oddly luminous.

Jordana turned to Pieter. 'Get her out. Will you get her out?'

'What's she thinking?' he muttered.

Jordana was almost in tears. 'Pieter, something's really *wrong*.'

Pieter stripped off his glasses, his shoes and socks and coat. Sometimes he only understood the weight of things through Jordana. Awkwardly, he lowered himself into the water. Its warmth surprised him. He took a few strokes, slowed by his clothes, then dove under.

Without his glasses, his daughter was at first a blob of dark and light. She let him catch her in his arms. He noticed, helplessly, the press of her breasts against him. They surfaced, gasping. Angie

9

didn't make animal cries, or rake her fingernails down her face, like in a movie. Instead she put her arms around his neck, beaming.

Confidentially, she said, 'I'll tell you my secret.' She leaned her forehead against his. 'I don't have to breathe.'

He glanced around; the pool edge was crowded with people.

Angie's hair, dark with water, lay flat and sleek against her head; her eyes reflected the intense blue of the pool. Droplets glinted on her shoulders. She smiled at Pieter. She was strong and young and healthy, her teeth white and even, and her smile was beautiful, at once joyous and knowing. He found himself starting to smile back at her.

Head up, she slipped from his grasp and took two short strokes away. Just before she dove back under the water, she said to Pieter – as though he had a choice – 'Now watch.'

Part One

Chapter One

Another windstorm had knocked the farm's electricity out, so the dining hall was lit by candles. She'd been here three months now, and they'd lost electricity three times. Angie liked how the flickering light made the movements of both Staff and Residents oddly holy, seeming to invest the smallest gesture – emptying a cup, unbuttoning a coat – with grace and purpose. In the candlelight, the tremor in her hands was barely visible. One of the things she hated about lithium was the way she shook, like an old woman. This half-light meant she didn't have to pull her sleeves down over her hands or turn her body so it was between other people and whatever she held. Angie didn't know what she was going to do about the trembling this afternoon, when Jess visited. Keep her hands in her pockets, maybe.

'Eggs and bacon,' said Hannah, folding back the foil from a pan. She lifted the serving tongs. 'What can I get you, Doug?'

'Yeah, yeah.' Doug was sitting on his hands; his long legs knocked against the underside of the table.

'You want both?'

'Yeah.' As he reached for his plate, a coin of scalp shone at the back of his hair where he'd begun to bald.

Hannah was Staff, one of the college students taking a semester off to work at the farm. She'd told Angie that she would write a paper at the end and be given course credit by the psych department. Most of the college students looked like hippies, with their long hair and rough shirts, but Hannah had crew-cut hair and overalls. She wasn't pretty, but she was graceful, and she stood out in a way the prettier students didn't.

She finished serving and closed the tinfoil back over the pans.

Doug had already wolfed down half his food, and he held out his plate anxiously. 'Can I have seconds now?'

'What's the rule, Doug?'

'Not until six-forty-five.'

'Yeah. I don't think everyone's up yet.'

Doug put his hands under his thighs again. He rocked forward. 'I used to have a car. A Honda Civic. It was green. They're good cars, aren't they? Aren't they?'

'Damn good cars,' Hannah said. Angie liked the way Hannah talked to Residents about whatever they wanted to talk about. Most Staff would have insisted on reality-checking with Doug every two seconds, steering him again and again back to the here and now.

The milkers came in, stamping snow from their boots. Sam Manning poured himself sap tea from the samovar. He had gray hair, cracked hands, wrists so wide he could have balanced his teacup on one of them. Sam was the only Resident who milked – the other milkers were on Staff – and he'd been down to the barn already this morning. He sat down next to Angie. When he reached for the sugar bowl, she felt cold air on his sleeve. His boots gave off the sweet, murky smell of cow shit.

'The big day,' he said.

Angie nodded and looked away. With Jess's visit only a few hours off, thinking about it made her feel as though she had something sharp caught in her throat. They hadn't seen each other in the time Angie had been at the farm. Sometimes Angie couldn't bring her memory of Jess's face into focus, which gave her the crazy fear they wouldn't recognize each other. At least the doctor had taken her off Klonopin completely now. She was fat and she trembled, but each word wasn't its own search-and-rescue mission.

'They're good, they're good, they're good cars. They're good cars. They're *good cars*. Mine was green. Not too slow and not too fast. Not too safe and not too unsafe. Not *too* safe. Can I have more bacon?'

'She said six-forty-five,' a Resident said reprovingly.

'She said, she said, she said bedhead.'

Hannah shrugged lightly. 'About ten more minutes, Doug.'

The door behind them opened, bringing the din of wind. Cold air rushed into the dining hall; the candle flames hunched low, wincing. The Residents who'd just come in had to struggle to close the door.

14

'Do you ever see any of your old friends?' Angie asked Sam. 'From before you got sick?'

'Before I got sick was a long time ago.'

'But do you?'

'I'm not like you.' He turned his big hands over, looking neutrally at the dirty nails a moment before looking up at Angie again. 'I've never been good with people. Really, my only friend is my sister.'

Angie still hadn't gotten used to the way people here said agonizing things so matter-of-factly. *He couldn't stay married to a mental patient. My mother says it would have been better if I wasn't born.* Angie said, 'You have lots of friends here. You have me.'

'You were asking about outside, though. You're nervous about your friend coming.'

'Not really,' she lied. Jess had been her best friend since second grade. Up until the breakdown, they'd seen each other almost every day. Now when Jess called on the pay phone, Angie sometimes whispered, 'Tell her I'm not here.'

Hannah yawned, covering her mouth with the back of one hand, blinking as her eyes watered. The yawn went on so long she looked embarrassed by it. Gesturing toward the long table behind her, she said, 'I've been up since four making bread. It's still hot, if anyone wants some.'

'I fed on dead red bread, she said. She said, come to Club Meds in my head.' Doug rocked forward, then back. 'Is it lemon bread?'

'Just regular bread. Wheat bread.'

Doug shook his head, making a face. He was too tall to sit at the table without hunching, and his knees hit against the underside, making the plates jump. 'Sorry, sorry.' He hunched even more. His scalp showed, waxy, through his hair.

Nurse Dave had the meds box. He poured three pills into Doug's cupped palm: Klonopin, a green pill Angie didn't recognize, and the same yellow and gray capsule of lithium she took three times a day. She looked away. Their movements were shadowed on the wall behind them, Nurse Dave straightening up, Doug remaining stooped as he reached for his water. The nurse watched Doug swallow his pills, then handed Angie her envelope, which she tucked beneath the edge of her plate. She'd only just gone from monitored to unmonitored meds, which meant no one watched her

15

take them. She wanted to wait a few minutes, to make being unmonitored matter.

'An engine is a thing of beauty,' Doug said.

A Resident muttered, 'Here we go.'

Hannah kept her voice casual. 'What did you do last night, Doug? Did you watch the movie?'

'An engine is a thing of beauty, a thing, a thing, thing of *beauty*. In*ject*or, *int*ake *man*ifold valve spring *timing* belt *cam*shaft *inlet* valve com*bust*ion chamber *pis*ton skirt alternator *cool*ing fan *crank*shaft *fan* belt *oil* pan gasket oil *drain* plug oil *pan air* conditioner com*pres*sor—'

Hannah glanced at the clock. It was only six-forty, but she said, 'Do you want some more bacon, Doug?'

'*Fly*wheel *en*gine block ex*haust* manifold exhaust *valve* spark plug *rocker* arm spark plug *cable* cylinder *head* cover vacuum diaphragm, distributor *cap,* in*ject*or, *int*ake manifold valve *spring,* timing *belt,* camshaft, *inlet* valve, com*bust*ion chamber, *piston* skirt *al*ternator *cool*ing fan crankshaft.' When someone rose, their shadow – huge and flickering – leapt up and slid across the east wall, stooped as they scraped their plate, straightened to set the plate in the sink. Doug rocked forward in his chair. 'Fan *belt* oil pan gasket oil drain plug oil pan air compressor – con*di*tioner – compressor flywheel engine block exhaust manifold. Inlet *valve*. Combustion *chamber. Piston.*'

At seven, they went in to Morning Meeting. Everyone wore jeans and work boots at the farm – Residents' usually newer and nicer, Staff's more likely to be worn and mended. Angie and Sam found seats together. Across from them, a Resident in a denim hat licked his chapped-to-bleeding lips, over and over. Staff whispered something to him and he stopped for a moment. Aside from the attendance sheets balanced on the Resident advisers' knees, Morning Meeting reminded Angie of Unitarian Church services she'd gone to a few times with Jess: folding chairs, announcements, singing with guitars.

To the east, against the mountains, the sky was purple with dawn. Some Staff were knitting, needles clicking softly. It would be nice to have something to do with her hands. Sitting here left too much room to think, so that Morning Meeting often turned into a half-hour meditation on ways she'd fucked up. The last time she'd gone to Jess's church hadn't been long before she jumped

16

into the pool, maybe a week. She'd gulped vodka in her room before church, trying to calm down – she'd been awake for days – and the combination of mania and alcohol meant she didn't remember much of the morning now. She did remember banners made of felt on felt, JOY, PEACE, an abstract chalice. She remembered screaming with laughter at the stupid banners, she remembered during the service talking loudly to Jess, she remembered falling down after the service, suddenly surrounded by legs. The way the noise was sucked out of the room. By her face was Jess's mother's ankle, stubbled with hair. The silence after her fall had probably only lasted a couple of seconds, but it had seemed much longer. On Mrs. Salter's ankle, she saw each black hair sprouting sharp from its follicle, each follicle a pale lavender indent, and under the skin the hair continuing down, ghostly, toward its root. Above the ankle bone was a small scar, white as a chalk mark. Angie could see Mrs. Salter in the shower, rushing a pink razor up her calf; the sharp, coppery taste that came into your mouth even before you consciously knew you were cut; the way that for a minute the area around the cut would have flinched back, and then the cut would have flooded with blood, not red but pink because her skin was wet, washing in a pale, wide stream down her ankle bone and foot; the way she would have cursed and pressed the cut with her fingers. Angie reached out and touched the scar. In the moment before Mrs. Salter reacted, Angie could feel a tiny seam beneath the tip of her finger, as though someone had taken two neat stitches there with white thread. Inside the scar was Mrs. Salter's soul. The soul was just that small, tiny and white as a star. For one moment she understood the realness of Mrs. Salter to herself, how to Mrs. Salter the world radiated out from her own body. Angie could feel that for every person in the room at once; she felt the room's hundred centers.

Mrs. Salter jerked her leg away.

The noise of the room had flooded back in. One of the noises was someone laughing, yelping, wildly. Someone had said, 'Is that girl okay?' Someone, Jess, had said, 'Stop it, Angie, stop it, *stop it*.'

Sam put his hand on her arm. 'Angie? We're supposed to be going out to the truck.'

Angie was bent over, arms around herself, face against her thighs. When they'd pulled her out of the pool, she'd been raving about the Olympics and breathing on the moon. Nothing, she was thinking – nothing, nothing – could make her fall apart in front of Jess again. She would be okay as long as she was careful, as long as she kept her hands out of sight, as long as she kept her thoughts on track. As long as she focused on the small details, as long as she made that be enough, as long as she made that be everything.

They rode the half mile to the barns in the back of a rattling Ford pickup. On sharp turns the key sometimes fell out of the ignition. The wind had died down to an occasional blast, sharp enough to pierce through Angie's coat. Though the sun was weak, the snow on the ground shone. They jolted slowly down the road, past the residences – Yellow House, White House, Ivy House – past the director's house, past the orchard, which in the summer held beehives. Sheep lifted masked, unsurprised faces to watch them. The llama had matted hair and a narrow, haughty expression. He detached from the flock and jogged mincingly toward the fence.

At the cowshed, the driver turned off the ignition; the truck continued to shake for a minute longer. Angie climbed up onto the rusty ledge of the truck bed, jumped heavily down. Pulling her scarf over her nose and mouth – as she breathed she tasted ice crystals and damp wool – she went around to the passenger-side door. Her hands were clumsy in her leather gloves, and it took three tries to unhook the baling wire that held the door closed. When the wire finally slipped free, she took a few awkward steps backward in the high snow, holding the door open. Sam Manning had been riding in the cab. He clambered down, and then together he and Angie wired the door shut again.

After the snow's glare, the inside of the barn seemed dim. Written above each stall were the names of the cow's sire, her dam, the bull she'd been mated with, and then the cow's own name: MOLLY, MAGGIE, JENNY. Angie helped unclip the cows from their long chains and herd them out into the frozen side yard. Jenny went uncomplainingly, but when Angie went back for Maggie, she balked at the doorway. Angie hit her, then set her shoulder against the cow's heavy haunch and pushed. Maggie set her hooves, tensing back. Her huge eye rolled wildly. Beneath Angie's cheek, the cow's coarse hair smelled of rumen, straw, and manure, at once pleasing and abrasive. 'Come *on,*' Angie said, banging the cow with her shoulder. Maggie didn't budge, and then all at once she gave in and came unstuck. As though it were what she'd

18

intended all along, she trotted out. In the yard, the cows crowded together, standing head to rump, their breath rising in dense white clouds. Angie unzipped her jacket and stood, hands on hips. Clouds of her breath – smaller than the cows' and more transparent – rose in the icy air.

Back inside, she pitchforked up yesterday's matted straw. Mixed in were crumpled paper towels, stained purple with teat disinfectant the milkers used. The barn was warm and close; Angie took off her jacket, hanging it on a nail. Another Resident, Betsy, turned on the radio, an ancient black Realistic balanced between two exposed wall studs, dialing until she found a faint heavy-metal song, fuzzed with static.

'No voices,' said Sam Manning.

'No voices,' the team leader agreed. Betsy rolled her eyes, tried to find another station. Finally she turned off the radio.

'They're all going to talk *sometime*,' she said. 'There's going to be *commercials*.'

In silence, they used brooms to sweep the floor clear of the last chaff. Then Sam Manning hosed down the concrete. Sam was more than twice Angie's age, someone whom – outside the farm – she would never have even known. In this new life, though, he was her friend, her only real one, the only person who laughed when she made a joke instead of looking worried. They'd first found each other on Movie Night because they both voted for videos that lost. They wanted *Chinatown* instead of *Crocodile Dundee, Witness* instead of *Top Gun,* anything instead of *Three Men and a Baby*. Angie went to the Movie Nights anyway; she had nothing better to do. She and Sam sat in back and made fun of the dialogue.

When Sam was twenty, voices had told him to kill his twin sister, then himself. He'd come to her college dorm and stabbed her in the stomach. She screamed and rolled away and his second thrust went wild, tearing open her arm. He managed to stab her a third time, in the thigh, before the resident adviser's boyfriend ran in and wrenched the knife away. Sundays, Sam's sister came to the farm, and they sat together smoking. She was also burly, also iron-haired. Her limp was barely noticeable, but if she pushed up her sleeve, a knotty scar ran from her right elbow down her forearm, almost to the wrist. There had been such extensive nerve damage that she couldn't use her right hand. It stunned Angie what could be lived around in a family: Surely it shouldn't be possible, their sitting together on the stone wall by the sheep barn. She'd seen the sister reach for Sam's lighter, dipping her left hand into his shirt pocket as naturally as if it were her own.

At nine-thirty, they took a break. Hannah drove down from the kitchen, swinging herself out of the truck cab. Her jeans were made up more of patches than the original denim. She reached back into the truck for chocolate chip cookies and a thermos of cider.

The cookies were hot from the oven. The Residents and Staff stood in the lee of the barn, eating the cookies and smoking, ashing into a coffee can of sand. Angie, not a smoker, wandered over to the fence and watched the cows.

Hannah came up beside her. 'Why do you think everyone here smokes?'

'Everyone did at the hospital, too. I don't know why.' Angie wiped the corners of her mouth to make sure she didn't have chocolate smeared there.

'It drives me—' Hannah cut herself off. 'It's annoying.'

Angie said shyly, 'I like your jeans.'

'Yeah?' Hannah looked down, considering them.

Angie's sweater snagged on the fence. She pulled it free, leaving a wisp of green wool in the rough wood. She rubbed her mouth again, in case there really was chocolate there. Hannah sometimes hung out with her like this for a few minutes when she delivered Morning Snack. Suggesting to herself things she might say to Hannah and then rejecting them, Angie pretended to be wholly absorbed in watching the cows. They looked miserable in the field, barely grazing. Melting ice dripped from the undersides of branches. If she closed her eyes, she could hear the drops all around her, running together into a sound like tap water. She probably looked crazy, standing with her eyes closed. She opened them and said, 'It's almost spring.'

'People say spring's a hard time at the farm. A lot of people have breaks.'

Angie glanced at her, but Hannah didn't seem to be remembering Angie as one of the group at risk for breaks. Trying to use the same casual tone, Angie asked, 'I wonder why in the spring? I'd think, like, a month ago, when it was so gray all the time. And, you know, cold.'

'Apparently the change does it. In winter people hold together as long as it seems things are going to get better. Then when things

20

do start getting better – I can't explain it well. We had a training on it. They said until things stabilize again midsummer, April's the last good month.'

All through lunch, she talked to Hannah in her head. She imagined telling how parts of her past seemed to belong to another person, a crazy girl who broke stuff, tore books apart. After the pool thing, when she'd been admitted to the hospital, they'd thought she was schizophrenic. The first antipsychotic they put her on, Mellaril, had made her more psychotic. It had also made her neck and jaw muscles stiffen so tight that she could barely talk. Sometimes she'd fallen out and been put into Isolation, where she threw herself against the wall until aides arrived to sedate her and the world stretched out thick and flat.

Hannah would say, *I can't imagine you like that. You're right, that's totally not you.*

Sitting in the TV room, waiting for the Town Trip, she told Hannah silently about her younger brother, the way he sulked and snapped on visits. She said, *You've seen him, right?* and in her head Hannah said, *I think maybe. Reddish hair?* She confided to Hannah that she hadn't taken her meds this morning; she hoped it would make her shake less. She was going to take a double dose tonight, as soon as Jess left.

Jess.

She was too wired to sit here. She had half an hour before the van left for Town Trip. Out on the front porch, she pulled her parka tighter around her body and started walking. Wind stirred up small eddies from the surface of the snow. She turned and cut up into the woods.

In the woods, the snow was deeper. Trees' black branches rubbed together, moaning. The high snow made walking hard; she stopped to unzip her parka. She thought about lying down to make a snow angel, then – as she started to lower herself – thought maybe there was something crazy about lying down in the snow and straightened and went on.

Hannah lived in one of the small Staff cabins out here in the woods, little houses without plumbing. In the winter Angie had helped deliver wood to these cottages. She'd still been on anti-psychotics, but Klonopin at least hadn't made her crazier like Mellaril had. Her few memories of the insides of the cabins had a

21

dreamy, unanchored quality: a red blanket, a shelf of books, a propped-up postcard of a painting.

The clearing between Angie and Hannah's cabin was wide and very still. Thin smoke twisted from the chimney. She saw a small brown hawk the moment before it launched itself from a tree into the air. There was the soft thump of snow falling onto snow, the *hush, hush* of wings. Walking through snow had soaked Angie's pants to the knees, and she shivered.

Just as she was turning to go, the cabin door opened. Hannah emerged, walked a few feet, drew down her jeans, and crouched. In the woods, everything looked like a pen-and-ink drawing: white snow, gray smoke, black trees and the cold blue wash of shadows at their bases. Hannah seemed drawn with ink too, as she stood again, pulling up her jeans. Short dark hair, the white undershirt she wore, then the closing of the cabin door behind her.

The wind paused. Angie walked toward the cabin. From inside came the chirrup of the woodstove door. A log thrown on the fire, and then a silence that stretched over the clearing to its edge, where the snow disappeared in the bases of trees. Where Hannah had been, the snow was pocked yellow. Angie felt oddly exhilarated. She crouched, using her teeth to pull off her mitten and put her hand above the surface, feeling warmth mixed with the cold air rising against her palm.

The Town Trip was to Sheepskill, thirty miles from the farm. Hannah parked the old van behind the health food store. Hitting the parking lot, the Residents were like a clump of fish being released into a tank, turning disoriented in place for a moment, then separating. Two of the lowest functioners headed together toward Sheepskill's supermarket. Others walked in the direction of the drugstore, the record store.

Angie lingered near the van. Kicking snow from her boot sole, she said, 'Today's the day I'm meeting Jess.'

'I remember.' Hannah finished writing the names of Residents who had come to town, then tossed the checklist onto the front seat. 'Are you nervous?'

Angie's stomach kept twisting, like a rag being wrung out. 'No. I guess a little. I haven't seen her in a long time.'

'It'll be fine,' Hannah said, pulling the van door shut. She reached and touched Angie's arm briefly. Then she took two steps backward, waved. 'Go on. It will be fun.'

As a meeting place, Angie had chosen the Daily Grind, Sheep-skill's less popular coffee shop, where they weren't as likely to run into other Residents. Walking down Main Street, she tried to see the town as Jess might. The stores had high square fronts and faux nineteenth-century signs, or else real 1950s ones. The banked snow was melting, filling the street with gray slush. In front of the gas station was a boy her age with a smudgy mustache, jaw raw with acne. He lifted a mop from a bucket of hot water, rolling the handle between his ungloved hands so the strings flared into a circle, then bent to swab the sidewalk. His body, beneath the blue-gray jacket, was beautiful. In the cold air, clouds of steam rose from the bucket. A handmade sign advertised free maps with a full tank of gas.

The Daily Grind was at the top of a steep hill. The slush made walking difficult; with every step, Angie slid half a step back, arms out to her sides for balance. Even with the hard physical barn work, she'd gained weight on lithium, and she reached the top of the hill breathing heavily. On the café's porch, while she tried to pull her clothes straight, a woman came out, holding the hand of a little boy. He had hockey-player hair, cut very short on top and left long in back. The boy said, 'Mom, I want—' and the mother yanked his arm, hard. 'I told you, don't say *I want,*' she hissed.

Jess stood as Angie came in. Angie's fear that she wouldn't recognize Jess had been crazy; she looked more familiar than Angie's own reflection would have.

Jess's long hair was pulled back in a ponytail. As she stepped forward, Angie stepped back, then realized Jess had meant to hug her. They bumped together awkwardly, Angie's hands still in her pockets.

'You look great!' Jess said.

'The coffee's pretty good here.'

'It's been so long since I've seen you!'

'Do you want some coffee? I'll get it.'

'No, I'll get it.' Jess reached back for her purse. 'My treat.'

Once, Angie would have said – what? Something sarcastic about Jess's generosity. She sat, then looked quickly around the café, relaxing when she saw she'd been right: no other Residents. Inside her pockets, Angie's hands were trembling, despite skipping her meds. She needed to calm down or she'd sound like a mental

23

patient: the response to *you look great* was not *the coffee here's pretty good.*

'Here,' Jess said. 'I got you a muffin too.'

If she gripped the cup hard enough, it stilled her hands. The coffee was black, bitter and delicious. The farm didn't have coffee. On town trips, Residents bought jars of instant and brought them back. At the farm, tablespoons of dried coffee were a currency as valuable as cigarettes, more valuable than real money.

There hadn't been coffee in the hospital either. The first morning last fall that she'd woken up on the locked ward, she had such a bad caffeine headache she'd shivered and vomited. She'd told the nurses she was dying, she had a brain tumor, she was descended from Scottish kings and she was dying on a shitty filthy mother-fucking ward. She took off her clothes and lay down on the floor of the bathroom. The small cold tiles under her cheek had, for a moment, brought her shockingly back – she said her own name to anchor herself, 'Angie, Angie, Angie' – but then the nursing aides tried to move her and she'd become terrified, scratching and biting, and that was the first time she'd ended up in Isolation.

Jess said, 'Your brother probably tells you everything about school.'

Angie shook her head. Luke didn't tell her much.

Jess visibly relaxed. She began talking about who had broken up, who had gotten into what college, the swim team. In the café were two geeky junior-high boys playing chess, a woman with a sleeping baby, a middle-aged man sketching. No one had any reason to think Angie was anything other than what she appeared, a girl in jeans, drinking coffee with a friend on a Saturday. She tried to listen to Jess, but her attention was on the street outside the door, willing Residents to stay away. So she wouldn't turn to look, she held herself stiff. Each time the door opened, she felt herself jerk in her seat. Jess smiled at something she was saying and Angie told herself, *Smile.* She was relieved to realize that Jess, in her narration of the last three months, wasn't going to mention why Angie hadn't been at school. Jess said some of the cheerleaders had been booted off the squad for coming to a game drunk. She laughed. Late, Angie laughed too.

Jess looked down at her cup. She picked it up and swirled it.

Outside, a car moved carefully up the street, headlights on. In the slushy snow, its tires made a sound like ripping silk. It was three-thirty in the afternoon, the light beginning to fade. Jess at last looked up. They smiled at each other helplessly. 'More coffee?' Jess asked.

If she drank more coffee she would be sick. She could just hold the cup and not drink. 'Sure. I'll get it.'

'Sit down, sit down.'

She sat down. Her hands were too trembly, anyway, to carry two mugs without spilling.

Jess bustled over to the counter, joked with the girl working. It was Angie, not Jess, who was usually good with strangers, but suddenly Jess had taken on the role of Competent Friend. On the way back to the table, she raised one hand – holding a full cup of coffee! – and used the back of her thumb to push hair out of her eyes. She sat down, saying, 'I'm so tired.' She bent her head, resting it on her arms.

While her head was lowered, Angie said quickly, 'The farm's like – my parents think I have to be there. The doctor doesn't even think I have what the first doctor thought I had. No one has a clue, really.' It seemed true as she said it.

Jess sat up. 'You must be so pissed.'

'It's not so bad. People are pretty normal.'

'In your letter you said they were pretty crazy.'

What had she written Jess? 'Well, some people. Not most people, though. I'm friends with this girl, Hannah, she's just taking a semester off from school.'

'So it's like that? I mean, some people are – some people need to be there, but other people are just . . .'

'Just there.' For the first time all afternoon, her footing began to feel sure, not just because she'd found a softened, not totally untrue, way to describe the farm but also because, next to Hannah, Jess would seem awkward and unremarkable. 'I mean, I wasn't going to come back to school in the middle of the *semester*. I think what I had before was a nervous breakdown, trying to do too many things at once. Everyone freaked out, but that was pretty much all it was.'

'You know, that's what I thought. I mean, it's not like you're psycho.'

'The hospital will make you psycho, though.' You weren't allowed to say words like *psycho* or *crazy* at the farm; using them felt like throwing off heavy blankets. 'When I was in there, at the

25

hospital, everyone was treating me like I was really sick. My parents were all—' She made her face pinched and solemn. 'And everyone was saying I'd have to take meds, *medication,* forever. You begin believing it.'

'In the hospital, I should've come see you.'

'No, you shouldn't have.'

Angie felt the conversation set its hooves and stall. She said one of the things she'd said to Hannah in her head: 'When I think of the hospital, I don't know who I am.'

'What's that supposed to mean, you don't know who you are?'

'I mean it's confusing. I think about things I . . . Jesus. I mean, it's the world that's fucked up.'

Jess pushed some crumbs into a line.

'I mean, isn't it?'

'I don't know. I guess so. I don't know.'

The door opened and shut. This time, they both turned. Sam Manning, stomping ice from his boots, raised his hand in greeting.

'Who's that?'

'A Res— someone from the farm.' At least Sam was normal. Wasn't he? She had the time he was in line to think what to say about him to Jess, but her brain felt slow. She raised her coffee and found she'd drunk it all.

Near them, a little girl was kneeling on the floor. Two women talked at the table above. Periodically, one of them called down, 'Are you okay, Liza?'

The girl didn't respond. She had straight bangs that fell into her eyes and a wind-up toy, an alien with arms hugged to its body and three eyes across its forehead. The little girl wound a key in its side and it ran awkwardly, body pitched forward so that with each step it teetered and seemed barely to catch itself from falling.

Angie said, 'They always make aliens look just like humans with one thing different.'

'What?'

Angie's hands were jumping on the mug. She put them between her knees, pressing to still them. 'Do you mean what did I say or what did I mean?'

'Which thing is different?'

'I don't mean there's a specific thing, I mean they change something.'

'What are you talking about?' Jess looked suddenly on the verge

26

of tears. 'You're not even acting like you're happy to see me. I don't know what's wrong with you.'

'Nothing's wrong with me!'

Jess flinched and looked away.

Sam was making his way over. He had a shambling walk – was that weird? – and blue down vest – weird? – and carried his mug carefully, watching to make sure it didn't spill. 'Hey, Angie.'

'Hey.'

There was a silence, then Jess introduced herself.

'I know,' said Sam. 'I've heard a lot about you.'

'You have.' Jess raised an eyebrow at Angie, who looked away. Jess asked Sam, 'Do you want to sit down?'

'I guess, for a minute.' Sitting, he looked around the café, cracking his knuckles. On his right hand, the fingers were stained dark yellow with nicotine. 'How long was your drive?'

'Four hours,' Jess said. 'The roads were pretty good.'

'You were lucky. Last night we had a windstorm.'

'In New Hampshire, we had a windstorm last year that killed two people. A tree came down on their car.'

Angie relaxed a little. This was a normal conversation. She was pretty sure. Sam asked about the colleges Jess had applied to, and Jess listed the places she'd gotten in and the places she hadn't. She thought she'd go to Bates. Had he gone to college? He had. Tufts University. 'But I didn't—'

Angie blurted, 'What do you think Hannah does on these trips?'

'Hannah?' Sam turned toward her. He was so big and so slow-moving. He said, 'Are you okay?'

'No. No. I just – right.' She lifted her mug – no, all gone; she put it down. Too hard: it skipped and started to totter and Jess grabbed to steady it. Jess and Sam had identical expressions on their faces. They looked like her parents had begun looking at her last fall, wary and assessing. She laughed loudly. 'You don't have to look like that.'

'Like what?' Sam asked.

'Like I've just run over your dog.'

'I don't have a dog.'

Angie laughed again. She rolled her eyes at Jess, then saw that Sam was watching her. She froze, halfway through the motion, mouth still open, eyes wide.

'Okay,' he said. He pushed back from the table and smiled

27

weakly. 'I guess you girls need time alone. I forgot how long it's been since you saw each other.'

Jess said, 'Stay, it's okay, we've had forever to talk.'

Sam shook his head. Angie remembered how he'd said his sister was his only real friend. She hated the emptiness of his life. When he stood and said, 'Well . . .' she let him walk away.

At four, ten minutes before the van would leave, Angie and Jess stood outside the café saying goodbye. The light had become grainy; in a half hour it would be dark. Low above the latched black branches of trees, the moon was barely visible against the equally pale sky. A parked car, finned and low, its headlights left on, floated at the curb like a blind fish.

'I have to go,' Angie said.

Suddenly, too late, she felt how much she'd missed Jess. They used to say goodbye like this, lingering at a corner. They'd call each other sometimes ten times a night. For a moment, it seemed homesickness would knock her down.

'Well, bye,' Jess said.

'You have a long drive.'

Jess shrugged. She bounced her keys in her gloved hand, looking off. Then she looked at Angie. 'You're okay, right? Are you okay?'

How many times removed was she from okay? She nodded, tightening her coat.

As she started down the hill from Jess, she could see – spread out through Sheepskill – other Residents, straggling back singly and in pairs. She saw the whole town as a pattern of streets, glazed with late-afternoon light, leading to the van. When she turned, Jess was still standing in front of the café, watching her. Angie gave a hearty whole-arm wave, the kind people on boats gave to people on shore.

At the van, a few people still milled around, taking advantage of the last few minutes off-farm. She put her hand into her pocket and found, still unopened, the envelope holding her meds.

Pretending to cough, she bent and dropped the crumpled packet in the snow, quickly burying it with her foot. As she straightened, her face burned, but no one seemed to have seen. Ahead of her in line, Doug chanted, 'Thing of beauty, thing of beauty.' Someone else – low, so Hannah wouldn't hear – said, 'Shut up, Doug,' and he did.

Angie walked hunched over through the van to a seat in the back. Two Residents talked loudly. Hannah asked, 'Julie, is your seat belt on?'

'Yup.'

'Angie? Seat belt?'

Out the window, the air was lined, as though with sleet: the last few moments between dusk and true evening.

'She's got it on,' someone said.

Hannah backed and feinted, backed and feinted, turning the van around. They drove slowly out of the lot. Angie leaned her head against the cold, rattling window glass. She felt like a small child, as though it were years ago and she was riding the school bus. In second grade, Jess had had a brown rabbit coat, so soft that Angie had found excuses – the bus going over a bump – for her hand to brush Jess's sleeve. They'd been best friends, by then, four months. During math time, they drew insulting pictures of each other naked. 'This is you,' Jess whispered, drawing salami-shaped breasts on a straight-sided woman. 'Well, this is *you*,' Angie whispered, and scrawled armpit hair onto her own picture, pressing so hard the pencil lines shone silver.

The van turned a corner and Angie saw the real Jess, head down, walking to her car. Angie started to duck, but Jess wasn't looking her way. She had her parka hood up and her arms around herself for warmth. As Angie watched, she broke suddenly into a run. Still hugging herself, she ran awkwardly, body pitched forward so that with each step she teetered, seeming barely to catch herself from falling.

Chapter Two

Spring air came, cold and green, through the opened window of Jordana's office, ruffling the papers on her desk. It was seven in the morning; she didn't need to be here for nearly two more hours. Though the office was ugly – low pocked ceiling; the thin tremble of fluorescent light – sitting here with the newspaper and her coffee was the part of the day when she felt least sad.

The Women's Clinic took up the fourth floor of an office building that also held a bank, real estate offices, a tax attorney, a hair salon, and two dentists. Before moving into this building they'd rented a Victorian close to the town center, but they'd decided it was too vulnerable to protests and sabotage. She pulled open the lower drawer of her desk, propping her feet on it, and stared out the window. From the bread factory across the street wafted the thin sweet smell of baking. On the building's side, a giant painted baker chuckled in a tall white hat. Blinking orange neon spelled out GOOD BREAD, with the outline of a brown loaf floating above the words.

Pushing back from the desk, she went into the lab room and measured more coffee into the machine. She leaned back against the counter with the bagel she'd brought for breakfast. Biting into it was as tasteless and dense as taking a bite out of the White Pages. Her jaw ached as she tried to chew; she stuffed the rest back in the bag. Coffee had just begun to spatter down into the pot, and for something to do she pulled on latex gloves and began to unload sterilized speculums from the autoclave. She held her breath, hating the singed smell.

Back in her office, she opened the newspaper. These days, concentrating enough to read a novel was usually beyond her; she skimmed and jumped ahead even when looking at *The White Moun-*

30

tain Times. The fear she'd felt when Angie was first hospitalized had worn down into an anxiety so persistent it almost felt like she'd always had it – a burning pressure in the chest, squeezing her lungs. The breeze from the window thumbed the edges of the newspaper pages. When she came across one of Ben's photographs, she felt a tiny, dim shock of pleasure. He called the paper a birdcage liner, but looking at it made her feel close to him.

Slowly, the clinic woke around her, the muffled noises of people putting away coats and finding the day's files and greeting one another. Four floors down, tiny people got out of cars, pulling briefcases and tote bags from backseats. A protester who came every day – he'd followed them from the old location – got off a bus, a plastic lawn chair under one arm, his Magic-Markered poster under the other. He was an old man with a roughly crumpled face and a blue parka that must not have been much protection on bitterly cold days. Because she knew what the sign said, she could read the letters from here: PLEASE PLEASE LET YOUR BABY LIVE. WE WILL HELP. Jordana spent so much time watching the protesters – some weekends there were a dozen or more – that occasionally at night she dreamed she was one of them, standing outside the clinic with a placard.

Midmorning, in the middle of an appointment, Iris buzzed her from the front desk to say Angie was on the phone. 'She doesn't sound so good.'

Jordana said, 'Excuse me a moment,' to her client, a girl about her daughter's age but claiming to be older; sometimes girls thought they couldn't have abortions unless they were eighteen or twenty-one. The girl shrugged and looked away. Jordana went into the labwork room down the hall. When she picked up the phone Angie was crying, a harsh, congested sound.

'What is it? Did something happen?'

'Everything is shit,' Angie choked out.

Not an emergency; she relaxed a little. 'Ange, that's not true. That's just not true. You're doing so well there—'

'Ma, I'm mucking out stalls!'

'You're getting up in the mornings, you're working—'

'That's nothing,' Angie said. 'You're not supposed to even have to think to do those things.'

'It's not nothing, Ange.' Holding the phone between her chin

31

and shoulder, she reached into the cabinet for a mug and poured herself more coffee. It had been on the burner all morning and tasted of scorch. Though she usually drank coffee black, she opened the lab room's fridge. Among the small, sealed bottles for culturing gonorrhea tests, they kept a carton of half-and-half. The cream sank in her coffee and then rose, a sudden yellow bloom.

She couldn't keep taking Angie's calls during work. She and Pieter already both talked to Angie every night after dinner, sometimes as long as an hour. Two or three times a week, Angie called Jordana in the middle of the night or at the clinic. It seemed like months that they'd been having this conversation. Her muscles ached with how little difference her assurances seemed to make. 'Listen. Angie.'

Angie's hard crying had dwindled to irregular, choked sobs. 'You're so good to me. I don't deserve it.'

Jordana leaned down, pressing her forehead to the cool of the aluminum lab counter. She could stand anything but another conversation about her goodness and Angie's unworthiness. But of course she'd stand it.

'It's so bad, Mom. It's so – you don't know what it's like, it's so *bad*. I can't think about this winter, the way I was this winter. It makes me feel like my head's going to come apart. I work and it's horrible, and Jess came and it was horrible, and my whole life, my life is horrible—'

'Oh, honey.' She couldn't think of a single helpful thing to say, and she had to get back to her client, who had tried to make herself miscarry by jumping off the low roof of a garage. 'It's not that bad. I promise it's not that bad. I'll call you tonight. Okay? Angie? Is that okay?'

'Do I have a choice?'

'You can talk to Samara if you need to.' Samara was Angie's *contact person* – farm-speak for therapist – a young woman with long skirts and a pierced eyebrow.

At $128 a day, the work therapy program at the farm cost a fifth of what the hospital did, but none of it was covered by their insurance. The three months Angie had been there had cost more than $10,000, money they'd saved for her college tuition. Sometimes Jordana found herself almost wishing that Angie would act just a tiny bit crazier, so that it would at least be clear they were doing the right thing. But then when Angie did slip and lose sight of herself like this, it was awful, nothing to wish for.

32

'I don't know why you even talk to me.'

'I love hearing about your days. But Angie, I'm with a client.'

'Don't go! *Please*. Just another minute.'

If Angie were a child again, not wanting to go to bed, this would be the moment she clung to Jordana's neck with all her weight. Jordana felt sick. Her daughter had supposedly stabilized; she was due to come home in three weeks.

Angie was crying again. 'You know that fairy tale, the one with the bad sister and the good sister? And the crone—'

'Angie, I promise, I *promise*—'

'—enchants her so that whenever she opens her mouth, what comes out are toads? That's me. That's what I feel like.'

'Baby, I love you. *I have to go.*' She kept herself from saying, *Okay?* Pointless to try for Angie's permission. 'I love you,' she said, waited a moment. 'Angie, God. I'll call tonight. I love you.'

In the hallway, she had to stop for a moment, put her hand to the wall. Where was she going? Her chest tightened; she was breathing too shallowly, and when she tried to force herself to take breaths into her stomach, she couldn't hold them. She needed to get back to her office, but Angie's calls made her feel pulled out of her body. She rested the side of her head on her hand, against the wall, gathering herself.

She could be knocked off balance at any moment. It could be something obvious, like Angie crying, or it could be something more oblique, like a girl begging change downtown. Worst of all, feeling glad at even the smallest thing – an unexpectedly beautiful day, the taste of sharp cheddar – would immediately remind her that she was sad. It was as though, between happiness and unhappiness, she'd discovered a trapdoor she'd never known was there, one she couldn't close.

In her office, the girl had both feet wrapped around the legs of her chair. She wore a navy blue dress, probably meant to make her look older but which instead made her look impossibly innocent.

Sitting, Jordana relaunched her speech about tab-gen abortions. 'Second trimester means a three-day process.' Pulling open her desk drawer, she found the demonstration set of lams, pale green matchsticks made of compressed seaweed. Inside the cervix they would swell, dilating it. She'd given this talk so many times her mind could unhook from the words. 'Once you start you can't go back.'

*

Four months ago, when Angie had been discharged from the hospital, she'd been stabilized but fragile, so bleary with medication that she walked into walls. She slept as soon as she got home from school in the afternoon, woke terrified in the night, could barely eat. Swimming was impossible, even the relatively easy practices they did between the winter and summer seasons.

In the third week after the hospital, Jordana had gotten a phone call at work: Angie was in the school nurse's office, crying and unable to stop. Jordana drove at twice the speed limit through Cort's tranquil midmorning streets. At the high school she ran, then forced herself to walk, then found herself running. The wide, empty halls echoed with her footsteps.

Angie lay crumpled on a cot. On the other cot sat a boy with a thermometer between his lips, and Jordana had to turn away, furious at him – for seeing Angie or for the banality of running a fever, she didn't know.

The nurse said, 'I thought at first – well, girls are very sensitive.'

Angie's body shuddered and bucked. She'd run out of tears. Her mouth opened and closed and opened, little gasps, almost soundless, like someone crying behind thick glass.

Jordana knew to kneel and hold her daughter, but she couldn't move. Up until now, she'd been going along with the doctors' advice, hoping the medications would work. She'd thought she was accepting her daughter's illness clearly and dealing with it practically, but now she realized that she'd been able to be methodical – checking that Angie was taking her meds on time, driving Angie to the clinic every Wednesday for blood work – because she'd held on to the secret belief that her daughter wasn't really sick. All the rituals of sickness had been to Jordana a kind of superstition: If she was good enough, she had believed, if she was obedient to the demands of calamity, she could divert the calamity itself.

The Onion's stained-glass chandeliers swung low over tables gouged with graffiti. Beneath their table, Ben held Jordana's knees between his own. The only other customer was an Abenaki woman, sitting at the bar in a lavender sweatsuit. Her cheekbones were sharp, as if hewn by an ax; the rest of her face was blurred with drink. She hit the bottom of her glass with one hand to dislodge the ice. The high, dirty windows strained the afternoon light.

'Did you know your left eye is bigger than your right?' Ben

raised his hands, squinting at her through the rectangle his fingers made. 'There are these pictures of Nixon made of two left sides of his face – they printed the left side of the photo, then flipped the negative and printed it again. And then next to it, a face made of two right sides. And they were totally different, like looking at two different people.'

With Ben, the knot in her chest loosened and she could breathe all the way in. 'So you're saying I look like Nixon.'

'Right, exactly. No, I'm saying faces are asymmetrical. Yours just more clearly.' Mixed into his brown hair were a few strands of gray; his eyes were yellow-green. He reached across the table, touching one side of her mouth and then the other. His hands still startled her, their softness compared to Pieter's calluses. 'Did you know people don't like pictures of themselves because they're used to their mirror image?'

'I don't like pictures of myself because I always look like I've just stolen something.' She was a little light-headed. 'I shouldn't drink in the afternoon.'

'A cheap date.' When Jordana frowned, he explained, 'You drink one beer. It's cheap to take you out.'

'Oh. I thought you meant cheap as in floozy.'

'*Floozy,*' Ben said. 'I don't think I've ever heard that word in real life.'

Sometimes, being older – thirty-eight to his thirty-two – made her feel assured and desirable rather than dowdy and staid. She reached across the table for his hand. 'Let's go to your place.'

'Let's have another beer first. I'll tell you my pig joke.'

'I'm already kind of drunk.'

Ben got up from the table, and her knees were suddenly cold. Turning, he rocked back on his heels to study her. He tipped his head to one side and raised his wide hands for a moment, framing her again, then dropped them. 'You're nice drunk,' he said.

Ben was the photographer for *The White Mountain Times,* but the paper was small enough that, as well as helping with layout and selling ad space, he also wrote some of the articles. Not long after Angie had left school for the farm, he'd come to the clinic to do a story about local response to a recent spate of abortion center bombings across the country. A young guy with unruly hair, corduroys worn to velvet at the knees, two cameras slung bandolier-style across his chest. He'd interviewed a number of protesters as well and –

35

anxious that he might be writing a hostile piece – Jordana had been brusque with him. Okay, she'd been rude. Angie's state then had been so precarious and frightening that Jordana was mad at everyone. After the article came out, she'd called to apologize.

She'd never thought of herself as someone who would have an affair. Truthfully, she still didn't feel that way. 'Affair' sounded torrid and agonized and *big;* being with Ben was easy. She was reminded of Pieter when she was with him, but it didn't make her feel as guilty as she would have expected, because Ben didn't threaten that other, real life.

At the bar, Ben put one foot up on the rail. He wore a black beeper, the kind doctors had, so the paper could reach him. Above his head, the ORDER HERE sign had been graffitied to read DISORDER HERE. She looked away, embarrassed, lust zagging through her stomach.

'So this guy is driving past a farm.' Ben slid back into the booth. 'And he sees a farmer holding up a pig to eat apples off a tree.'

Later, lying tangled in the sheets of Ben's futon, the room sank so gradually into dusk around them she didn't even realize it until Ben reached over her to switch on a light. The shapes of things sprang back into focus.

'It's late. I should go.' It was hard to feel urgency, though; it seemed impossible that a whole other life awaited her. And when she got home, she knew, that other life would swallow her whole. She would hardly believe Ben existed. She bowed her head quickly, kissing his shoulder, then his neck.

He said, 'I haven't felt this way before.' He touched her jaw. 'Did you know you have a freckle right here? Under your chin? A really dark one.'

'A freckle?' She tried to sound light, though her breath felt caught in her throat: *I haven't felt this way before.*

'Exactly like a poppy seed.'

An hour later, she walked into her house, into the tornado of obligations and attachments, lights blazing, the phone cord pulled taut up the stairs and into Luke's room, bills stuck in the frame of the front-hall mirror along with a scribbled note to buy stamps, her husband shut in the living room with Beethoven's Ninth crashing around him. She stood for a moment on the threshold, door still open behind her. Then she let the door shut and went into the living room, where Pieter lay on the couch.

36

He was so tall, six-foot-five, that his feet hung way over the armrest. He'd been born in the Netherlands: he had almost Asian eyes, slanted and narrow, as though he were squinting or laughing. The white in his hair just made him look blonder.

He jumped up and changed the record. 'I was listening to this just a minute ago.' The needle skated over the outer band of the record and into the first groove. 'It's magnificent, isn't it?'

She stole a glance at the cover: Henryk Górecki. 'Górecki?'

'I knew you knew it.' Pieter could hear a piece of music once, and then years later hear it again and know exactly what it was. He could hear a few bars of a recording he'd never heard before and guess the soloist or chamber group. While he recognized that not everyone could do the same, he found it unfathomable that Jordana couldn't. She'd lived with musicians her whole life. She thought that, to Pieter, recognizing a composer was as natural as recognizing the taste of a lemon or the color green. Because she wanted him to admire their intimacy – their united front in an often-senseless world – she lied about music as much as she dared. She said, 'I thought Górecki was sentimental.'

'He is. Still. When you get to the second movement . . .'

Instead of the wall-to-wall carpeting the last owners had put into the rest of the house, the living room had a hardwood floor, now scarred and gouged by Pieter's endpin and the endpins of his students. For a moment, she felt the guilt that normally eluded her.

She pushed off her shoes and crawled onto the couch next to her husband, lying along the edge, holding on to him so she wouldn't fall off. Closing her eyes, she breathed him in. Pieter didn't always let her cling to him like this; it distracted him. Part of what she'd fallen in love with when she was fourteen and he was twenty-nine had been Pieter's reserve, the way he seemed unreadable and self-contained.

He smelled of soap and resin. Through her shirt, she could feel the calluses on his fingertips where they held her shoulder. 'Wait, listen,' he said.

The orchestra dropped away, leaving the soprano's voice alone, like a vertical shaft of light. Pieter's lips moved just slightly, chin lifted. Jordana pulled herself against her husband's body, holding on to the soft cotton of his button-down shirt. Why did she sometimes let herself forget him?

Pieter looked down at her. 'What is it?'

'It's nothing,' she said.

Chapter Three

At night, Luke's stereo covered the noise of opening the window. He stepped from the chair to the desktop to the sill and leaned back to turn off the music. Crouching, he stretched one hand out to the scaly bark of the dogwood tree. The branch was just far enough from the window that he couldn't hold it with both hands before jumping, and every night he had a moment of vertigo – he forgot it immediately afterward, until he was standing here again – when he thought he couldn't jump.

Then he jumped, left hand sliding down the alligator bark before he got a grip, his body swinging wildly in the air, heart pounding in his chest. The branch jerked and shuddered, blossoms raining to the driveway below. He kicked to get his feet up around the branch and pulled himself on top of it. Crawling backward, he worked his way down. When he got near the heart of the tree, he felt behind him, his foot in empty space and then brushing a low limb, and he inched that foot down, lowering his weight slowly until he was squatting. When finally he let go of the upper branch, his hands ached, from holding on and also from the cold; it was late April, the days bright but not really warm, and the nights still sharp.

He shuffled back a few inches on the branch until his back hit the trunk, then spent a minute squeezing one hand with the other, uncramping them, before reaching into his pocket for gloves. As he pulled them on – the leather stiff with cold – a light came on behind him.

Fuck. His heart hopped unpleasantly.

But the light wasn't in his room. It was in the empty room next to his, Angie's. After a moment his mother appeared through the window, fists jammed deep into the front pockets of a pair of too-big paint-splattered jeans. She wandered to Angie's shelf and pulled down a book, flipped through it, then stuck it back. She wrapped her hand around the swimmer on one of Angie's trophies. Then she drifted over to the desk chair and sat. Folding her arms on the desk, she rested her cheek on them. From where he crouched in the tree, maybe six feet below her, he couldn't tell if her eyes were open.

She can't see you anyway, he reminded himself. It felt weird, watching someone who didn't know she was being watched.

She'd always been younger than his friends' mothers. Something about her still seemed young, even though she was almost forty. She stood, put both hands into her already-wild hair, and shook them, as though shampooing, which she did when she was frustrated. She wheeled around and out of sight; the light in the room winked out.

He stayed crouched in the tree. If it had been him at the Funny Farm, he couldn't imagine his mom coming into his room and mooning over his stuff. His parents didn't even realize they favored Angie; they'd always been more focused on her, even before. It was actually good, because he could pass under the radar without much trouble.

He jumped the last six feet to the ground. His sweatshirt was covered with bits of bark and dead leaves. Kristin wasn't there tonight, a relief. Not that he thought she'd tell his parents or anything; he just didn't want to have to talk to her or else not talk to her. Back in eighth grade they'd been assigned to work together on a social studies project and had spent three weekends in a row in his basement constructing a three-dimensional cardboard model of a Soviet commune. Ten o'clock the night before the project was due, as she'd painted a tiny Young Pioneers emblem on the side of a building, he remembered her asking, 'So what exactly is this assignment supposed to prove? We can cut up boxes?' She'd had a crush on him then, but it had seemed to go away after a few months of his not being interested. Then one night last autumn – Angie'd already begun falling out, so it must have been about October – he'd been drunk at a party and apparently had talked to Kristin for hours. After that she'd begun appearing in the yard.

With his gloved hands, he brushed himself off as well as he could and then, because his heart was still beating fast, he ran the three blocks to Khamisa's. On Wanderwood he slowed to a walk,

39

getting his breath. Khamisa and her mother lived at the end of the street in a duplex, the right-hand side of an old square house. Standing at the bottom of the porch steps, he could see through both front windows. On the left side, a woman in a nightgown walked with a baby, talking to it and bending her head to eat potato chips from a bag. On the right side, Khamisa and her mom lay on the couch, sharing a blanket. Their faces, unself-conscious, lit blue by the television, looked more similar to each other than to either of their daytime selves. Khamisa had curly – she said frizzy – gold-brown hair. She was pretty but she looked ugly right now, her face slack in the TV's flickering light. The way she looked made him want to stay outside and also made him want to run up the stairs and knock on the window frame and startle her face out of its looseness.

At his knock, she jumped up and came to the window smiling. 'You're here,' she said, voice faint through the glass.

'Are you going to let me in?'

She shook her head no and put her lips to the window. He leaned down, kissing the glass over her mouth. The pane was cold, and when he drew back a print of his lips stayed there for a moment, white, before fading. Khamisa reached over to the front door – it opened directly into the living room – and undid the locks.

Khamisa's mother waved from the couch. 'Luke.'

'Hi.' He was supposed to call her Pam, but it felt too weird, so he usually didn't call her anything. Pam had had Khamisa at seventeen, even younger than his mom had had Angie. When he'd started dating Khamisa a few months ago, Pam had sat them down to talk about birth control. He and Khamisa hadn't looked at each other as Pam said to him, about six times, *Don't think with your dick*. If he'd met Khamisa's eyes, he would have started laughing, or else he might have fled the room. Since then, though, Pam had been totally laid back. He couldn't tell if she was really cool or, like Khamisa said, she was just trying to be cool. Either way, she let him stay over at their house.

'What's on TV?'

'You've got sticks in your hair,' Khamisa said, picking one out.

Pam said, 'This movie: A guy breaks into a house and steals a locked box he thinks is going to be like a safe, but it turns out to be full of this woman's diaries. This married woman's diaries. And he falls in love with the woman from her diary, and turns himself

40

into her fantasy man, and they have an affair.'

'Is it good?'

'Trash,' said Pam. 'You two should go to bed, you've got school tomorrow.'

'No, we'll watch with you,' he said. It wasn't just to be polite. He liked how Khamisa and her mother did things together, though Khamisa complained they were more like sisters. They shared clothes; Khamisa told her mom gossip from school. Once, when Luke was over, Pam had suggested they get takeout. Khamisa had said, 'Do you know how many times we've had takeout this week? I wish you'd sometimes cook a fucking meal,' and Pam had slapped Khamisa. Without pause, Khamisa slapped her back. 'You *cunt*,' Khamisa said. They glared at each other, Pam's hand still raised, and then the corner of Pam's mouth had tweaked, and Khamisa'd huffed through her nose, and they'd begun laughing.

He settled into the chair to watch the movie. Khamisa and Pam sat against opposite arms of the small couch, their knees drawn up, feet by each other's hips. 'Did I ever tell you how I got my name?' Khamisa asked now.

She had, but before he could say so she continued. 'This is, like, a perfect illustration of my mother. She was living in Santa Fe, and there's chamisa brush growing all over there – c-h-a-m-i-s-a.'

'It's the sound of it that matters,' Pam said mildly, eyes on the television, eating ice cream from the carton. With her other hand, she pushed Khamisa's shoulder lightly. 'Don't be a bitch.'

On television, a man rubbed sun lotion into his bare chest while a woman, presumably the diarist, gulped and looked away guiltily. 'She wrote about that in her journal,' Pam said. 'It's her fantasy. The sun lotion and all.'

'And she doesn't know he's the robber?' he asked. 'Isn't that going to make her suspicious?'

Khamisa rolled her eyes. She wrapped her arm around her mother's knee, resting her chin there.

Khamisa's room was tiny and crammed with stuff. She'd stuck so many photographs into the mirror frame that only a photo-sized scrap of mirror remained; earrings and flimsy scarves and incense ash and dried-out roses, the red petals edged tan with age, and a pack of brown Indonesian cigarettes, and little bottles of scented oil cluttered the top of the bureau. Clothes hung on one wall. Amid

41

the jumble, her bed an island, narrow and carefully made.

He liked being here not just because he loved Khamisa but also because escaping his own house was such a relief. He wouldn't have thought he'd miss Angie, and he didn't, not exactly. But things were even more fucked up with her gone than they had been with her there. His father, more distracted than usual, might easily forget a whole conversation he'd had with Luke the day before. Luke's mother plunged into frenzied projects – pulling everything out of the hall closet, for example, to box up donations for Goodwill – and then lost heart. At the moment, their hallway was half blocked by partly filled boxes and an enormous heap of down parkas, mittens, hats, red rubber boots from about kindergarten that still had bread bags inside to make them easier to pull off.

He picked up a magazine from the floor, flipping through it. Happy teenagers grilling hamburgers in their bathing suits, a quiz that he was glad to see Khamisa hadn't bothered to fill out, a column called 'Was My Face RED!' (*I was in line at the bank in front of this really cute guy. When I opened my purse, a tampon fell out – on his shoe!!!*)

'Do you like this?' Khamisa asked, from the other side of the room. She'd taken off her shirt and was holding something small and black in her hands.

'What is it?'

'I found it at that thrift store downtown. Seventy-five cents.' She put it on her head – a small velvet hat with an asymmetrical veil. She looked at him over her shoulder. 'Do you like it?'

'When would you wear it?'

She shook her head. 'I just like it.' She put it back on top of the bureau. She was always showing him things she'd bought and wanting him to comment. He took off his sneakers and sat on the side of the bed while she continued fiddling with stuff on the dresser – she brushed her hair, put it up, then took it down again. The straps of her bra shone pink against her shoulder blades.

'Come here,' he said.

She shrugged. Mostly, he was happier here than anywhere else, but she got into these moods. It seemed like there was something specific she wanted him to do, but she wouldn't tell him what. He looked at her clock: nearly midnight. He'd have to leave at five, which meant tomorrow was another day he'd sleepwalk through school.

42

'Khamisa, I have to get up in a couple of hours.'

She crossed the room, turned off the light. He heard her take off her jeans and unhook her bra. In the dark, she opened a dresser drawer, took out clothes to sleep in. When she got into bed he tried to embrace her but she turned away, managing – despite the small-ness of the bed – to lie without touching him.

'Are you pissed because I said we'd watch the movie with your mom?'

'I'm not pissed.'

'It seemed rude to just come upstairs.'

'I'm not pissed.'

'Fine, you're not pissed.'

'I'm *not*.' She was silent a minute, then burst out, 'You never even tell me when you're going to come over. I'm supposed to just wait around.'

This wasn't how he understood things between them at all. He could feel Khamisa beside him, rigid, arms crossed over her chest, staring at the ceiling. 'Right,' he said, rolling away. 'Whatever you say.'

He must have fallen partway asleep, because when she kissed him it startled him awake. She rolled over on top of him and he ran his hand down her back, then up under her T-shirt to one of her smooth, heavy breasts. Although he knew they were allowed to do this, he put his hand over her mouth as they made love, so her mother wouldn't hear.

Chapter Four

The drive to the farm took them down to Northampton, then west along the Mass Pike, leafy green, punctuated every twenty miles by a service plaza: always McDonald's, Boston Market, Dunkin' Donuts. Twisted toward him in the passenger seat, Jordana used both hands as she talked.

'You know, one good thing that's come out of all this,' she said. 'Angie and I are closer. Not that I want this to have happened, but now that it's ending . . .'

The cello was the instrument that sounded most like the human voice, and to Pieter his wife's was the human voice that sounded most like the cello, vibrant and rich. In her happiness, she skipped from topic to topic: the clinic, the summer ahead of them, a movie she wanted to see. Had they seen a movie since Angie had gotten sick? He couldn't remember. Now, at last, their life had doubled back to where they'd been before; they would become themselves again. Jordana's hands moved together and apart and together, as though cat's-cradling invisible yarn.

'. . . So now I'm thinking, why not?'

She paused, clearly waiting for a response. He said, 'Why not—?'

'You weren't listening to me.'

'I was listening. I just—'

'Goddamn it, Pieter. Forget it.'

She undid her seat belt and arched back to reach into her bag, which sat on the floor behind her. The last few weeks she'd almost seemed to be seeking arguments; things she usually didn't balk at drove her crazy. Pulling *Crime and Punishment* from her bag, she thumped back into her seat, opened the book, and began to read. Defensive about her intelligence, self-conscious because she hadn't

44

finished college, she would never read anything that wasn't recognizably serious.

Pieter held off as long as he could before saying, 'Jord—'

She looked at him, brows raised.

'Your seat belt.'

She pulled it over her lap, went back to her book. He envied that she could read in the car. Even checking a map made Pieter carsick, and carsickness flung him back to the Atlantic crossing he'd made when he was six. He could smell the salt and the diesel fumes, feel the unending chop of the sea and the crawly headaches that had accompanied his nausea. After escaping the occupied Netherlands for England – his parents had sent him out and stayed behind – he'd sailed to New York on a ship full of children, mostly British. Miserably homesick, miserably seasick, they abused each other in miniature dramas of dominance and submission. Against the madness of this tiny society, unrelated groups of children formed rough family relationships. A three-year-old girl, Beatrice de Groot, had attached herself to Pieter. He had fed her with a spoon, as though she were a much younger child, a baby. Feeding his own infants, who smiled and babbled and grabbed for his hand, had never moved him in the way he'd been moved at six by Beatrice de Groot, her eyes fixed on his as she let herself be fed.

In Stockbridge, they exited the pike for the smaller roads of western Massachusetts, then eastern New York. Phone lines dipped and rose across the sky. After a time, Jordana looked up from the book, marking her place with a finger, and looked out the window. Although it was late May, there had been snow the night before. Fields clicked by, white, smoothly parted by barbed wire.

Angie was walking in circles, picking things up from one spot in her room and putting them down someplace else. The carpet was covered with piles of sweaters, papers, mud, glazed and unglazed pots, boots, yarn. An opened-mouthed box held a tangle of dirty laundry.

'You were supposed to *pack,*' wailed Jordana.

'I am packing.'

Pieter asked, 'What time is our meeting with Samara?'

'Things aren't even sorted,' Jordana said. 'What have you been doing?'

Angie looked pleadingly at Pieter.

He said, 'The three of us, working together, we can do this in an hour—' Jordana turned and glared at him. He stiffened. 'I'm just being pragmatic.'

'Pragmatic,' Jordana said, as though it were something disgusting. He shook his head – he didn't want to argue in front of Angie – and turned, picking up a box. 'Do you have a marker?' he asked his daughter.

'There's a pen around somewhere.'

They located a ballpoint in a drift of work clothes that were caked with mud and dried manure. He labeled the first box TO WASH. The writing looked shuddery and skeletal, bumping over the corrugations invisible beneath the cardboard's skin. Already he felt discouraged.

He'd envisioned this homecoming: They would carry Angie's boxes to the car, Angie and Jordana chattering. If his wife's voice was a cello, his daughter's was usually the lowest, most open notes of the flute, though when excited her voice went to the higher, closed notes. After packing the car, the three of them would meet for a final time with Samara, in her office decorated with lumpy weavings. She would close Angie's file, stand up, shake their hands. He'd imagined his daughter's excitement as they pulled into the driveway of their house. In his mind's eye, she rushed into the kitchen and hugged Luke, who looked embarrassed and pleased.

As he packed, Pieter tried to sort and throw out and fold. Jordana didn't fold but at least she sorted. Angie just threw things at bags, sometimes missing, tapes and clothing and papers all crumpled together. He found on the floor one of the activities calendars that showed the farm's schedule of town trips and hikes and contra dances, classes on yogurt making and beekeeping and spinning wool into yarn. The farm seemed to him a huge over-reaction to Angie's breakdown, but the calendar made him feel the weird hollowness of loss. Angie could at least have taken advantage of more there.

'Did you learn to spin?' he asked.

'I learned to knit.' Angie gestured toward a heap of brown yarn.

'It might have been interesting. Spinning.'

'Might have been.'

There was a knock on the doorframe. A tall boy stood there, very thin, red hair, red face. He lowered the headphones of his Walkman so that they hung around his neck. The music was turned up loudly enough that Pieter could make out isolated words: *instruct . . . monkey . . . rocket.*

'You packing?' the boy asked Angie. He jittered from foot to foot. 'That's cool, that's cool.' He threw a few punches in the air. '*Bam. Bam.*'

Angie got up unsteadily, then stumbled. 'Shit, my foot's asleep. These are my parents. This is Tim.'

Tim nodded hello, threw another punch. '*Bam. My* parents tried to poison me. *Bam. Bam.*'

Jordana threw Pieter a startled look. He was used to her knowing what to say, but it was Angie who seemed unfazed. 'Are you going on Town Trip?' she asked.

'Yeah. You?'

'No, I'm leaving.'

'That's right. That's right. You're leaving. That's right, you're leaving.'

Angie talked easily with Tim, diverting him back to concrete topics when the conversation began to veer off. She seemed deliberately not to look at Pieter or Jordana, though Pieter could sense her awareness of them, the unnaturalness of not looking around as she spoke. She was demonstrating something, but he wasn't sure whether it was that she belonged to the world of the farm or transcended it, whether she was rebuffing or reassuring them. He wondered if she knew.

'So,' Pieter tried, when there was a break in the conversation. 'Where are you from, Tim?'

'Everyone knows where I'm from. Carlisle, Pennsylvania.'

'How far is that from Philadelphia?'

'You don't have to talk slow, Dad. He's not retarded.' Angie went out onto the porch with Tim so he could smoke.

They'd planned to leave the farm by two in the afternoon, but it was nearly seven when they finished. By the end, they were packing things that they would have thrown out earlier in the day, just to be done. Their daughter squeezed into the backseat with the boxes and plastic garbage bags of her belongings. Jordana drove, the car bumping down the dirt road from the farm, through eastern New York and onto the Mass Pike, lined with darkening trees. At least, now that they were finally on their way, Jordana was calmer. Her hand, when she didn't need it to shift, rested on his knee.

47

Glancing into the rearview mirror, she asked Angie, 'What do you want to do first when you get home? What's the very first thing?'

'I don't know. You keep asking me that.'

He could see Jordana was trying to be quiet. After a few minutes, though, she said, 'Maybe we could go to the Lobster Shack. To celebrate.'

Angie shrugged, turned toward the window.

'Or ice cream.'

He revised his fantasy of the homecoming. Angie was probably not going to embrace Luke so enthusiastically that his feet lifted off the ground – but in a few days she would be used to her family again, less worried, adjusting back to her old life. Her plan was to swim this summer, as always, and then retake her senior year at Applefield. He and Jordana had suggested that she go to a different school, that she give herself a break from competitive swimming. She was adamant, though, that everything be the same, and he found himself relieved by this, her surety that she could pick up where she'd left off.

They were passing tobacco farms now; the rich brown smell filled the car. Pieter turned on the radio, searching until he found a news station. A muffled thump came from the backseat, as though something in the pile of Angie's things had shifted and settled.

Pieter turned just as there was a second thump. Angie swung her head toward him, then back into the window. 'Angie?' Jordana said, then, 'Stop. Angie, *stop.*' Angie's temple hit against the glass twice more, a dull, regular thud, before Pieter grabbed her, digging his fingers into her knee.

'You can't,' he said.

Angie stared back at him. Then her body relaxed and she looked away, giving in.

'Angie, God, you can't do that,' Jordana said. Pieter shook his head and she caught herself, closing her mouth.

By the time they reached the pike, Angie had fallen asleep, her cheek against the black plastic of one of the garbage bags holding her clothes.

He let go of Angie's knee and they drove in silence, leaving the pike at Northampton for 91, then taking the exit for 121. They passed the art school and New Hampshire State's Cort campus,

48

then Jordana's clinic; they reached the railroad tracks just as the gate arm lowered, flashing and clanging.

Boxcars flashed by. On trains, Pieter had sometimes had the illusion that the landscape was moving slowly backward while he stayed still. Now he had the same experience in reverse: For a moment he didn't know whether it was the train moving or their car, sliding away beneath him.

His shoulders hurt from twisting toward Angie, and he slid low so he could lean them back against the seat. 'What are we going to do?' Jordana asked.

'It's okay. She was . . . They said she'd be anxious.'

When he looked at his wife's profile, he saw it from below, her strong jaw, the flare of her nostrils. To his surprise, she laughed – a loose, unhappy sound.

Chapter Five

Back from the farm two weeks, Angie went to the first Summer League practice but made it only as far as a changing stall in the locker room because she was shaking so hard she felt she might throw up. The stall had a plastic shower curtain, patterned with bikinied fish, that shielded it from the room. From outside she could hear, dimly, splashing and the shrill of a whistle. Pawing through her bag she found her new lighter, nearly dropping it, and lit an absolutely prohibited-within-fifty-yards-of-the-pool-house cigarette.

Deep inhalations of smoke calmed her enough that she could sit. The coach called, *Gather round!* By the time a mother and, from the sound of it, two toddlers came into the locker room, Angie had the presence of mind to stub out the cigarette, pushing it down the metal floor drain. She pulled herself into the corner of the changing stall, knees to chest, head down. Her breath sounded very loud. It was 8 a.m. and still cold.

'Do you need to go wet-wet?' the mother asked. 'Go wet-wet while I put on Julia's suit.'

'I don't need to.'

'Will you just try? Try sitting on the toi-toi.' In a lower voice she muttered, 'Smells like an ashtray in here.'

At last she got both kids into their suits, got all their belongings gathered up, and sailed out toward the wading pool. Angie, alone again, picked at the bench's varnish, which was peeling in brittle yellow curls.

Summer teams – made up of any kids who belonged to the local pools – were low-key, much less competitive than the winter high school league. She'd always loved summer practices, especially the morning ones, the misty cold, almost no one else at the pool, wispy silver vapor lifting off the surface of the water.

Midway through practice, someone came into the locker room. Angie pulled her knees more tightly to her chest.

'Ange, I know you're here.' Jess. She walked over to Angie's cubicle. 'Luke said you came together.'

Water dripped from Jess's suit onto the turquoise-blue tiles at her feet. Angie said, 'Since when have you had a toe ring?'

'Can I come in?' Jess waited a second, then pushed aside the curtain and scooted into the cubicle, sitting on the wood bench next to Angie. She wore a green bathing suit over an orange one. Angie had on two suits as well: it increased drag in the water, as did letting her leg hair grow out between meets. Not that she particularly needed increased drag, since she still had ten pounds of lithium weight.

Jess worked her hands under her butt, sitting on them. She looked at the curtained door of the stall. 'Luke asked me to find you. I didn't even know you were *back*.'

'It's just been a few days,' Angie said, also looking ahead at the curtain.

'It's not like I'm your best friend or anything.'

'You are. I just—'

'Just what?'

'I don't know,' Angie said miserably.

From outside came the noises of splashing, the coach's whistle.

'You're going to get in trouble,' Angie said. 'You should go back.'

Jess shrugged. 'I'll say I got my period.'

They sat side by side, Jess swinging her legs, Angie still hunched into a ball.

'Your period? Really?'

'Jerry will turn, like, bright red and start waving me away. Do you want to hear about graduation?'

She said that graduation had been so hot that one person fainted crossing the outdoor stage. Because of the heat, and because they were drunk off their asses, some of the boys hadn't worn anything under their gowns; after receiving his diploma, Avi Goldman had turned and mooned the audience. There had been a party out at the radio towers, and the cops found them but looked the other way.

'I'm sorry,' Angie burst out.

'It's okay. It's not like you're doing it on purpose or anything.'

The words soaked her with relief. Until Jess said it, Angie hadn't even known what she dreaded: that people thought she was being an asshole, that she *was* being an asshole. 'Luke really asked me to find you? I mean, asked you to find me?'

Jess nodded. She stood, running a finger under the edge of her suits' leg holes, pulling them down. 'There's only so long I can pretend to be dealing with my period. Are you coming?'

'It's too obvious,' Angie said. 'I'll come to this afternoon's.'

'I'll pick you up at your house.'

'You don't have to do that.'

'I know I don't *have* to do that.'

Afternoon: the white concrete apron of the pool hot beneath her feet; pool a surreal blue. Jess walked beside her, for which Angie was grateful. She wished she could talk to Jess, seem truly like this was no big deal, but her heart beat too fast. Mothers read heavy novels from the library, looking up occasionally to shout warnings. On vinyl-webbed lawn chairs, girls and a few boys sunned themselves, the glib smell of Hawaiian Tropic rising off their warmed skin. Two little girls just finished with the twelve-and-under practice lay on the edge of the pool, arms tight to their sides, trying to soak up the concrete's warmth. They had poochy little stomachs, like porpoises, and their teeth were chattering, but they were also clearly enjoying the heat after an hour in the pool, clearly enjoying the grown-upness of having suffered, especially now that it was over. They were pale; by fall they would be the same brown as the leaves.

The coach, Jerry, was a college kid with a stupid goatee. He looked like he was going to say something to Angie about this morning's missed practice, then quickly shut his mouth and concentrated on his clipboard. People were looking at her. She began to feel light-headed, as though her cheeks were hollow, as though her elbows and knees were made of glass. When she got to the edge of the pool, she dove in quickly. The shock of wet and of cold. She broke through the water, down toward the pool bottom with its squiggling white reflections of light, its thick black lane markings.

Normally she remembered interrupting the swim meet the way she would remember a dream, in sharp fragments and with the same loss of logic. She didn't remember the Emergency Room at the hospital, and she only remembered bits and pieces of the first few days she'd been in the locked ward, like the brownout of being drunk. Now the cloudiness of chemicals, the slow bicycling of legs treading water above her, brought back something she'd forgotten: the car ride to the hospital, her mother and brother sitting on either side of her. She and Luke and her father all dripping wet, the car filled with the sharp yellow scent of chlorine, her mother's arms around Angie. She'd thought that her mother was filled with admiration and awe, and Angie's newly enormous love for her mother had been edged with pity. Now she could see that her mother had been terrified. The memory of transcendence felt stronger – more true and clear – than the knowledge that she'd been psychotic. Jesus, *psychotic*.

She burst to the surface of the pool, gasping.

Two kids were shoving each other at the pool edge, and someone called someone else a faggot, and Jerry said, *Okay, gather round,* just as one of the shovers succeeded in pushing the other into the pool. *Gather round.* It was a thin line to hold on to, but one instruction led to another, and in this way she got through practice, and the next, and the next and the next and the next.

'My mom hates this car,' Jess said. 'I think she's hoping I'll crash it.'

There was no backseat in Jess's father's red Miata, so Tris Wu perched on Angie's lap. Tris had long black hair and an appealingly crooked smile. She was cooler and more popular than Jess or Angie; they'd never been able to decide exactly why she was friends with them.

Jess let the clutch out jerkily; Angie grabbed Tris's waist and Tris grabbed for the dashboard.

At the radio towers, they parked far down the road; too many cars together and the police would know there was a party. As they hiked back, Angie wished she'd brought Ativan. She'd been trying not to take it because she hated feeling like she needed a pill to get through things. She stopped and found her cigarettes, turning her back to the wind. Her lighter didn't work at first and she shook it to moisten the wick. When she looked up, Jess was standing next to her.

She reached out and patted Angie's arm, saying for the fiftieth time, 'I don't care about this party. We can leave any time you want.'

'I'm fine.'

'I'm just saying.'

Fireflies hung in the weeds on the road's shoulder. At the curve, Angie and Tris and Jess turned off the road, jumping the ditch. They shouldered through high grasses, calling when they lost sight of one another. Angie held her hand with the lit cigarette above her head, using the other hand to push grass aside. From all around came the keening of insects.

'I can't believe you smoke now!' Tris called back. 'You're, like, Super Athlete.'

At last they emerged into a broad cleared field, the radio towers winking atop small hillocks. The moon, almost full, hung low and greenish-yellow. If no one's parents were out of town, this was one of two places for parties; the other, which they used more in winter, was a house in the woods that had been abandoned after a fire. Clumps of kids stood around drinking from plastic cups. Angie would allow herself one beer. She hadn't thought to bring water or a soda, any more than she'd thought about Ativan. She hadn't been to a real party since she got sick.

Someone stopped Tris to talk to her; Jess stopped too, but Angie mumbled hello and continued toward the keg. 'Ange!' Tris called, and ran to catch up.

'How are you doing?' Tris asked.

'I'm just going to get a beer.'

'Are you okay?' Tris patted her arm, brows pulled together.

'I'm fine,' Angie said, moving a step away. 'I'm just getting a *beer.*'

Abe McGirr pumped the keg. He didn't go to her high school – he went to St. Gregory's, which was private, Episcopalian, all boys – but as kids they'd swum on the same summer team. He handed Angie a cup. Her hand was almost steady.

Stepping away from the keg, he asked, 'So, where are you going?'

'Going?'

'To school?'

'Oh. Where are you going?'

'Harvard,' he said, trying to look casual. 'I think the coach there pulled some strings.'

Abe had protruding, froggy eyes and brown hair that went in every direction. Back when they'd swum on the same summer

54

team, they'd both been singled out at ten to swim the thirteen-and-up practice, which had meant that Angie had been very aware of Abe while at the same time carefully avoiding him. He'd avoided her also, both of them wanting the acceptance and company of the older kids. When his family had moved to the other side of town, and therefore a different summer team, she'd been glad.

She said, 'I'm-taking-some-time-off-before-college-what-are-your-summer-plans?'

'My summer *plans*?' he asked. He was grinning at her, as though she might be joking, but then he seemed to realize she wasn't. The question must have sounded like one a parent's friend would ask, and his answer sounded polite in the way you'd be polite to a parent's friend. 'Well, I'm swimming for Patton. I'm working at a record store. You know Stars?'

'Me too. I mean, I'm working. At Full-Beli Deli. It's very orderly.'

Abe laughed.

'What?'

'Oh.' He stopped laughing. 'I thought you were making a pun. Very *orderly*? Orders? Like lunch orders?'

'I meant more like you don't have to make choices. People say white bread or rye or wheat bread, and you do that. Fritos or potato salad.'

'It must be boring.'

She raised her cup to her mouth too fast, slopping some beer onto their shoes, onto the ground.

'Whoa. Slow down a little there.'

'I'm going to go find my friends,' she blurted.

Abe leaned toward her. 'Do you want to know a secret?'

'I don't know. Do I?' He was so close they almost touched.

'The cameras in the record store? The ones that're supposed to keep people from shoplifting?' He looked around exaggeratedly, then leaned close again. He raised the collar of his shirt and behind it whispered, 'Fake.'

'*No.*'

'I shit you not.' He straightened, dropped his collar, and said in a normal voice, 'A real closed-camera system would cost like a thousand dollars, so they just have these plastic cameras. They have a battery that makes a little red light flash, which makes it look like they're on and doing something.'

55

'Does it work?'

'I have no idea.'

'Okay. I'll tell you something about the deli.' She lifted the neck of her T-shirt, but the only images she could summon were spreading mayonnaise with a rubber spatula, the bleach-soaked paper towels laid over the counters at night, the black grease pencil she used to write sandwiches' names on the white paper in which she'd wrapped them. She whispered, 'Actually, there's not a single thing to tell.'

'That's a disappointment. It looks so sinister.'

'Right. Is it the Coke signs that look sinister or the pictures of football players?'

'Football players,' he said. 'Definitely.'

She had said something semi-clever. It had never occurred to her to find Abe McGirr attractive. She wasn't sure whether she found him attractive now or whether she was responding to being with someone who didn't know what had happened last winter.

Down at the edge of the field, Luke emerged from the tall grass. A moment later Khamisa followed, brushing chaff from her curly hair. She was a sophomore. No: a junior now. Luke was going to be a senior. Jess was going off to Bates, Tris to UNC. Violet, Luke's ex-girlfriend, was going to some California school – Pomona, or maybe Pitzer? It was as though Angie had traveled away on a rocket, returning to find everyone but her had aged and moved ahead.

Luke said something to Khamisa and left her to come over.

He and Abe greeted each other, shaking hands. 'How are you doing?' Luke asked Angie.

'I'm fine,' she said, giving him a warning look: brows raised, eyes hard. 'How else would I be?'

'Are you supposed to . . . is that okay?' He nodded at the beer.

Abe said, 'Well, it tastes like horse piss.'

'Drunk much horse piss?' It came out more barking and aggressive than she'd meant. Abe straightened up.

There was an awkward silence. Then Abe said, 'I'm going to go say hi to some people. So. I guess I'll see you around.'

Abe loped down the hill and she turned on Luke. 'I'm allowed to have one stupid beer,' she said.

He touched her shoulder, about to speak.

She shook him off. 'Why does everyone keep *patting* me?'

*

To her surprise, Abe came into Full-Beli the next day. Later in the week she went and bought a CD at Stars – when he was watching, she pretended to stuff the case under her shirt. *Real life,* her brain was singing. On a night she worked late, he picked her up from the deli and they walked around the closed and quiet downtown, looking into the windows of stores.

'My mom hates these places,' Angie said, outside of the Sandpiper, which sold candles and silver-plated shells and pretty cards. 'Actually she hates a lot of random things.' Even though it was true, she felt guilty saying it; she remembered at the farm how relieved she'd been every time she heard her mother's familiar low voice on the phone.

The bank fountain was still on. They sat on its lip, feet in the water. The plashing water sent up a mist that dampened her face.

They looked at each other seriously, then laughed and looked away, then looked at each other again and kissed. Angie could feel coins beneath the soles of her feet.

'I can't believe how beautiful you are,' Abe said. 'I didn't know if . . . I thought you might just want to be friends.'

Truthfully, she wasn't sure what she wanted. A year ago, she wouldn't have been interested in Abe. The granite lip of the fountain was cold against the backs of her bare legs. Slipping her hands under her thighs, she leaned forward and kissed him again.

New Hampshire's summer days were hot, muggy, the high chatter and whine of insects all around. She worked at the deli from nine to four-thirty, coming in with her hair wet from morning practice and leaving just in time to bike to afternoon practice, sun glancing off the downtown windows. Saturdays, she had meets in the mornings. She came in to work around two, still vibrating from competition, and worked until close.

Wednesdays she had off, and Abe changed his schedule at Stars so he could take Wednesdays off too. They liked to go to matinees, the sudden cold of the dim theater lobby. They brought sweatshirts to wear over their T-shirts, and sometimes, as one movie finished, they strolled as casually as possible to the next screening room, coming in at the middle, watching through to the end. If it seemed worth it, they'd stay through the emptying of the few occupied seats, the straggling in of the next small audience, and see the movie over from the beginning, pushing right up until four-fifty,

57

when they had to run from the theater to Abe's old Galaxie 500 and drive to the pool for Angie's afternoon practice.

Angie argued for her lithium to be lowered, and as her dose went from 1200 milligrams to 900 and then 750, she felt a heaviness lift from her shoulders. At the deli, she was pleasantly bored, arranging salami in overlapping circles, tossing crusts into the crust bag, wrapping sandwiches in white paper before slicing them in half, the sliced edge of paper instantly soaking yellow with mustard. A soft-rock-from-the-seventies radio station crooned meaninglessly in the background. She remembered Sam Manning saying, *No voices*. She'd liked the farm, but now it seemed like quicksand she'd been lucky to escape, and she held her eyes wide for a minute, breaking off the memory, focusing on the next sandwich. She performed the same actions so many times they followed her into sleep; all night she dreamed of making sandwiches of RB or TUR, with AM CH or SW.

One morning she and Abe went to Cort's Historic Village Green, which had a new-made-to-look-old sign proclaiming it as such. They sat on the steps of the gazebo, where some nights a swing band played. Facing the square were a steepled church, the town hall, the public library, all of them white with shutters and doors painted a green so dark it was almost black. Later would be stunningly hot, but at 6 a.m. a chilly haze hung in the air.

Sitting hip to hip, they drank from a shared Styrofoam cup of coffee. Abe would leave for Harvard in three weeks. He'd gotten a postcard from the housing office with his roommate's name: Evan Johansson, from Bemidji, Minnesota. Angie took the postcard, turning it over in her hands.

'He's a seven-foot-tall cross-country skier,' she said. 'He's going to wear Nordic sweaters and drink lite beer and seduce a different girl every night.'

'They won't put me with another athlete.' He took the postcard back from her, tucking it into the front pocket of his sweatshirt. 'He stutters. He's like five feet tall and he's a virgin.'

Abe's leg, pressed against hers, was tanned and muscular, with pale curly hair. Angie was in love with Abe's legs. She wasn't sure if she was in love with Abe, only that she wanted to see him every day. After he dropped her off at night sometimes he called to say good night, and her heart leapt (really, her heart leapt) with gladness. Did that mean she loved him? They'd had sex for the first time a week ago, in the backseat of the Galaxie, sweet and awkward. He'd hit his elbow once, hard, on the window, and they'd laughed. Afterward, he'd clutched her, breathing raggedly. 'Thank you,' he'd said. 'That was ... thank you.'

She was going to tell him about the hospital. A car passed, then another. When a third car went by she'd say it.

'You're awfully quiet this morning.'

She faked a yawn, stretching out her arms. The faked yawn set off a real yawn, which made her smile. 'I never get up this early,' she said, and then realized she used to get up this early at the farm. For that matter, she'd gotten up this early all the way through high school because of swim practice. She blushed. A low blue station wagon passed, rattling. 'Can I have the coffee?'

He handed her the cup. She drank the dregs, silty with sugar. A fourth car passed. Seven cars and she'd say it. Angie pushed off her flip-flops and tucked her knees to her chest, pulling her sweat-shirt down over them.

Abe claimed he'd had sex before, with a girl on a ski trip. Angie didn't believe him, but it made her feel affectionate rather than annoyed, especially since he immediately said, 'But it was nothing like this.' She said, 'Me either.' She'd lied in the other direction, reducing her experience to just her ex-boyfriend Thad, editing out the freshman boy at a party and Luke's friend Cole and a half memory, possibly a dream, of desperately rubbing against someone, a *girl,* in the hospital Activity Room. She'd been manic during that time, so she wasn't exactly lying; she was telling an alternate truth, what should have been true.

The sprinkler bowed, sweeping a slow silver parabola of water across the dark grass. Abe stood and pitched the empty cup at a green metal trash can. 'I need to get you to the pool.' He reached down quickly, touching his toes. 'Will you visit me?'

'At Harvard?'

He pulled her up and kissed her, running his hands down her sides. 'If Evan Johansson is such a stud, I'll have the room to myself sometimes.'

'I was in the hospital for a few days,' she blurted. 'About ten. I mean, I was in the – the hospital was ... on a psych unit. It's called bipolar, there's – I have a chemical missing, like diabetics don't produce insulin?' She took a breath and finished lamely, 'So anyway, that's what I wanted to tell you.'

59

'It's okay.' His hands rested easily on his hips.

'That's all you're going to say?'

He raised and dropped his shoulders. 'I knew.'

'You *knew*? Who told you? You *knew*?'

'No one told me. I don't remember who told me. I heard about it last winter.'

'You've known the whole time?'

'It doesn't matter to me,' Abe said.

She walked away. The grass was cold and wet and stuck to her bare soles. She moved as fast as she could across the green. Catching up, Abe put his hand on her arm. She shook him off without slowing; he caught up to her again. She was beginning to feel melodramatic, like a bad music video, so she stopped and turned. Not out of amusement or happiness – she guessed out of embarrassment – she couldn't stop smiling. She hid her mouth with her hand.

'It doesn't matter,' Abe said again.

'Why didn't you tell me you knew?' Her face burned, and an awful giggle escaped.

'I thought you knew I knew. Cort's not that big.'

'Oh, shit,' she said, and began laughing in earnest. 'Oh, God. I'm sorry. I guess everyone knows. *Shit.*'

She laughed until tears began to leak down her face, and then she forced herself to stop. Abe's face, its suspension between relief and worry, almost set her off again; she turned around, took deep breaths.

Tentatively, he reached out, gathering her hair into a bunch behind her. 'Blow off practice. Let's get breakfast.'

'I can't.'

'Yes, you can. What's your coach going to do?'

Nothing. She'd known since the first day of the season, when Jerry had decided not to say anything about the missed practice. Anyone else would have had to do extra laps or pick trash off the lawn. Exactly because there would be no consequence, she couldn't blow off practice.

She went back for her flip-flops. They were quiet most of the ride to the pool. Angie usually took meds now, at seven. She'd only skipped that one dose, the day Jess visited her out in Sheepskill, and then had been awake all night sure she was going to become manic and end up in the hospital. She might as well take her meds in front of Abe, since he knew.

Everyone knew.

She picked up an open Coke can wedged against the seat. 'When's this from?'

'Yesterday?'

She tipped her pills into her palm, then into her mouth. The soda was warm and flat, delicious.

Abe asked, 'What would happen if I took one of those?'

'You wouldn't get high, if that's what you mean. You'd shake and have cottonmouth. Want one?'

'Yeah, right, really fun.'

She propped her feet against the dash and fiddled with the radio, tentatively happy. Actually, maybe lithium would get a normal person like Abe off, but the idea bothered her.

They pulled up to the low pool house, its white paint grimy, its wide front window shuttered. 'We met here,' she said, realizing.

'Bleah.' He made a face. 'I was such a little brat.'

'You *were* kind of a brat.'

She got out of the car. When she leaned down to say good-bye, Abe said, 'I love you.'

She wouldn't have imagined he'd be able to say it like that, looking at her, not touching his toes or stretching his shoulder muscles.

'I love you too.' As she said it, it became true. She slammed the car door, ran up the steps to the pool house.

That morning she swam the hundred-meter butterfly in 1:11.87. It was the closest she'd come all summer – though it wasn't very close – to the record she'd set last year.

She'd been dreading Abe's departure, but as she climbed out of the pool, then stood doubled over with her hands on her knees, panting, exultant, she felt a stab of yearning. She wanted the summer over.

She'd pushed herself hard and she was dizzy, blood pounding in her temples, her feet shriveled, white, weirdly distant. Everyone knew, and this fall was going to be much harder than she'd let herself understand, but she wanted it to come, she wanted Abe gone and the summer over so she could know she'd managed to not fuck it up, know that it was safe.

Chapter Six

The alarm went off at ten of five, and Luke reached over Khamisa to turn it off. Then he reset it for six-thirty, when she needed to get up. Over the summer, he'd been able to go back to bed after getting home from Khamisa's, but since school had started up again two months ago, he'd had to wait for weekends to catch up on sleep.

Groggily, she said, 'I had the strangest dream. You were, like, a car, but also you—'

'I have to get up,' he whispered. He found his cold sweatpants on the floor by the bed and pulled them on. Leaning back, he kissed her quickly but she put her arms around his neck, pulling him into a longer kiss. He reached behind his neck, unhooking her hands. 'I have to go.'

'You were a car, and there was this tower with water in it, and those little rectangle windows. And you were floating in the water . . .'

He shoved his feet into running shoes. Going back through his window via the dogwood meant getting up at four or risk bumping into his dad. Instead he wore sweats to Khamisa's. That way, coming back into the house, he could claim to have been out jogging.

'Kiss me again.'

'I really have to go.' He leaned over and kissed her breast quickly, where it was flattened against the mattress.

Downstairs, he pulled the front door closed. Late October. No snow yet, but the cold air pierced through his sweatshirt, through his T-shirt, to his skin. He began to run, muscles stiff. When he lifted his hand to tug at the sweatshirt's neck, his fingers smelled

62

musky, like sex. Quite suddenly, he was very happy. The gray half-light made the houses indistinct, like buildings under water. That he was the only person awake made the world seem full of promise. He jumped up to hit a low-hanging branch.

His family's house was rectangular and brick, shouldered between two white clapboard houses with green shutters. It was the only house on the block with a light on. His father stood at the front kitchen window, looking blankly out into the yard. Luke circled around to the back door, and his father turned as he came in.

'How was your run?'

Luke shrugged. He got water at the sink – it was very cold and tasted of iron.

'Chilly morning,' said his dad.

'I guess.'

'Leaving at five-twenty?'

'We always leave at five-twenty.'

Upstairs, he pulled on his swim trunks, then his sweatpants again. The room was freezing – the window had been open all night, and he went to close it now. Luke glanced at the clock; if he was late, Angie would leave for practice without him. From outside, he heard her car cough, then shake alive.

He jogged downstairs and out to the driveway. The open sides of his letter jacket knocked softly against his chest.

Abe hadn't taken the Galaxie to Harvard and was letting Angie use it. Luke opened the front door so he could reach back and undo the back door lock.

From the driver's seat, Angie asked, 'What are you doing?'

He crawled into the backseat. 'I'm wiped out.'

'You're lying down?'

'I just want to sleep till we're there.'

'No way,' Angie said flatly. She turned off the ignition. Her eyes in the mirror were pale blue. 'You can sleep in front but I'm not chauffeuring your ass.'

'Jesus, Ange.' He flopped over on his side, his face against the hard plastic seat. Muffled, he said, 'Why do you care if I'm back here or up there? Just pretend you're alone.'

'I'm not going anywhere with you in back.'

'Fine.'

'Fine.'

63

She turned the key, but just to switch on the radio. She found a rap station, then lit a cigarette.

'You know, I'm being nice enough not to tell Coach Nawrocki about you smoking. He'd kill you.'

She turned the radio up.

This summer she'd been pretty normal. Once or twice she'd even spoken to Luke without having first been spoken to. One night after Abe dropped her off she'd said, 'His clothes are a little too perfect, don't you think? They should be more worn out.' Luke noted in his head: *more worn out.*

Another night he'd been lying on the bed, listening to the Meat Puppets. Occasionally he glanced up to see if Kristin was under the tree outside. He tried to check without moving his head, so she wouldn't know he was aware of being watched. Angie appeared at his bedroom door with a small plastic film canister. 'Do you want this?' she asked, and tossed it to him.

He sat up to catch it. The canister was so light it felt empty; it must hold pot. 'You don't want it?'

'I'mfuckedupenoughwithoutdrugs.' He could tell she'd practiced saying it before coming to his room. She took a breath. 'Anyways, it's old. It might not even be any good.'

He popped off the lid, picked up a bud: pale green, shaped like a tiny horseshoe crab. He wasn't used to Angie lingering. Rolling the bud between his thumb and forefinger, he asked, 'Do you still think you're sick?'

Her blond hair was pulled back into a messy ponytail. She wore a dark pink cotton tank and cut-off jeans, the sunburnt tip of her nose peeling a little. She'd squinted at him and he'd thought she might yell, but her voice had come out uncertain. 'I don't *feel* sick.'

The backseat smelled of old Coke spills, and stuck in the crack were dozens of crumbs like sharp, tiny stars. An ad for diamonds came on the radio. He couldn't think of anything stupider than paying thousands of dollars for a piece of rock, then wearing that rock on your finger. The radio announcer made some extravagant claims for the station. He tried to sleep. When he found that he couldn't, he concentrated on the appearance of sleeping, holding his body still, breathing as slowly as he could.

Angie was smoking with the window up, so that smoke filled the car. After maybe two minutes, Luke said, 'Shit piss *fuck.*' His

64

sister would sit there all morning. When he pushed himself over the front seat, tumbling awkwardly, she calmly turned on the engine and rolled the window down partway, letting out the smoke. Without speaking they drove to the Y.

The air indoors was thick and warm, mugginess pierced by the sharp smell of chlorine. Luke stepped out of his sweatpants, balling them and tossing them up into the scored metal bleachers, high enough not to get splashed.

Fluorescent lights flickered high above the pool room. The tall, dark windows mirrored people as they pulled off their clothes. Steam rose off the pool in dense wisps. A sophomore boy sat on the pool's concrete apron, legs straight out in front of him, back bent so that his forehead touched his knees, hands wrapped around the arches of his feet. Farther over, a girl stood with her hands on her hips. Another girl stood behind her, slowly pushing the front girl's elbows together until she cried out sharply. The back girl let go; they both laughed.

His sister was taking off her sweat clothes, folding them carelessly. Her pale hair was silvered by chlorine. As kids they'd been friends, but in about junior high Angie had lost interest in Luke. Mostly they just didn't have much to say to each other; Angie was Supergirl, all honors classes and Student Government, and he didn't care about that stuff. For a long time, swim team had been the one place they really connected. Last fall, when his IM relay won against Whitman High, Angie had screamed and screamed through the whole race, then given him a hug so exultant she'd lifted him off the ground. Of course, that had been when she was doing crazy things: running through a party naked (other people had streaked too, but all guys), stealing shoes from Goldman's, standing to make a funny, rambling speech at an all-school assembly.

Before the hospital, Angie had been so much better than anyone else on the team that it wasn't the kind of thing you got jealous about. Lots of people swam butterfly well, but you admired them because you could see how hard it was. With Angie, the stroke seemed so natural that you didn't even appreciate it until she raced and you saw how thrashingly other people swam, how inefficient their movement was. If she'd been at Regionals last year and not in the hospital, their team would have come in second, possibly

65

first; without her, they came in fourth. Weirdly, though, her being gone had been a kind of relief. The scale for achievement shrank; it was possible to just be good.

Coach Nawrocki, who was also Luke's algebra teacher, blew his whistle. He'd written the workout on a whiteboard, which he wheeled to the side of the pool: a four-hundred-meter warm-up, a ladder of timed intervals, two four-hundred-meter IMs, some stroke practice, a warm-down. Sometimes, between intervals, Luke saw Angie in the pool. She wasn't the way she used to be. Partly she'd lost conditioning, but also she didn't seem to care very much. She got by because her form was so good.

When they finished, the windows were hard with the white light of New England winter. He showered in the tiled bathroom, only realizing now how exhausted he was. Because the bathroom had no windows, it could have been midnight. Afterward, he studied himself covertly as he combed his hair. Since Kristin had begun coming to the yard last year, he'd looked in mirrors more, but he didn't look any different. He still had a big forehead and eyebrows that met in the center and hair that looked shaggy no matter what, unless he crew-cut it. Sometimes at home, he locked himself in the bathroom and took off his clothes, standing on the toilet lid to see himself full-length in the mirror above the sink. *This is the body I'll be in until I die,* he'd say to himself, and sometimes for a moment he'd feel awe, but then it would be gone.

The air in the parking lot, during the hour they'd been at practice, had gone from darkness to thin gray dawn, sharply cold, scented with gas fumes. Trucks ground by on the highway in clouds of white exhaust. His sister was standing in front of the Y, frowning, near a knot of girls. She was bigger than them, and wearing a shapeless, shabby overcoat of his dad's. She barely spoke to her teammates these days, even though Martha Packer was lingering near her, obviously hoping to be noticed. Martha, with her triple-pierced ears and black lipstick, was one of the girls who had recently become infatuated with his sister. Since her breakdown, Angie had had satellites, girls who wrote poetry about the poignant beauty of dead roses and doodled razor blades in the margins of their class notes.

She saw him and said, 'Finally.' She stomped out toward the Galaxie.

Martha called hopefully, 'See you at school?'

Angie kicked a chunk of snow, which burst into powder. She wore flip-flops, her toes pink and hard-looking in the cold.

At school, stowing his stuff in his locker, he found a letter Kristin had pushed through the slats. He didn't have to look down the hall to know she was watching him unfold the paper. Written in ball-point pen, it began:

So, it's 11 on Tuesday night and my mother is downstairs drinking wine with her 'boyfriend.' This one has been around for exactly two weeks, and I give the relationship another two weeks, max. That's an optimistic forecast, though, since the last 'boyfriend' I was introduced to I never saw again. I could see him anytime I want, of course, if I just walked into the Onion after about four in the afternoon. And now you could too, though I doubt you will.

If you did go in, the 'boyfriend' (now 'ex-boyfriend')'s name is Mike, but rather than going into the Onion and shouting, 'Mike! Mike!' you could just look for a guy who looks a little like a basset hound – big oniony (ha!) rings under the eyes, no cheekbones – and who (according to my mother) drinks Bloody Marys into the evening and plays Johnny Cash on the jukebox. She confessed these details during the why-doesn't-he-call-do-you-think-he's-going-to-call? (um, no, Ma) week after she slept with him, before she gave up and went out and found the current boyfriend. Are you even allowed to drink a brunch drink at night and while listening to Live at San Quentin?

Apparently so.

Anyway, it's eleven, and I can't come see you because even though my mother probably wouldn't notice or care, once I left when a boyfriend was here and the whole time I was away I was imagining coming home and finding her strangled in bed, á la Looking For Mr. Goodbar. *(Did you see that movie?) Not that it ruined your night or anything, but anyway.*

Sometimes I get this awful chill and know how maybe this all seems out of proportion, considering we aren't even exactly friends or anything. But then I think about how that night when we talked, it was like I'd finally met the one person who got it. Before that, I'd decided you were just a jock with your jock friends, and now that I know differently, I find I can't go back

67

to seeing you the way other people do.
I wish you'd just let me know you don't hate me.

Khamisa came up behind him. 'Another note?' She took it from his hand, skimming it, and muttered, 'God, she is so weird.'

'She's right down the hall,' he said.

'So?'

'So it's going to embarrass her if she sees you reading that.'

Khamisa turned away from him, holding the note up in the air, and waved it. 'Fuck her,' she said.

'You want me to fuck her?'

'Very funny.' She kissed him, hard.

He wished she wouldn't. A *jock*. Was he really a jock? As spooky as Kristin was, he didn't quite want her to stop coming to the yard. This summer, there had been two weeks she hadn't shown up, and he'd felt almost lonely. As if he existed less. He opened his eyes but couldn't see, past Khamisa, whether she was still there.

Chapter Seven

Waking up, there was a moment Angie didn't feel bad. Then it descended again onto her chest, like a cat that had merely stood to change position and was now settling more securely. It was three in the morning. She had to go back to sleep, or she would be a wreck at school.

She lay awake for an hour, watching the green numbers of her digital clock. Nights had been getting steadily worse. Finally, she decided she could at least get something done if she was up anyway. It was a comfort to have an excuse to get out of bed, but then as soon as she sat at her desk she felt exhausted again. She forced herself to pick up the first of the blank college applications, heavy tan paper with a blue seal. *What one experience would you say has most shaped who you are as a person?*

What happened last fall had made a mess of her transcript. She'd failed a class and gotten pity-Ds in two more, though, bizarrely, she'd held on to an A in Spanish. And she'd aced her SATs, a 1560; that had been late October, when she'd been a little manic but hadn't yet gone off the rails. She was applying to Yale and Brown and Wesleyan and Middlebury and Cornell, as she'd originally planned. Her parents thought she should, and she didn't have it in her to figure out a new list of schools. Her mom kept saying, 'One bad semester won't matter if you just tell them what happened.' Her mother's theory was that colleges were full of students having breakdowns. According to this theory, Angie would be attractive *because* she'd gotten her breakdown out of the way.

She picked up a pen and stared at what she'd written on a sheet of loose-leaf, a few lines about losing a swim race that would have qualified her for the Junior National team, the day she'd realized she wasn't Olympic material, not even close, as much as she could dominate regional meets. She imagined sentences, the words lined up like railroad ties into the distance. The essay would be easy to pad and fill out. She'd describe the meet, her hopes, her dashed hopes, and what she realized now, or at least recognized she should realize now – that losing sometimes was necessary and good. She put her head down on the desk, on top of the pile of applications. It wouldn't be so hard to do this essay, and then she could change it to fit the other schools' questions, which all basically asked what made her different. She didn't have to do it yet: a thin strand of relief.

At practice she had to force herself through every lap. Her arms and legs felt like they had weights tied to them. She wanted to stop, sink, but that would just mean flurry and attention and someone diving down to pull her up. The energy of the scene – the image of people lifting her from the pool, thumping on her back – exhausted her. Luke would be standing off to the side, disgusted. She managed a leaden flip turn, pushed herself forward.

As soon as she completed her last lap of warm-down, she pulled herself out of the pool and walked, wobbly-legged, toward the bathroom. The rest of the team was still around the pool, getting their things, talking about school. Her brother and his friend Cole stood, listening to a girl. She was much shorter than they were and was telling a story, gesticulating wildly. Luke and Cole both had towels wrapped like skirts around their waists, arms crossed over their chests, identical smirks. Cole was much more handsome, but Luke always had a girlfriend and Cole never did. Luke and Cole glanced at each other over the girl's head, and Angie looked away quickly, hatred prickling in her throat. When she'd fucked Cole, it had been here, sneaking away to the showers in the middle of practice. It had been fun and funny. Afterward, whenever she and Cole saw each other, they grinned without speaking. Since her break, though, Cole had been distant, as if she was just a friend's older sister. No: more like a friend's mother, someone you were polite to but didn't really see.

Their team used Cort's Y from 5:45 to 6:45; now people were arriving for the open swim, the first lithe old women and the double-amputee guy in the wheelchair. If she looked at them, her thoughts would get too fast. She kept her head down.

In the shower room she turned on the water, very hot, and stood

70

beneath it with her arms up to her chest, fists tucked under her chin, eyes closed. Hot water striking her shoulders was the only thing that felt good anymore. Showering and smoking. Food didn't taste like anything; thinking about sex made her feel exhausted and sick. Sometimes thinking about Abe relieved her, but she had to be careful; she returned to memories of him so often that they were wearing thin. Some had actually begun to tear along their folded and refolded creases. The first time he said he loved her – had she been in the car or getting out? The first day he came into the deli – hadn't he lingered, reading the descriptions of sandwiches, working up to coming over, waiting for the place to clear? Or was she thinking of another time?

'Did you write the paper for English?' Alice Newman asked from under the next showerhead. Angie'd been friends with Alice Newman for a long time, and she forced herself to be normal for a minute.

'I think so,' she said.

Other girls came in, turning on showers. As they called to one another, the steam held their voices. 'Does anyone have a tampon?' Marcia Davis was asking. Someone else said, 'They were all over each other. I mean, *all* over.' Through the steam, their bodies were blurred and indistinct, like the illustrations fronted with tissue paper in old books. Angie's vision of the girls swam up out of the fog – a girl took three steps across the room, bent to pick up a bottle of Finesse – and then sank away.

During the day, moving from anatomy to European history to art, she grew heavier and heavier until she could barely walk. She couldn't skip classes. Skipping classes would bring her too close to last fall. She wasn't taking chem., but otherwise she had most of the same teachers that she'd had a year ago when she spun out; the first class she missed they'd be on the phone. She could have eaten lunch with girls from swim team, but instead she spent lunch period in the library, head down on one of the tables but unable to nap or even close her eyes.

She'd worried that people would ask about the hospital, but the only people who had were Abby and Tracy, two juniors. Angie hung out with – or maybe just near – them between classes on the school's back steps, where you were allowed to smoke. Abby and Tracy listened obsessively to The Cure. Not only listened to The Cure but dressed like Robert Smith, the lead singer: long black coats, black eyeliner and black lipstick, and hair dyed dead black. They wanted to know about shock treatment, which she hadn't had, and bizarre suicide attempts, which she said she didn't know about. A lie: people in the hospital and at the farm talked about suicide all the time.

She wasn't shunned, exactly. She still had friends on the swim team. Sometimes other kids stared at her, but as soon as they realized they were staring, they'd look quickly away, busying themselves. If people made fun of her, they weren't doing it to her face. She probably had Luke, at least in part, to thank for that: in people's minds he'd neutralize some of her weirdness.

The bell rang for the end of lunch, and she rose from the library table slowly. In the hallway, the pay phone was free, and she gave in to the desire to call Abe. She'd tried to reach him twice today already and had just gotten the machine.

Abe sounded surprised to hear her voice. 'Aren't you supposed to be at school?'

'I am at school. In C Hall, in front of the trophy case.' Abe thought it was funny that the public high school's buildings were lettered; St. Gregory's had been too small to need anything like that. She twisted the stiff metal-wrapped phone cord around her wrist. 'Do you love me?'

'You know, I did last night, but today I woke up and thought, Hmm, no, not so much anymore.'

'Not funny.'

'Well, you always ask. I love you.'

'I have class,' she said. 'I've got to go.'

She shouldn't have called. Now she'd wasted her one thing to look forward to for the day. Midway through Spanish, so jittery she hadn't heard a word of the lesson, she got the hall pass and called Abe back. Usually when his machine answered she hung up, but now she said, 'It's me. Are you there? If you are, I guess you don't want to talk. I'm sorry I was so weird. You're probably not there. If you are it's okay. Never mind. Sorry, I'm sorry.'

After Spanish she had AP English, then calculus. Midway through that class she got another hall pass.

'Are you there? Abe, really, if you're there, please pick up . . . Okay, you're not there, I guess. Ignore this call. Pretend I didn't – sorry, I'm being – you're just never there when I fucking need you, and it's fucking getting to me, I guess. This is stupid, talking to your machine.'

She hung up, walked toward calculus. Math classes were held in F Hall, dim and low-ceilinged, with orange lockers stretching into the distance. At the far end of the hall were heavy doors with wire-reinforced glass windows at the top letting in some light from the stairwell. Angie had a moment of vertigo, thinking of the hospital; for a moment she felt locked in. She turned back, ran to the phone.

'Hi, guess who? That's right, it's me. Ha-ha. Anyway, I just wanted to say, I shouldn't have – I take that stuff back, I know you're busy – I'll talk to you later, I guess. Will you call me later? I'm sorry. This is stupid. Sorry. Sorry.'

She had to stay after school to talk to Mr. Diebhorn about her lab reports. Her drawings were sloppy – 'dashed off,' he said – and her test scores had been slipping. He had a broad nose, wide nostrils filled with hair. The hairs, dark, locked together, made her feel sick and hot.

'I know you had some trouble last year.' When he said *trouble* he cocked the first two fingers of both hands. *Little Bunny Foo-Foo, hopping through the forest.*

Angie glanced down at her lap. Her hands were shaking. She realized she'd dressed like a blind woman: a stained Yale sweat-shirt over a wrinkled green silk blouse. She had on Docksiders from eighth grade and ancient beige corduroys, too short, so you could see her socks. She tried to remember choosing clothes this morning but couldn't.

'I don't plan to start making allowances that allow shoddy work—'

Had she walked around like this all day?

Mr. Diebhorn looked at her, templing his fingers. It was her turn to say something. She tried to replay his words through the noise in her head, which was like a phone left off the hook, persistent and distracting. She wanted not to think of last fall, she pushed against it with her mind, but pictures came, the boys she'd slept with. She'd been sure her physics teacher, Mr. Ridge-back, was in love with her, and on a day when he'd asked her to stay after school she'd tried to seduce him. She could still feel the silly, sexy smile she'd had on her face, walking toward him across the room.

She had to say something. She forced herself to look toward Mr. Diebhorn, focusing on the periodic table behind his head. Lithium

73

was the third element, *Li*. Because she'd been thinking about sex, she imagined, unbidden, Mr. Diebhorn naked, his penis pushing raw and red through thatched pubic hair. She felt completely disgusting.

Whispering, she said, 'I forget what you asked.'

He exhaled noisily. Not looking at her, he asked, 'Whom do you think I'm teaching up here? Am I entertaining myself?'

'I don't know.' Even with her eyes closed, she could see his awful penis. She pressed her hands over her face.

'You don't know,' Mr. Diebhorn said, loading the words with sarcasm. Then, oddly quiet – though she sensed his sadness was for himself – he said, 'No, I suppose you really don't.'

The second-floor bathroom had three metal-doored stalls. It had just been cleaned: the toilet seats were all up, and there was the smell of chlorine. She thought of when she'd thrown herself into the pool. Everything in her head was a way she'd humiliated herself. Here was jumping into the pool, here was falling at Jess's church, here was trying to get into Thad's room the night he broke up with her. She wrapped her hand around Mrs. Salter's ankle. Lizzie Travnor burst into the room where she was having sex with the freshman; Lizzie said, 'Whoops, sorry,' shut the door, and then started laughing. Inside the room, above the freshman, Angie laughed, and laughing she ran toward the lip of the pool. She walked toward Mr. Ridgeback, unbuttoning her shirt. She opened the door of the chemistry room, shut it behind her. Lizzie Travnor laughed. *Am I entertaining myself?* She walked toward Mr. Ridge-back, smiling, reaching up for the top button on her shirt.

For some reason toilets at school didn't have lids; there was no place to sit. She closed herself in a stall, wedging herself beside the toilet so that her back was against the wall. She put her hands over her mouth and screamed. *Fuck,* she yelled, the word backing up into her head. *Fuck! Fuck! Fuck!*

The door opened and shut; footsteps crossed to the sink, then paused. 'Angie?' said a girl's voice.

Angie scrambled to her feet. Fuck again.

'I saw you come in here. It's Kristin. Kristin Cannon?' Footsteps echoed in the small room as she crossed to Angie's stall and stopped outside. 'Are you okay in there?'

'Fine.'

74

'I was hoping I could talk to you.'

'Go right ahead.'

Kristin giggled nervously and was silent. Fuck, fuck, fuck for real.

Angie straightened her sweatshirt and flushed the toilet, then pushed open the stall door and strode past Kristin to the sinks.

She twisted the knob for HOT; water sang in the building's old pipes.

'Do you think ...? Your brother used to talk to me ... I can't sleep, I have no appetite. I just – I know there's nothing you can do, but maybe if I could just talk with you—'

Angie looked at Kristin in the mirror. 'Are you *serious*?' Clearly she was, her face pinched with unhappiness. In the last few months, Angie had become excruciatingly aware of degrees of outsiderness, but Kristin was normal enough, even kind of pretty. She had teased bangs, dark eyeliner, a long colorful sweater over tight black stirrup pants – the look of almost every girl at Applefield High.

'I know it's ridiculous,' Kristin said. 'You're probably laughing your ass off. I should stop. Coming to your house, I mean. I even could; I just don't want to.'

Carefully, Angie turned off the sink. Hoisting her bookbag onto her shoulder, she walked away, pausing in the doorway to say, 'You've got no chance with Luke because you're totally fucking crazy.'

She let the door slam behind her; it echoed in the empty hall. The lockers – blue metal in A Hall – stretched narrowly away, lock after lock after lock. Angie's quick footsteps rang.

She turned from A Hall into E. At the far end, a custodian was polishing the floor. She moved the heavy polisher slowly, with both hands. The way she turned slowly to the right, then slowly, slowly, to the left, reminded Angie of the people you saw on the beach in Portsmouth sometimes with metal detectors, headphones covering their ears, eyes down as they scanned the sand.

Angie stopped short. Oblivious to her presence, the woman moved away up the hall, smaller and smaller. Angie held her breath, praying the woman wouldn't see her before she got hold of herself. She was going to get hold of herself. She was going to Yale.

75

Chapter Eight

'Don't move,' Ben said.

He jumped up from the futon and moved naked across the room, penis bobbling between his legs. Above him, clothesline strung with prints crisscrossed the apartment. The air from the electric space heater made the photos twist, their shadows dappling the floor.

Grabbing a camera from where it hung on a chair, Ben turned back to the bed. 'Your hair looks amazing all spread out like that.'

Jordana smiled lazily and he took her picture. Then, feeling loosened and slow, she rolled onto her stomach. The shutter clicked; he reached and pulled the sheet down and clicked the shutter again.

'Stop,' she said, because she didn't want to seem vain. She sat to reach for the sheet and twitch it up again. He took a picture of her, then another when she made a face at him. He laughed, and she was secretly pleased.

Holding the sheet around herself, she stood and approached him. Ben danced a step back and took another picture. She advanced and he retreated, stumbling a little and laughing, until she'd backed him against the table. The camera almost touched her face. He took one more picture, put the camera down, and kissed her. 'Do you want some wine?'

'It's three in the afternoon,' she said.

Ben shrugged and moved away, opening a drawer and scratching around for a corkscrew. Though he was only a few years younger than she, she sometimes thought of him as closer in age to Luke: how unattached he was, maybe, or how he seemed to take things as they came. Whereas Jordana had turned – even before

Angie's break, she realized – into someone who *worried*.

The first time they'd slept together, Ben had touched her hip, which was so jutting and sharp that he'd jerked his hand back: 'What's *that*?' She'd started laughing, and then he had. She laughed often and easily with him. When she'd told her best friend, Beth, about Ben, she'd had trouble articulating why she liked being with him, other than that it was ... *fun*. The word seemed weak, as did *comfortable* or *sweet*. But she loved the relationship's sweetness, its comfort.

On the clothesline hung photos Ben had taken for the paper: a homecoming parade, a single-car crash. Between the newspaper and wedding photography and the occasional odd job – he used his truck to haul brush or move furniture or, with a blade attached in winter, plow snow – he cobbled together a living. His juggling of bills was one of the self-consciously bohemian details he was proud of and brought up often, pretending to disparage it. But other things, things he seemed not even to notice, impressed her more. He had no credit cards, no television, no bureau – he kept his clothes in an open duffel bag on the floor. No stereo, just a cheap Sony boom box. He'd turned the small kitchen into a darkroom and moved the fridge into the living room, where it left rusty water stains on the carpet. A folding table that served as both pantry and kitchen held cereal, rice, canned soup, an electric hot plate. His belongings would have fit in the back of his truck.

She turned on the radio, fiddling the knob. An evangelist, a ZZ Top song, heavy metal, easy listening, The Cars. It seemed like any time she turned on the radio anywhere in New England she found a Cars song. Normally she would have turned to the classical station, but it felt weird to do that here.

Sitting down on the couch, she tilted her head back to see the pictures hung above her of a wedding Ben had photographed the previous week. The necessary shots of bridesmaids lined up, of bride and groom dancing. The bridegroom smashed cake against his new wife's mouth.

'You know what this is called?' Ben asked, holding the wine bottle with two fingers.

'I'm pretty sure that's called wine.'

'No, this space here.' He pointed to the bottle's neck, above the wine and below the cork.

She still hadn't gotten used to his earnestness. It made her sarcasm feel prickly and cheap.

He said, 'It's called *ullage*.'

'I can't believe there's a name for that.'

'It's true. I photographed a story on wine making in New Hampshire.'

She managed not to say anything, though wine making seemed like just what New Hampshire was totally unsuited for, with its freezing winters and muggy gnat-clouded summers. People wanted to be able to do everything. She pointed her chin at the photograph of the bride trying to smile, her face smeared with frosting. 'What happened there?'

'You haven't seen that? A lot of guys do it.'

'Is it supposed to be funny?'

He nodded, pulling out the cork with a tiny grunt of satisfaction.

'It seems so aggressive,' she said.

'Yeah, like, "You made me go through this whole spectacle, now fuck you."' He poured the wine into two glasses – one a juice glass with a peeling decal of Snow White on the side, the other an actual goblet that he handed to Jordana. He wandered a few steps away, running a finger along the bottom edges of photos. Unlike Pieter, Ben wasn't self-conscious about being naked. He raised his arms to unclip a photo and reclip it more securely, then turned and walked back toward the couch. Though they'd just had sex, desire twisted her stomach. His brown curls stood up all over his head, and his eyes were the yellowish-green of olive oil. Sitting on the floor, he hooked one arm up over her knees.

She stood at the door of her daughter's room. Angie sat at the desk, a pile of textbooks at her elbow. In the next room, Luke had the stereo turned up so loud the bass thumped in the floor beneath their feet. This was when Ben felt most unreal to her, immediately after she'd been with him.

'Can you work with all that noise?'

Angie shrugged. Her hair fell into her face, and Jordana stopped herself from walking over and pushing it back. She'd been yelled at for doing that.

Angie's room contained both the detritus of girlhood and the clichés of a teenager: her old Nancy Drews, a collection of glass hippos, taped-up magazine pictures of Olympic swimmers, milk crates of records, photos of her with Jess or with Abe. Her swim-

78

ming trophies lined the windowsill, bodies straining toward invisible water. The floor, like all the upstairs floors, was covered in green wall-to-wall carpet, and the furniture, like all the furniture in the house, was heavy, dark, inherited from Jordana's parents. Angie had (without asking) painted it white and maroon, which only made it look more lumbering. Nothing suggested that Angie could have spent five of the last twelve months in psychiatric care. Jordana didn't know whether the room's blandness was reassuring or strange.

'What are you working on?'

'Homework.'

'What kind of homework?'

'Anatomy and physiology.'

They went through a few more rounds. Was anatomy interesting? Not really. Was it hard? Not too hard. How was school? Angie shot her a look, and Jordana said (she heard, hated, but couldn't help that she was whining), 'I'm just *asking*—'

'You ask every day, Ma. It's okay. I'm okay. I'm taking my meds. I'm not going to go crazy again. Okay?'

'I know you're taking your meds.'

'Yeah, that's why you watch me every single time I take them.' With exaggerated patience: 'Could you get out of my room now? You're not exactly helping me concentrate.'

Angie made Jordana want to grab her, either to shake or embrace. Before she could stop herself, she reached forward to push Angie's hair behind her ear. Angie jerked back. 'Ma!'

'It was in your face!'

Angie unhooked the lock of hair, shaking it in front of her eyes again. 'You're always *around*.'

'Okay.' Jordana had to force herself to start moving. 'How are college applications going?'

'They're fine. They're almost done.'

Jordana made herself not push. She stooped, gathering a sticky plate, some cups. Just as she put her hand on the doorknob, her daughter said, 'These questions are so pointless.'

Jordana paused, unsure.

'Like this one,' Angie said. 'Like it really matters if you know the formula for lactic acid buildup.'

Jordana took a hesitant step back into the room. 'Do you want me to take a look at it?'

79

Angie shrugged. Jordana was terrible at anything mathlike, but she bent down to see the question, something about calculating carbon dioxide in the blood.

'Have you been *drinking*?' Angie said.

Jordana's hand flew to her mouth and she took a step back. 'I had a glass of wine with Beth after work. She'd had a difficult morning.' Angie looked at her strangely; she was talking too fast. 'I'll go brush my teeth.'

'It's not a big deal.'

'It will just take a minute—'

'I need you to help me.'

Jordana moved back into the circle of light cast by the desk lamp. She bent cautiously over her daughter's work, lips clamped.

They worked on the first problem until they both got frustrated, Angie near tears, saying, 'Forget it, I'll come back to that one,' and Jordana saying, 'Why don't they explain this better? Are you sure the formula isn't here?' She took the book, flipping backward through the pages.

'I'll go *back* to it,' Angie said, twisting the book away. Then: 'No, don't go. Help me with this next one.'

Jordana knew she wasn't helping. But she didn't want to leave, and her daughter clearly didn't want to be alone. 'Scootch over, then. My back is killing me.'

'God, your breath stinks.'

She took a deep breath and perched on the edge of Angie's desk chair, hip to hip with her daughter. They began on the second question, about the rate of oxygen pumped into the blood during exercise. The lamp threw a circle of yellow light over her daughter, now really in tears; the penciled formulas; the erasures that turned the paper gray and nappy. They worked that way together, Angie giving up on problems and insisting she'd come back. Sometimes, they came up with answers that seemed wrong to Jordana but that Angie insisted were right, they were fine; could they just go on? Jordana breathed through her nose. When Pieter's voice rose up the stairs, calling them for dinner, it was startling to remember the world still going on outside the room.

Chapter Nine

Angie bought her bus ticket for Boston, and then she and her mom went to the grubby doughnut store that took up an alcove at one end of the station. Angie got a cup of decaf and her mother got regular. 'Should we split a maple bar?'

'*Mom.*'

'What?'

'You don't think I'm fat enough?'

Her mother's shoulders tightened. 'You're not fat.'

'Whatever you say.' Angie took her coffee over to one of the little tables, the sticky floor pulling softly at her boots. She hadn't seen Abe since he'd left at the end of August, more than two months ago. A bald man with gingery tufts of hair above each ear hunched over a magazine two tables over. He looked up as Angie sat. She smiled; he looked back down at his reading.

God, why had she smiled at some stranger? Why did she have to be so weird?

She looked to see if her mother was coming, but she'd stopped to talk to the girl behind the counter. Her mother always talked with girls and women working shitty jobs. She would also do things like go over to a woman yelling at her son in the grocery store and offer to help out. Somehow, she did it in a way so that the woman actually consented. Angie's mother would pick up the crying kid and plant him on her hip, talking softly. She would hand the child her keys to play with, and then walk around the store with the mother, chatting, gently jiggling the child. Angie, left standing by their own cart, would watch as they disappeared around the corner.

Though she hadn't slept much the night before, she kept her eyes

81

open. It was bright outside, snowing weakly. Next door, a bunch of teenagers – a year or two younger than Angie – hung out in the slushy parking lot of the Cumberland Farms convenience store. Two guys with longish feathery hair messed around, pushing each other. A girl perched on the hood of a car held a paper-bagged bottle between her knees, probably peach schnapps or Bailey's Irish Cream. Behind them, the stubble of a November-blue field.

Recently, Angie had begun thinking about hurting herself. It wasn't that she wanted to hurt herself but that the images wouldn't leave her alone. She saw herself go into the kitchen and slash her palm with a knife, stab herself in the thigh. Cut off a finger. She saw herself going into the garage after the garden loppers. If she closed her eyes even for a second, she imagined her own forearms slashed with long lozenge-shaped wounds.

Taking a deep, shuddering breath, she tried to concentrate on Abe.

She was sick. She was really sick. She really was sick.

Abe. They were supposed to go see some play.

Everything had begun to look like a weapon: nail file, bleach, window, book, belt, bathtub. Screwdriver (eye). Pen (eardrum). Stove (forearm, cheek). She avoided being in the kitchen alone, or down in the basement. She peed as quickly as possible. She hadn't given up cigarettes (lashes, face, stomach, inner thigh, hair, hands, hands, hands), but she had given up smoking alone. In front of people, she trusted herself to maintain.

Finally, her mother turned, balancing a maple bar in one hand. She wore a narrow oat-colored sweater and long tinkling earrings of coral and silver; she'd begun buying new clothes, something Angie and her father had been begging her to do for years. Her hair still went everywhere, she still wore old jeans of Luke's, but the nicer things made the messy ones seem part of a deliberate effect.

She put the maple bar down on the table, saying, 'You don't have to have any, it's for me.' The glaze had a dent, the size of a fingertip, cracked and hazy. 'So, what are your plans?'

'My plans.'

'For Cambridge.'

Angie shrugged. It made her too anxious to think about how she was going to get through the three-day weekend. Abe had said something about a party tonight. 'Harvard is beautiful,' her mother said.

Angie bit down hard on the edge of the cup. The Styrofoam tasted satisfyingly bitter, which helped keep her mind back from hurting herself.

'I don't want—' her mother said hesitantly. 'I know Abe cares about you, but—'

'So, like, I say I don't want a doughnut so you put one in front of me? Is that how it works?'

'He's in a new place,' her mother continued doggedly. 'He'll have new friends, and—'

Angie crossed her arms over her chest, eyebrows raised, looking at her hard.

'I just – I don't—'

'God, just say it, whatever it is.'

'I don't want you to be disappointed if it's not all you've hoped.'

'I'm *crazy,*' Angie said, 'not stupid.'

'You're not crazy,' snapped her mother. Then, more softly, 'And you're not *fat.*'

This was one of her mother's involved, protective days; she either acted intensely present like this, or else busy and distracted, impatient, easily irritated. She pulled her broken-strapped watch from the pocket of her jeans. Angie looked away from her, at the man two seats over bent close to the table, where his magazine was laid out. As he turned the page, a picture flashed for a moment: two teenage girls in fingerless black leather gloves, their long-nailed hands on each other's naked breasts, tongues meeting in the air.

Angie stood, knee hitting the table. One of the cups capsized, coffee sloshing up onto her mother's oatmeal-colored sweater. Her mother jerked up, eyes wide. 'What is it? What's wrong?'

'Nothing. I just think we should go.'

Her mother sank back. 'You could be a little more careful. We have fifteen minutes.' She pulled a napkin from the dispenser on the table, wet it with her tongue, and blotted at the coffee stain.

Angie bounced from foot to foot. 'Can we *go?*'

'It's not coming out. Damn it, Angie.'

The man looked up from his magazine, head tilted toward them.

'*Please,* Mom. Please can we go?' She was almost shouting.

Her mother looked up, about to say something, then caught herself; she actually jerked a tiny bit backward. She nodded and rose, gathering up her cup and soggy napkins. She carried them to the trash, wiped her hands on her jeans.

When she came back, she put her arm around Angie's shoulders. 'Are you okay?'

'I'm fine.' More forcefully: 'I'm *fine*. God.'

'You know, you don't have to go to Boston.'

For just a moment, the idea washed Angie with relief. She imagined climbing the stairs at home, getting into her clean, cool sheets, sleeping and sleeping. But even more than she was scared of going, she didn't want to be someone who stayed home. Twisting out from under her mother's arm, she said, 'Don't be dumb.'

Sometimes she remembered Abe as more handsome than was true, other times as uglier, but here he was at Boston's North Station: just Abe, with his flat wide mouth and beautiful shoulders, holding flowers. He seemed so wholesome, so normal, that she began crying with relief. She rushed to him and pressed against his warmth and solidity, wishing her body could melt into his. The gaudiness of the flowers – a confusion of mums, carnations, roses, the tulle of baby's breath, a big orange lily – moved her.

She continued crying on the T, Abe's arm around her. 'What is it?' he said. 'What can I do?'

'It's nothing. I don't know. I'm fine. I'm good.'

Harvard Square was a jumble of street musicians, T-shirt sellers, panhandlers, students, café tables. A man played the bagpipes a few feet from another man playing the harmonica, the strains of 'Amazing Grace' tangling with wheezy blues. Angie and Abe joined a surge of people crossing the street against the light; cars honked. And then they passed through a brick arch and into the hush of Harvard Yard, the chill of shadows across its lawn, the crunch of dark red leaves underfoot, students moving across the yard, two others standing still, talking. One wore an orange wool scarf so long it touched the ground behind her; crumbs of dead leaf clung to its fringe.

Abe's room in Thayer Hall was the inner of a two-room double. His roommate was out, and as they passed through his room Abe opened the closet: velvet, silk, what looked like tiny steel links. Angie reached out a finger to touch them.

'Chain mail,' Abe said. His letters were filled with stories of Evan Johansson, who had turned out to be a sullen Creative Anachronist. 'He's probably out jousting.'

'Does he wear this stuff to class?'

'Sometimes. And the thing is, I still don't really believe it. Like he still might turn out to be kidding. Even though clearly he's not.' Abe closed Evan Johansson's wardrobe and opened the door to his own room. 'Ta-da!' He put Angie's suitcase down beside the desk. 'Plus he's up all night and then sleeps all morning.'

'What can I do with these?' she asked.

Abe took the flowers from her, looked around, and stuck them in a coffee mug where they splayed out awkwardly.

'Why's he up all night?'

'He says his circadian rhythms aren't like other people's.'

The room had ebony-framed windows and elaborate ceiling moldings. The elegance of its architecture contrasted with the stolid furnishings: blond wood headboard, blond dresser, blond wardrobe, blond desk. The bed was neatly made up with a red blanket. Before Abe left for school he'd asked Angie for a photograph, which now sat, framed, on the blond bedside table. Above his bed hung R.E.M. and Elvis Costello posters he'd gotten from Stars.

'At last: we are alone,' Abe said. He started the sentence off stagy and Dracula-like but ended in a normal voice, as though he'd gotten self-conscious midway through.

She went over to hug him. If she could always be in arm's reach of Abe she'd be okay. Breathing him in, she made the mistake of closing her eyes a moment and saw her gashed arms again.

'What?' Abe said.

'What?'

'You made, like, a sound.'

She reached over to pick up the photograph of herself, studying it as though she hadn't seen it before. It had been taken a little over a year ago, before her break and before lithium. She sat on a picnic blanket, looking over her shoulder, smiling at the person (her mother) taking the picture. They'd been having a family picnic, the kind of occasion that Angie and Luke called Enforced Voorsterism. She'd been smiling because it was a photograph, not because she'd been having a particularly good time. She wasn't stupid enough to think that before she got sick everything had been perfect.

'Do you tell people about me? I mean, do you tell them about . . . that I was sick?'

Abe shook his head. 'That has nothing to do with who you are.'

85

He took the photo, tossed it on the bed, kissed her. As long as she kept her eyes open, she could stay okay. Abe moaned and put his hands on her hips, pulling her against him.

Kissing her, he began to tug her sweater up. 'I've missed you so much,' he said.

She tried to go through the motions, trying to think what the right motions should be.

Abe stopped and pulled back. 'Is everything all right?'

She reached up and put her hand over his eyes. 'Don't look at me, okay?'

'What?'

'Just, right now – I just ... Close your eyes.'

Evan Johansson turned out to be stocky, with a dark circular beard, like he'd pressed a dirty glass to his mouth. It was five in the afternoon and dark; outside the window, wind gusted up old leaves from the grass. To Angie he said, 'You must be the H.T.H.'

'This is Angie. Angie, Evan.'

Angie said, 'H.T.H.?'

'Hometown Honey.' His accent, flat and midwestern, contrasted bizarrely with his voluminous wine-colored cloak. Perched on one shoulder was some kind of stuffed animal – no, an actual taxidermied raven. Angie winced. Its scaly feet had been sewn directly to the cloth.

'How was jousting?' Abe asked.

Evan turned away to hang his cloak in his closet. '*Sparring*. Did you see horses?'

'Sorry.' Abe made a face at Angie. 'How was *sparring*?'

'Would it mean anything to you if I said I scored six touches?'

'Nope.'

'Well, that's how it was.' He finished arranging the cloak on the hanger, shut the door of the wardrobe, turned, and faced them with his legs planted wide apart and arms folded across his chest.

'We're off to the Union.'

Evan said, 'For a change.'

'Do you want to come?'

She should admire Abe's niceness, but actually it annoyed her: always believing the best of people made him obtuse. Clearly Evan Johansson despised Abe. She imagined he saw Abe – saw both of them – as conventional and untroubled. Also dumb in a way that unconventional, troubled people didn't have the choice to be. She was sure Evan Johansson would sigh noisily and turn Abe's invitation down. Instead, he sighed noisily, turned back to the wardrobe, pulled out his cloak again. She couldn't believe he walked around with a dead bird on his shoulder; was that even legal?

A needle going through the feet, the tug of thread as it pulled through her flesh.

'Ouch.' Abe jerked his hand from hers and shook it; she must have been clutching too hard. 'Careful, there.'

She groped for his hand again. 'I'll be careful. Sorry. I'll be careful.'

The three of them went out into the hallway, which was filled with the noise of people getting drunk and shouting. Angie had imagined something different for Harvard, a greater solemnity. Instead, paper banners festooned the hall, not unlike the paper banners at Applefield High, advertising events in Magic Marker: a room-to-room party; a movie – *The Shining* – to be shown in the Common Room.

Evan said, 'So, you're the one who leaves all the fucked-up messages.'

'I guess.'

'You *guess?*'

She blurted, 'Abe tells me you're from Minnesota.'

'Do we really have to do this?' Evan Johansson grimaced. They were crossing the dark, windy quad; dry leaves scuttled across the sidewalk like crabs. 'The whole where-did-you-go-to-high-school-what-do-you-think-your-major-is-going-to-be bullshit? The whole name game – "You know Cindy Meyerson? Oh, my God – *I* know Cindy Meyerson!"' For this last, he pitched his voice into a sudden, painful squeal; several people jerked around, startled. He put his face close to hers and whispered loudly, 'When really no one *gives* two *shits.*'

'So,' she said, looking into his eyes. 'Abe tells me you're from Minnesota.'

He tilted his head, a corner of his mouth tweaking into almost a smile. He must have been used to making people back down. Angie felt triumph and then, immediately, regret. Why did she care if she impressed Evan Johansson?

'Minnesota.' He straightened up so he was no longer in her face.

87

'Land of butter. Land of the Norse.'

They'd come to the Freshman Union, where Abe handed her an ID card. 'It's a friend; she went home for the weekend.'

'But she's black.'

'They don't check.' He was right; the cashier swiped the card without looking. When she handed the ID back, Angie looked at it more closely: Marisol Thompson was smiling, pretty, thin. Angie's therapist was always saying that she couldn't compare her insides to others' outsides. Still. There was no way Abe was going to stay in love with Angie when he was surrounded by pretty, smart, interesting, normal girls, girls not retaking their senior year of high school.

Ducking her head, she followed him into the Union.

Sunday, Abe took her on a long tour of campus, showing her the buildings where each of his classes met, the library where he studied, the upper-class house to which he hoped to be assigned. At the statue of John Harvard, he told her the story of the three lies, the same story she'd heard two summers ago when she toured Harvard. For lunch, they went to Café Pamplona, where he kept saying, 'Isn't this place cool?' It was a basement room, tiny, white-washed, the ceiling so low Abe had to duck when he came to a beam. The only food on the menu was a ham, cheese, and butter sandwich; it came wrapped in white paper, ham sliced so thin you could see through it.

'Isn't this great?' he said. 'Don't you love this place?'

And Angie, who had already cried twice today – once with Abe when he tried to get her out of bed for breakfast, once alone in the shower – fought not to cry again. If she opened her mouth, she would be lost, so she just nodded and tried to smile. She had never felt so lonely.

What did she feel like doing this afternoon?

She shook her head; she didn't know. Why had she come on a three-day weekend and not a normal two-day? If tomorrow weren't Veterans Day, she'd be leaving soon.

See a movie? Abe suggested. Go into Boston? Walk down by the river? Quincy Market?

The air was so heavy she could barely breathe. Even shaking her head was exhausting. The only thing she could imagine doing for the afternoon was crawling underneath the table and sleeping.

88

Something warm and light touched her cheek, and thinking a small insect must have landed there, she tried to wave it away. No. Fuck, she was crying again.

'I'm not like this,' she said. 'This isn't me.'

'I know it's not.'

She covered her face with her hands, taking deep breaths. 'Okay.'

'We could go to the aquarium.'

'*No.*' She'd gone to Boston's aquarium on field trips in grade school. 'That's someplace you'd take, like, your grandparents. Someone you didn't know what to do with.'

'What then?' Abe said, finally frustrated. 'What do *you* want to do?'

'I don't know! I don't know! Stop hammering at me!'

'I'm sorry,' Abe said after a moment. He reached for her hand. 'I'm being an asshole.'

She jerked her hand away. 'You're not being an asshole, I'm being *horrible* to you. Why don't you yell at me?'

'I love you.'

'You should just break up with me. You're going to sooner or later, anyway. You're going to meet someone who's nice, and who's smart—'

'Jesus,' Abe said, flopping back against the whitewashed wall of the café. He closed his eyes. 'I don't know how to be with you when you're like this.'

'Do you think *I* do?'

Abe shrugged. It was around two in the afternoon, and the restaurant had mostly emptied. The waiter cleared plates and crumpled paper napkins. Drab light filtered into the room from the staircase that led down from the street. The woman who had been working behind the counter got herself a cup of coffee and came out to sit at a table, tiredly unwrapping a sandwich. She must eat ham, cheese, and butter every day.

'A walk,' Angie finally offered, hoping she could make good on it. Her legs felt very heavy. 'A walk would maybe be nice.'

And she did feel better, walking along the Charles. As they made their way downriver, Cambridge changed: more and more faces were dark; more and more buildings were boarded up or blackened by fire. They walked as far as MIT, then turned and made their

89

way upriver again. Back near Harvard, Abe sat behind Angie on the grass, wrapping them both in his wool coat. On the water, sculls rowed past. The air was cold and fiercely bright, wind rattling last leaves from the trees.

'See?' Abe asked. 'That wasn't so bad, was it?'

'It's so peaceful by the water.'

Another scull passed. The rowers bent forward together, straightened, bent forward. At this distance, they seemed like people genuflecting in prayer.

'What I said before . . .'

Abe waited, then asked, 'Which part?'

'If you broke up with me. I couldn't – oh, damn.' She stopped before she started crying again.

Abe wrapped his coat more tightly around them. 'You know those NRA bumper stickers: YOU'LL HAVE TO PRY IT OUT OF MY COLD DEAD HANDS?' He put his warm cheek down against her temple and whispered, 'I want to be with you when we're both, like, eighty and have no teeth.'

By the time they made their way back to Harvard Square it was around four-thirty, edging toward twilight. The bagpiper was playing again, and a man sat on the pavement, head bent. In front of him were a paper cup and a sign: OLD, SICK, TIRED, HUNGRY. Chattering students parted around him and then closed again, a brook moving around a rock. A woman sold jewelry, silver spread out across black velvet on the sidewalk, and Abe bought a ring for Angie, tiny chips of green turquoise between two narrow strips of silver. A band played behind the T station: two guys and a girl, all with guitars, plus a drummer who wore sunglasses despite the sun being down, the streetlamps lit.

'I've seen her before,' said Abe, pointing with his chin. 'She's a sophomore.'

The girl's hair fell forward, covering her face; she didn't look at her audience. She sang 'I Wanna Be Sedated,' a song meant to be fast and hard but that she sang slowly, soft and urgent. The members of her band watched her with what seemed like total concentration. Passersby would pause, listen a moment, occasionally drift over to the stairs to sit down.

The band moved on to The Beach Boys' 'Be True to Your School,' then a Violent Femmes song that had been popular a few years ago. Making bouncy songs slow and eerie seemed to be the band's one trick, but it was a good one; it turned the songs inside out. The girl sang that she'd waited her whole life for just one kiss, her voice a desperate-sounding whisper.

At the end of the song, she looked up at her listeners for the first time, shaking the hair back from her face, giving a small self-conscious but delighted smile at their applause. Sadness rose again in Angie, gusting through her, blowing any sense of safety out like a match.

They saw a play with a group of people, and then went out to a place called Civili Tea. Angie couldn't concentrate on the hundred varieties of tea and picked the third thing on the list, something called green tea, which sounded light and fresh. Abe's new friends tried to involve her in the conversation, but it was like hearing surface noise when you were swimming underwater: faint, bright, foreign. Her tea tasted like charred grass. She had to ask them to repeat their questions; then she would dredge up a one-word answer, and Abe would jump in and help. (*Angie's a swimmer,* he offered. *She won All-State last year. Angie's probably going to Yale.*)

They complained about roommates and classes and how someone's suite was smaller than suites in Massachusetts Hall. The luxury of their concerns made them seem conventional, untroubled, dumb.

They were quiet walking back to his room. Abe closed the door behind them, turning to her and asking, 'What is going on with you?'

'You really like those people?'

'Why, don't you?'

On the phone he'd told her about this or that spoiled rich kid, or about the new weird thing Evan Johansson had done, or about the Teaching Fellow for his econ class. In discussion section, the TF blew and blew his nose until the pile of used Kleenex on the table in front of him was as big as his head. On especially bad days, he ran out of fresh tissues and had to hunt and peck through the pile for the least soggy of the used ones. Angie loved when Abe told her stories, but she hadn't realized until this minute that she wanted him to be unhappy at Harvard.

'You have a whole life here.' She willed him to contradict her. 'I'm a distraction.'

91

'Please tell me you're not doing this again.'

Looking him in the eye, she said, 'So get out, if you want out.'

'This isn't happening to us.' He slapped the wall with his hand. '*Fuck*.' He hit the wall again.

God, what was she doing? 'I'm sorry. I'm sorry. I know I'm being crazy. I just love you, and you act like this is just some fun thing or something.'

'Fine. I act like this is just some fun thing. What can I do? Tell me what more I could be doing and I'll do it.' He was yelling, but his voice broke on the last words.

'Like—' But she couldn't think of anything. 'Never mind. It's not important. It's okay.' She put her arms around his neck, trying to kiss him, but he shook her off, saying, 'I don't exactly feel like it right now,' and she cried and clung to him until he felt sorry for her and apologized and held her while she sobbed into his soft blue T-shirt. She should never have come to Harvard. She was terrified to think that tomorrow she would have to leave.

They made love. As soon as they finished, she wished they could start again. She felt like she'd just drunk salt water for thirst.

Abe seemed unsettled, too, though differently. 'It can't keep being like this,' he said. 'I don't know what I can say to prove I want to be with you.'

She felt, starting up in her, the itchy desire to argue, to say *so maybe we should break up,* even though breaking up was the last thing she wanted. She needed to get out of this room. Standing, she fumbled on her clothes. 'Maybe I'll take a walk,' she managed to say.

'It's nearly one in the morning.'

Dumbly, she made her way to the door, down the hall. The air would clear her head. Ten minutes of walking and she'd be free of this panic, able to go back to Abe's bed and sleep.

'Wait. Where are you going?' Abe had caught up to her, a sheet wrapped around his waist.

'Just out. I just need . . . just let—'

'*Now?*'

She wrenched away from the hand he'd put on her shoulder. 'I just have to get *out*.'

She stumbled down the steps of his dorm. It was very cold. Wind lifted leaves from the ground; they rose and then banked, like a flock of startled birds. Pulling her sleeves down over her hands, she began to walk as fast as she could.

Harvard's freshman dorms faced each other in a neat rectangle. One of the buildings had a white sheet suspended between two windows, advertising a party. From inside came music, the bass so heavy Angie could feel it in her feet. A group of students talking on the front stairs suddenly cried out and looked up; a guy stood at the edge of the roof, pissing, the urine splashing a few feet from the group. One girl yelled, 'Fucking asshole fucker – oh, hey, I *know* you.'

'Hey, hi.'

'You're in my astro class.' The girl took a stumbly step back. 'You should come over later.'

Angie had to get off this campus.

The news kiosk in the center of Harvard Square was dark, but music came from some of the restaurants. Near where the girl had sung earlier, a man settled into the lee of the T station, pulling newspaper over himself.

She took a deep shaky breath. Okay. She was going to be okay. It was good to be out of Harvard Yard. She took another deep breath and began walking up the street. This was good. A man leaned close to her; startled, she looked into his face. His nose was red and seeded, like a strawberry.

'Big tits,' he said. 'You have nice fat titties.' She veered away from him. 'Maybe someday you let me suck your fat titties,' he called.

She began to run. Crowds of people were coming out of the bars. She bumped into someone who said, 'Hey, watch it.' She took a step back, bumping into someone else, turning. In the dim neon light, faces seemed elongated, dark holes where mouths and eyes should have been. She moaned, stumbled back, and felt hands on her shoulder blades. 'Whoa, there.' There was a hole in the crowd; she lurched toward it. Behind her, someone said, 'That girl's going to have one hell of a hangover tomorrow.'

She caught sight of her own reflection in a shop window. Her face looked haggard, almost unrecognizable, and she realized with a shock that she wasn't wearing a coat.

She started back toward campus. The thought of Abe's room, though – its darkness and heavy warmth – was suffocating. She veered off, turning down a side street, then turning again, finding herself on a brick sidewalk, some of the bricks loose, wobbling under her feet, so that she felt as though she'd just gotten off a boat and had sea legs. Ahead of her, dark buildings, then just darkness: the river.

She crossed the highway and stood on the bicycle path that ran parallel to the water. She hadn't noticed earlier, but the river smelled of fish. A car passed, headlights briefly illuminating the grassy bank. She was surprised to notice that she hadn't thought of throwing herself in, and then that was all she could think of. She huddled behind a tree, where she couldn't see the water, holding her knees to her chest, shivering. The cold felt as if it came from inside her bones. Cars passed, and passed, and then one slowed and pulled over. It was a taxi. The driver, a tall black man, got out.

'Where do you want to go?' he called. His accent was foreign, musical.

She shook her head.

'It's not safe, a girl down here by herself.' He swept open the back door of the cab with a flourish.

She scrambled up and bolted in the other direction, toward the bridge. Her ankle struck something, a branch, and she fell hard, catching herself with her hands. Someone screamed, a face right next to hers, gray hair streaming, a few teeth jagged and yellow. Angie yelled, scampering away on all fours, whimpering even as she realized that she had stumbled over a sleeping woman. She gagged. 'Oh, God, I'm sorry.' She ran, fell, picked herself up, and kept running, still panting *Sorry, sorry, I'm sorry*.

Chapter Ten

After dropping her daughter off at the bus station, Jordana drove to Ben's. The first time she'd visited him, she'd thought Ben would live in an old industrial space or at least in one of the run-down Victorians crowding Cort's outskirts. Instead, the Bonne Chance apartments: headache green, with external metal staircases.

She'd been looking forward to seeing Ben, but as she climbed the rattling stairs to the second floor and knocked on his door, she found herself resenting him. Clouds rolled in, dampening the light. She'd hated watching her daughter board the bus for Boston, shoulders hunched, hair hanging in her face. But what would have been better? Angie holed up in her bedroom for another weekend?

Ben opened the door, sweeping his arm behind her to bend her back in a kiss. She took a step away, righting herself. 'You're in a good mood.'

Ben straightened. 'Those pictures turned out really well.'

'Pictures.'

He turned and unpinned photos from the clothesline, handing them to her. Oh, those pictures. Her black hair puffed out on his white pillowcase; her sharp clavicle and hipbones contrasted with the wrinkled sheets and hazy smile.

She realized that she'd expected the pictures to make her pretty. It wasn't rational; she'd never looked pretty to herself. Still. In one shot, her mouth was half open, and she looked at the camera from the corner of her half-closed eye with an ugly, sly expression that clearly meant *get it?* She must have said something she thought was funny.

If she'd been alone, she would have studied the photos, but she felt embarrassed looking at herself in front of Ben. She tossed them on a chair, then stepped forward and kissed him, hard, pulling him down to the floor. They had sex with her straddling him, holding his wrists down, moving so slowly that he groaned and bit his lips, and she didn't know where the line was between wanting to give him pleasure and wanting to make him unhappy. She would have gone on for an hour if she could have, not letting him come, but he muttered, *Oh, God, fuck me,* and moved his hands from her grasp – he was too strong for her – grabbing her hips, pulling her down onto him.

Afterward, they lay side by side. The photos overhead cast rippling shadows across their bodies. He moved his hand between her legs but she pushed it away, saying, 'I should get home.'

He turned on his side, trying to look over his shoulder. 'I think I have rug burn.'

'I don't see anything,' she said, barely glancing. Standing, she found her underwear, pulled it on. If she had come, they would be even, whereas now she was owed, somehow morally superior.

'What are you doing tonight?' he asked.

She buttoned her jeans, found her sweater, dropped it over her head. Although she needed to leave, she flopped down on the couch. 'I don't know. Nothing.' Reminding herself to ask about him – sometimes she forgot his life existed outside their time together – she said, 'You?'

'Movie.'

'Which one?'

'I have a date, actually.'

'*Oh.*' She stood. She picked up a glass of water, lifted it to her mouth, then put it down. 'Really? You have a date?'

He smiled and shrugged. 'You won't talk about where this is going, so I have to assume—' He shrugged again, opening his hands wide, but the words had come out too practiced: his nonchalance, his expectation she would also be nonchalant, were an act.

She went into the bathroom to wash her hands. Keeping her voice casual, she called, 'How old is she?'

'I don't know.'

'You don't know? How do you know her?'

'I don't, really. She's just someone I see at L'Isola. That café.'

'I know it's that café. Christ.' The mirror above the sink showed that about half her hair had escaped from its ponytail. She yanked off the elastic and, with wet hands, tried to smooth her hair. 'So, what? You asked her out? She asked you out?'

'We just got to talking.'

'I don't know how these things work.' She looked around for someplace to dry her hands. 'This towel's filthy.'

'Hmmm?'

She pulled his bath towel off the rack and carried it into the living room. 'This is filthy.'

Ben sat on the carpet, still naked. He scratched his stomach. 'There's another in the closet. Top shelf.'

'You live like you're still in college or something.'

'In college I had six roommates. You're glad you didn't know me then.'

She held up the towel. 'This is *ridiculous*. Grown-ups don't live like this.'

'Why do you care? You don't live here. You come over here, get your fuck-fix, and then you go home.'

'A what? A fuck-fix? Are you *twelve*?'

'Isn't that what this is?'

She dropped the towel on the floor. 'Enjoy your date.'

'I plan to.'

'Good.'

'Good.'

By the time Jordana got to the grocery store from Ben's, it was four-thirty. The kids called the IGA the Igga, which she'd begun calling it too. She hurried through heavy puddles, gray sky sagging above the parking lot. God, a fuck-fix. *Fuck* him. It was still light out when she went through the Igga's automatic doors, but fifteen minutes later she emerged into darkness. A thin, stinging snow had begun.

She shoved her groceries into the back. Scooping the keys from the ashtray where she'd left them, she held them up to the weak overhead light to find the one she needed. On the second try the car shuddered and then caught and she sat for a minute, blowing on her hands and letting the engine warm. She should have asked if his frat brothers taught him that phrase. No: she'd sounded immature enough. *God.* Wincing, she buried her head in her hands and sat hunched, shivering, the heater blowing tepid air. She'd lived in Cort sixteen years and still didn't adequately anticipate the cold: she had on a cotton sweater – now coffee-splotched – and a

97

red and black Applefield High letter jacket that Angie no longer wore. The orange lights above the parking lot showed a thin glaze of new snow over black asphalt. Plowed snow, gray with exhaust fumes and gravel, was banked all around. She shifted into reverse, then stopped to pull down the knit cuffs of the jacket, balling the ends in her fingers.

She drove like that, fisted hands balancing the steering wheel without gripping it. The wipers spanked the windshield's bottom edge on each downstroke. Patting the seat beside her, she found a cassette tape. The tape, when she slid it in, was a scratchy recording of a quartet. Schubert. Where the cello should have entered in the fourth measure, there were only the violins and viola playing around the empty spaces. It must be one of Pieter's rehearsal tapes, his string quartet playing without him. She knew this piece so well she could hear his part, ghostly beneath the violins and viola, rising as they fell, falling as they rose, a twisting ribbon of silence.

At home she parked without turning off the engine and sat, blowing on her hands. When the piece ended, she realized she'd been waiting for it to end, that she'd forgotten how late she was getting home. Hurrying out to open the back door, she dragged the grocery bags across the seat toward her. She took all four, two in each arm. She slammed the car door with her foot, then stumbled a few steps back, unbalanced.

Jordana spent that evening and all Sunday staying busy. She finally finished packing up the Goodwill donations that had half blocked the hallway for six months. She dragged Pieter on a chilly hike. Angie would come home Monday afternoon. She didn't call to say whether everything was going all right, and Jordana had to remind herself that was a *good* sign: high school seniors visiting their boyfriends at college didn't call their mothers.

Sunday night Pieter asked if she'd checked that the back door was locked and Jordana lied and said she had. They had just made love. She didn't want to get out of bed and make her way downstairs, turning on lights as she went, and she didn't want, either, for her husband to get out of bed and leave her. She was curled away from Pieter, soles of her feet pressed against his calves.

'Are you sure?'

'*Pieter—*'

He moved closer, arm over her rib cage so that the calloused tips of his fingers rested on the underside of her breast. Jordana pulled the sheet up over her naked shoulder. She said, 'Tell me about when we met.'

'You know about when we met.'

'Tell me anyway.'

He sighed and pulled closer into her back. Pieter would sometimes go along with talking about the past, but he didn't find it very interesting. 'All right. My first job after Juilliard was for the New York Opera, which was a huge, huge coup. I had the last seat, but the first cellist took me under his wing. He thought I was talented. I used to go over to his apartment, and we'd play duets or chess. And his daughter was this funny little girl who used to hang around and watch us.'

'I borrowed clothes from my friends just for those afternoons.'

'I never won at chess. I don't know why I kept agreeing to play.'

'Because my father loved winning more than you cared about losing. I remember you winning sometimes. But I was so bored. If you played duets, at least there was something to listen to while I stood around in three-inch heels waiting to be noticed.'

'Mmmm.' Pieter was falling asleep.

'I'd bring you tea and you'd smile at me like I was eight years old.'

'You *were* eight years old to me,' Pieter said.

Jordana, sixteen, watched her mother fumble around the kitchen, two glasses of wine already drunk and dinner not really begun. Jordana's father insisted that when they had guests – Pieter was bringing his girlfriend to their apartment for the first time – they weren't going to serve something cooked by the maid. Three boiled lobsters in various stages of disassembly littered the Formica countertop, which had a pattern of gold sunbursts on pale blue. The apartment, on the Upper East Side, had been a wedding present from Jordana's mother's parents, who were astonished and grateful at their daughter's last-minute (she'd been thirty-one) rescue from spinsterhood, even if it was by a Jew. Jordana's father had filled the rest of the rooms with velvet and leather, dark wood, heavy draperies, but no guest ever visited the kitchen, so he left its Formica and turquoise-blue carpet alone.

A tall, heavy woman, Jordana's mother wore a beautifully fitted green dress and pumps of buttery leather, dark hair pulled back from her face in a perfect French twist. With a fork, she clawed the meat from a lobster. She put the pieces of its shell onto a baking sheet and slid them into the oven to dry. When she turned, tiny stars of grease speckled the front of her dress.

'You're going to have to change,' said Jordana.

'Of course I'm going to change. This is a day dress. Is there really nothing else you could have done with your hair?'

'There really *isn't*,' Jordana said, in mock sorrow. From when she was eleven until earlier this year, when she'd refused to go anymore, a black hairdresser at 125th and Amsterdam had straightened Jordana's hair. The chemicals burned her scalp and made her eyes water. A cab ticked in the street outside, her mother sitting upright in the backseat; kids would gather at the beauty shop's window to look in at the white girl.

Untreated, Jordana's hair puffed like black smoke around her face. She had dressed carefully in careless-looking clothes. She would let her father greet Pieter and Em. She herself would wander out in twenty minutes or so, *Ulysses* in one hand, and profess surprise: *I didn't even hear you come in.*

A soft wheezing came from the oven as the pieces of shell dried. 'Get those out.'

'"Please?"' Jordana suggested.

'Just get them.'

Jordana drooped over to the oven, pulled out the baking sheet, and then drooped back to her stool.

She had no idea where her mother's time went. It wasn't that it was unusual for women on the Upper East Side not to have jobs – in fact, Jordana had only in the last few years become aware that other women in New York, tens or maybe *hundreds* of thousands, worked all day. But besides grooming herself or being groomed, what did Jordana's mother do? Not tennis, or meeting friends for drinks, or sitting on committees, like the mothers of Jordana's friends. Her time just disappeared, water dribbled into sand.

Her mother pulled the lobster tail apart with her hands. 'If he hasn't married her yet, he's not going to marry her.'

'Who are you talking about?'

Meat hung down from the lobster shell, a tattered skirt that Jordana's mother tore at. Mouth twisting with distaste, she lifted the second lobster. She held it upside down and cracked a claw, letting the liquid run out into the sink. She didn't bother to answer: They both knew who.

Jordana hated when her mother acted like she knew anything about Pieter. 'Not everyone believes marriage is the solution to everything. You can be just as committed to someone without some piece of paper.'

'Well, aren't we radical.' Her mother slid the mortar and pestle over to Jordana. 'Grind those shells, if you want something to do.'

Jordana picked up a piece of shell and then dropped it. 'It's *hot*.'

'You're the one who's so smart.'

Fingers stinging, Jordana used a dish towel to transfer the pieces of shell to the mortar. She pounded them to a fine dust. When she tried to slide the mortar back over, her mother nodded at the *Joy of Cooking*. 'Under *lobster butter*.'

The four different parts of the recipe, separated by hundreds of pages, had been bookmarked, and she flipped through: Lobster Newburg . . . Newburg Sauce . . . Lobster Butter . . . About Lobster:

The uninitiated are sometimes balked by the ferocious appearance of a lobster at table. They may take comfort from the little cannibal who, threading his way through the jungle one day at his mother's side, saw a strange object roar overhead. 'Ma, what's that?' he quavered. 'Don't worry, sonny,' said Ma. 'It's an airplane. Airplanes are pretty much like lobsters. There's an awful lot you have to throw away, but the insides are delicious.'

Jordana read the paragraph a second time, to make sure it really was as stupid as she thought. The doorbell rang.

She was out of the kitchen, through the living room, in the foyer opening the door before remembering that she'd planned to be cool and aloof tonight. She hadn't thought to rinse her hands; she reeked of lobster.

Pieter's eyes seemed an even starker blue than she'd remembered, his hair an even paler blond, his cheekbones higher and sharper. Seeing him, no matter how she tried to prepare herself, she always had the same physical reaction she had now: her heart seized and knocked, her stomach contracted. She had a vague impression of a tall woman beside him, but couldn't bring herself to look directly.

101

'Em, this is Jordana. She's a pain in the neck.' He punched Jordana lightly on the shoulder. Normally, she would have poked him back; then he would have tried to tickle her, and they would have half wrestled until they heard the approaching footsteps of Jordana's father. Pieter would have straightened, tucked in his shirttails, shook Jordana's father's hand, and then – when her father turned to lead the way to the library – winked at Jordana. Flirting, she'd thought. She loved those moments of feeling Pieter's ribs beneath his soft cotton shirt.

'Nice to meet you,' she muttered, looking at Em's collarbone. Jordana had assumed that her own gauzy skirts and Gypsy earrings were close to how Em, a modern dancer, would dress, but Em wore a powder-blue linen shift. She had stainless-steel posture and a flat chest, even flatter than Jordana's.

Em said, 'Pieter's told me so much about you.'

Startled, Jordana looked into Em's face. Late twenties, no makeup, hair pulled back in a low ponytail. Em and Pieter had a whole life together. They discussed Jordana's family.

Lightly, Pieter hit Jordana's shoulder again, asking her, 'What's the matter? Is she having a bad day? Is she asleep?'

She turned toward him, feeling as slow and stupid as a bear teased at the zoo. He put up his fists, dancing back, feinting once toward her. 'Aha!' he said. 'She awakens. Go ahead, put 'em up.'

If he did this in front of his girlfriend, it didn't mean what Jordana had thought. Pieter bounced on his toes. Em gave her a long, considering look. Jordana's face burned, but she forced herself to return the gaze.

When they were seated for dinner, Jordana's father announced, 'I discovered the most remarkable recording of Bedrich Smetana.' He leapt up from the table and disappeared from the room. A minute later he reappeared, sliding a record from its sleeve. He opened the sideboard to reach the hi-fi – every room of the apartment had at least one. Holding up his hand for silence, he closed his eyes. Two soft pops as the needle skated toward the music. Jordana's mother stopped in the act of serving cream of asparagus soup, ladle dripping.

Jordana's father was a small man with a crest of white hair that rose over his forehead. He wore a gray suit and red cravat. As the first notes sounded, he brought his fist down softly, face squeezed into a grimace. No one moved. The music rose around them, orchestra bearing down on the rippling melody carried by the string section.

Jordana's father opened his eyes. Bounding back to the table, flicking a napkin onto his lap, he smiled at Pieter. 'Isn't that fantastic?'

Jordana's mother resumed serving soup. Em said, 'I've never even heard of – is it Smetina?'

Jordana's father gave her a quick, pained smile, lips closed, chin turning briefly toward her but not his eyes. To Pieter, he said, 'Stone deaf when he wrote this. He's the only one of the Romantics without sentimentality. Later, of course, he went mad.'

Jordana's mother sighed, put the tureen down on the sideboard, and dropped into her chair at the foot of the table. The soup was matted with fibers of asparagus stalk; Jordana gulped wine to wash it down.

'I think each course should have its own music to go with it, don't you?' Jordana's father said to Pieter. 'Tonight we'll have Smetana as an appetizer, Berg as a main course, and for dessert— ?'

'Bach?' Pieter guessed.

Jordana's father twinkled at him. 'A man after my own heart,' he announced to the table.

'That's interesting,' said Em. 'Like having different wine—'

'Of course,' Jordana's father said, still to Pieter, 'there's also Purcell to consider. Or one could even dash to the other end of the spectrum—'

'Someone like Schoenberg.'

'Exactly!' Her father beamed. 'Something angular, to offset the sweetness. But then naturally we can't have Berg as our main course ... Mussorgsky? Too rough?'

It had been Jordana's father who'd insisted Pieter bring Em. She had two small spots of color high on her cheeks. Jordana, though happy at Em's discomfort, was taken aback by Pieter's apparent unawareness. Before dinner, she'd wanted to change into tidier clothes but had known that would make her more ridiculous in front of Em. Now she was glad that she had instead crayoned even more kohl around her eyes, come to the table barefoot, silver bracelets jingling. Fuck them both.

'Mendelssohn was a sentimentalist,' Pieter was saying.

'What do you mean, he's sentimental?' Jordana broke in. 'Who are you to say that?'

Pieter turned his gaze to her. To fit his long legs under the table, his chair was pushed back perhaps a foot. He shrugged, almost lazily. 'Maybe you're right.'

'He's a great composer. You're just in an orchestra.'

Her father looked between them, eyes sparkling with amusement, one finger folded over his lips. He leaned forward, chest almost touching his crossed legs, waiting to see if they'd go on. When Pieter didn't respond, her father seemed disappointed, but he just straightened up and said lightly, 'So, no Mendelssohn. And of course the equation falls apart somewhat if the food can't support the music.' He held up his left hand as, with his right, he lifted his spoon and tasted the soup. He coughed and pushed away the bowl. '*Uhhhh.* Please don't be polite. You needn't eat it.'

'It's good,' Jordana said.

Em and Pieter glanced at each other and said together, 'It's very good.'

'No, no, no,' said Jordana's father, holding up his hands. 'Please. Perhaps the next course will be edible.' He turned to his wife. 'What *is* the next course, my love?'

As an adult, Jordana would understand this scene far better than she'd understood it at the time. She would realize that her father had been confusingly, painfully infatuated with each of the young men he 'took under his wing' from the orchestra. His manic cheer as he presented Pieter with esoteric recordings and glasses of single-malt Scotch was cover for his agitation. She came to understand, at least partially, her father's cruelty to her mother, a woman with money – money that, now Jordana's, helped pay for Angie's treatment – but without charm.

That night, though, Jordana had followed Pieter into the library to choose more records, shaking with – adoration? disappointment? She stood behind him as he looked at the spines of her father's record collection.

Pieter turned, about to speak. He might have been about to suggest a piece of music; he might have been about to say something about her father's behavior. She couldn't have stood either.

'I love you,' she blurted. 'I've loved you forever.' She kissed his astonished mouth.

It had always been that Pieter couldn't sleep and she could, that she wanted to be held when they slept and he felt too hot. Now, though, he slept beside her, arm draping her hip.

Had she really ended things with Ben? She couldn't stand lying still like this, thoughts racing. As gently as possible, she freed herself from Pieter, finding clothes by feel on the floor of the room.

Downstairs, she checked the back door. She had forgotten to lock it after all.

It felt like if she could be with Ben for five minutes, she'd be all right. Putting her hands to her head, she walked blindly through the rooms. It was just after midnight. She could call Ben, apologize; then she would be done with that. She rushed to the phone, dialed the number. Ben's deep voice answered on the second ring. She hung up, hands shaking. She moved to the sink, pressed her forehead to the window above. The glass was cold. 'Okay,' she said out loud. 'Okay, okay.'

She shook out her hands. Listing stacks of dirty dishes filled the sink. Taking a steadying breath, she reached for the soap and squirted it over the dishes, ran hot water, then gripped the edge of the sink and wept. It was almost soundless, eyes closed and mouth stretched into a grimace, a dry chugging of air in her throat. She gasped, trying to stop, then bit her lip as hard as she could.

Her friend Letty had left a husband of fifteen years for a man she'd known three months. *I'd given up on finding my soul mate,* Letty had told Jordana, *and then I met him. I think – I think the universe would be angry if I turned my back on this.*

Jordana hated Letty's desire to believe she had no choice. In her mind she always called her own relationship by its ugly name, *affair,* not allowing herself to call it *falling in love.* She felt the draw of blaming fate, but her life was dishonest enough as it was. If she was falling in love with Ben, it was not because it had to happen but because she had allowed it to happen. It was a betrayal, and shitty, and the worst possible timing, but she had let it happen.

Fishing an envelope out of the trash, she scrawled on the back that she couldn't sleep and was going to Papa Toby's to read. *Back soon.*

She grabbed her book and her wallet, then let herself quietly out the front door. Frozen grass crunched softly under her feet. Something moved under the big oak.

The girl stood up from the lawn and then squatted, bouncing,

105

probably to uncramp her legs. Standing again, she reached down for something, hefted it to her shoulder. A bookbag. She didn't seem to hear Jordana's approach.

'What are you doing?'

The girl jumped and gave a cry, quickly covering her mouth.

Jordana asked, 'What do you think could possibly come of standing on our lawn?'

The girl closed her mouth and raised her chin, as though Jordana weren't there. She moved left. Jordana moved too, blocking her. The girl ducked right; Jordana reached out and grabbed her wrist hard, pulling it up.

They stared at each other for a moment. Then Jordana felt the absurdity of it and let go. The girl pulled her arm to her chest, making a show of rubbing the wrist.

'Where do your parents think you are, all these nights?'

She stiffened. 'Just my mom. She's fine with it.'

'I'm not going to call her.' It struck her that most adults would have done exactly this. Somehow, she had never made that transition fully away from identifying with the children to identifying with the parents. But why had Pieter not called? As soon as the question formed in her mind, the answer formed alongside it: He didn't like messiness.

The girl's glance slid away and, following her gaze, Jordana twisted around. Luke had just come into his room. He pulled off his sweater, moved out of the frame of the window. A moment later he reappeared, shirtless, brushing his teeth. He crossed in front of the window and Jordana drew back.

'He can't see you,' the girl said disdainfully.

Luke bent one elbow, drawing it straight up over his head, a stretch, and then bent the other up and back. For all that he acted annoyed by the girl's presence, he was playing to her.

The girl said, 'I tell her I'm going to a friend's house.'

Late at night, the traffic lights in Cort flashed yellow. The roads were nearly empty. Turning left onto York, Jordana descended the long hill toward the highway. An oil truck passed in the other direction, gears grinding as it lumbered uphill. She imagined being someone who was up every night this late, a truck driver or maybe a security guard, someone for whom darkness was just a condition of work. It was very cold, stars blistering the sky, and the dark

106

seemed full of mysterious promise.

She was underdressed again. Ben's apartment complex was in western Cort, down Route 121. By halfway there she was shivering, driving with one hand, the other beneath her thigh for warmth. She passed the clinic and the bread factory; its sign was broken, so that instead of GOOD BREAD it just blinked GOOD.

It was only when Jordana was out of the car, up the stairs, and standing outside Ben's apartment door that the wild energy pushing her there dissipated. He might not even be awake still. And if he was awake, what did she think would happen? Had she been thinking at all? It was nearly one in the morning. She'd shown up in the middle of the night a few times before, but they hadn't been fighting then. What if he'd seen his date again tonight? She could be there, sleeping next to him.

Now she was terrified Ben would wake. She moved down the stairs quickly. Reaching the parking lot, she saw that she'd left the car's headlights on. She got in, turning off the lights, and sat still for a few minutes, looking at the dark building in front of her.

She drove halfway home, then made an illegal U-turn and drove back toward Ben's. When he opened his door, she said, 'I've spent the last hour trying to get here.'

'What time is it?' His hair stood up all over his head. 'What are you doing here?'

'I was horrible yesterday.'

'The First Fight,' he said, in a deep sports-announcer voice. He held out his arms, and she felt gratitude slide down through her as she moved into them. 'The First Reconciliation.'

'How was your date?' she asked, muffled against his shirt.

'Boring.'

She was letting something shift between them, letting something be settled: She would be the impetuous one, given to blurting and scenes, and he would be the one whose affection for her triumphed over his exasperation.

'What I think of this – it's not what you said before.' She couldn't bring herself to say *fuck-fix*. 'That's not what this means to me.'

'I know that. Not me, either.'

'I'm completely crazy about you.'

What was she doing? Why couldn't she leave well enough alone? And yet she felt only relief and something like deliverance as she pulled herself more tightly against him, as he said her name. He thrust both hands deep into her hair, putting his head down on her shoulder, the world around them dark and sleeping on.

It began raining in the night. By four-thirty, when Jordana said goodbye to Ben at his front door, it was pouring. She felt so happy that dashing to the car only relieved a fraction of her energy.

She couldn't walk into the house grinning like this. It was not only Pieter but also Luke she might run into. Being only a good, not brilliant, swimmer had never seemed to bother him, but in the last six months he'd suddenly added long morning runs to his workout, coming back just in time to change clothes and leave again for practice.

She turned on the radio: The Cars, singing about the *fineness* of a best friend's girlfriend.

And she held on to happiness, not allowing it to fade out even though the road was filled with water and the drive took too long, held on to it by force of will. She passed the clinic and the bread factory, its sign blinking GOOD, GOOD, GOOD. When she pulled up to the curb and turned off the engine, it was a shock to see the stoic brick of her house unchanged, lights shining warmly in the windows. Pieter must already be up. *A lighthouse* she thought: a house filled with light.

It was raining harder now. Jordana ran toward the house, slipping a little on the wet lawn.

Halfway to the kitchen door, she was stopped by her view of Pieter, bending over the dishes she'd left in the sink. Light, tarnished by rain, shone a little way out onto the lawn. His thin face seemed heavy. Standing in her front yard, beyond the patch of light silvering the wet grass, Jordana felt longing rise in her throat. The scene was so worn and domestic that it seemed there must be a wife just outside Jordana's vision – that from here Jordana might see that other self rise, touching her husband's shoulder as she crossed the room to lock the back door.

Chapter Eleven

Pieter, waking at one-thirty, found Jordana gone. She'd never dealt calmly with insomnia. Frustrated to the point of anger by even twenty minutes' sleeplessness, she would jump out of bed, pull on clothes, and drive to the diner, where she could be around other people who were also awake. Since Angie's homecoming, her sleeplessness had become more frequent. The next day, she would seem energized, almost manic, shadows under her eyes dark as bruises.

In the kitchen he put water on to boil, found carrots in the fridge, cut off the tops. Putting back the carrots themselves, he washed the feathery leaves – wet, they were as dark and silky as seaweed – and curled them into the bottom of the teapot. Bean came and wove around his legs, and he leaned down to lift her. He stroked her, feeling the round bones of her skull beneath the fur, saying, 'Yes, you're a good cat. Yes, you're a very good cat.' She hooked her head under Pieter's arm, purring. Last year, when he'd remembered in the midst of Angie's hospital intake to tell Jordana about Bean, she'd looked at him blankly and said, 'A cat?' as though she wasn't sure what the word meant. Those first days and weeks, they'd operated in such a state of emergency that they'd just absorbed the cat into their lives. Now, though, he liked having her. Holding her with his left arm, he moved to the refrigerator, opened the milk carton with one hand. They still hadn't fixed the fridge thermostat, and slushy chips of ice ticked together as he poured the milk into Bean's bowl. She leapt lightly down from his arms.

The air in the house felt thin. Ever since childhood, he'd been able to tell by feel how many people were in a house, but tonight

– though he'd heard Luke come home hours ago – Pieter felt alone. The oddness of having both his wife and his daughter gone in the middle of the night must be throwing his sensitivity off. When the water boiled, Pieter poured it over the carrot leaves, added honey and a few drops of orange juice, then carried the pot into the dark living room.

Two in the morning. He put on a recording of Baroque Flemish songs, turned down low, and wished Jordana were there. If she were awake they could sit together companionably; if she were asleep, he'd know that eventually he'd be returning to the warmth of her body in bed.

At the same time, he loved that she was impulsive and restless, that she was so different from him. On the night more than twenty years before, when Jordana had kissed him in her father's library, he'd pushed her away. After, he'd still thought of her as a little girl. But he no longer teased her; she no longer perched on the arm of his chair while he played chess with her father. Eventually, they almost didn't speak to each other at all. That went on for some months until one day – he'd just come into the apartment and said hello to her – Jordana turned and threw her coffee cup at him. The cup struck his chest and fell, shattering on the parquet floor. Jordana, stricken, wheeled and ran down the hall. Kneeling down awkwardly to gather the thin white shards, Pieter had thought, *I've never done one unpremeditated thing*. It stunned him.

Now he stood at the living room's dark bay window, sipping from his cup. Carrot tea was a remnant of his childhood, something his mother had drunk during the war and had continued – why? – to drink after she emigrated. It tasted sweet and grassy, run through with the faint metallic note of dirt. He could feel nostalgic, drinking it, because he hadn't nearly starved, as his mother had. Pieter drank two cups, washed out the pot, climbed the stairs to bed.

An hour later, he startled, sitting straight up, not knowing what had awoken him. An enormous white rabbit loomed over him, and he said *Jesus Christ,* and then the phone rang again and the rabbit dissolved into the light cast by the streetlamp outside.

He felt toward Jordana's side of the bed, still empty. Another ring. He fumbled in the dark through two more rings before finding the phone. He said into the receiver, 'A moment,' then

110

held it against his chest, trying to quiet his breathing. And then another alarm rolled through him. The phone call meant something seriously wrong.

It was Abe. Angie had gone out and not come back. He'd been out searching for two hours.

Oh, God, Pieter thought.

He told Abe they were on their way and hung up. But maybe it was better to stay here. By the time they got to Harvard, Angie might be long since returned. Or what if they didn't go down, and two hours from now she was still gone, and they might have been there by then? He could go down and Jordana stay here, or vice versa. He couldn't think; his mind kept jamming.

Downstairs, he pulled out the White Pages and found the number for Papa Toby's. The cashier who answered put the phone down briefly – faintly, the ephemera of a restaurant came over the line, chatting, a cook calling, 'Order *up!*' – and then returned to say there was no tall dark-haired woman there alone.

Jordana was already on her way home, then; it wouldn't take more than ten minutes.

He started upstairs to wake Luke. But if they didn't drive to Cambridge, there was no reason for Luke to be awake. He hesitated, mid-staircase, torn between not wanting to wake his son and not wanting to be alone. Jordana would be home soon. He turned and went back to the kitchen, put the kettle on. Angie and Abe might have had a fight, she might have stormed off; it would be ridiculous for her parents to show up. Jordana would know what to do. The kettle boiled and he turned off the stove but didn't pour the water. He paced the dark first-floor rooms, picking things up and putting them down, starting upstairs and then coming back down. Twenty minutes. Twenty-five. He picked up the phone, began to dial Papa Toby's, hung up.

Thirty minutes.

He could be almost to Manchester by now.

He dialed the diner to ask how long ago Jordana had left. This time the cashier sounded annoyed. She put the phone down and called, 'Sue? It's that guy who's lost his wife.'

Another woman came on the line. He began to describe his wife; the waitress cut him off. 'Are you talking about Jordana?'

Of course his wife would have talked to the waitresses. She said, 'I haven't seen Jordana in . . . I don't know. Weeks.'

111

Heart knocking, he made for the stairs, beginning halfway up to run. He banged hard on Luke's bedroom door, though the weight-lessness of the air – he should have trusted himself – said his son wasn't there. He tried the knob. Locked. Going to the linen closet, he ran his hand under the stack of towels, feeling for the skeleton key, knowing it would be gone and at the same time so able to imagine its flat, crooked shape that he could almost feel it beneath his fingers. He pulled the towels off the shelf to be sure: only the ancient shelf paper, a design of little girls rolling hoops. He ran back to Luke's door, banged again, rammed his shoulder into the wood, then backed up and ran at it. The door shivered in its frame. He ran at it again. On his third try, a muscle in his back twisted and ripped just as the lock gave.

The room was still, dark, peaceful, Pieter's ragged breath the only sound. He leaned against the doorframe, back flashing with pain.

Where was his family?

Flipping the light switch, the room's dim shapes leapt into focus. A tap came at the side of the house, then another. Rain. In the evidence of Luke's escape – empty bed, the open window, the slick black branches outside – Pieter understood that his wife was with someone else.

Jordana's closet revealed nothing, nor did her bedside table with its stacks of books and notepads. He opened the top drawer of her dresser, which held boxes of jewelry she never wore, handed down from her mother and grandmother. Nothing, and nothing in the T-shirt drawer or the drawer that held jeans. The air in the room was so thin his heart beat crazily. He sat at the edge of the bed. Rain gusted against the side of the house.

From downstairs came the softest click of a key being fitted into the lock. Pieter went to the head of the stairs, turning on the hall light. Below, Luke was just closing the door behind him. His hair and sweatclothes were soaked with rain. Blinking, he turned.

Pieter started down the stairs. The pain in his back flared.

Luke looked uneasy, as though he thought he might be in trouble but was going to brazen it out. Water dripped onto the carpet at his feet, darkening it. 'Why are all the lights on?'

The hum of the wheels over highway. The car's heater was on high. Lying on the backseat, Pieter felt every bump; he closed his eyes and tried to still his breath.

112

They'd driven an hour. He could almost feel normal, but it was like being poised on the crest of a terrible wave. Each crash down was terrible, but weirdly a relief. Jordana's upper arm had the asterisk of a polio vaccination scar. Someone else had touched that scar, even kissed it. He wanted to put his fist through the window. The smash of glass, his wife screaming.

As soon as he imagined the act, there was no longer a possibility of doing it; it would be self-conscious now, theatrical, ridiculous. Laboriously, he turned over to face the front of the car. The pain in his back had receded to a kind of glittering buzz. Moving stirred it up, a hive of bees.

'Were you ever reading?' Pieter asked. 'Any of those nights you were gone?'

He thought she was ignoring him, but then she said quietly, 'I can't believe – it's like I went crazy or—'

He reared up. 'Don't. Don't talk to me. I don't want to hear you.'

She gripped the steering wheel, shaking it. Slowly, stopping when it hurt too badly, he rolled from his side flat onto his back, putting both feet on the seat, his knees bent. The rainstorm had stopped, or they'd driven through it. Telephone lines stitched the hazy sky. His wife's wet hair stuck to her skull. In a gesture he had seen thousands upon thousands of times, she lifted the back of her hand to rub her eyes, tiredly.

'I don't know if I can live with you anymore,' he said.

She wilted. 'Don't say that. Please, Pieter.'

He felt oddly clear and calm, as if he'd been climbing a forested mountain and had suddenly emerged to the barren rock, thin air, and long views above the tree line. More than clear and calm: disdainful.

'Please take it back,' she said.

Savoring the words: 'I don't think I can live with you.'

Abe waited on the steps of his dorm. They'd made it to Cambridge in an hour and a half, some kind of record. Seven in the morning, darkness just beginning to pull back and soften.

Abe was talking before they reached him: '—campus police. Or supposedly. They're "keeping an eye out on their rounds." My roommate's still out looking. I came back to meet you.' He wore a wool turtleneck and a backward baseball cap, and Pieter felt

113

some of his animosity shift onto Abe.

'I've been all over campus. She was so – I should have stopped her. I keep trying to think where – there's nowhere to *go*.'

Pieter knew that now Jordana would step forward and hug Abe, say it wasn't his fault. She didn't move, though. Turning away sent a spasm of pain across his back. He jerked and stood motionless, grimacing. Jordana reached toward him.

'Leave me alone. I'm fine.'

'You're in agony,' she said.

'Leave me *alone*!'

Abe said, 'And what if someone . . . if something happened. There are lots of places she shouldn't be, and it's been hours now, hours and hours. Last month, there was a girl jogging by the river—'

'Stop it,' Jordana said. 'We're going to find her.' She was the woman Pieter knew again.

To Abe, Pieter said, 'We should have been here earlier. Getting here so late, it's unpardonable.'

'Why didn't you leave without me, then?' Jordana didn't look at him.

Jordana had the flashlight from the car. They decided she would go north, Abe east; the roommate had apparently gone toward the river. Pieter stayed behind, in case Angie returned to the dorm.

He sat on the cold stone steps, which immediately chilled him. Wrapping his arms around his torso, he rocked forward, conserving body heat. Jordana had a habit of running her thumb over his cheekbone – after sex in particular, but also when they just lay in bed, or looked up at the same moment from newspapers, or waited for their food in a diner. He thought of that gesture as theirs. But of course, it was hers. He heard himself make a strangled noise, part sob, part gasp. Putting his head down on his knees, he struggled not to let himself go. He bit the inside of his cheek until he tasted blood. He heard himself say *Getting here so late is unpardonable*. How stiff he'd sounded, how formal and absurd.

Getting here so late is unpardonable. He jumped up and began to pace around the building. When he put weight on his right foot, pain zinged through his back. He had to go up on his toes, which made his walk a stumble: a heavy stride with the left foot and then a quick, high step with the right. He lurched around the building. Stupid, he should have just sat. But when he reached his place on

114

the steps and sank down, his thoughts rose, smashing and grinding and he jumped up again. He realized he was speaking: 'No. No.'

When he rounded the building the third or fourth time, a wide cloaked figure was lurching toward him from the other end of the quad.

Pieter wiped his eyes with the back of his hand. The figure limped, holding something beneath its arm. Nearer, the person resolved itself into two: a boy he'd never seen before – the room-mate? – and Angie, both of them wrapped in an enormous cloak.

Pieter went cold. He had forgotten his daughter.

Her eyes appeared to be closed, and she was stumbling a little. The shaggy boy held her up, half dragging her. Pieter couldn't move. A bird swayed on Angie's shoulder, its feathers a dull greenish-black. It appeared to be anchored to the cloak; when Angie and the boy moved forward it swung down, as though nipping at her, and then reared back, curved black beak glittering in the weak winter sun.

Chapter Twelve

Luke had bought records at Stars, and, walking the mile home from downtown to his house, his bad mood of the last weeks softened for a moment. He liked the way winter afternoons turned dark and cold, wind scudding across the ground, lifting small cyclones of snow. He liked the knock of the bag against his knee; he liked the decorations still up on the houses and the way the snow reflected the colors of flashing lights. He had to get through dinner at home, but tonight there would be a New Year's party out at the Burnt House. Luke stuck to the side of the road. Cars passed him; an Indian man in a white turban fought to keep his old black bicycle upright against the wind.

At home, his dad met him in the hallway, holding the phone message pad. He said, 'Cole, Warren, Khamisa, Khamisa.'

'Okay.' The bad mood was instantly back, a tightness in his chest and behind his eyes.

The front hallway was dark. His dad, in his old-man cardigan with leather elbow patches, seemed to be waiting for more.

The night six weeks ago when his father had come downstairs with that haunted, accusatory look, Luke had thought *condoms, pot* – maybe he'd forgotten to lock his bedroom door, and his father had found something incriminating there. But his dad had just said, 'I thought you were your mother.'

'Mom's not here?'

'That,' said his father, 'is something of an understatement.'

Upstairs, he'd found his bedroom door hanging from one hinge, like an arm dislocated from its socket. The window was still open, and rain blew into the room. There were puddles of water on the desk. He closed the window – carpet squelching under his shoes –

116

and went to bed. Downstairs, he heard his father in the kitchen. Headlights flared across the hall ceiling as his mother's car pulled to the curb, and he put his pillow over his head. He didn't want to hear.

Hours and hours later, he woke to find his room hot, bright with afternoon sun. His father stood in the doorway, screwdriver in hand, fixing the hinge on the door. Luke sat up, pushing off the too-hot covers.

'Angie's sleeping in her room. There, that should hold.'

'She's home?'

His father gave a funny little salute and bent to put his screwdriver back in the toolbox.

Nothing more had been said about his sneaking out by either of his parents. After a week or so, Luke started going out again, more often than before. He stopped waiting for his parents to go to bed: he went into his room, locked the door, and went straight over to the window and down the tree. Sometimes he went to Khamisa's house; other times Cole would be waiting for him at the end of the street in his old Volvo. They'd get stoned out at the radio towers or they went to Paisano's Pizza, where the waitresses didn't care. Sometimes they just drove around.

His father held out the sheet of phone messages. Luke took it, jamming the paper into the front pocket of his jeans. For something to say, he asked, 'Is Angie home?'

'Working on her college applications.' Angie had been working on applications for two months. Out of nowhere, his father said, 'Last night of *Nutcracker!*'

'I guess.' His dad hated December, when the orchestra did six *Nutcracker* performances a week, but what was Luke supposed to say about it? He ducked around his father and went upstairs. At the top, he knocked on his sister's door. 'Ange?' When she didn't answer, he pushed the door open.

She was halfway out of bed, headed for the desk, but when she saw it was just him she lay back down. She still had on that sweatshirt, the stained gray one she'd gotten at Yale two summers ago, and her hair looked as though she hadn't washed it in a few days.

'That sweatshirt's gross.'

'You could knock.'

'You could close the window. It's freezing.' He crossed the room to push the frame shut, then turned and leaned against it. 'I

117

did knock.' Some papers had blown onto the floor. Leaning to gather them up, he saw a raised blue crest, a raised maroon crest. There were the beginnings of essays on stray pieces of paper, but the applications themselves were blank. *Who is the person, alive or dead, you'd most like to meet?* A few pages later, *What would you say is your 'moral code'?*

'There's nothing on these.'

'Jesus, Luke, leave it *alone*.'

He put his record bag down on the desk and moved to perch on the edge of her bed. It made him nervous. Her body gave off a murky, pinching smell, like frying onions. 'Ange, how're you going to finish this?'

She buried her face in the pillow. Along her part were thick flakes of skin. Not thinking, he started to brush one away, then pulled his hand back and stood up. They didn't just touch each other.

'Do Mom and Dad know?'

Her head jerked up. 'Don't tell them!'

He shrugged, annoyed; he didn't tell his parents anything.

'I mean it. Don't tell them.'

'Fine.'

'The essays are done. I just need to copy them over onto the forms.'

'I said fine.'

Angie put her head back down on the pillow.

Clothing was heaped all over the room. He bent and gathered up an armful, carried it to the closet. Balled up with the sweatpants and flannel shirts were two sweaters he'd never seen, tags still attached to the cuffs, and her prom dress from two years ago, its blue taffeta creased and wrinkled. He crouched to reach under the desk, where there were T-shirts, shoes, a pair of underpants with a smear of blood at the crotch. Embarrassed, he jammed the underwear into the middle of the pile. When he'd dumped all the clothes on the floor of the closet and shut the door – this was how he cleaned his own room – everything looked better. He took the books and cups off the desk, arranged the college applications in a stack.

'Here,' he said, coaxingly. 'All's you have to do is fill in the blanks.' He held the pen out, waving it a little, the way you'd try to interest a baby in a toy.

'I'll do it.' She turned to the wall. 'Just go away, Luke.'

Jordana dressed in a flowered dress she'd worn when pregnant, a white apron, a cameo pin. Her friend Beth, and Beth's husband, Stephen, were having a costume party – a Masquerade Ball, they called it, to make it sound New Yearsy – and she and Pieter were going as the *American Gothic* painting. Pieter had left already for his performance, taking his costume with him, and would meet her at the party later.

Since that first night, he'd brought her affair up only a few times. Once, sitting in the kitchen, he'd asked suddenly, 'It's over now?'

In her nervousness and relief, she dropped the toast she was buttering. She crouched down to retrieve it from under the table. She'd spent so many hours thinking what she would say that now all the sentences logjammed in her head. 'I love you so—'

'*Stop.*' He stood, eyes narrowed. 'It's bad enough that it happened.'

Another time, they were lying in bed – she'd thought he was asleep. 'If it had just happened once,' he said suddenly. 'If you'd been drunk . . .'

She waited for him to go on. Instead, he threw back the covers, got out of bed.

'Pieter. Wait, don't go.'

He left the room. A few minutes later, the faint strains of Bach rose from downstairs.

He did that, just took himself away. Every few days, he might let a few words slip, a conversation come unstrung. She could have better withstood anger, accusation. If she pressed, though, Pieter would only retreat further. One morning, she'd come upon him in the living room, looking through pictures from when Angie was a baby. 'Pieter?' she'd said.

He looked up with his mouth agape, as if he didn't recognize her. Then he pulled his knees up to his chest and began to cry, gaspingly, rocking forward.

'Pieter—' She'd rushed forward and he lifted his face, which was twisted and wet.

'Get away!' he bellowed.

These six weeks, she'd done any conciliatory thing she could think of. She didn't spend too much time with Beth, or alone, or even reading on the living room couch. She took Angie to doctors' appointments. She made dinner, shopped, did laundry, picked up her clothes instead of letting them fall where they might.

Pulling her hair back into a bun, she went into the bathroom. She was a mess. She tried slicking her hair back with water, but it was too kinky, and when she passed a mirror a few minutes later she saw that she had a fuzzy penumbra around her head. Glad of the excuse, she went and knocked on Angie's door.

Scuttling noises. 'Angie?' Jordana said. She knocked again, waited a moment, then pushed open the door. Angie sat at the desk, forehead in one hand, pen in the other, hard at work.

'Do you have hair spray or something?' Jordana asked.

Hand still on her forehead, Angie turned to look incredulously over her shoulder. She'd been holed up for three days, finishing her college applications. She didn't look like she'd even showered or changed clothes. 'Mom, I'm *working*?'

'I just wanted to see if you had something . . .' Jordana suddenly felt embarrassed, slightly pathetic, for having wanted so badly to see her daughter. Trying to maintain authority, she said, 'What was all that noise, anyway?' She twisted the doorknob back and forth. 'You're sure you don't want me to read them? Even proof-read them?'

'I told you I'd tell you if I needed anything. I'm fine.'

This fall, had she missed signs that Angie needed more help? Had they been too eager to believe Angie was stable? Worst of all, had the affair kept Jordana from paying enough attention? But then what was Pieter's excuse?

Angie had already turned back to her applications. Jordana said, 'Okay, then. I guess I'm going.'

Her daughter wrote something carefully.

'I guess I'll see you later, then.' Leave, she told herself. She made herself step back, pulling the door closed – but slowly, in case Angie called her back.

Angie lay down on the bed. She was cold but she didn't have the energy to pull the covers up.

Dr. Tepper had asked some questions about Cambridge, muttered 'Mixed-state,' and wrote something on his prescription pad. 'This is an antipsychotic,' he ripped off the slip of paper, holding it out toward her. 'A very low dosage to start.'

She put her hands behind her back. 'I can't take those. Anti-psychotics. I can't take them.'

'Haldol is very mild.'

'You don't think I need to . . . you don't want . . . I thought, the hospital?' she whispered. She'd hated being hospitalized last year, but she'd accustomed herself to the idea of having to go back in; now she realized she'd begun to long for it. She just wanted to rest.

'This should begin to work almost immediately,' Dr. Tepper said. He seemed cheerful; he lifted his hands and wiggled the fingers, saying, 'We'll fiddle-faddle around until we hit the right combination.'

Haldol didn't knock her soul out of her body, like Mellaril, and it didn't make her feel as if she was on Jupiter, the gravity so strong she could barely move, like Klonopin. It did dry out her mouth even more than lithium alone; she drank water constantly and so had to pee constantly. The images of hurting herself retreated. She didn't like the idea that her brain chemistry could manufacture obsessions without her consent. Maybe all the things she thought of as her personality were really just neurons firing around randomly.

The images' disappearance relieved her, and then it didn't. She still felt awful, and she couldn't blame it anymore on visualizing her gashed wrists. On the phone, she broke up with Abe before he could break up with her. When she saw Dr. Tepper, she said she felt great. Really great. Even if she failed at everything else, she could be a good patient.

At Beth and Stephen's party, a woman wore heavy black eyeliner and the letter P pinned to her shirt. 'I'm a black-eyed P!' she cried out and laughed.

'I bet she didn't come up with that on her own,' Jordana said to Beth. She wished she had more of an independent life; then, when she was alone in social situations, she missed Pieter. Somehow parties invariably ended up like this, leaning against a wall with Beth, talking about the other people there. 'Someone else did that at another party and she stole it.'

'Probably.' Beth ate a carrot stick. She was always on a diet and never lost weight. She and Jordana had worked at the clinic together since it was just starting out as a grassroots egalitarian center, where they'd all taken turns mopping the floor and woman-

121

ning the front desk. Beth brought brownies to staff meetings and never forgot birthdays and cooked casseroles topped with corn-flakes for families when there was a sickness or death. Jordana had initially distrusted her: too nice. But Beth, not critical or brusque herself, had a surprising taste for those qualities in Jordana.

Beth dunked a cucumber spear in dressing. 'You know, giving parties sounds like such a good idea in the abstract, and then when they actually happen I just want to go hide in my room.'

'We never have parties. I don't know why that is.'

Across the room Beth's husband, Stephen, turned to the black-eyed P and smiled. Jordana couldn't stand Stephen. Even if she hadn't known from Beth that he cheated, she would have known from the distinct tang of willingness that he gave off – leaning too close when he talked to women, throwing his head back when he laughed, as he did now across the room. She supposed she'd lost her right to judge Stephen, but if anything her dislike of him had grown stronger.

She and Ben had been supposed to meet the day after they'd last seen each other. She hadn't gone, of course. She hadn't called, either, to tell him she wouldn't be there. Just the thought of dialing his number had filled her with guilt.

Let him wait. Let some small part of the consequences be his.

Ben called her at the clinic the next day. When she said her husband had found out about them, he'd said quietly, 'Oh, shit. I'm sorry.'

'*Oh, shit, I'm sorry*? That's all you can say?'

'I don't know what to say. Jordana—'

If he hadn't had his stupid date, if he hadn't said that thing about a fuck-fix, she wouldn't have torn out of the house in the middle of the night. And why was he seeing a married woman anyway? Because she wasn't a threat to his look-at-me-I'm-so-bohemian lifestyle. She'd hung up on him, breathless with rage.

A man with a gray ponytail stopped next to her and Beth. He wore a studded leather collar and a pinstriped suit over a leather vest. He asked Jordana, 'Who are you?'

'Jordana Voorster.'

'Who are you *supposed* to be? Are you a pioneer?'

Jordana had nearly forgotten she was wearing a costume. She looked down at the baggy calico. 'It's half of a painting,' she said. With Pieter, her costume had seemed funny, but now she felt

122

frumpy. Looking around the party, she realized most of the couples had dressed as other couples: the dish who ran away with the spoon, Han Solo and Princess Leia. Stephen had on black-rimmed eyeglasses and a bow tie, Woody Allen to Beth's scarves-and-fedora Annie Hall. There was something claustrophobic about it, everyone so paired that they stayed that way even when pretending to be someone else. Princess Di and Prince Charles – a younger couple Jordana didn't know – wore crowns from Burger King.

'What are you?' she asked.

The man stepped back from her, holding open the sides of his suit jacket, sticking out his chest. The leather vest had two holes through which his nipples showed, flat and putty-colored. She shook her head.

'Stocks and bondage,' he said.

'Clever.'

It actually was clever, so why was she being a bitch? Not that he'd noticed. He seemed to be the kind of person too satisfied—

You're always doing that, Ben's voice said in her mind. *Saying 'the kind of person who.'*

Fine. This man seemed like the kind of person who would hardly notice irony. And indeed, he had launched into a description of his corporate job. So there, Ben.

She'd accused him, during another post-discovery phone call, of getting out scot-free.

'Is that what you think?' Ben had said.

'Aren't you?'

'You tell *me*. You know everything.'

Her anger at him had held her together, these last weeks. She bit harder on her lip. Stocks-and-Bondage talked on. The gestures of active listening were so ingrained in Jordana from the clinic that she could hum and nod and lift her eyebrows without having to hear a thing. From her lip, she tasted the faint acidity of blood.

Playing the same music every night depressed Pieter, as did the corps of anorexic ballet students dressed as snowflakes, a different Clara each year, the same Snow Queen and Sugar Plum Fairy two or three years running. How thin the girls were, skin so translucent you could see the shape of their skulls, the knobs of their cheekbones. On this tracing-paper skin, they painted splotches of color: blue eyeshadow, fuchsia lipstick.

This year's Sugar Plum Fairy was a twenty-year-old named Lisa. Most of the third act she spent sitting between Clara and the Nutcracker Prince to watch the Russian Dance, the Tea Dance, the Waltz of the Flowers, a tight smile on her face. She had a knee injury, not disabling but so painful that she collapsed backstage after every show. She'd showed the younger dancers how to fill the toes of their slippers with Super Glue, then zag more Super Glue across the shoe's arch, to reinforce it. This way, she could make a pair of slippers last two days of rehearsal instead of one. The younger dancers' respect for her advice was mixed with condescension that came of being sure they would go farther than she had. Pieter recognized the mix of respect and disdain from himself, back when he'd been sure he'd be a soloist, the orchestra rising behind him as he carried his cello into the hall. Back then, he'd written and rewritten in his head the biography he imagined would someday appear in program notes: *Pieter Voorster stunned the music world in 1973 with his recordings of . . .*

After the performance, Pieter packed his cello, a 1880 Trapani. From his vantage in the orchestra pit, two young couples lingering together in the aisle appeared foreshortened. One of the women was beautiful, with dark hair brushed smoothly back from a wide brow and a fur coat just a shade lighter than her hair. The husband held a little girl, maybe three years old, in a green velvet dress and white tights. Pieter remembered those tights from Angie's childhood: the way they snagged, small balls of thread roughening the knees and seat. He saw himself kneeling to buckle his daughter's patent leather shoes, his forehead resting against her leg.

Angie. His stomach ached. He tried to hide his anxiety from her – if she saw that he pitied her, she'd only feel worse – and it seemed to have taken up permanent residence in his gut instead.

'No more 'rinas for a year,' said Nita, the concertmaster. She called the dancers 'rinas when she was feeling charitable, bunheads when she wasn't. She loosened her bow with two quick twists of her wrist.

'What are your plans now?'

'Home and bed,' said Nita. 'I have a wedding in the morning.'

'I had one this afternoon.'

'Did they have lots of metaphors about the new year?'

'Yes. But tomorrow, your bride and groom will also be hung over.'

Nita snapped shut the violin case. 'I can't wait.'

He and Nita often played at weddings together as part of a quartet. She was given to elaborately sequined clothing and had a raft of small pimples on her chin, where it rested against the violin. They'd known each other for nine years without ever quite crossing the line into friendship. These last few weeks, he'd realized sharply that he didn't really have friends. His last real friendship had been with Jordana's father, and that had ended bitterly when Pieter fell in love with his daughter. There were couples they saw together, and the men were sometimes referred to as 'his friends,' the women as Jordana's. Stephen, for example, Beth's husband, though Pieter's conversations with Stephen were generally halting and superficial. After a night with Beth and Stephen, he and Jordana would talk lazily on the ride home, along the dark winding road that followed the curves of Morrill River. She would take his hand from the stick shift, putting it onto her knee. She kept her hand on his, even when he had to shift gears. He'd thought he knew his own life; she'd robbed him of that.

Nita was looking at him strangely. He realized he'd paused in the middle of strapping the Trapani into its case.

'Are you okay?' she asked. 'You've been—'

He bent to snap shut the clasps of the heavy black case. 'The other thing about the wedding today was that everything was in Christmas colors. The bride had a red bow tie for me to wear, and there were children dressed as elves.' It worked: Nita smiled and began to tell him about a wedding where the first view of the bride had been as she stood on a pedestal at the back of the church, her back to the congregation. Then the pedestal, mechanized, had rotated slowly, until the bride faced the aisle.

To grin and nod was so painful he wanted to drop to his hands and knees.

'And she beams like Miss America—' Nita said. Pieter smiled and made a humming noise of sympathy and assent.

'Your sister's here,' said Cole.

Luke looked down the Burnt House stairs to the wide foyer, where silver beer cans piled like snowdrifts in the corners. Angie was wrapped in the long wool coat of their dad's that she'd started wearing this year. Underneath, the Yale sweatshirt. She was with Tris Wu and Jess Salter, back from UNC and Bates.

Luke said, 'All month she's been like, "I have to finish my applications." Tonight, I go in and she hasn't even started them.'

Cole had a beer in one hand; the other he rubbed across his chest. He had begun dressing recently like a fifties hood: white T-shirt, zip-front jacket, dark blue jeans turned up at the cuffs to show white socks. On his right hand, a grooved brass ring, once part of a faucet. Everyone else at school wore rugby shirts. Luke would never in a million years be as cool as Cole. Last summer, Cole's parents, both doctors, had wanted to buy him a Jeep, but instead he'd gotten a silver '62 Volvo station wagon, stick-shift. It was so old it had a starter button instead of an ignition key. Bubble-faced dials lined the dashboard. Luke had been disappointed the first time he saw the Volvo, and then gradually he'd realized it was the perfect car. He had fantasies of Cole tiring of the car and selling it to him, and one fantasy – guilty but honed – in which Cole died and his parents gave the car to Luke.

Angie and her friends started up the stairs. Jess said, 'Luke, hey!' and peeled off toward him. Angie didn't glance up. She trailed after Tris, toward the beer.

Jess gave him a hard one-armed hug while he said, 'Hey, wow, hi.'

'Long time no see.'

'Yeah.' Not like Jess'd ever talked to him when she was still in high school. Jess had a crew cut now, and she kept running her palm over the top of her head.

He drank some beer. Jess looked down over the railing at the people in the front hall. The house was way out in the woods and a few years ago, when a grease fire had started in the kitchen, the fire department had gotten there in time to save only part of the house. The right side remained more or less intact, but on the left just an outline remained, blackened framework that showed where the walls had been, the pitch of the roof.

Downstairs, someone had made a pipe out of a green apple, the murky smell of marijuana smoke rising. No west wall, so moonlight flooded in. On that side, nearest where the house ended, the ceiling was bumpy and blackened, like alligator hide. Over Jess's shoulder, Cole pointed at the stairs and started down. 'High school parties,' Jess said. 'Wait till you get to college.'

The thought of going away made Luke light-headed with relief. Cole and Warren were going to UNH. Luke had been planning to go there too, but he'd given in to his mother and applied other

126

places also, Wisconsin and Maryland. Now he said, 'I might be going to UW. If I get in.'

Jess seemed to find this ambition unremarkable, which was good because it made UW seem within reach. She said, 'Madison's supposed to be cool.'

Tris Wu walked up to them, handing Jess a beer. Her long dark hair was pulled back in a bouncy ponytail. He liked Tris, the least overachieving of Angie's friends.

Luke asked, 'Where's Angie?'

Tris shrugged and held Jess's gaze around Luke, the way teenagers communicated when there was a parent there. Then she smiled at Luke. 'How's it going?'

'Good, good. How's North Carolina?'

'"Go Tarbacks!"' said Tris. 'Everyone's in a stupid frat.'

Uneasiness about Angie was trying to jiggle free in his head. 'Are you going to transfer?'

She shook her head, lifting her cup to her mouth. 'God, the beer's even worse there than here at a *high school* party.'

'Where's Angie?' he asked again.

'Abe dragged her off to talk.'

For some reason, he couldn't lose himself in the party. When he had conversations, he felt like he was watching himself talk. Khamisa wanted him to do tequila shots with her and he did a couple, thinking they'd make him less self-conscious. It didn't work; everything he said sounded stupid and loud.

The dining room had a heavy table, scorched at one end, and long shredded drapes that might have once been red. He crawled out the window – the house no longer had a back door – to the back porch. Halfway out, he saw that Abe sat on the back steps. He started to pull back, but too late: Abe had turned and seen him. Reluctantly, Luke pulled himself the rest of the way through the window.

'What is going on with your sister?' Abe tore a long splinter off the porch railing and hurled it toward the woods. 'I try to talk to her and it's like there's soundproof glass there or something.' He ripped off another piece of the railing. The air was no colder on the porch than inside, but the smell of pine for some reason was stronger.

'She can be kind of a bitch,' Luke said.

Abe twisted around on the porch step. 'Kind of a bitch? My

God. It's like she's dying right in front of us.'

Luke felt something like a drop in barometric pressure, subtle and heavy. But Angie had doctors and his parents, monitoring her. 'You guys broke up. Why do you even care?'

'Why do I care?' The sentence started out sarcastic, but by the end Abe seemed to be asking himself. He lifted his chin toward the party. 'You just want to get back in there, don't you?'

Even though he'd been unhappy inside, now he wanted nothing more than to get back in there. He lifted his hand, tilting it back and forth: sort of.

'What's stopping you, then?'

'Nothing's stopping me.'

'That's right,' Abe said. 'Nothing's stopping you.'

At Beth and Stephen's, Pieter lifted his cello case carefully from its seat, jutting his right hip to meet it. In his left hand he had a pitchfork – borrowed from a French Hornist whose wife kept some horses – and the duffel bag with his costume. The night was dark and icy, and he picked his way carefully along the sidewalk, the cello's familiar weight against his right hip. He slipped once and caught himself, the instrument banging his thigh hard. The pain felt ridiculously personal: an affront, a betrayal.

Coming into the party, he looked automatically for his wife. She stood with a woman dressed in a toga. It was clear to him that Jordana was bored, but the woman talked on. He thought of Jordana's emotions as transparent, but maybe he just knew her too well.

He touched her shoulder. She turned, her face lighting. 'You're here. Your costume—'

Why had he come over to her? 'I'll put it on upstairs.'

'No, use the guest room. I'm glad to see you.'

Her lower lip looked strange, swollen, almost like she'd been kissing someone. He lifted the cello. 'I need to put this down.' He just wanted to be away from her. It had returned to him that, for all her transparency, she'd deceived him for months. Once a week? Every day? He wanted to ask and didn't want to ask. Answers were like junk food: after each bite, he felt vertiginous satisfaction and then was immediately hungry again.

'I'll come with you—'

He frowned, shaking his head sharply.

128

In the first-floor guest bedroom, an orgy of coats covered the bed. He closed the door behind him, not bothering to turn on the lights. Through the door, the noise and laughter of the party came faintly from down the hall. He pulled on the faded overalls and collarless shirt Jordana had found for him at Goodwill and got his rimless reading glasses from the inside pocket of his tux. Moving toward the door, his reflection moved with him in the mirror above the dresser. He stopped, then found the light and switched it on.

He'd tried on the costume once before and had been, despite himself, impressed with Jordana's ingenuity. But now he saw how stooped he looked, how old. No wonder—

He shook his head sharply to block out the thought and switched the light back off.

For so long, he had depended on Jordana to help him interpret the world. It had been she who pointed out the contradiction between Nita's restrained demeanor and her look-at-me clothes. She had told him that Fidel, the conductor, couldn't stand the orchestra's artistic director, and he'd immediately seen that she was right, though he'd watched them interact for years. If asked what his children were like, Pieter fumbled: *They're swimmers* or *Angie's a straight-A student*. Once, asked the same question, Jordana had said, 'Angie engages with everything. She rides out into battle. Luke's happier just taking things as they come.'

Of course that was who his children were. He never could have articulated it. And Jordana had told Pieter about himself. He hadn't realized his own tendency to get very quiet when he disagreed, rather than arguing. He hadn't known that sometimes he stopped dead in the middle of the sidewalk, staring at nothing. Nor had he known that when he laughed it sounded rich and surprised, and that people would glance over, smiling themselves. In some way, Jordana carried his identity more than he did. What happened to that enormous part he'd given over to her if she thought so little of it she could want someone else?

He opened the door to the hallway. From the party a woman's voice rose above the mutter of conversation. 'A black-eyed pea!' she cried. 'A black-eyed pea!'

He'd come to this party because he didn't want people to see that anything was wrong – it would have seemed strange if he hadn't been with his wife on New Year's – but now he found he couldn't make himself go out into that babble. There were chairs around the

TV, near the door; he went and sank down in one. The television reflected him bulbously, swelling hip and shoulder and cheek, his feet and profile shrunken and tight. In the hall behind him, one and then several people lined up for the bathroom. They were so close Pieter could have turned and grabbed at their pant legs; in the television their reflections were large and distinct. A woman in a pinafore, a man in a Burger King crown.

'That's the thing,' Crown was saying to Pinafore. 'You *are* the Buddha. Each one of us is the Buddha.'

'Uh-huh, uh-huh.'

Pieter pulled his knees farther in to his chest, resting his cheek on them. In the dark screen of the TV, he looked faint and unfamiliar, and for a moment he left his body. There was a roar like traffic, the metallic taste of nausea. Then he felt his weight again, the cushions beneath him, the faint persistent twinge in his back that lingered from breaking Luke's door.

Leaning his head against the back of the chair, he waited for the light-headedness to pass. He didn't feel he had enough of a self to talk to other people – to smile, to pour a drink – without ripping in two.

The guest bedroom looked out onto the driveway. Pieter crossed silently to the window and pushed it open. Sitting on the sill, pain flickering between his shoulders, he awkwardly pivoted his legs out. The ground was only a foot or so beneath his shoes; all he had to do was stand up to walk away.

'Avez-vous la période?'

'What?' Angie said. She and Tris were crouching in the woods to pee. She wasn't supposed to have beer with her meds, but it calmed her down. She might have drunk too fast, though. Time kept skipping.

She'd decided, finally, that she just wouldn't apply anywhere that had a January first date. The applications weren't that hard; she could surely get the January fifteenth ones in.

'Do you have your period?' Tris said. She gestured toward Angie's lap, where the creased edge of a pad showed.

Angie stood quickly, pulling up her pants, embarrassed. She'd begun wearing a pad all the time because she was afraid she could get her period and not realize it right away. They made their way back into the Burnt House, up the wide curving staircase. The bathtub held bottles of beer.

130

'I feel kind of dizzy.'

'Maybe you shouldn't drink, with your period and all.'

'Oh, shit,' Angie said, and put her hand out for the counter. The bathroom walls were graffitied with black marker, a hole punched into the wall labeled *Daniela Moore's cunt*→. Her vision went dark at the edges, like burning paper. For a moment she thought she'd throw up; then it retreated. 'No, I'm okay. I'm okay.'

She could hear that someone had started a contest downstairs, throwing bottles out the missing wall to crash against trees.

Sounding like Jess – voice dipping low with concern – Tris asked, 'Are you sure you're okay?'

'I'm fine! I keep saying I'm fine.'

Jordana waited for Pieter to come out of the guest room. It had been twenty minutes, then thirty. Finally, she went after him. His cello case stood in the corner; his tux hung neatly over the foot-board of the bed.

'Where is he?' Beth asked, when she came out.

'I don't know. His cello's here, so he must be. He's walking or something.'

Jordana let herself out the door of Stephen and Beth's house, into the shattering cold, and walked up and down the block, wider and wider circles. Her husband's car was nowhere. Pieter would never leave without his cello, but he had.

She stood, letting it sink in. Then, bending her head, arms crossed over her chest, she began walking swiftly, without desti-nation. Gradually the houses gave way to stores. The blocks became longer; she was walking parallel to Route 121, moving toward the commercial part of town. She passed the backs of build-ings she drove by every day, and then she passed the back of the bank building that held the clinic.

Donut Haus smelled of sugar and Clorox. There were no customers. A woman, pink skirt pulled tight across her hips, leaned over a bucket of gray water, wringing out a mop.

'I wonder if I could get some coffee.' Jordana put a dollar on the counter.

The mopper stood up slowly and turned. She was pregnant and very young. Her gold pin said LAURETTA. 'Where you are, I just mopped there.'

'Sorry.' Jordana stepped back.

'I already closed out the register.'

Jordana had only come in because the little store had been right there, and lit, and empty. She hadn't really wanted coffee and so was shocked to find herself close to tears. 'Is there any way—?'

'You can have it if you want it that bad.' The girl leaned the mop against the wall and, skirting the wet floor, came around back of the counter. Above her was a clock with WHAT TIME IS IT? written across the face, and D·O·U·G·H·N·U·T·T·I·M·E· in a circle instead of numbers. Lauretta picked up the coffeepot and sniffed, then shrugged and poured a mug. 'Just don't tell my boss.'

It was warm in Donut Haus; Jordana put her cheek down on the counter. The store's wide front window reflected them: the pregnant girl in the pink uniform, Jordana dark and pinched, still wearing a long white apron. Steam rose from the mop bucket, breaking apart in the air. The clock hands hovered just before the D, then clicked forward. Midnight.

Pieter pulled into the driveway of his house and turned off the ignition.

There was something pathetic about the pull of home for him; it only occurred to him now that he might have gone somewhere else, might have gone anywhere. Now that he was here, he couldn't imagine going inside. He grasped the steering wheel with both hands, pulling himself forward. He wanted to scream, and hated that he couldn't bring himself to, and the pain of that – his decorum and absurdity – did make him scream.

At the Burnt House, they screamed the last seconds of the year: 'Three! Two! One!'

Luke pulled Khamisa to him and kissed her. Then to be nice, he kissed Kristin, who was standing right by his elbow. Her lips were very soft and she tasted of mint gum. He touched the tip of her tongue with his. She gave a little moan and he realized what he was doing.

He pulled back quickly, looking for Khamisa, who – thank God – was turned away to hug a friend. Around them people shouted; champagne bottles popped.

Afterward, people still yelled, trying to keep the moment going. Khamisa kissed Cole on the lips.

'Where's Ange?' Luke asked Jess.

132

She looked around, then nodded toward the stairs. Angie stood at the edge of the top step, next to Tris. Even from here, Angie looked pale. She swayed, put her hand out for the banister. He started toward her, smiling at the girls who stopped him to kiss his cheek. He wasn't quite to the stairs when Kristin grasped his shoulder. She had what looked like angry tears in her eyes.

'What the fuck was that?' she asked.

At the top of the staircase, his sister folded up and began to fall.

She fell with stoned slowness, end over end like flip turns, the jarring thuds of her shoulder, her feet, her head. Luke shook Kristin off and bounded up three stairs. He tried to catch his sister but her weight knocked him over and they slid down the last steps, tangled together.

Angie sobbed. No, she was laughing. Her hair had a line of blood in it. She raised herself to her hands and knees, laughing and crying, then fell onto her side. Mascara streaked her face, and her jeans had ripped at the knee. Through the hole he could see her kneecap. He put his hand there, over the rip. The warm arch of his sister's knee fit his palm. Angie stilled, blue eyes enormous, and in the long moment before he looked away and the noise of the world returned, he felt himself falling, as she had, end over end.

Chapter Thirteen

The ice of the river was wavy, and in places weeds had frozen into it, dark warping of the surface from beneath. Pieter had learned to skate so young, on the canals near his boyhood home in Haarlem, that he couldn't remember a time he hadn't known how. The Morrill River narrowed here, this short stretch almost like a pond. It was midafternoon but overcast: sky dark gray, air heavy. In the middle of the river, the ice shadowed to lavender.

It was their family's tradition to skate here on New Year's Day. He hadn't wanted to come, but he hadn't been able to think of anything he could stand to do at home, either. Now he wished he'd stayed behind.

He skated to the edge of the ice, where the Girl Scout troop had set up a card table to sell hot drinks; a Magic-Markered sign said HELP US in orange, with purple smiley faces. One Girl Scout, maybe thirteen, had thick glasses and wore her green sash over her parka. Behind her, two other Scouts, much younger, sat whispering together on a Styrofoam ice chest. He felt sorry for the older girl, officious and uncool, her forehead breaking out. As she handed Pieter his hot chocolate, it slopped a little over the cup edge and onto his rabbit-lined glove.

The chocolate had a dry artificial taste, but its warmth felt good. He turned to watch the skaters. His wife was easy to pick out. She hadn't learned to skate until adulthood, and she did it slowly and with concentration, staying close to the ice's edge. Angie and Luke were skating together, racing and deliberately bumping into each other. Strange to see them enjoy each other's company.

There was something about Angie's face. He skated closer and took her chin, turning her face so the cheekbone caught the light:

134

a bruise and, up near the hairline, a cut. 'What's this?'

Angie glanced at Luke.

He said, 'The party last night? Mandy's mom had just mopped their kitchen. Lots of people slipped.'

'You slipped?'

She nodded.

'You know, you're not supposed to drink with your meds.'

Luke said, 'She wasn't,' and threw himself back into their game of pushing.

When his kids were in junior high, they used to spend Saturdays at the skating rink downtown. Pieter would pick them up as a last errand, after the hardware store, after buying stamps at the post office, dropping his concert shirts at the cleaners. Driving toward the rink, those late winter afternoons, the dark trees had seemed to hold the last of the old light against the sky.

And then he'd park and walk into the rink, every time the same song, or so it seemed, someone singing they wished that they had Jesse's girl, lights flashing magenta and yellow and blue across the ice, Angie skating with a boy who came up to her shoulder and had perfectly feathered hair. Black rubber mats squeaking under Pieter's hard-soled shoes, the air smelling of pizza. The rink was over-bright and tacky. It seemed to him, now, that he'd had everything.

A few yards away, his wife relaxed and unlocked her knees. Then, as though noticing her ease, she froze and crashed.

He slowed his stride, keeping his eye on her. She was no longer seeing Ben Webster, but did that make her all the more likely to pine for him? Did she have to hide her longing from Pieter, pretend it didn't exist? The idea seemed more terrible than the affair itself. Jordana put her mittened hands on the ice and tried to push herself to her feet, but her skates skittered and she fell to her knees again. Angie skated over and hoisted her up. Despite Angie being wider and fair, they looked alike to him: not in the way of mothers and daughters but more the way old married couples sometimes came to resemble each other. As they passed him, Angie reached back for Pieter. He let her pull him for a few yards, then smiled weakly and extricated his hand. 'I'm going to rest awhile.'

He made for a bench at the edge of the river, passing an older couple waltzing without music and then a high school couple who had stopped skating and were just standing on the ice, holding on to each other. And then, standing under a tree: the girl from the yard.

It was her shape he recognized more than her features. She hunched in the cold, hands under her arms. Her aloneness seemed terrible.

He looked back, to where she was looking. Luke had joined Jordana and Angie, grabbing Jordana's other hand, helping to pull her across the ice. They wore heavy jackets, bright hats. Laughter floated through the cold air. The three of them looked like a family, a happy family.

Part Two

Chapter Fourteen

The summer before his senior year of college, Luke bought his first car, a blue '78 Datsun. It had been through too many Wisconsin winters: along the fender, salt had corroded a ragged gray coastline into the paint. The man selling it, Roger, had a broad sunburnt face and a yellow mustache. He'd duct-taped squares of heavy cardboard over two holes where the floor was rusted through. A sleek cream-colored cat snaked a figure eight, over and over, between and around the guy's ankles, its tail whispering against the stiff denim of his jeans.

'We have a Siamese at home,' Luke said, glad at this point of connection. He needed Roger to go down on the Datsun's price. 'My sister rescued it from a breeding factory.'

'I don't think anyone's going to try to breed this lady.' Bending down, the man scooped up the cat. He held her under the armpits, so that she faced Luke, the rest of her body hanging down. The cat was blind, eyes a cloudy eggnog-white. Roger began to swing her slowly side to side, a heavy pendulum. Lazily, she closed her eyes, tongue flicking out once to lick her nose.

Luke had already driven the car around the block a few times. The clutch felt smooth; the noises from the engine were loud but not alarmingly irregular. He liked the car's compactness. The others he'd looked at had been low and lurking, with the long snouts and round eyes of alligators.

'Seven hundred's a lot of money,' said Luke. He was lifeguarding at the Nat for the summer, making minimum wage. Nine hundred in his checking account, and he hadn't paid last month's bills yet. His phone bill, in particular, was depressingly high.

Something in Roger's face shut down. 'That clutch isn't even a year old. That cost me five hundred bucks, alone. I've got the receipt.' Handing the cat to Luke, he turned and went into the house.

After a moment's shock, the cat began to squirm. Luke gripped harder, but with a yowl the cat corkscrewed herself out of his hands. Dropping to the pavement, she tore around the corner of the house.

Roger reemerged a few minutes later with a pink carbon copy. 'It's a little torn,' he said.

'Your cat wanted to get down.'

Roger thrust the carbon paper at Luke – 'It's a little torn,' he said again, 'no big deal' – and crouched down, calling, 'Pretty? Pretty?'

The receipt showed the clutch had been replaced for $423. The upper right corner was ripped, where the repair date should have been.

Still squatting, Roger shuffled forward a few steps, crooning, 'Here, Pretty, Pretty, Pretty.'

Luke wished the clutch hadn't come up – he hadn't even been worried about its age before. He wanted the car. Driving it, shifting from second gear up to third, he'd felt incredibly happy. He liked the car better for being unpretentious, for having vinyl seats and a ceiling so low it brushed the top of his hair. The gearshift knob had been replaced with a devil's head whose eyes lit up when he braked.

Roger had coaxed the cat out; it curled around the brick corner of the house, meowing resentfully. Scooping her up, he stood and turned to Luke. 'I should get a better filing system.'

'It's fine,' Luke said quickly. 'I'll take it.'

Down the street was a pay phone, between the gas station and IHOP. Luke tried Angie, letting the phone at the halfway house ring and ring. He kicked at some pale weeds that grew through cracks in the concrete. Finally, after twenty-three rings, he hung up.

The night she'd fallen down the stairs at the Burnt House, almost four years ago, he'd gotten it – really *gotten* it, for the first time – that she wasn't faking. It was like that optical illusion where you saw an old woman and then realized the picture could be a young woman as well: a tiny shift, but it had rearranged everything.

He'd helped get Angie through the last semester of high school, making her do her homework, talking her out of bed when she was too depressed to move, lying to their parents. He hadn't realized how aimless he'd felt before – that was part of why he did it, and part was guilt. But he also found he just liked being around his sister. She had a wry sense of humor, a funny off-center way of looking at the world. By the end of summer, she'd been more stable; she'd made it through seven months at Middlebury College before overdosing on lithium and being hospitalized. She lived at home, then a group house, then home. She stabilized and got jobs, went off her medication and lost them. Off meds, she picked up men she didn't know, gave all her money to panhandlers, bought extravagant and senseless presents, destroyed possessions, went back to the hospital. But she'd been doing well these last few months, sticking to her therapy schedule, working as a cook. She even talked about returning to college, maybe UNH this time.

He tried calling her one more time, then gave up and drove to Wendy's.

Nine a.m. The lawns were green and shady, and from all around came the high chant of insects. He loved driving, even on these short, slow streets. His housemate had a Honda Civic that Luke occasionally took to the grocery store or a movie, but it felt different to be in his own car. Wendy lived in a big gray house on Gorham. He pulled into the side driveway, under the chestnut. The house had once been a mansion but was now divided into many small apartments; there was a perpetual red and white FOR RENT sign jammed crookedly into the front lawn.

He let himself into the building, then into Wendy's apartment, which took up the right side of the first floor. He called out, and Wendy called back, 'Kitchen.'

The air smelled of frying butter. The apartment was smaller than Luke's place, which he only shared with two people. Here Wendy and another girl had the dining room, and four other roommates split the two bedrooms. There were high ceilings and elaborate moldings around the windows and stained brown carpet covering the floor. During the school year, the space always felt chaotic – ringing phone, dishes on the table, rinsed-out underwear hanging over the shower rod – but most of the housemates had gone home for the summer, and now the apartment felt airy and quiet.

When he came into the kitchen, Wendy glanced over her shoul-

141

der and smiled. She was barefoot, her dark red hair pulled back in a neat knot. They'd been together two years but he still hadn't gotten used to how different she looked at different times. Sometimes at night, when he unfastened her hair from its bun, she was ethereally beautiful. Other times, she seemed plain, with her pale lashes and wide forehead and freckles everywhere. Wendy should have been a senior like he was, but she'd spent her first year in Madison waitressing, to qualify for residency and in-state tuition.

She was cooking a grilled cheese sandwich for breakfast. She didn't like cereal: too soggy. Pointing with her spatula, she asked, 'Want one?'

'Sure.' He wanted to tell her about the car but found himself nervous about it, suddenly sure he'd made a mistake. Going to the window, he peered out toward the driveway but could only see the edge of the front bumper.

He turned, watching Wendy cook. He liked the way she did things without wasted motion, with matter-of-fact grace and precision. She lifted out the sandwich with a spatula, sliced it in half diagonally, and handed it to Luke on a plate. Buttering two more slices, she arranged them carefully in the pan.

He bit into the sandwich, Swiss cheese and thinly sliced tomato. The bread was almost burnt, the way he liked it. Wendy said, 'Oh, look at this.' She stretched out one arm to where her purse hung over the back of chair and pulled out a tract: Your Ticket to Eternal Salvation. 'Someone left this last night instead of a tip.'

'So, hey. I bought a car.'

Wendy froze. 'You *did?*'

'Want to see it?'

Clicking the stove off, she brushed past him toward the front door. He followed her, nervous, the car deforming in his imagination into something twisted and scabrous. When he saw the actual car, he didn't recognize it for a second: shiny, compact, with only a freckling of rust along the bumper. He'd been right to buy it.

Wendy walked around it. 'How much was this?'

'Five hundred dollars,' he lied. 'Do you like it?'

'Are you sure it even runs?'

'I'll take you for a drive.' She didn't have to be at work until late afternoon; he didn't work on Saturdays.

She opened the door. 'What is this? Cardboard?'

'It's fine. It's nothing. The floor's a little rusty.'

142

'Did you get underneath the car?' She looked at his face. 'Oh, *Luke*. The whole underside could be about to go.'

'It's fine. I looked at all the records.' She looked doubtful and he said, more harshly than he'd meant, 'Wen, forget it, it's fine.'

Only a few miles north of Madison was farmland. Lush green fields surrounded the road. The barns looked like the Fisher-Price barn he'd had as a child: red, with wide doors and perfect silos. The air smelled plush and wet. 'Isn't this great?' He motioned with his arm. 'We should come out here more.'

Wendy shrugged, unimpressed. She'd grown up in a farming town in Iowa. 'You see that?' she asked, pointing. 'That big brown thing? That's a cow.'

'No way.' He put his hand on her knee, then had to take it off to downshift. 'Hey, can you drive stick?'

She nodded. Of course she could. She could walk on her hands, beat him in pool, fix a clogged pipe. When he'd first seen her, she'd been waitressing, pouring two coffees simultaneously, barely glancing down at the cups.

She pointed past him to a field. 'That black-and-white thing?'

'Don't tell me that's a cow too.'

'I'm afraid so.' She turned on the radio, which spat and hissed like a cat. A song came faintly through the static. Taking off her shoes, she put her feet up on the dashboard, in the sun.

It was a beautiful day. Luke rolled down the window, the sun warming his bare arm. He loved driving. It felt great to be out of Madison. Up on the road ahead was an Amish buggy, black with a reflective orange triangle on the back. Luke slowed down and passed carefully. As he braked, the devil's eyes lit up red. Wendy said, 'Oh, my heck.'

'Isn't that great?'

'Who'd you *buy* this from?'

'A little old lady. She said she only drove it on Sundays, to church.'

Wendy threw back her head and laughed. He loved the way that she never pretended to find something funny just to be nice; laughter always seemed to take her by surprise.

The girls he'd dated his freshman year, before Wendy, had been hip and pretty. They were from Philadelphia or Washington, D.C. They listened to obscure bands and took photography classes and

143

talked about the inner-city kids they'd tutored during high school. Dating them somehow seemed easy. It wasn't that they were undemanding, exactly; just that he'd always known how to act and approximately how they'd react.

Wendy had worked places like McDonald's during high school; she'd been a cheerleader and got straight A's. When they were alone, she could be warm, almost heartbreakingly sweet. Other times, she was prickly and easily annoyed. They might be lying in bed after making love, happy and whispering; he'd get up to go to the bathroom, and when he returned Wendy would be already dressed and saying she had to get to the library, shrugging away when he tried to hold her. If he'd thought she was playing games, it would have turned him off, but her stubborn self-sufficiency was compelling. That she didn't try to accommodate or impress him somehow made her seem whole in a way other people weren't.

They passed a store advertising Amish-baked pie; glancing into his rearview mirror, he made a squealing U-turn. 'Let's get a pie,' he said. He still wanted to try and make this feel like a holiday. He pulled into the parking lot of the store. Wendy started to speak but he broke in quickly. 'I'll pay. I owe you money.'

'From what?'

'From when you bought aspirin the other week.' He came around to her side of the car, opening the door, then dropped to a squat, retrieving her sneakers from the floor. 'Here, give me your foot.'

She said, 'That aspirin was about two dollars.'

'Not with interest.' He hated the way she still couldn't accept things from him. She paid her own rent and tuition, things his parents covered for him; she was always broke.

She reached down to retie the shoelace he'd just done. 'I'll pay. You bought gas.'

He turned his head and kissed her knee.

'What?'

'I can't stand when we go out and I know it's killing you, I can see the gears in your head, thinking how you're going to eat rice all week or something to make up for being bad.'

'That's not—'

'Wen, come on, it *is*. You don't let me do anything.'

'Okay,' she said. 'You can buy the pie.'

'Hooray.'

144

'I thought that's what you wanted—'

'It is,' he said quickly. 'I'm sorry. It's good.'

Inside, they picked out a blueberry pie, still warm in its box. They ate it from the center, sitting outside on a grassy hillock. The thick yellow air felt like it had grown ten degrees hotter in the ten minutes they'd been inside the store.

The pie was delicious, crust flaky with butter. 'Your teeth are purple,' he said.

She ran her tongue along them, under closed lips. 'There was this rule in my high school,' she said. 'I mean, not a rule, but the popular girls didn't eat in front of their boyfriends. If they came into McDonald's, they'd just get a Coke.'

'Did you do that?'

'I wasn't that popular.' With her fingers, she broke off another bite of pie. 'What do you need a car for?'

'We can go places. It will be fun. We could go to Chicago.'

'I hate to break this to you: I don't think that car's going to make it to Chicago.'

'It could. I don't know, Wen, *grocery* shopping. We can go to movies.' He stood up, nodding at the phone at the edge of the parking lot. 'I want to try calling Angie. I couldn't reach her before.'

Wendy looked at her watch. 'I have to be at work by four.'

'It's two.'

'I'm just saying.'

He walked across the tar – springy in the heat – and shut himself in the little booth. The phone's silver surface was cloudy and scratched. He dialed the long string of familiar numbers: first the access code for AT&T, then his calling card number, then the halfway house.

This time the phone rang twelve times and a woman picked up. She had the slow, heavy voice Luke had come to associate with taking antipsychotics, and when he asked for Angie there was a long pause before she said she'd get her.

Through the glass of the booth, the car shimmered with heat, crouching over its parking space. His sister said, 'Luke?'

'I'm on a pay phone. I just wanted to check in.'

'I'm fine. I think this thing might work.' Her doctor had decided to wean her off lithium and onto a new med. 'I feel ... I really feel pretty good. I'm sorry, I know I'm boring about this.'

'No, no, it's great.' In truth, though he was glad the Depakote seemed to be working, she *was* a little boring about it, so anxious for it to succeed that she tracked every hiccup in mood. 'I bought a car. It's really cool. I mean old, but cool.'

'You bought a car!' she cried.

'I did. I can see it from here.' He looked out at his car and laughed aloud.

Chapter Fifteen

Their bedroom, with the shades drawn, was cottony gray. It wasn't quite seven in the morning, though Pieter had been up nearly three hours, practicing. Quietly, he pulled off his shirt, dropping it into the hamper. He felt creaky with fatigue. Because he was about to leave on a week-long tour with the orchestra, he'd stayed up late the night before, packing, talking to Angie on the phone.

Jordana slept in their bed, but as he sat gingerly on the edge of the mattress to ease off his shoes, she turned and rolled toward him. 'Be close to me,' she said sleepily. She put her arms around his waist and her cheek on his back.

Gently, he unhooked her arms from around him and stood. 'I need to get ready to go.' He began pulling clothes from the dresser. 'It's six hours to Clementine.'

Jordana flopped onto her back, staring at the ceiling. 'Why won't you touch me?'

'You're exaggerating.' They made love almost as much as they used to. It did feel far more loaded to him, though. Sometimes, he wouldn't initiate sex because he needed her to want him. Other times it was the opposite, and the knowledgeable, insinuating stroke of her hand – its assumption that he was just *available* to her – sickened him.

'What *is* it then? Tell me what to do and I'll do it.'

He needed her to say that she loved him. That she wouldn't leave, that she wasn't thinking about leaving.

She had said all those things; if he asked her to say them again she would. She'd be exasperated but also relieved, pleased, amused, reassured. How easily the power could tip back to her. How easily she could feel sure of him, and therefore bored, and therefore all the more susceptible to an affair.

'Did you even hear me?' said his wife.

'Of course I heard you.' Leaning against the open bureau drawer, he pressed his fingers to his eyes, exhausted. He didn't want to go on with this talk, but he couldn't make himself move toward the shower.

'Listen,' Jordana said. 'If you can't touch me, what about this? What if you hold me and I touch myself?'

He couldn't think of anything more terrible. He shook his head.

'*What*, then?' she said.

When he didn't answer, she sat up in bed and pulled off her nightgown. Beneath her arm, the smudge of stubble. 'Okay,' she said, and closed her eyes, running her hand across her small breast and down her stomach.

He'd seen her touch herself before, if he was behind her during sex; it had aroused him then.

'Don't,' he said.

She opened her eyes. Her expression was almost fierce. He looked back, hating her, thinking his glare would shame her into stopping. But she went on. She went on and on and on, rubbing and working. The blue morning light showed waxy wrinkles around her eyes.

How had Clementine, Maine, come up with the money to bring the orchestra there? Most of the cost of their trips around New England came out of the states' arts funding and the orchestra's own budget, but a town still had to find nearly fifteen hundred dollars a day. Nor could he imagine why Clementine – population seven thousand – believed that enough people would attend concerts to warrant having the orchestra for two days of its tour.

In small towns, the orchestra was usually put up in people's homes. Pieter didn't mind cost-cutting, but he minded the way Jean, the orchestra's manager, always presented financial decisions as being about something else – in this case as 'building a community's connection to the arts that goes beyond the usual one-sided relationship of audience to artist.'

Pieter and Vladimir Andronovich, the orchestra's timpanist, were staying with the Stevenson family: Vlad in the guest room, Pieter in the master bedroom. Mr. and Mrs. Stevenson themselves had taken the basement rec room's pull-out couch. The Stevensons were in their sixties. They were almost the same height, and both had short gray hair and sweatshirts – his black, hers red with a quilted snowman.

'We thought we'd have an aperitif on the veranda,' Mrs. Stevenson said. She led them into a sunroom off the kitchen, where a bottle of white wine sat next to a platter of complicated-looking hors d'oeuvres: folds of ham on little toasts, topped with sour cream and pennants of pimento. The sunroom was carpeted with green synthetic grass that scrinched underfoot.

'We so love classical music,' Mrs. Stevenson said. She was the designated talker of the two. An old couple, Pieter thought, and then: I'll be sixty in three years. It seemed impossible. Why had Jordana chosen this morning for a fight? Things had been good between them recently. Angie's going on a new med had felt like watching together as she tried to cross a high, rickety bridge. Each day that she got a little farther out, the bridge still holding, he and Jordana had relaxed a tiny bit.

Turning to Pieter, Mrs. Stevenson put her fingertip to her cheek. 'Now, how did you decide to become a cellist?'

He was touched by the effort they'd gone to and by their evident nervousness. At the same time he just wanted to escape upstairs to the bedroom and not have to perform. He said something quickly about his uncle, who had taught him the basics of playing on an old cello. He could see he was disappointing them. He might have gone on to talk about the degree to which he'd taught himself, the music-store owner who had let him copy sheet music by hand when he didn't have the fifty cents to buy it. They would probably have loved those stories, but they embarrassed Pieter; they seemed melodramatic.

And – something he tried to keep secret even to himself – he was hoarding these stories in case he ever became famous. It wasn't going to happen, and yet he'd gotten into the habit of saving up for imaginary interviews, not letting the stories wear shiny with handling.

Anyway, Vlad fulfilled the role of storyteller. He was doing his parents now: 'They said – in Russian, of course – "The drums? Vee come to the U.S. so you can *boom, boom, boom*?"'

Pieter hung the garment bag with his tuxedos – he had two regular ones and a third faintly grayed by age, as though covered in a light film of dust, that he had to include on longer trips. Vlad knocked at the half-open bedroom door and walked in. He was short and muscular, with a black mustache and beard. Across his forehead and cheeks he had acne scars, craters the size of olive pits. 'That tree is something else, no?'

'Tree?'

Vlad threw himself down on the bed. Pieter was annoyed, then amused by his annoyance; he'd already begun thinking of the bed as his.

Vlad wiggled his back, getting comfortable. 'In the living room? You step in, a little ficus tree lights up and Mozart starts. You step back out, *poof,* gone.' Vlad had been born in the States; Pieter wasn't sure whether the very slight accent and sometimes-stilted grammar were affectation or genuine remnants of growing up with immigrant parents.

The bed was so enormous that there was nowhere else in the bedroom to sit, so Pieter crossed his arms and leaned against the closet doors. He realized he had no idea what to say. Vlad had rolled onto one hip, though, and was working something out of his pants' pocket. 'So. I have this.' A small enameled box that Pieter knew held cocaine. Vlad shook it, raising his eyebrows questioningly at Pieter, who shrugged: sure.

Pieter had done cocaine a few times, always when the orchestra was traveling, with Vlad or a group containing Vlad. They sat on the edge of the wide sink top in the master bath. Pieter went first, an order he'd noticed Vlad always adhered to: funny that something as seedy as using drugs in their hosts' bathroom would have strict etiquette. The cocaine made his throat dry and itchy. There was a mirror opposite the sink as well as the one over it, and so the two of them were reflected, over and over, infinitely but growing smaller and smaller, like an echo bouncing between canyon walls.

Vlad leaned back and held his finger under the faucet, then tipped his head back, dripping water into each nostril. 'Here is my theory,' he said. 'Every person has one drug that is their perfect match. Your job is to go out into the universe and find it.'

Pieter let his feet kick gently against the below-sink cabinets. 'You sound like you're talking about a soul mate.' Before he'd first tried cocaine, he'd imagined it would make him feel euphoric, transformed. The actual effect was less artificial and so, in its own

150

way, even more seductive. He felt the way he did when skating: bright. Certain. Happy.

'It's much harder to find your soul mate, though,' Vlad said. 'Drugs there are only – what? Fifty?'

'You believe there's one person in the world you're supposed to find and be with?'

Vlad spread his hands and shrugged, a very Slavic gesture for *sure, of course,* his lower lip jutting out. Pieter didn't actually much like Vlad, who was boisterous, sarcastic, a womanizer. Jordana said Vlad reminded her of a sperm – all blind aggression.

'What if you never find her?'

'I've already found her. I fucked it up.' Vlad's accent and stilted grammar were gone. He turned his attention to the soaps, shaped like teddy bears. He picked up a pale blue one, the color of cue chalk, and turned on the faucet again.

'I don't think those are supposed to be used.'

'Oh, they're definitely not supposed to be used.' As Vlad washed his hands, the bear's features flattened. Then he carefully replaced the soap in the dish, its face buried in another bear's crotch.

Vlad held up the enameled box. 'Before dinner, one more?' The accent was back. He didn't wait for Pieter to respond before tapping out lines.

Dinner was in the basement of the public library, a large room set with folding tables. As one after another official and townsperson rose to make hyperbolic too-long speeches about the necessity of bringing the arts to Clementine, Pieter realized again how much it had cost this town to have the orchestra there. He tried to keep their effort at the front of his mind, and not his irritation, as the librarian struggled to her feet (she had on a full-length taffeta dress, as though she were attending a prom) and began a rambling account of the decision to have a concert here. Under the table, Pieter jiggled his crossed legs, fast.

'They said we couldn't do it!' the librarian said. *They?* 'To them I say: We. Have. Done. It.' She raised her arms; the hall applauded. 'We have done it!' she cried again.

He hated them, these people with their preference for Mozart and Vivaldi, hated the smallness of their ambitions. And then, just as suddenly, his hatred turned in against himself. Who was he to

151

feel contempt for these earnest people, who had saved and schemed to bring him here?

And, as always happened when he let his guard down, his wife's affair rose in him. He had to get out of this room.

'Bathroom?' he gasped, sotto voce.

Mr. Stevenson pointed, frowning. He looked concerned, though Pieter wasn't sure where his concern was directed. Pieter's health? The rudeness of leaving mid-speeches? Standing, he stumbled a little, just as the librarian had, and began to make for the side door. People were looking at him. More and more people looked over. He was making a spectacle of himself. No: they thought he was about to speak. Some clicked their water glasses with their forks. Someone clapped, uncertainly.

He called their house from the pay phone in the library's dark hallway. The phone rang ten times before he hung up.

Sometimes Pieter didn't even know if he still loved Jordana. He looked so assiduously for hints of her infidelity that when he found one, no matter how weak – she was out! at seven at night! – his first reaction was triumph. And then the sensation of unhingement. He felt literally as though he were being *unhinged,* the parts of him gently, stealthily moved apart. His elbows and hands felt cold and buzzy, and he thought he might throw up. He shoved through the library's heavy side door.

Outdoors, he leaned over, hands on knees. He was panting, as though he'd run.

He felt he should have gotten over the affair, at least enough to think of it with philosophical rue. Instead, it had lodged itself jaggedly in his chest. If Pieter talked to a young man, any glimmer of humor or kindness radiated threat. And at the same time, he sought them out, the ones he thought Jordana could possibly fall in love with. Young, not necessarily handsome, but probably artistic in some way. If he saw Jordana talk to someone at a party, he had to talk to them also. Partly he was trying to minimize danger – he acted friendly and interested, on the theory that suspicion would only make the other man competitive. There was also an element of fascination, though, like seeing cars about to collide. He actually thought Jordana probably wasn't cheating. But part of him wanted the crash.

After a few minutes, he became aware of the cold. He took a

152

step away from the building, then turned and looked back at it. Even these small, depressing towns often had stately public buildings. The library was Federalist in design: square, three-story, with greenish-black shutters and doors.

'Pieter?' Vlad said, poking his head out the door.

Pieter had to clear his throat twice before he trusted his voice. 'I'm fine. I just don't feel very good.'

'That's natural when you're coming down.' Vlad hesitated a moment. 'You should come in soon.'

Pieter waved and tried to smile.

After Vlad had gone back indoors, Pieter imagined a different exchange. He could have said, *Not physically unwell. I mean inside.* And Vlad might have said *That's what I meant, too.*

His loneliness seemed without bottom.

After a time the worst passed. He straightened, dragging his hands down his face. He took a few deep breaths, then made for the door from which he'd exited.

Light came murkily from a crude wooden chandelier, high above. He could hear the noise of the 'banquet' downstairs – voices so clear they must be traveling through heating vents, the words oddly indistinguishable. He found the narrow basement stairs behind one of the hall's wooden doors. The walls were brown in the process of being painted white, or else white in the process of being painted brown.

Descending the stairs, it seemed what mattered wasn't the dramatic stuff: Jordana kissing him in her parent's apartment, or Luke being born in the cab on the way to the hospital, even Angie throwing herself into the pool. What truly made up his life were the moments like this one, when something – maybe only the cocaine's polluted wake – took him out of himself. All he wanted was a life that had coherence and a little grace. It didn't seem like such a big thing to ask, yet here he was, leaning against a half-painted wall, as somewhere below floated a crowd, their faint cheers rising around him.

Chapter Sixteen

At the halfway house, Lily was making her slow progress down the driveway, clutching Teresa's hand. Angie, on the way home from her day program, stopped to watch. Staff tried to have the house Keep a Low Profile because there had been protests about their moving into the neighborhood. Some of the houses still had signs up: NOT HERE. Residents weren't allowed to smoke on the front porch, only the back, and they couldn't wear nightgowns or pajamas outdoors. Once a day, though, Lily had to walk, which was in no way low profile.

Angie thought, *We're here, we're queer, get used to it* – a gay rights slogan, but she liked the feel of it against the inside of her head. Lily weighed probably close to three hundred pounds and had only two expressions: catatonia and terror. She was twenty-eight but looked forty, with her lank hair and thick glasses. Trembling all over, almost to the mailbox, she said, 'That's close enough, that's close enough.'

'Keep going. Just a few more feet.'

Lily was afraid of stairs, water, night, cars, people speaking foreign languages, dark liquids, children, and the outdoors. She touched the mailbox, stretching as far as she could to avoid taking another step. Then she held her hand out toward Teresa, who dug Lily's daily pack of cigarettes out from her pocket. Cigarettes were the only way to make Lily do anything. Lily grabbed the pack and barreled back to the house, moving so fast now that Teresa could barely keep up.

Angie followed them into the dirty light of the front hall. A sign leaned against the hallway wall: BRIGHT FUTURES. It was the name of the halfway house, but the less-than-brilliant late realization that they needed to Keep a Low Profile meant the sign had never been put on the lawn – as though without the reminder, the neighbors would forget that the six patients and three staff at Bright Futures weren't really just a big, jolly family. The bathroom door was closed; Bill was probably jerking off. He spent about three hours a day in there.

The kitchen linoleum, walls, and cabinets were all a pale yellow someone must have hoped would brighten the small room, but which succeeded only in looking grimy. Angie would bake a cake. The refrigerator's sole magnet held the chore wheel. Lily wasn't on the wheel: because of the water phobia, her chore was always to vacuum the living room. (She also didn't have a turn making five o'clock coffee. Dark liquids, she insisted, might be made of ground-up bugs.) Russell hadn't done the breakfast dishes again, and Angie couldn't cook if the sink was full of dirty dishes, so she washed them. Not wanting to put them away on dusty shelves, she took everything out of the cabinet. The supposedly clean dishes were sticky to the touch. In her head, accelerating and stuck, like an advertising jingle: *we'reherewe'requeergetusedtoitwe'rehere we'requeergetusedtoitwe'reherewe'requeergetusedtoit.*

She washed the counters, the gunk that built up on electric cords and stove buttons, the dirty moldings. She'd meant to make a cake! No chocolate in the house, but oranges. Orange cake. She turned on the oven, found her – clean clean clean, thank you very much – sifter, sifted flour. Some flour got on the floor, and she found the broom, which wouldn't budge a large black spot; she got the steel wool and knelt to scrub it. Down close like this, she realized that about half of what she'd taken to be the linoleum's pattern was actually gunk. Filling a pot (there was no bucket, natch) with soapy water, she worked on her knees, scrubbing in small concentric semicircles. The linoleum turned out to be beautiful, with a pattern of pale green leaves vining against the lemon yellow. She was forgetting the cake. She sprang up, sloshing and almost upsetting the water; she'd deal with it in a minute. The fridge drawer was labeled PRODUCE! She'd said once, 'It's like a communist exhortation,' and the staff person, Mark, articulating slowly as an ESL teacher, said, '*Pro*duce. *Pro*duce is things like lettuce and apples.' 'Oh,' Angie had said with false brightness, 'fruits and vegetables!' and Mark had beamed at her as though she were a particularly bright student.

In the *pro*duce drawer, she found the oranges, along with carrots that had sprouted roots. And potatoes! You weren't even supposed to keep potatoes in the fridge; they went starchy and inedible. Maybe even poisonous, she didn't remember, but they were related to deadly nightshade. She'd get rid of them in case. She pulled out the potatoes, the gone-soft celery, the carrots with their soft white fringe of new roots, piling everything on the floor – she'd bring the trash can over in a minute. The whole drawer smelled faintly rotten. She pulled it out, dumping it into the sink. She should defrost the fucking freezer, now that she'd started. She bet none of this had been done in months. It was outrageous, that she paid to be here and Staff was paid to be here. She should become Staff somewhere. God knew she had enough experience. She'd been places where Staff were crazier than the clients. It took a certain kind of craziness to want to live in a halfway house. Teresa was idealistic and would burn out, and Mark – Angie would swear to it – had all the negative symptoms of a schizophrenic: the inability to read social cues, the over-loud voice, the sudden, awkward exiting of conversations. The center drawer, marked FRIGID MEATS, was sticking.

'You're home,' Trevor said, from the doorway. 'Are you trashing the kitchen?'

'I'm *cleaning* it. Help me with this drawer.'

A silence: his meds meant it took Trevor longer to process things. He had a narrow, handsome face, and his dark hair, long in front, fell into his eyes. 'It looks trashed.'

'Make omelets, break eggs. Are you going to help me with this drawer?'

She worked her hand into the narrow opening she'd been able to make already. Pulling out the plastic packages of bologna and ham, she tossed them onto the floor. Together they wrestled the drawer out.

'The trash can,' said Angie, but as she rushed across the room to get it, she slid on the water she'd meant to mop. 'Hey, look,' she said, sliding again. 'This is my dad skating.' Angie clasped her hands behind her back, looked down, frowned, and swept rapidly across the kitchen floor. 'Now this is my mom.' She fell showily on her butt and said, 'Fuck shit damn.'

'. . . Your mom says *fuck shit damn*?'

Trevor was two years younger than Angie, twenty. Although

156

romantic relationships weren't supposed to be allowed at Bright Futures, she and Trevor had been together six of the six and a half months she'd lived here. She lay back on the floor. The lamp was of dusty red glass like in a pizza parlor. 'I'm looking up its skirt,' she said.

'. . . What?'

'Come here, come lie here.'

Trevor didn't say, On the *floor*? He lay down, a potato rolling away from his foot and under the stove. Angie looked for faces in the water stains that moved like clouds across the ceiling.

Trevor rolled close and took her hand. 'Who was the first person you ever knew who was crazy?'

'Not till the hospital, I don't think. Before that, I had a babysitter who tried to kill herself. Not while she was babysitting us. I think her boyfriend broke up with her.'

The pause. Talking to Trevor was like talking on a bad overseas phone connection. Then he laughed. 'How did she do it?'

'Cold pills. Contac.' Residents weren't supposed to talk about the subject but they did, all the time. They were a house of failed suicides, five of the six of them having made attempts. Usually multiple attempts.

Keeping her eyes on the kitchen light, she put her hand under his shirt. Even in heat like today's, Trevor wore long sleeves. He didn't let Angie see the burns on his body, but she could touch him. His stomach reminded her of one of those topographical maps in elementary school, at once bumpy and plastically smooth. Trevor had almost died when he'd set fire to himself in front of his parents, three years ago. He was the one resident, though, who didn't count as actually having made an attempt: he'd been messianic, psychotic, not suicidal.

'If I was crazy, this place would make me crazier,' Trevor said softly.

'Tell me about it.' Beneath his armpit, her fingers found the rough place where the blanket his parents had used to smother the fire had fused to his skin. A few fibers had been left – cutting them out would have meant doing one more graft – and his skin had grown around them. He drew her hand away, up to his lips.

The water on the floor had begun to soak through her clothes. Plus she was getting bored. She started to get up. 'I want to make my cake.'

157

He didn't let go of her hand. 'Stay here with me.'

'I'm making a cake.' She jerked from his grasp. 'I'm fucking *making* a fucking *cake.*'

Nighttime. Lily already snoring heavily, stoned on Ativan. Rachel perched on the edge of her bed, biting the hair off her wrist. Rachel was twenty-five, African-American, very pretty: men always tried to talk to her when she and Angie went downtown. She had survived two attempts, the second a jump from a high bridge. Jumps were higher status than overdoses like Angie's. If you jumped, you were seen as having really meant it. Her red welted arm glistened with spit. Lifting her head, she turned her arm over, searching, and then with a small grunt began gnawing at a spot where she must have seen a minuscule hair regrowing up through the weals.

And Angie, wide awake, wide wide wide awake, lay under the covers, legs thumping the mattress, running in place.

Chapter Seventeen

Wendy woke at six. Quietly, she found her work clothes and dressed without waking Luke. Before this summer, she hadn't realized how much he slept. She liked how guiltlessly pleasurable it seemed for him. Sprawled on the futon, he looked smaller and younger, vulnerable in a way he never seemed awake. The blockiness of his forehead was offset by the fullness of his lips – open now, with a damp spot on the pillow beneath. His rusty hair, usually pulled back into a ponytail, fell into his face.

Downstairs in the kitchen, she touched her toes, pressing her forehead to her knees. She liked these early mornings, when Madison was cool and still. The whole town emptied between May and the end of August, which meant that she and Luke seemed to live in a pocket of time – eating bread and cheese for dinner, going to movies at the Orpheus, calling each other during work – that scarcely touched their real lives. Lately, she'd been sleeping at Luke's every night. Semi-living together broke several of her rules for herself, but instead of making her feel panicky and out of control, she felt a strange, lazy complacency.

Pulling her hair back, she turned on the kitchen tap and bent to drink the running water. Outside, a rattling green Galaxie bumped to the curb. Wendy wiped her mouth, swung her ankle up onto the sink edge to stretch her hamstrings. A big blonde girl emerged from the car. She turned in circles, then bounded up the walk, knocked on the frame of the screen door, and – without waiting – walked into the kitchen. She seemed jittery but happy, wearing cut-off jean shorts and a man's tattersall shirt, sleeves rolled up to her biceps.

'I bet Luke's still asleep. That car,' the girl announced, pointing, 'has a *mind*. The heater doesn't turn off. All the way across

159

Pennsylvania, which is a huge state; you don't think of its being huge, it's so innocuous and rectangular, I mean, I think of Philadelphia, Pittsburgh, and the Amish, and then I run out of associations – oh, Hershey's – but you're on the highway and both sides are crusted with houses of windows and there are these hundreds of lives going by every second – you know those *blink and you'll miss it* signs? You look away and you've missed seeing about a hundred houses, all of them full of people's lives and their ideas, their *radios,* talking to them. All those garages full of Black and Decker stuff. Hershey's isn't even automatic, I don't see it in the store and remember Pennsylvania. You must be Wendy. You don't look like a cheerleader. And Quaker Oats, and Quaker Oil. Can you imagine, like, Hindu Oats? Baptist Oats? They'd be horrified. Hor-ri-*fied.* No one'd buy it.'

'That was high school,' Wendy said, of the cheerleading. Her brain was several steps behind. This must be Angie. She looked different from her pictures, heavier but more cheerful. Luke had just talked to her two nights ago on the phone, and Wendy was pretty sure he and Angie hadn't discussed her visiting.

'You're not blond, though. I actually went through Hershey, not that it's exactly on the way. There's the factory on one side of town, and a few miles away is a paper mill.' She spoke so fast the sounds pushed together, hard to separate into words, the way people talked when they were very tipsy but not yet drunk. 'So you smell chocolate – it's so *strong!* – and then the wind changes and you smell wood pulp, it sounds like a good smell, wholesome, right? but it's more, God, closer to burning shoes, I would have bought some chocolate, but this was like two in the morning; the factories must go all night, chocolate and paper. Do you have any coffee?'

'Luke's housemates might have left some. You drove here from New Hampshire?'

'Luke still doesn't drink coffee. I don't understand people who don't drink coffee. You're not Mormon, are you?'

'Lutheran. Kind of. I was.' Should she wake Luke? She found herself looking through the cabinets for coffee. Finally, she located a can in the freezer, its red sides misty with frost. She held it out and Angie said, 'Oh, God, I *love* you. You're wonderful.'

'That's the coffeemaker on the counter,' Wendy said unnecessarily. 'I'm going to go tell your brother you're here.'

In the bedroom, she touched his shoulder. He grumbled and

160

pulled the sheet up.

'Luke.' She shook him a little. 'You should get up.'

Luke half woke, reaching out and pulling Wendy down beside him. 'You're back,' he said. Eyes closed, he began to fumble with the rubber band of her ponytail; he liked to sleep with his fingers in her hair, hand cupping her skull. The first time he'd done it, it had made her feel so protected she might have cried if she'd been a crier.

'Luke,' she whispered, catching his hand. 'Luke. Your sister's here.'

His eyes opened.

'I think it's her. I mean, it *is* her. Making coffee.'

'Oh, crap. Oh, crap.' He threw off the covers, found his boxers on the floor. 'What's she like?'

'She seems pretty—' She knew the word was *manic,* but she was embarrassed to say it, like she'd be appropriating something of Luke's, pretending greater sophistication than she had a right to. Hedging, she said, 'I don't know what she's usually like.'

Standing up, Luke had none of the softness he did in sleep. He was tall, with rough features. His long hair fell into his face; he pushed it back with both hands. 'Is she talking a lot? Like almost too fast to understand?'

Wendy nodded, for some reason beginning to feel scared, as though she'd done something wrong.

'*Crap,*' he said again, pulling on a T-shirt. She followed him downstairs. Angie was jerking open kitchen cabinets; she'd taken down a tin of baking powder, a plastic Tupperware bowl with a warped green lid, a jug of Gallo wine, all the coffee cups.

At his appearance, Angie threw herself across the kitchen. 'Luke!' she said. 'My baby brother. You're so skinny! Look how skinny he is!'

'What's happened? Why are you crying?'

'Nothing's happened. I'm just happy to see you. Can't I be happy to see my little brother? My skinny baby brother I haven't seen in months?'

'I thought you were working.'

'I quit; it was ridiculous, cooking all those fucking eggs; this trapper kept asking me out, *black* teeth, and he ate his bacon and eggs on flapjacks with syrup; we're in New *England* and it's seventy-five cents extra for real maple syrup, otherwise you get that brown sugar water. Scrambled eggs you just kind of chop with

161

the side of the spatula right before they go out. I need to be cooking somewhere where my talents can be used; it's ridiculous to be chopping up eggs for five dollars an hour; the *trapper,* in the back of his truck, had pelts nailed to boards, beaver, the town pays him to trap beaver because of the trees—'

'Ange, slow down.'

'Sorry. I'm sorry.'

She was pacing the kitchen; some coffee spilled from her cup without her noticing. Wendy grabbed a sponge from the sink, knelt to wipe it up. She couldn't put her finger on what Angie sounded like. Then she realized. It was like hearing her own thoughts, spoken without any editing.

Angie said, 'I'm just glad to see you. I want to see Madison, I want you to take me where you like to go. The drive here, it was amazing, I only had to stop once between Pennsylvania and here, I'd look at the gas gauge and it would be on the half mark, and then I'd look back an hour later and it would still be at half; it was like Hanukkah. God, this coffee is so *good;* what is this coffee?'

'Coffee?' Luke said.

Wendy said, 'Like Hanukkah?'

'You know, lamp oil, only supposed to last a day but it lasts eight.' She glanced at Luke and said, '*Joke.* I'm not manic.'

'Okay.'

'Okay. Christ, Luke. You're looking at me like I just ran over your dog.'

Luke put his hands over his eyes.

Angie glanced at Wendy, looking both nervous and defiant. Crossing the room, she touched Luke's arm. 'Sorry. I'm sorry. I didn't sleep. It makes me stupid.'

'Are you taking your meds?' he asked, muffledly.

'Are you?' Angie snapped. Wendy could see her struggling to get calm; she balled her fists and exhaled hard. 'I'm taking them. All right? I'm not manic, I was just stressed out at home. And I'm glad to see you.' She hit him softly in the stomach. 'I'm glad to see you.'

'I can't believe you still have that car. It was about to fall apart when Abe left it.' Luke sighed and let his hands drop. 'I should call Mom and Dad.'

'They know I'm here.'

'Yeah, right.'

'They *do,*' she insisted. 'They *do.*'

162

He rolled his eyes, but he smiled. She laughed. They seemed to have forgotten Wendy was in the room, and when she spoke – 'Well, I guess I'll go to work' – her voice came out abrupt and loud. She let the screen door bang behind her.

Tuscan Sky was on State Street between a store that sold tie-dyed shirts and a Mexican restaurant that advertised BURRITOS AS BIG AS YOUR HEAD. Every time Wendy looked for a job she promised herself she'd find something other than waitressing, but nothing paid as well. Besides, she'd worked at restaurants since she was fourteen. She'd never been good at joking with customers, but she was good at always staying polite and attentive because she didn't lose her calm during rushes. In fact, rushes were her favorite part of the job. She liked the order of waitressing, the hundred details you brought into line to get people's meals out.

All morning, as she served omelets and Bloody Marys, Wendy remembered how Luke had covered his face. He was usually so easygoing; she only saw him really upset when his sister was in trouble. His sister was also the one person who could make him howl with laughter. When Luke answered the phone, Wendy always knew if it was Angie because of the animation that came into his face. They could stay on the phone for hours. Sometimes Wendy lost patience – especially if it was the third time that week – and picked up her things to leave. Luke would say to Angie, 'Just a minute. Bye, Wen.' He would tilt his mouth up to be kissed, then down to the phone again. 'Okay, I'm back.'

In the kitchen, she entered the codes for quesadillas, 516, and blueberry pancakes, 1114, into the computer without glancing at the cheat sheet. Her own competence calmed her. She closed out another check and wrote *Thanks* across the bottom. She signed it *Meredith;* in restaurants, she always wore the left-behind name tags of ex-waitresses. She couldn't stand customers calling out 'Wendy,' using her name like they knew her.

In her imagination, Angie had been wildly sad, frail with suffering, pulling her sleeves down over her hands the way that sad girls always seemed to do. The real Angie seemed closer to someone who might come up to you on State Street, wanting you to listen to some cockamamie idea, less tragic than annoying.

Carrying four plates, she walked to the heavy kitchen door and in one practiced movement kicked it open and turned her body to

163

slip through. After she tipped out the bussers and the bar, she usually made about sixty dollars for seven hours. Brunch wasn't really simpler than dinner to serve, or much cheaper to buy, but people were shocked when the bill came and they realized how much they'd dropped on breakfast, which made them prone to undertipping.

By three in the afternoon, weekend brunch had leaked away. Only a few cranky families remained, and a four-top of hair-sprayed Kappas getting drunk on mimosas and trying to maintain hilarity. The manager was upstairs, so she and the other waitress ate olives and sliced oranges out of the bar tray. It used to be that mis-cooked or sent-back food was given to the staff, but this new manager had decided that policy would encourage errors, so now they had to throw out mistake food. By this time in the afternoon Wendy was starving. She looked out at her tables, trying to calculate how much longer she'd be here. The Kappas had maybe ten more minutes; their mirth was collapsing. At least one of them would stagger off to the bathroom to make herself throw up, and the others would exchange meaningful glances. For Wendy, as for the customers, Saturday brunch started out well, seeming like a good idea. Now the restaurant felt dim and claustrophobic, the last diners snapping at each other before raggedly gathering up their purses and windbreakers and emerging at last back into the bright, spent afternoon.

When she got home, Luke and Angie were lying on the living room floor, Angie's head propped on Luke's shins. Smoke from Angie's cigarettes made the air hazy, like early twilight. Next to each other, they looked more alike than Wendy had thought this morning. Angie was fairer and didn't have Luke's heavy forehead, but they both had narrow blue eyes and high ruddy cheeks. A song that had been popular when Wendy was in seventh grade – probably the time in her life she least liked remembering – played on the stereo.

'Why are you home?' Wendy asked Luke.

He grinned. 'Called in sick.'

'Oh.' She held his gaze. It made her obscurely angry, though it wasn't like it should matter to her. Anything he made from his job was just extra spending money.

'Did you bring us presents?' Angie asked.

'What? Presents?'

'No presents,' Luke said, mock-sad, to Angie. He reached up to

164

encircle Wendy's ankle with his hand, rubbing gently through her sock.

Angie said, 'What kind of girlfriend is that?'

Wendy couldn't think of words to play along; her terrible honesty always forced her to say something like what she said now: 'I was at work.' She looked down at them, sprawled on the floor. Her hair and clothes reeked sweetly of bacon grease and the Comet she used to scrub down the side-work station.

From the stereo came the sound of bagpipes: 'Come on Eileen,' another song she hated from junior high.

'Oh, God. I love this song.' Angie jumped to her feet, tottering for a moment before finding her balance. She ran to the stereo, turning the volume up so high Wendy felt the words in her chest more than she heard them.

'Dance with me,' Angie said. Wendy shook her head. Angie pulled on Luke's arm. 'Dance with me, dance with me.'

'He doesn't like dancing,' said Wendy.

But Luke let himself be pulled up. Angie let go of his hands and jumped around the room, jumping onto the couch and from there onto the chair. Luke jumped up on the couch. They bounced, shouting along with the song. Angie jumped to the coffee table; Luke jumped to the La-Z-Boy, which tipped precariously. He shifted his feet apart, riding the wobble of the chair like a surfboard, his sister laughing.

When the song slowed, Angie grabbed the floorlamp and sang like Elvis, her voice deep and gargly. Luke doubled over, laughing. Angie made her eyes go heavy, hips jerking.

As soon as the song ended, Wendy said, 'I'm going to the grocery store.'

'No, I'll go,' Angie said. She let go of the lamp, which tottered. Wendy grabbed it before it fell. Still in Elvis's deep warble, Angie shouted over the music, 'You guys are putting me up! I'll make dinner!'

As soon as she left, Wendy turned down the stereo.

Luke said, 'God, she's manic.'

'She said she wasn't.'

Luke shrugged. 'She's the smartest person I know. I mean, she's smart enough to be self-aware.' Talking about her, he looked happy even through his concern. 'She's a mess. She's funny, though, isn't she?'

'She's nice.' He hadn't noticed Wendy was wearing her long

165

hair loose the way he always bugged her to. She felt a wince of hurt at Luke saying Angie was the smartest person he knew. Sometimes, anything he admired about someone else seemed like a way she herself fell short. 'She didn't ask anything about me.'

'She's *manic*.'

'I *know*. You've said that, like, ten times.'

'Well, you're acting like she made a social faux pas. It's serious.'

She sighed. 'Did you call your parents?'

'Not yet.'

'Don't you think you should?'

'Wen, I've been dealing with this for a long time. I think I can handle it.'

'Fine.' She turned away from him to begin fixing the living room. 'They're not worried. Don't call them.' Why was she being a pain about it? He was right; she had no idea what she was talking about. But he looked at her, hands on his hips, then sighed and went into the kitchen. The phone chirped as he lifted it.

Wendy had first met Luke during the year she was getting residency. Luke used to come into Cleveland's for breakfast, sometimes alone and sometimes with different girls who looked radiant and disheveled, wearing his clothes. He was a big, shaggy boy whose accent marked him as East Coast and whose worn-out sweaters and holed sneakers marked him as well off: no poor student would dare look like that. If he was alone, he'd read for twenty minutes and then, apparently bored, get up and find an issue of the *Isthmus* or the *Onion*. He'd been growing his hair, and it was at an awkward chin-length stage.

Usually the college students who came into Cleveland's alone were intense and pretentious, smokers, bad tippers. Luke was different, but he annoyed her anyway: out-of-state and therefore paying full tuition, casual about his studies and his right to be here. And casual about the women he slept with, since Wendy rarely saw the same one twice.

He used to try to talk to her, but she didn't respond except to say *A few months; it's fine; the tips are fine.* Then, pretending to forget that he always ordered hot chocolate, *Some coffee?*

A year later, when she was enrolled as a student, he came up to her at the Union when she was studying. 'Katy,' he'd said, which

166

was the name tag she'd worn at Cleveland's; it impressed her that he remembered. After they'd talked for half an hour with Luke leaning on the back of a chair, she invited him to sit down.

Almost the first thing he'd told her that day was that he had a manic-depressive sister, and Wendy had pretended to have more than a vague idea what that meant. She'd been flattered that he'd told her, not aware it was one of the first things he told everyone. She'd even been tempted to say something about her dad's drinking, which she never talked about.

She asked Luke to walk her home, planning to sleep with him right away. She'd only slept with one person before, a high school boyfriend everyone had assumed she would marry. She was tired of being careful and good, tired of how she finished papers days before they were due, of how she could agonize for fifteen minutes about whether to buy the second-cheapest shampoo rather than the cheapest. Tomorrow she would be the radiant, disheveled girl that he took out to breakfast, and that would be the end of it. But at her door Luke had asked for her phone number and loped off into the night. He'd been the one who insisted their relationship go slowly, and she had felt both lucky and disappointed.

Wendy heard Angie's car approaching from blocks away. Its engine made a rattling sound, like coins in the dryer. Luke's car had surprised Wendy when he'd bought it last month; it was so modest, and she'd liked him for that. Now it struck her as one more way in which he'd connected himself to his sister.

When Angie burst into the house, she had three paper bags of groceries in her arms. 'They started to give me plastic,' she said. 'At home I use my own bags. Probably paper's just as bad, but it used to seem healthier. Not after that paper mill. I shouldn't have gotten paper. I love your grocery store, though. There's more out in the car. I was listening to the most amazing radio program on the way over here, I had to get off the road so I could really pay attention. In Norwegian. I didn't know I could understand so much Norwegian! I hope you like rhubarb. I got a lot of rhubarb.'

Angie had also gotten a lot of tinned oysters, a lot of granola, small apricots the size and color of walnut shells, three spiral notebooks, a set of camping pots, four kinds of shampoo, a carton of saltines, six kinds of pasta, frozen coffee cakes, lox, a club lock for the steering wheel of Luke's car and a second club lock for Wendy (who didn't have a car), two packs of Hershey bars, bacon, a video of *The Little Mermaid* ('Because you have the same hair,' Angie told Wendy), three flavors of melting Häagen-Dazs, green, red, and yellow apples, tangerines, a ten-pack of blank tapes, Jell-O mix, nonfat milk, low-fat milk, reduced-fat milk, whole milk, two more cans of Maxwell House coffee, two dozen gladiolas, and a scraggly handful of carnations, dyed green and lilac. There were nine paper bags in all, and when Wendy felt around on the floor of the backseat – her back, bad from waitressing, spasmed once as she bent – she found gravel and felty Kleenex and pennies and also things that had fallen: more shampoo, boxes of cake mix, celery. Against the dirty car floor, the celery's narrow ribs gleamed like jade.

About the carnations, Angie asked, 'Aren't those the ugliest and best things you've ever seen? I watched this woman picking through for the best ones, I loved her, she had on one of those plastic *rain scarves.*'

Wendy asked, 'How did you afford all this?'

'Visa.' She lit a cigarette with one hand. 'Visa Visa Visa, baby.' She smoothed the empty paper bags with the palms of both hands, her movements quick and repetitive. In the window behind her, darkness began to gather in the branches of trees. 'I'm going to return these now.'

Luke said, 'Ange, it's night. It's dinnertime.'

Angie hesitated. Her hands still rapidly smoothed the bags.

'Let's make dinner. I'm going to get you a glass of juice.' Luke took the paper bags from Angie's hand. Wendy hadn't seen him focused like this before, concerned, parental. It made her oddly lonely. 'Sit down at the table.'

'I don't *want* to.'

'Just for a minute. Here. Your juice.'

Angie took the glass meekly, then looked at him. He said, 'Drink your juice.'

Later that night, in bed, Luke used his mouth and hands to make Wendy come, over and over.

'Do you wish I was different?' she whispered.

He pushed her hands down, holding them against the mattress, and lowered his mouth to her again. In the light that came in around the blinds, his face looked hard and unfamiliar. She wished she could at least touch his cheek, to erase his strangeness.

168

Chapter Eighteen

More than fifty years later, ice forming on water – the way it spread in frail sheets; the way the river paled with it; the almost metallic smell, like biting into an unripe plum – took Pieter back to Holland. Other things worked on him the same way: the opening chords of Grieg's *Holberg Suite* or a cold shirt pulled on in a dark room. The ridged plastic tops of Crest tubes felt like the old radio's Bakelite knob, tiny serrated ridges between his thumb and first finger. The scent of wet ground could bring Haarlem back, or the smell of boiling potatoes, or dry mold, or lavender cologne. Once, in Queens, a pair of dusty wingtips thrown up over a telephone wire took his breath away; they were the same shoes his father had worn when he was alive. And more than once a white kite, a white banner, laundry glimpsed from the corner of his eye, had brought back the flash of excitement and shame he'd felt the day of the invasion. His mother had roused him and they'd stood in the yard watching the white mushroom shapes of German parachutists sink gently toward the earth, outlined against the black smoke of bombing.

After decamping for Madison and returning, Angie had seemed to stabilize for a few weeks before falling apart again, worse this time. Depakote wasn't working. As he drove toward the halfway house, the river revealed and hidden and revealed by the woods, Dutch words came back to him unanchored by meaning: *aardappen, duur, Woensdag, Donderdag*. In the passenger seat, Jordana sipped coffee from a dented thermos cup. She wore a bulky sweater, once Luke's, stretched over her knees, which were pulled up to her chest. She'd gotten too skinny. At night, when she took off her clothes, her body swam into view, thin, pale, like the wavering flame of a candle.

169

He said, 'You need to eat.'

'I mean to. I forget. I just . . . I forget.'

There was new snow on the ground. Jordana's hair, black threaded with coarser strands of white, was pulled back into a rough ponytail. She looked out the window, chewing at her already-short nails. After a while he reached up and gently took her hand away from her mouth.

'*Pieter,*' she said, pulling free. Instead of biting the nails again, though, she fisted her hand and pushed it under her thigh, saying, 'Sorry.'

The houses thinned after Westfield, and towns, when they came, were smaller: just a church, a post office, a gas station. An old woman standing at a mailbox looked through her letters, flipping each one up against her chest. There were fields of cows, kids straddling their dirt bikes by the COLD ICE boxes of small stores, sometimes nothing but dark ponds frozen around marsh grass, telephone lines stitching the sky.

Towns became denser again before the ragged outskirts of Manchester. They drove through the city, turning from Bridge Street onto the improbably named Koscioszko Street, and then onto the very probably named High Street, Church Street, Amherst Street. Were there New England towns that didn't have streets with those names? Pieter made a left onto Orange Street, which took them to the east side of town.

Jordana asked, 'What are you *whistling*?'

He didn't know. He frowned, listening to himself. '"Oranges and Lemons."'

'Please don't. Don't whistle right now.'

He felt a stab of disgust at himself. The song backed up into his head:

> *Oranges and lemons,*
> *Say the bells of Saint Clement's.*
> *When will you pay me?*
> *Ask the bells of Saint Rémy.*
> *When I get rich,*
> *Say the bells of Saint Nick's.*
> *When will that be?*
> *Say the bells of Saint Glee . . .*

170

Surely it couldn't be Saint Glee. He wasn't sure, in fact, if he had very much of the song right. Even more annoying was that he heard the song in the high-pitched voices of a child choir. Luke and Angie had had a 45 of the song when they were kids, and a little record player of ocher plastic. He remembered teaching them to lower the needle. He remembered the scratchiness of the built-in speaker and thought again of the radio his family had owned in Haarlem, on which he'd first heard classical music; later the Germans had confiscated it, after he was gone. If not for the war he would have lived his whole life there. His father might still be alive. If Pieter hadn't been a child immigrant – lonely, watchful, out of place – he would probably never have become a cellist.

Thinking of Holland, he steered them closer and closer to Angie.

On Angie's street, half the homes were kept up; the other half had dirty paint and dying front lawns, on which rested cars without tires and chipped plaster animals. The halfway house was of the kept-up kind, but despite its new green paint and neatly cut grass, it looked a little ragged – listing mailbox, blanket covering one window from inside.

He and Jordana had gone to the town meetings when the house was about to open and the newly formed Neighborhood Association protested that property values would plummet. A woman stood up and said that, while a halfway house might not be a bad thing in itself, it didn't belong here. 'I just don't think they'll *fit in,*' she said. 'I just don't think they'll be *comfortable.*' Others, less indirect, talked about how this was *a family neighborhood,* as though somewhere there existed neighborhoods without families.

'How would you feel if your kids couldn't play on the street?' a woman finally said, struggling not to cry. 'How would you feel if your daughter was late home from school and you had to imagine her being dragged somewhere, raped, killed?' Later, when the halfway house had been approved, that woman's family had been one of three who put their homes up for sale.

Pieter pulled in behind a Lincoln Town Car already parked in the driveway. Instead of moving to get out, Jordana sighed, looking blankly at the windshield. 'Sometimes she seems so close to getting well, and then . . .'

'She just needs to go back on lithium.'

'I know,' she said. 'I know. It's just – I feel like it never stops.'

Jordana was almost never pessimistic about Angie's illness.

171

'Oranges and Lemons' began again in his head:

When will that be?
Ask the bells of ennui.

He definitely had the words wrong.

Jordana got out of the car. It was a beautiful day, the kind that tourists hoped for when they came to New Hampshire: crisp, the trees blazing red, the sky heart-stoppingly blue. A yellow bus rumbled up the street behind them. It slowed, lights flashing, a STOP sign unfolding creakily from the side.

What do you wish?
Ask the bells of dead fish.
I do not know,
Say the bells of old snow.

The living room had a stack of shabby board games on the coffee table, a poster of a puppy standing on another puppy's head (EVER HAD ONE OF THOSE DAYS?). A television played to the empty couches. Jordana crossed the room, clicking the program off.

She paced; Pieter sat on the couch. One of the board games was called Martian Autopsy. PLAYER WITH THE MOST MARTIAN ORGANS wins! trumpeted the side of the box. On the top were pictured a wife, husband, son, and daughter, laughing, one holding a small piece of brain-shaped plastic aloft.

'What's taking so long?' Jordana asked.

He opened the game and, using the tweezers, removed the heart and put it to one side, then the kidneys. He started to remove the liver. As he lifted it, the tweezers brushed the edge of the liver's cavity and the Martian's eyes flew open, red and huge. It gave a high, ululating cry.

When Teresa came for them, they followed her up the narrow staircase with its olive high-traffic carpet. Residents watched them surreptitiously as they turned into the second-floor office. Dr. Brown was there, a walrusy man in gray, and Mark, the other staff person. And Angie, pacing, her hands moving as though tearing invisible paper. 'You've brought the cavalry,' she said, glancing at her parents. 'Plenty of people to keep things in check if the crazy girl does something crazy. Where are the German shepherds,

172

though? Where are the hoses?' She was shaking. 'It must be a disappointment, your fat fuck daughter.'

She looked awful, her long hair ratty with tangles, skin a dull gray. She lay down on her back on the floor, arms and legs spread.

'Get up from there,' said Jordana.

'Leave her,' said the doctor. 'It's all right.'

'It's all right?' Jordana said. 'What about this is *all right*?'

'Jordana—' Pieter put his hand on her arm.

She wheeled on him. 'What? Jesus, Pieter, am I embarrassing you? Do *you* think she's all right?'

Pieter shook his head and walked to the window. Across the street, a toddler in a blue jacket was being encouraged by its mother to jump into a pile of leaves.

'You're trying to smother me,' said Angie.

Pieter – though he should have known better – looked over his shoulder at her. 'We're trying to make you well.'

'Wells are for water!' she shrieked, and collapsed into laughter. 'Well, a *well* well's for water. Poisoned wells are for witches.' She rolled onto her stomach and began to grind her hips into the carpet.

'Stop!' Jordana shouted. 'Stop it, Angie!'

Mark and Teresa exchanged a look; Teresa put her hand on Jordana's shoulder. Pieter turned back to the window. Across the street, the toddler climbed out of the leaf pile, stumbling almost drunkenly with joy. Pieter forced himself to tune in to the conversation behind him. Dr. Brown was saying that he would commit her to the hospital unless she voluntarily went back on lithium—

'What's voluntary about that?' Angie said.

—and she'd need to be on an antipsychotic until the lithium kicked in.

'Fine. God. *Fuck*. I'll take it.'

And then Pieter stopped hearing again. He touched his left thumb to each of the fingers of his left hand; his thumb made little wooden clicks against the calluses. When he looked up, Angie had a paper cup in her hand. Teresa was checking Angie's mouth to be sure she hadn't cheeked the meds.

'Lift your tongue,' said Teresa.

Angie lifted her tongue. 'La, la, la, la, la.' Then, '*Happy* now? Are you happy? Are you *happy*?'

Mike's Lobster Shack was housed in a low flat-roofed prefabricated building between a used-car lot and a doll store. Dusky green lobster swam in tanks. Behind the restaurant's scarred counter, a girl read *Cosmopolitan*. It was late afternoon, too early for dinner and past lunch; except for them, the restaurant was empty. He and Jordana ordered at the counter. When Jordana asked for coffee, the girl said, 'Just beer or soda.' She jerked her head toward the used-car lot. 'They have a machine, if you're desperate.'

Jordana shook her head.

They paid and sat down to wait. 'Look.' Jordana lifted her chin to point through the window at the sign next door. 'The cars aren't *used,* they're Pre-Owned.' Her lips began to tremble; she covered them with her hand. 'Oh, God. I can't stand it, Pieter. I don't know how to stand it.'

With his hands he pushed back from the table. 'I'll get you coffee.'

Outside, it was cold and bright. He walked across the parking lot, fed quarters into the machine. A Styrofoam cup tumbled down, and he righted it. There was a dark, odorless stream of coffee. He wished that, like Jordana, he could feel toppled by grief. He hated that his brain moved immediately to separate *this is what we can fix* from *this is what we won't think about*. In a way, he even envied how Angie was affected by everything around her. Once, very depressed, Angie had been trailing him around the grocery store and they'd seen a woman roaring at her small son, '*I don't give a shit!*' – the kid, only about three or four, frozen, staring at his mother. Angie had barely been able to get out of bed for two days afterward. She couldn't forget the things you had to forget if you wanted to live in the world. It made her the most and the least reasonable person he knew.

The coffee had slowed to a trickle. He put his hand against the machine's red glow. It kept coffee hot and milk cold beside each other, but from the outside there was no difference in temperature, only tight vibration.

Back inside the restaurant, he handed Jordana the cup.

She said, 'At the halfway house, it's like you weren't even there. You barely react.'

There was nothing to say; they'd had this conversation so many times. Tiredly, he scrubbed his hand across his eyes. 'Let's talk about something else for a while.'

He expected her to get angry, but she just looked away. They sat in

174

silence. Maybe they really couldn't talk about anything but Angie.

Their lobsters came in plastic baskets. They cracked the shells, pouring the juice off into a battered metal bowl. He pulled the claw from its shell, the pink meat freckled with red, polished and curved like the petal of a lily. The first bite set off a small explosion in his brain, so that for a moment all he felt was deaf pleasure.

Jordana asked, 'So do you want to hear a joke?'

'A *joke*?'

'This man is driving by a farm, and he sees the farmer out in the orchard, holding a pig up in the air.'

'You're telling me a joke?' The absurdity shocked him. Then he smiled that he could be shocked.

'Shh. The guy's so curious he has to stop.' She sipped her coffee. 'Oh, hot.' He sometimes forgot how beautiful she was, in her harsh gypsy way. 'He pulls over, gets out of the car, and walks into the orchard.'

The joke wasn't funny yet: it was anticipation that made him laugh nervously.

'So as the guy gets closer, he sees the farmer is holding the pig up around its middle, so that the pig can eat apples off the tree.'

Jordana demonstrated, pretending to be first the farmer, then the pig, front legs waving, mouth working, eyes squinched and darting around.

He laughed so hard he could barely get his breath. 'Stop. Stop, you're making my stomach hurt.'

'So the man is astonished. He asks what the farmer's doing, and the farmer says, "The pig likes to eat apples."

'"But why don't you just leave the pig on the ground and climb up into the tree yourself?" the man asks. "You could throw twenty apples down to the pig in a few minutes. It would be much faster." And the farmer looks at him, incredulous, and says: "What's *time* to a *pig*?"'

Pieter bent double, hands across his stomach. When finally he'd caught his breath, he took off his glasses, still giggling, and wiped his eyes. 'It's not even funny!' he said, which set him off again. Jordana leaned against the back of the booth, also laughing a little but staring at him, arm across her stomach. Then suddenly, she pushed back from the table, came around to his side.

Kneeling on the floor, she laid her head on his thigh. 'We have to be together,' she said.

There were so many ways he might take that; he didn't have the energy to parse it. He put his wrists on her shoulders, his buttery hands arching away – like small wings – so they wouldn't touch her sweater. They stayed that way, the lobster growing cold on the table. Behind her, through the dirty front window, he could see the Pre-Owned parking lot. The sun was setting between two black pines, turning the windshields of the used cars gold.

Chapter Nineteen

Angie hated being back on lithium, and she hated, *hated,* Haldol. Her thoughts felt like water bugs, skating rapidly over the surface of a tiny body of water – a sink – trapped and blind and hitting the sides. She dragged herself down to the halfway house's basement, dumped her laundry into the washing machine, and then had to stop and get a hold of herself – the routine seemed so futile and neverending – before she could reach for the garish box of Tide.

Back upstairs, she threw herself into a chair in the common room. A too-warm Sunday, the air still and ocher and close. From outside, faint and disturbing as the buzz of insects, the cries of children playing floated in. She stood and paced the common room, then sat, then paced, then sat, too unhappy to move and too unhappy to sit still.

Time felt more like spiral than line to her. When she was manic, she felt closer in time to other manias than to recent flat periods; depression reconnected her with her last depression. Feeling like this, simultaneously exhausted and ramped up, meant she was tuned to the All Fuck-Ups All the Time channel. She saw the day she'd wrecked her room at home, wrenched her mind away and found herself on the day she'd leapt into the pool; then flipping out in front of her parents the other week. Evan Johansson finding her under the bridge at Harvard. Showing up in Madison to rant in front of Luke's girlfriend. Her overdose at college.

Luke had helped her write her college application essays, surprising her with his ideas; he was such a mediocre student that she'd let herself dismiss him. Two of her teachers wrote letters of passionate recommendation. Yale still rejected her, but both

177

Middlebury and Wesleyan had accepted her spotty grades offset by the great SAT.

She chose Middlebury because no one else from her high school went there. When she began, she almost believed it would work out. Her doctor lowered her lithium dose – too low, it turned out, but at first it felt great, burning off the fog she'd lived in for almost a year. Everyone at Middlebury was so good-looking and healthy, playing Frisbee on the lawn, raising their hands in class, talking over plastic cups of beer at Mr. Upp's. Angie's first semester she'd run around, meeting new people every day, going out at night, orange leaves crunching beneath her hiking boots, writing papers in an hour, sledding on dining-hall trays down the hill by Stewart. She stayed up late almost every night with her roommate, Stephanie, talking and drinking vodka mixed with Country Time lemonade.

Over break, she was able to talk about college life with Jess and Tris; she even had a drink once with Abe. He'd been cautious and slow to speak, and when he finally told Angie he had a girlfriend at Harvard, she realized he was nervous she'd have a movie-style crazy-person fit. Clearly he'd been prepared to reject a pass, but when she didn't make one he kissed her outside the bar, almost angrily. 'I've never felt this way about anyone else,' he said. She led him back into the alley, leaning against the brick wall, his hands under her skirt, faint music and laughter from the bar drifting around them. She had never felt so irresistible or gorgeous.

During J-term, the gears in her head began moving too fast, clanging and gnashing; in February, they caught and locked to a grinding halt. She couldn't read; she recognized each word without having the ability to string them together coherently. Going to class was an effort. Showering was an effort. She slept in her clothes, didn't answer the phone. It wasn't sadness: feeling sad would have been a relief. She couldn't feel anything. Couldn't talk, couldn't study, couldn't sleep.

The images of hurting herself began coming back, but this time it was a single consistent image. During her good time, she'd become friends with a junior, a woman who lived off campus and had a bathtub. Angie imagined cutting her wrists – longways, she knew – in that tub, in the dark, lying back in the warm water and going to sleep. She felt deadened and frantic, her mind like two sticks being rubbed together to make a fire, rubbing faster and faster, no room for coherent thought, only the panic of friction. She didn't know how she would ever talk her way into Viv's tub, but she had twenty-four lithium and sixteen Ativan.

She dragged herself to Student Health and whispered that she needed to talk to someone. The guy behind the desk – he looked like an undergraduate, maybe *was* an undergraduate – said there was a mental health appointment opening two days from now.

'This isn't an emergency or anything?' the guy remembered to ask, halfway through writing down Angie's name.

She still had some pride. 'Um, not really. I don't think so.'

Walking back toward her dorm, head jangling, she imagined her bed, cool and narrow, waiting for her, its white comforter mounded like snow. She longed for and dreaded the familiarity of her bed. She'd been spending more and more of her days and evenings there, mostly unable to sleep but occasionally dropping off for a few minutes, half an hour, the best part of her day.

Long black shadows of trees lay across the icy grass, which glimmered in the late-afternoon light. She was reminded power-fully of something. She stopped, searching her mind and then found the image, a momentary clear space amid the din: standing outside Hannah's cabin at the farm, how the world had seemed starkly revealed.

Outside the gym she hesitated and then, without knowing why, went in. She'd spent some time here the semester before, and as she stood in the hall, she felt the momentary brush of the happy mood she'd been in at that time. Then it was gone. She wandered through the hallways until she came to the window overlooking the swimming pool. The water was the unreal blue of mouthwash, tiny figures churning up and down the lanes.

Farther down the hall, she came to the window of the fitness room: elliptical trainers, rowing machines. Students biked nowhere, or rowed nowhere, or ran nowhere. On one of the Stair-Masters was her roommate, Stephanie, hair pulled tightly back into a ponytail, a horseshoe crab of sweat darkening her T-shirt. This was why she'd come, of course, to find Stephanie, who came to the gym every afternoon. It stunned her that after all this time and however much psychotherapy, she could know her own mind so little.

Stephanie had barely spent any time in the dorm these last few weeks – which had been fine with Angie, since at least her loser-

179

dom seemed less public that way. Watching as Stephanie climbed imaginary stairs, though, face clenched and red and dripping sweat, Angie realized that Stephanie had been avoiding their room.

Angie took a step back from the window. Everything she touched turned to shit.

The realization freed her. Relief moved like a cold breeze under her heart, lifting it. With the first real energy she'd felt in two months, she went back to the dorm. She took off the clothes she'd been wearing for however-many days, showered, dried her hair, dressed in clean jeans and a blue sweater. She put on a CD and cued it so that Stevie Nicks would sing 'Gold Dust Woman' over and over. She got into bed with a glass of water and took lithium until the world blurred and bled and then went dark.

The dose had been lethal. She'd thrown up, though, which meant she hadn't come close to dying, although she'd absorbed enough to be very, very sick. Probably she wouldn't have died no matter what, because Stephanie found her so soon after. Had Angie remembered on some level that Stephanie would be back to change clothes? As she'd swallowed the pills, she'd been sure that she was serious.

And the weirdest part was that she still thought of Middlebury with nostalgia. She could know how terrible it had been and yet she remembered the beautiful kids lying on the lawn or flirting in the vaulted reading room of the library – things she'd lost all access to even when she was there – and wished she could go back.

She was pacing the room faster now. With her hand she hit the side of her head, like a television whose picture might be brought back, then hit it again, again. Her doctor kept reminding her that this period of readjustment to lithium had a purpose, that she'd begin feeling better soon, but everything inside her bashed so loudly that she couldn't imagine how she'd hold on that long. Trevor was away for the weekend, visiting his family, unmooring her all the more. When finally it was time to head down to the basement to move her clothes to the dryer, she almost welcomed the errand. After laundry, the afternoon yawned out in front of her. And after that was the evening to get through. After that, night.

Halfway down the stairs, she heard a moan and stopped. Something moved desperately against the washing machine. Bill Morrison was jerking off, his pants around his ankles. No, not jerking off; Lily was beneath him, leaned over the machine, ass in the air. She turned her big blank face toward Angie, jaw slack. Between schizophrenia and meds, Lily's thinking was agonizingly slow. Angie could see recognition rising slowly in her, like an air bubble in water.

'Angie,' Lily said, triumphant at remembering the name.

Angie screamed at Bill Morrison. 'Get the fuck *off* her.' She jumped down the rest of the stairs and pushed him.

She'd pushed hard enough to disengage him, but instead of grabbing for his pants, as she'd expected, he put his hand on his erection, pointing it toward her.

'What, Angie?' he said. 'You're not getting enough from Trevor? You have to go breaking up other people?'

'You're sick.' She turned her back. 'Lily, here. Put these back on.'

Bill said, 'No, *you're* sick.'

She knelt down, untangling Lily's underwear – beige, the color and size of a plastic grocery bag – from her pants. She lifted Lily's heavy, unresisting leg, hooking the underpants over her foot. The dryer made the room warm, and Angie began to sweat. Because of Lily's water phobia, Teresa had to force her to bathe once a week. It had been a few days since the bath, and Lily's body – as Angie struggled to pull the underpants up her legs – smelled swampy, like sex and smoke and anxious sweat.

Bill said again, 'No, *you're* sick, Angie. You go around acting like Miss Hot Shit, like you're on staff. Like you can go around telling people what to do. Miss Hot *Shit.*'

'Lift your foot,' she said to Lily.

'Sex is just for normal people. Oh, I forgot – and for Angie Voorster.'

'Just shut up.' She pulled the nylon underpants over Lily's pale, heavy thighs. She felt better, less vulnerable, once Lily's pubic hair was covered, those sparse, stiff hairs like an old woman's chin.

Bill grabbed Angie's arm and jerked her up. She'd liked Bill until today. They played pool down in the room next to this one, on long Sunday afternoons when there was no Group. Sometimes as Bill racked the balls – the eighth game, the tenth – she'd feel a wave of despair and boredom, as though she couldn't stand to start another game. In the next room, the washer would pause, then launch itself from soak to spin. And then the game's momentum

181

would set in, the soft blue chalking of cues and the crack of balls, Bill and Angie passing each other as they walked around the table to sight from another angle.

She yanked her arm free, grabbed Lily's hand, and began pulling her toward the stairs.

'You're hurting me,' said Lily.

Angie jerked harder, half pulling Lily across the laundry room. Lily was heavy and slow, and halfway across the room she stopped completely. 'My cigarettes.'

'I'll go back for them.'

'Bill has cigarettes.'

'Oh, Christ.' She stopped and stared at Lily. 'You were having sex for cigarettes?' Did this mean Bill was taking less advantage of Lily or more? 'I'll give you cigarettes. Any time you run out.'

'Yeah?'

'Just ask me.' It wasn't Lily's fault for being so crazy, for caring about nothing but smoking and *Days of Our Lives*. Still, Angie was having trouble liking her.

At the stairs, Lily balked. 'I'm not going up those.'

'You came down them.' No response. 'Christ.' Angie grabbed both of Lily's wrists and, backward, took the first stairs. Lily started to cry. Angie couldn't actually drag Lily up, but she could pull hard enough to hurt, and then Lily groaned and took a step, tears coursing down her wide, stupid face. Angie's arms shook with the effort. They paused a moment on the landing, both breathing hard, not looking at each other, and then Angie said grimly, 'Okay, let's go.'

'Another minute—'

'*No*. I said let's go!' She felt behind her with her foot for the next stair, pulling Lily with all her strength. The next stair, the next, and with her shoulder blade she pushed open the door to the first-floor hall, stumbling backward, which pulled Lily up the last step. Angie spilled into a group of strange adults. Teresa was saying, 'We have many activities—' People jumped back as Lily crashed into the hallway behind Angie.

Still holding Lily's wrists, Angie stared around at the group. She couldn't tell if the people were parents, or donors, or if a few potential new patients were mixed in. She could see Teresa trying to decide whether to say something, whether to react to Angie towing a woman wearing only underpants and a dress-for-success blouse.

182

'Bill Morrison is a fucking rapist,' Angie said to Teresa over the group's heads. She was suddenly furious: at Bill, at Lily, at Teresa with her stupid over-lined lips, at herself, at the polite faces turning, blank as sunflowers, toward her voice. 'If you get down there, you can get him. He's probably still got his pants off.'

'Angela—'

'Laundry room, no pants.' She let go of Lily – let Staff deal – and started toward the front of the house. A man in the group said, 'What just happened? What just happened? What just happened?' in an insistent, mental-patient monotone. Turning, she saw Teresa tense. Angie could say anything she wanted.

'I know his family pays the full rate,' she said. 'He still better get kicked out.' Then she charged out the front door.

Chapter Twenty

The houses on his street always looked to Luke like a row of people perched on bar stools: too close together, trying to look natural and keep their elbows in. He hadn't been home in almost a year, since last Christmas. He turned off the car engine and for a moment just sat, hands on the wheel. He'd been driving for seventeen hours. Closing his eyes, he felt himself still moving forward.

He got out of the car, heaving his duffel out after him. He hadn't felt sick traveling, but out in the fresh air nausea caught up with him. In the silence his head buzzed. He bent at the waist, hearing the blood chant in his ears, body suddenly prickling with sweat. His stomach contracted – he tasted the doughnuts he'd had at a rest stop – and then subsided.

He was standing there, hands on his knees, when his mother came out onto the porch. Her mouth opened in astonishment. She dropped the trash bag she was holding and rushed toward him, hugging him so tightly he couldn't breathe.

'That's a little hard,' he squeezed out.

'Sorry.' She let go and stepped back, squinting a little as she looked up at him. 'What are you doing here? You *drove*? From Madison?'

He gestured back toward the Datsun. He was astonished that it had made it. 'Any news?'

His mother shook her head. Her eyes filled with tears; she looked away and took a few rough, deep breaths, trying not to cry. Angie had been missing for four days, without meds. She'd called Luke once, the first day, to tell him he was a fucking selfish asshole. When he'd tried to break in, find out where she was, she'd

184

screamed in frustration and hung up, leaving him shaking. This was hardly the first time she'd ever taken off, but it was the longest she'd gone without contact. He reached out and touched his mother's shoulder, and she gave him a tremulous smile, patting his hand.

After a minute, she straightened up and pushed some graying hair out of her eyes. Long hair used to make her look younger than other mothers; now it made her look old. She dressed like the girls at UW. Not like Wendy, but like some of the girls he'd dated before Wendy: holey fisherman's sweater, boys' jeans, canvas sneakers. Also girlish was the way she stood, one foot hooked behind the other ankle. 'What about your classes?'

'So I'll miss a few classes.' He picked up his duffel bag. 'Just a week. I'm going to get some sleep.'

'Isn't it almost midterms?'

He'd looked forward to seeing her; now that he'd gotten here, she was bugging the shit out of him for some reason. 'I haven't *slept*, Mom.'

He shouldered past her, into the house. In his room he put down the duffel bag and crossed to the bulletin board, looking at the photos pinned there. Himself with Cole after an IM relay; they stood with towels wrapped around their waists, hands on hips, heads shaved. A later picture, drunk at prom with Khamisa. She wore outrageous green chiffon, a dress she'd bought for five dollars at the Salvation Army for what she called its fuck-you-ness. They'd chosen the tackiest backdrop the photographer had, a palm-treed beach at sunrise. A picture of him and Angie camping together, summer after his sophomore year of college. She hadn't let him stop at Mobil because of the Gulf War, or at Exxon because of the Valdez oil spill, or at Shell because of its connection to South Africa. They couldn't go to fast-food restaurants because they all used Styrofoam or beef farmed in former rain forests. He'd been so annoyed he hadn't spoken to Angie the whole afternoon. Angie's obstinacy was compulsive, he knew, but it seemed like most people had things they were stubborn and inflexible about, just more privately. When Wendy studied, she had one Steve Miller tape that she listened to over and over on her cheap Walkman, and she always wore a sweatshirt from her high school, though he couldn't get her to admit she thought she couldn't study without it. She took Reading Week literally, spending it on a grim sixth-floor landing next to the elevators in Memorial Library. He brought her tea sometimes, smuggling the thermos into the building under his coat, and she would let him perch on her desk for a few minutes.

He hadn't known how to tell her he was leaving Madison; it had been easier just to leave.

In the picture of him and Angie camping, they were grinning, hands on hips – no sign of the fact that they'd argued most of the weekend. They both had shoulder-length hair. Hers had lost that silvery-green undercast it used to get from swimming.

His mother tapped on the door, then pushed it open. 'Luke?' She pulled her hair back, twisting it into a bun and then letting it drop, another of her oddly girl-like gestures. 'I'm going down to Manchester to talk to the staff again. Will you be here? If she calls?'

He turned his back, unzipping the duffel though he didn't need anything from it. 'Where else would I be?'

He woke, gasping, in a dark room, the sky dark outside. For a long vertiginous moment, he didn't know where he was.

If Wendy were beside him, her long red hair would spread across the pillow. All month as Angie had seemed more sick, less sick, more, less, more, more, Luke had felt off balance, as if he might actually fall over if he stood up too quickly. Studying had gotten harder and harder, the letters black stitches taken in white cloth. He wanted to stay in Madison with Wendy, and he felt selfish for wanting that.

After Angie took off from the halfway house, he'd felt too jumpy even to eat. Finally he'd jammed some clothes into a bag and thrown it into the backseat of the car. He felt dread for her, but he also felt – he could barely admit it – relief. Finally things had gotten bad enough that the choice was made for him.

He pulled his hair back into a rough ponytail, fastening it with a rubber band, then went out into the hallway to the phone. One of Wendy's ten thousand housemates answered. When Wendy finally came on the line, he said, 'Guess where I am.'

'Where you are? The Rat?'

'Yeah, right.' He hated the Rat, the depressing beer cellar at the Union.

'I don't know,' she said. 'When are you coming over?'

'I'm in New Hampshire.'

Dead silence. Finally – her voice high and tight – she said, 'Wow. That was a fun guessing game. Thanks for making me play.'

'I had to get out of there,' he said. 'Just a few days.'

'I saw you *yesterday*.'

'Angie's in trouble.' For a moment, startlingly, he felt the pressure of tears against his Adam's apple. 'Everything's so fucked up. It will just be maybe a week I'm gone. I have to be back for midterms.'

'For midterms.'

'Wendy, I really miss you.' Holding the phone was like holding a seashell to his ear: the same whooshing distance. 'A *week*,' he said again, almost pleading. He needed her to say it was all right. 'A week and a half at the most.' *Say it's all right,* he thought. *Say it's all right.*

Chapter Twenty-One

In Angie's imagination of the shelter, she just walked in. She had no place to sleep, so they would come toward her, making soft noises of concern. They'd wrap her in a blanket, lead her to a chair, feed her broth. Her room would be small and clean, a nun's cell, bare yellow light through the window. No words. The throttle in her brain would ease back. It would be a place where she had no history, a place to start over.

The outside of the shelter was squat and tan, not how she'd imagined. Angie walked in and asked the man behind the counter, 'Are you Staff?'

'I'm a Resident Advocate.'

'Does that mean you're a resident?'

'No, it means I'm Staff. Could you hold on one moment?'

He turned his attention back to a woman Angie'd barely registered. She was well dressed, holding two shopping bags. '*You're* homeless?' Angie blurted. Or thought she'd blurted. Both the others ignored her.

'Oh, gosh, I don't know. A thousand dollars?' said the woman with bags.

Angie's head was chattering. *You look great the coffee's good what's wrong with that girl get off, Angie, get off get Angie we're here we're who am I teaching up here I love him but I can't live yeast infection swimmers take your marks not here not here.*

'Now. Can I help you?'

'What happened to that woman?' Every word was hard to push out past *you're dwelling, dwelling in a dwelling smelling of yeast beasts.*

Staff was looking at her expectantly. *I love you please look at*

188

me you fucking rapist oh no not Angie Voorster. Had he already responded to her question? 'Did you say something?' she asked.

'I said, "How can I help you?"'

Angie laughed. He wanted to fuck her but she wouldn't let him. She was going to get her room. 'You know.'

Staff sighed. 'We don't take walk-ins here.'

'She left her bags! That lady left her things!' She dropped to her knees. 'She's going to need these things! Her winter coat's here.'

'Those are donations, ma'am. I'm going to give you a shelter list—'

'These are *old*. She needs these, she's going to freeze—'

'Ma'am. Ma'am. Please get up.'

He glanced behind her, and she turned to see that a small group of residents were watching her. How had she gotten onto the floor, surrounded by a nest of old clothes? She couldn't make out what he was saying – something *loan phone moan* – from the jabbering in her head. She pulled an old white turtleneck sweater onto her lap, twisting it. *Those are* your *CDs do you want room for cream ma'am please put the donations down down downed plane off the coast of Sri Lanka a thousand I can give you family neighborhood she's cranked up I can give you a shelter list and ten minutes on the phone these aren't even written on Angie* she saw herself asleep on a bench and a man came toward her, he was going to rape her and then slit her throat and she screamed, hands over her ears, someone trying to pull her to her feet, the voices still there but drowned under her own voice and she screamed again and screamed and screamed.

'What's that?'

'Those are your things,' said the discharge nurse. 'Sign here.'

Angie's motions were slowed, like water ballet. She watched her hand float toward the pen, and then the pen was gone and the nurse was gone, no, the nurse had bent down and was straightening up, the pen in her hand. Angie's legs buckled and she caught herself on the edge of the counter.

'Hold on tight,' said the nurse, closing Angie's hand around the barrel of the pen.

'This isn't my stuff,' Angie said. The nurse had piled on the counter an old white turtleneck sweater, some rocks, *Great Expectations* and *Cold Feet,* a doll-sized white apron, a crumpled

189

typewritten list. 'The books are mine. The rest—'

'This is what you came in with, Jessie.'

Angie smiled. She'd given Jess's name and her own Social Security number, but with two digits reversed.

Like Jess would have, she said, 'It's not *Jessie,* it's Jess.' *Miss Salter if you're nasty.*

Sigh. 'Jess. The shelter has a bed for you. You need to come in with a week's supply of meds. Do you have a way to get there? Are you sure there's no one I can call for you?'

'What did you guys give me? I feel – God, I feel drunk.'

'Let me look on your chart.'

Angie picked up her books and turned away, trying not to stagger. 'Throw that shit out. I don't want any of it.'

She walked. Her shoes kept her from feeling the road so she took them off, lining them together neatly, like her father kept his wingtips and dress shoes and his single sad pair of old red tennis shoes. She felt better after she left her shoes behind. The sun rose in the east. Carrying her books against her chest, stones pressing warm into her soles, she walked east toward the sea.

In the morning a man found her asleep on the church steps and took her to another shelter. When was the last time she'd used heroin? asked Staff, reading from a list of smudgy questions. Cocaine, crack, crank? Then, 'Do you need to get your things?'

'I don't have things.'

She slept and woke to darkness. The dorm had filled with women and children. A little boy screamed as his mother – *You're going to get it* – wrestled clothes onto him. The dorm had bunk beds and cribs set up between the beds. Over the windows, whimsical curtains with seals balancing red balls on their noses.

'What time is it?' Angie asked.

'Six.'

A.M. or P.M.? She didn't want to sound crazy, so she didn't ask. Her head pounded. She started out of the room, but when she opened the door, the way had been blocked with a wall of paper towels and toilet paper, gleaming white.

An older Asian woman with dyed-red hair touched her arm. 'It's that way.' She pointed in the opposite direction.

Angie leaned close and tried to whisper, through the static, 'Is it day or night?'

She must really have managed to get it out, because the woman patted her shoulder. 'Suppertime, honey.'

The front room was bright, the last light of the day shining through the front window. Outside, the maples burned red. Someone said, 'You need your shoes.'

Angie shook her head. Her feet glowed with heat.

'Come into the office,' said Staff. She held open the half door. 'Sit there. Now, let me see your feet ... Oh, my God.'

'You see why they can't be covered? They spun the room around but I got out ... Has anyone told you about that woman? She's been following me all week—'

'Slow down, Jess. Slow down.' Staff sat on a stool. 'Okay. I want to take your temperature, and then I want you to wash your feet so I can bandage them.'

'*No*. If you do that I won't be able to see. This way I have three-hundred-and-sixty-five-degree vision.'

Staff looked up crookedly at her. Angie could hear the woman's thoughts singing like crickets, in sweet shrill arcs. She pulled on gloves and, with surprising gentleness, picked up Angie's glowing feet.

'Isn't that amazing?' Angie asked.

'I always get the crazy ones on my shift,' the woman muttered. She reached for a bottle, poured something onto a cotton ball. 'This is going to hurt like hell, Jess. Hold on tight.'

Chapter Twenty-Two

Home from work, Jordana stripped off her itchy wool pants and stood in her underwear and sweater, going through the mail. Outside, a cold, sulky rain. She read a Christmas letter, then another. Normally, she would have ignored them – their bragging and false cheer – but she didn't know what to do with herself. Her concentration was so bad these days; if she tried to read a novel, she lost track of events from one paragraph to the next. The Radners had a new grandson. The Hoffheimers enclosed a picture of the whole family in snorkel masks in Belize; the Hardings had moved again. Water drops crept down the glass window, their shadows dappling the hall wall.

Jordana kept trying to remind herself that Angie had taken off before, but it only temporarily pushed fear back to the edge of her brain. They knew Angie hadn't had her wallet with her when she left the halfway house. But she could have hitchhiked, and if she could have hitchhiked, she could have been raped or killed.

She hadn't hitchhiked. She was more likely to be scared, hiding someplace near Manchester. Jordana and Pieter had met with police in three counties, had made flyers. The flyers showed Angie above the words MISSING – ILL – MAY BE DISORIENTED, and then their phone number. Jordana thought the posters might help, and at the same time they shamed her; the words felt like a betrayal, exposing their daughter at her weakest.

Luke's Datsun turned into the driveway. After a moment, she heard his footsteps on the porch, his key in the lock. He tossed his keys, then his scarf, onto the stairs. Shutting the door, he leaned back against it.

'Anything?'

He shook his head, then grimaced. 'What are you doing?'

'Sorting the mail.'

'In that?'

She glanced down at herself, then laughed. 'Oh! *Shit.* Sorry. I guess I'm just used to you and Angie being gone.' Looking around for her wool pants, she saw the letter she'd opened earlier. She held it up. 'Can you believe some people are already getting their Christmas letters out? *Lisa is finishing her senior year and applying to law school . . . Chuck and I continue to work on the summer house . . .*'

'Aren't you going to put something on?'

'I guess. These must be people your father knows.'

'So I went out to that farm Angie used to be at, since you asked. I thought Angie might have gone back there.'

'You drove out there? It's three hours each *way*.'

'Jesus, Ma, I can't talk to you dressed like that.' He went past, into the kitchen.

She pulled on jeans upstairs, then went down to join him.

'There's nothing to eat,' Luke said. He shoved a bag of popcorn into the microwave and turned it on. The microwave's hiss reminded her of when Ben used to call from the static-ridden car phone *The White Mountain Times* had given him; she waved her hand in the air, pushing away the thought.

Pieter's coping strategy was to throw himself into rehearsals: his string quartet was meeting nearly every night this week. Left to themselves, she and Luke cobbled together dinners – as though, she thought, they were snowbound. Box of frozen string beans, a hunk of yellow cheese and slightly stale Lay's potato chips. Rolling Rock beer and pancakes made from a mix.

She didn't think they were going to find Angie just by driving around southern New Hampshire, but all three of them did it. Yesterday – a drizzly Sunday morning – she'd tried to occupy herself cutting back the forsythia. She'd abandoned the project halfway through, when she realized she was breathing so shallowly she felt dizzy. Yanking off her gloves, she left them with the clippers on top of a damp heap of branches. She snatched up her wallet and keys from the house, flinging herself into the car and driving south, still in her mud-splattered clothes. She knew that the police had a better chance of finding Angie than she did, but just doing something lessened the constriction in her chest. She drove all day, staple-gunning telephone poles with flyers: Angie's face among all the lost cats. The gas gauge trembled onto empty and she'd forced herself to stop at a Mobil station. When the attendant, on his way to the office with her credit card, had paused to talk with a customer, she'd wanted to scream *What are you* doing?

The buttery smell of popcorn rose, its rat-a-tat coming in short bursts. The other week she'd noticed that if she held her hand near the microwave, it gave off warmth. Did they all do that, or was it leaking in some way, one more thing to deal with? She meant to check the one at work but kept forgetting.

Luke leaned on the counter, staring into the microwave as though it were a television screen or an oracle. She opened her mouth to say something about radiation, then decided not to. Exhausted, face drawn, he looked like a grown man.

Luke blamed them for Angie's disappearance. If she and Pieter had done enough, he seemed always to imply, then Angie would have been found. His disapproval pissed her off, but that always collapsed into just feeling tired and sad. She couldn't sustain resentment: Luke's love for his sister was so protective, so fiercely loyal. And tinged with guilt, Jordana suspected, for being hard on Angie after her first break.

She found a carton of orange juice in the fridge and drank from it.

'Popcorn?' he asked.

'Sure. OJ?'

These meals were the closest time between them, leaning against the counter, trading containers. As soon as she felt coziness, though, it turned lonely. The most companionable moment of her day was with her barely-speaking-to-her son.

After dinner, Luke went upstairs to make his long nightly phone call to the girlfriend in Wisconsin. He didn't talk about her, and questions made him even more bristly than he already was. From Angie, Jordana knew that Wendy came from one of the midwestern vowel states and had red hair to the middle of her back. 'Pretty boring,' was what Angie had said of her. 'Like she's so scared of saying something dumb that she only states the completely obvious.'

Jordana turned out the light in the kitchen. One of Pieter's cardigans hung over the back of a chair; she sat, wrapping it around herself, smelling his familiar blend of wool and Dial soap. She was so wiped out. She'd never felt quite this way before, this tangle of alarm. Instead of galvanizing her, it made her feel slow and stupid. She kept thinking of Angie, scared and lost. She thought of someone from one of the handful of family support meetings she'd attended, a woman whose daughter had hanged herself in the mother's closet. With the mother's favorite belt. *Stop it,* she told herself.

Hugging her knees to her chest, she rested her head on them. She imagined Ben there, the weight of his cheek against her back. She'd been sleeping only a few hours a night since Angie disappeared; the chair felt like it was on the deck of a gently pitching ship. Recently, she'd begun talking to Ben in her head a lot, telling him about her days, saying *I'm so scared for her.* Strange to miss him now, and with such longing, after years when thinking of him filled her with panicky aversion.

She stood. What could she do? Not read. She turned in place; there was no direction that held out promise. TV would only depress her more. Rain outside. She could sort through old magazines, but the idea overwhelmed her.

Going to the base of the stairs, she called up, 'Luke?' She waited. 'Luke? Want to play cards? Scrabble?'

No response. His music was on. She climbed the stairs until she stood outside his door. She knocked. 'Luke?'

He yanked the door open. 'I heard you the first time.' He had the phone receiver pressed against his shoulder, and she thought, strangely, of holding him against her when he was a baby. He hissed, 'No, I don't want to play Scrabble. Jesus.'

Chapter Twenty-Three

Luke woke earlier than he ever had without an alarm, getting breakfast at fast-food drive-throughs. All the women in his life hated McDonald's – his mother and Angie for various political reasons, Wendy because of working there in high school – but the Egg McMuffin trumped any argument. He had no idea why it was so delicious.

Because it has, like, five thousand grams of fat, he imagined Angie saying.

He drove, and when he could no longer stand driving, he parked and walked. He'd already been home ten days, the longest he'd thought he'd stay. He could still be back for midterms – and maybe salvage his grades – if he started back to Wisconsin in six days. Seven at the most.

He had a stack of his parents' flyers, though he didn't have a lot of faith in them, and he carried pictures of his sister, which he showed around anyplace she might have visited. He stopped at shelters and soup kitchens. She loved coffee shops, where a dollar could buy a whole afternoon at a table. ('Tourist of the normal,' she called herself.) Fast-food restaurants and pet stores she hated enough that she might go in and lecture the workers. He was trying to pretend his search had an essential order, but he knew that if he finished visiting every coffee shop and pet shop in one town today, Angie might arrive there tomorrow.

Angie had left the halfway house in a mixed state. He'd just found out his mother called Angie's manias light or dark, which was kind of funny because he also had his own names for them. To him, mixed states were *dirty manias* – unlike the pure mania Angie had been riding when she'd showed up in Madison – and they scared the hell out of him. Not because she was incoherent or violent, though she could be both. Dirty mania meant he barely recognized his sister. Even very depressed or manic, Angie was basically kind; she had moments of dark humor and self-aware-ness. When people used the term 'he isn't himself today,' it had always seemed ridiculous to him. But in mixed states Angie could become truly not herself.

He showed Angie's photo to a kid sitting in Memorial Park sixteen or seventeen, shivering in his T-shirt and windbreaker. There was a scab – nearly black – on his upper lip. He took Angie's picture to study it. With one finger of the other hand, he worried the edge of the scab. 'She's pretty.'

In the picture, Angie sat on a picnic blanket, looking over her shoulder, smiling, hair caught back in a messy ponytail so that strands framed her face. Luke had chosen this picture because Angie looked so normal in it, which might make people sympa-thetic. But also part of him was embarrassed by the thought of showing another photo – Angie glowering and sullen in a dirty sweatshirt, or Angie in a low-cut shirt and heels, smiling with her mouth wide open, as though she were about to swallow the camera.

The kid hadn't seen her. Neither had the woman with swooping eyeglass stems who worked at the St. Anthony's thrift shop. 'I'm sorry, hon. Maybe try back through that door. That's the soup kitchen.'

The kitchen he entered had stainless steel appliances and butcher-block counters, much more sleek and industrial than he'd expected. An older black man in a baseball hat measured dried basil and oregano out of plastic containers the size of milk jugs; a youngish woman opened enormous cans of stewed tomatoes. She wore a knee-length navy blue jumper and a small gold cross.

'We're making spaghetti,' she said.

'Smells great.' Luke was just being polite, but as he spoke saliva rushed into his mouth. He took out the photo.

'We don't get a lot of young girls in here, unless they got kids.' The man held the picture toward the woman opening tomatoes. 'Sister?'

Sister: a nun. The unfashionable jumper, the sober brown clogs, the cross. She wasn't much older than Luke himself. It seemed exotic that she could have decided her whole life already. She glanced at it, started to shake her head, then squinted and said,

197

'Maybe ... Does she have short hair now?'

'Not that I know of.'

The nun held Angie's picture at arm's length, finally shaking her head. 'Three or four days ago I was at CVS. But I'm really not sure it was her ... A woman, a young woman, was standing in the middle of the aisle, and I asked if she was okay and she walked away. That's it. But she had much shorter hair than this.'

It was a tiny thing to go on. It was nothing to go on. Still, Luke felt ecstatic. On the way out through the thrift store, he bought a parka for six bucks. It had fake white fur around the hood and the name of a football team on the back.

When he got back to the kid in the park, Luke said, 'Here.' He thrust out the jacket. 'Hope you like the Cowboys.'

It was the kind of thing Angie might do. It made him feel close to her. And feeling close to her – he knew it was irrational – made him feel closer to finding her.

That night, talking to Wendy, he asked, 'Do you miss me?'

'You'll be back in a few days.'

'Ever practical.' Phone calls weren't their best medium: Wendy got irritable and shy, he got messy and nostalgic. 'Hey, I met a woman who'd seen Angie. A nun.'

'Mmmm.' It was her all-purpose noise recently. Humming meant she wasn't going to respond, but it was impossible to call her on it.

'At a drugstore.' He didn't say that he'd gone to the CVS, where he'd walked the aisles as though Angie – if it had even been her – might have hung out there all this time. He was going to add drugstores to his rounds. 'What do you think a nun buys at the drugstore?'

'What if you don't find her by Friday?' Wendy asked.

'The nun?' he said. Wendy didn't laugh. He sighed. 'I'll come back anyway.' He didn't want to be here, but he couldn't tell Wendy that; she was so opposed to his having left school that he always ended up defending it. His first midterm was next week. He had all his books with him to study, but the letters still seemed like meaningless glyphs; he could force them together into words but couldn't force the words to make sense.

When he told Wendy he loved her, she made the humming noise.

They hung up and he lay back on his bed. Wendy was right; he was never going to find his sister. What did he think, that he could just drive around until their paths crossed? The other times she'd taken off, she hadn't gone very far – except when she'd driven to Wisconsin, and that hadn't been dirty mania, and this time she didn't have her car. Still, even on foot, she could have gone a fair distance by now.

Wednesday, he drove down to Portsmouth. He parked near the deserted dock, which advertised summertime sunset cruises among the Isles of Shoals. Hills of trash and dirty salt, two or three stories high, rose all along the waterfront. He walked through the touristy shopping area. His parents' flyers hung on some of the downtown notice kiosks; they made him feel lonely, for some reason. He passed the library: *shit*. How had he not thought to include libraries on his rounds?

It was hopeless, but he didn't know what else to do, so he stopped and left a flyer at the library. By four, he'd been back to the libraries in three towns. It was now five days before he'd have to start back to Madison if he wanted not to flunk everything. Bruisy-purple twilight had fallen, sharply cold; in fifteen or twenty minutes it would be night. He didn't feel as effective when he couldn't see as far, but he wasn't ready to go home, so he pulled out the map. He'd skipped Huntstable; he'd retrace his steps a few miles, go to his places, and then call it a day.

He pulled onto Route 33. Routes in New Hampshire might follow one road for a while, then jag off onto another road, and then jag off again onto another. The road you were on would change; you'd be driving on 35, and if you missed the small road that hooked off to the left, you'd suddenly be on 211. It drove tourists crazy. Thinking of tourists made him remember when he was a kid, how he and his friends would drop to their hands and knees in downtown Cort to bark at the day-trippers.

An old man limped along the shoulder of the road ahead. He had wild white hair and staggered, drunk. As Luke got close, he could see that the man's feet were bare, despite the bracken edging the road, and despite the biting cold. He thought, *Angie would stop for him.*

Luke slowed to a few miles an hour, lurching across the front seat to roll down the passenger-side window, still driving with his left hand, glancing between the window and the road ahead. 'Hey!' he called. 'Are you in trouble?'

The person turned, and Luke realized he wasn't drunk. His lips were pulled back from his teeth, his face so twisted by pain it seemed inhuman. And then, knowledge dropping into Luke like heavy coins: not a man. Not old, not drunk. She'd lost a lot of weight and butchered her hair; her face was red with windburn and streaked with dirt. She started to raise a trembling hand to her mouth, then let it drop by her side.

He yanked on the parking brake, taking his foot off the clutch so fast that the car jumped and stalled. Forcing himself not to move too quickly, he got out. He went around the car and very carefully put his arms around her. 'I can't believe I really found you.'

She was stiff in his arms. 'I need to go to the ocean.'

'Let's get in the car.'

'I mean it. I'm not being crazy. I need to *go* there.'

In the car she couldn't sit still. She kept making partial gestures, switching mid-movement – reaching for the window crank and then starting to touch the ceiling. He pulled into the road. He'd never seen her this bad; he wasn't sure he could get her home. Where was there a hospital? It would be better if he could get his mother first; she would know what to do. His hands shook on the wheel. He realized his motions were still slowed-down and gentle; he was driving way below the speed limit. He sped up, keeping Angie in the corner of his vision. From this angle, her constant movement looked almost like dancing.

'Angie.' She jerked toward him, and he said, 'I really found you.'

'I need to get to the ocean.'

'Okay. We're going to the ocean.'

She turned on the radio, scrolling back and forth down the dial, a squawk from one station, then the next and the next, joining together in a single nonsense phrase. She tensed and stared at him. Something had tipped her off. 'We're going home,' she said.

'We'll swing by home to get what we need to go to the ocean.' His voice was full of forced jollity; he barely recognized it.

She turned and scrabbled frantically for the door handle.

'What are you doing?' he yelled. With his elbow he jammed down the lock on his own door; the other locks clicked down. He slammed his foot onto the brake, trying to steer toward the shoulder.

She turned on him, going for his face with her nails. Her face was so distorted – teeth bared, eyes glazed with pain and fury – he thought for a second it wasn't her, that he'd picked up a stranger after all. The car lurched left, into the other lane, and he jerked the wheel back the other way. Using his right arm to block her hands, he cringed, trying to steer. 'Stop it!' he yelled. 'Angie, stop!' He was braking but still in third gear and he couldn't reach the shift. The car shook, surged, and the engine died, throwing them both forward.

Angie wasn't wearing a seat belt; her head hit the dashboard and he got his own belt off, scrambled over the gearshift and parking brake, and grabbed her wrists, straddling her body. She seemed dazed, but as he shoved her hands down and knelt on them, she began to struggle. She made a high, keening sound, like the whistle of a kettle.

'Goddamn it, Angie. It's me!'

She lunged for him, and though he wrenched away her teeth closed on his shoulder. He screamed and hit her in the face. He had never hated anyone like this. 'I'm helping you!' he screamed, and hit her again as hard as he could, and her teeth released his shoulder. He undid his buckle, yanking to free his belt from the belt loops. He grabbed up one of Angie's wrists and then the other and bound them with the belt, pulling it tight.

'Oh God,' she said, then screamed. 'Oh my God, oh my God, oh, fuck, oh my God.'

He got her seat belt around her, strapping her in, then collapsed into his own seat.

'Oh *God*. Oh my *God*.'

He pressed his trembling hands over his eyes. The acrid smell of urine reached his nose. His sister screamed. 'Oh, *God*!'

He'd heard her scream to be dramatic, or to provoke someone, but this scream was deep and filled with horror. He needed to think what to do. He needed to think, but her breath was ragged and quick and he was suddenly drenched with sweat, and he pushed his hands into his temples and screamed back at her to shut up.

Chapter Twenty-Four

Jordana had never known her daughter to wear the hospital clothes. But here Angie was, in a gown with a faded-almost-invisible pattern and sad beige socks with white rubber skids on the bottoms. In the center of her forehead, like the third eye of a Hindu god, a bruise from where she'd hit the dashboard of the car almost a week earlier. She lay in bed, curled on her side, eyes open.

'Mom.' She said it dully, but not as dully as she had yesterday. Any progress counted.

'Baby.' Jordana kissed her daughter's temple, pushing back her greasy hair. 'How do you feel?'

'Like shit.' The ghost of a smile.

When Luke had called last week from the hospital in Concord, Jordana had raced to Pieter's rehearsal – he'd tried to pack up his cello, and she'd said, 'Go, we need to *go*' – and they'd made the forty-five minute drive in thirty minutes. Her son had been in the waiting area outside the emergency room, sitting on the edge of a molded plastic chair. When she touched his back, he'd stared up at her and Pieter through his fingers. He looked as though he hadn't slept in days. Some mean part of Jordana's mind thought, *Good, now you know what it's like.*

Angie had been transferred here to Hayslip-Balsbrough, where there was an open bed. To bring her down, she'd been given such massive doses of antipsychotics that she'd been essentially catatonic. Now, as the doctors backed off the Thorazine, she was coming alive a little again.

Jordana reached into her bag. 'I brought you some stuff to read.'

Angie moved her head, neither a nod nor a shake. Her face looked blurred, like watching a filmstrip the projectionist kept trying to focus. Jordana found space on the bedside table, already piled with the books and magazines she'd brought on other days, a hodgepodge because she didn't know what Angie might want. Answer: nothing. Still, she continued to bring them. There were also two paperbacks that Angie had had with her: a fat Dickens novel and a mystery whose cover showed a wedding cake with a plastic bride next to a fallen plastic groom. Pieter usually visited during evening hours, bearing CDs; those were piling up too, here and on the dresser. Luke hadn't been to see her.

'Do you want to take a walk?'

Angie's face wavered. 'I don't know.'

'Let's try.'

Jordana had to help Angie pull back the sheets. Angie swung her legs heavily over the side of the bed; her nightgown was ruched up around her waist and Jordana looked away from her daughter's hands fumbling the hem, the shadow of pubic hair visible at the edge of her underwear. 'I don't know,' Angie said again.

'We won't go far.'

Angie stood, swaying a little, her hands over her eyes.

'Come on, honey.' Jordana put her arm around Angie's waist.

'I don't think I can.'

'Just to the nurse's station. Just take a step, Ange. Can you do one step? Good. Hold on to me. One more.'

'One more,' said Angie.

'Good. Now one more. One more.'

A nurse passing in the hall boomed, 'We're getting some exercise!'

'We sure are!' Jordana boomed back. Angie laughed a little through her tears. She had an arm around Jordana's shoulder, her weight dragging Jordana down on that side. 'Oh, shit,' Angie was saying. 'I can't.'

'You can. Look how close we are—'

'Stop making me!'

Angie slumped and Jordana staggered to keep her from falling. A nurse in turquoise scrubs hurried down the hall, and the two of them got Angie back to bed.

The nurse pulled the curtain closed around them. Angie had stopped crying. 'I'm sorry,' she said dully. 'I'm as bad as Lily.'

Who was Lily? Jordana pushed back Angie's hair, trying not to show her distress. 'We'll try again in a couple days.'

203

'Yeah, okay.' She clearly didn't mean it.

The nurse came back in, said, 'Meds.'

Angie nodded. She took the paper cup of pink and red pills, tapped them out one at a time, then bent her head to lap them from her hand.

It took Ben more than a minute to answer his door. She must have woken him from a nap; his hair stuck up, and he'd pulled on a pair of boxer shorts. 'What are you doing here?'

'I don't know.'

He slid out through the half-opened door, reached back to fiddle with the knob so he wouldn't lock himself out, then closed the door and leaned back against it, arms folded.

She said, 'There's someone here.'

'Kind of, yeah.'

'I'm sorry. I know I – we haven't—' Frustrated, she closed her eyes and exhaled. 'I just wanted to see you.'

Tightly, he said, 'Well, your timing sucks.'

'Because of—?' She pointed her chin at the door to indicate whoever was inside.

'Because you refuse to talk to me – you disappear for, like, four years – and then you just show up like no time has passed. *Jesus,* Jordana.'

Years had gone by in her family, but it was true that she felt like no time had passed in her life with Ben. She said, 'I'm sorry. I wasn't very fair to you.'

'It doesn't matter anymore.' He reached out and pulled her hair back out of her face, twisting it into a bun. 'I don't know why you don't wear this back more often.' Then he dropped his hands. The gesture had somehow not been tender, but she still felt her stomach twist.

'I shouldn't be here.'

'No.'

All the conversations they'd had in her head rose up in her, as if evidence of a closeness Ben was willfully ignoring. She wanted to cry. She'd formed – she realized now – a picture of sitting on Ben's couch, letting him make her espresso. She had wanted to tell him about Angie in the hospital. She had wanted to resist, then give in to, going to bed with him.

She hated that she felt outrageously sorry for herself. 'How

204

long—?' She nodded toward the shut door.

'Not that long. You know *me*.'

Involuntarily, she glanced at his face; did he realize the intimacy of the phrase? No sign. 'How old is she?' she asked. He raised his eyebrows, and she said quickly, 'Don't answer that. I need to go.'

She made for the stairs, not looking back until she was in her car. Ben still stood at the railing, looking down. She'd waited this long to talk to him, then blown through her chance in five minutes. He raised his hand to her, then turned back toward the door, bending quickly to pick up the afternoon newspaper.

When she got home, Luke was lying on the living room floor, reading through the Christmas letters, long hair loose from its ponytail and falling across his shoulders. She couldn't get used to seeing him as a grown man.

He waved a letter in his hand. 'Who are the Saylors?'

'People your dad knows, maybe.'

He'd called and rescheduled his first midterm so he could stay longer, though he hadn't used the time to see Angie. What *had* he done? Watched a lot of TV. Slept away the afternoons. He'd driven down to Durham once to see Cole. And here it was Monday; he was leaving tomorrow.

Her hands felt shaky, still, from seeing Ben. She hated that she'd apologized for being unfair; she'd said it not out of remorse but because she'd wanted to hook him into talking about the past. *It doesn't matter anymore.* She shook her head to get his voice out. Trying to sound normal, motherlike, she asked, 'Have you thought about stopping by the hospital on your way out of town?'

Luke moved his hand, a gesture that might have meant anything.

She sat next to him on the floor. 'How's studying going?'

'It's going.'

She picked up a Christmas letter with three caroling penguins at the top. She skimmed it without registering a word, then dropped it back on the floor. 'Dr. Morgan wants Angie to have ECT.'

'Shock?'

'He keeps saying, "It's not like *One Flew Over the Cuckoo's Nest*."'

'You're going to let them?'

'You don't even go! You don't know what she's like.'

'I know what she's like. That doesn't mean she should have her brain fried.'

She'd argued against ECT; how was she now in the position of defending it? 'He said it takes more effort to get a plane into the air than to keep it aloft once it's up.' Luke frowned and she said, 'He means meds aren't enough now.'

Luke shook his head but didn't say anything. She couldn't believe she'd used up her chance to talk to Ben – impulsively, without even thinking. So fucking *stupid*. She wanted to cry with frustration. She held very still, and after a moment the urge receded.

Luke rolled over onto his back and lay there splayed, looking at the ceiling. He felt around himself for another Christmas letter. 'The Lings hope our year was as blessed as theirs. Nicole's taking her M-CATs.'

'Hooray for Nicole.'

Luke dropped the letter. He made his voice deep: *'The Voorsters had another exceptional year.'*

'Right. Exceptional.'

'No divorces and only one near-death, so keep your fingers crossed! We're sure Pieter will turn up, though he's temporarily AWOL—'

'Luke, he's not.'

'Angela seems to be recovering nicely on Thorazine after her psychotic break.' His voice, beneath its false cheer, sounded forced. *'Our son, Luke – yes, we have a son! – left UW with only a semester and a half left. Go, Luke, go!'*

'But you're going *back*.' As Jordana said it, she knew he wasn't.

Luke looked startled, as though he hadn't known either, until this moment. Jordana wanted to grab his shoulders and shake him. He was sabotaging himself, as if it were his fault Angie wasn't in college. Trying to sound neutral, she said, 'You have a life out there.'

'It's just for now I'm not going back. For now.'

'God!' Springing to her feet, she rushed from the room, then jerked to a stop in the hallway, unsure where to go. She was trembling.

Such a pointless waste. 'Stop,' she said, not loud enough for Luke to hear, not even sure who the words were meant for. She put shaking hands over her eyes. 'Stop. *Stop.*'

Chapter Twenty-Five

Luke taught his 7 and 8 A.M. classes the same things he'd been taught as a child: to put their faces down in the water and blow bubbles, to do the dead man's float, to dive for small objects. These were adults who had never learned to swim, and in the water they were nervous and hopeful, sometimes almost fierce when he'd set a difficult task. He had ten women and three men. One woman worked as a printer at *The White Mountain Times:* when she dove into the water, faint vapor trails of ink streamed from her hands and arms. Afterward, his students used the Y's shabby locker room to change into work clothes, blow dry their hair, put on makeup and jewelry. Transformed into their day selves, they got into noisy old Celicas and Marauders and drove off in different directions: the bank, the hospital, the Igga. A man who came to class gray-faced from the night shift at UPS went home to bed.

Once Luke had said to him, 'If you're ever too wiped out, you don't have to come. We have makeup classes.'

'Oh, *no.*' He seemed upset at the idea. 'I look forward to this all night. This is the best part of my life right now.'

It seemed impossible that Luke could be responsible for the best part of someone's life. He'd taught classes like these for the last three summers: he felt like he could do it in his sleep, and sometimes like he *was* doing it in his sleep.

This life back in New Hampshire – staying in his old room, working at the Y again – seemed unhinged from time. Even his sexual fantasies had reverted back to those he'd had as an adolescent. He came upon a beautiful woman on the beach, standing with her back to him. From behind, he slid his hands into her bikini top. Just the weight of her breasts falling into his hands, the press of her nipples, was all he needed.

In his Intermediate class he taught backstroke, flip turns, the frog kick. A few mastered those and learned butterfly, Angie's old stroke. On beginners it looked desperate, like drowning: arms smacking the water, head rearing to suck in air. At ten, he taught a private lesson to a guy who'd lost his legs in a car accident; then he taught a Guppy class.

He finished work around one. He told himself he would go visit Angie at the hospital, but as usual, as soon as he got into his car, he was overtaken by such deep tiredness that he almost couldn't lift his hands to the wheel. He drove home and stumbled up to his room, where he slept for the rest of the afternoon.

When he woke, it was dark inside and outside the house. The clock said five, and he had to search his memory before deciding *afternoon*. He'd slept in his clothes, and his skin felt clammy. Turning onto his side, he drew his knees up against his stomach. He felt so emptied that it was hard even to breathe. What was he doing here? If he were waking from a nap in Madison, Wendy would be beside him. She would have a textbook open on her knees, hair pulled back, the lamp throwing a yellow circle of light on the page. It was stupid to be here – he wasn't doing Angie any good – but he couldn't see himself anywhere else. Madison, that life of drinking beer in the afternoon with his housemates, doing laundry with Wendy, sitting in lecture halls, felt closed off to him now, no longer available.

Putting his hand beneath the waistband of his jeans, he cradled himself. It comforted him, a little.

Chapter Twenty-Six

Angie woke with a dry mouth and a pounding headache. There was a piece of gauze on her arm over the IV mark, and a place on her temple that felt tight. She touched it: adhesive that hadn't all been swabbed off. She couldn't remember being awakened or coming down here for the ECT. She felt like a pot whose insides had been scoured with steel wool: that empty, that dry.

A nurse, wearing a cardigan that obscured all but the first letter of her name tag, K, brought Angie water. Angie tried to say something about aspirin. She must have said something because K nodded and left, returning with a fluted paper cup of water and another paper cup holding two red pills. Angie swallowed them and lay back on the gurney. Closing her eyes, she felt herself floating, the way she used to feel after swim practice, when she lay back in the water, exhausted, muscles aching. Except that then she'd felt relieved and happy. Now her head burned; immediately, she threw up the water and the melted white nubs of aspirin.

While she was still leaning over the edge of the gurney, pawing her face, a doctor stopped next to her. He put his hand on her shoulder, 'You had a very good seizure.'

She felt a dim flash of accomplishment. A nurse used a cotton pad to swab adhesive from her temples, and Angie remembered a day a couple of years ago when Jess had taken her to a salon. Brow waxing was a very girly thing to do, not really Jess's style – or Angie's. She'd been in very bad shape, though, and Jess must not have known what else to do to cheer her. Angie lay on a vinyl exam table while a woman used a tongue depressor to swab hot brown wax between her eyebrows. She pressed a small piece of muslin against the wax, then yanked it off. Angie had cried out. Cheerfully, the woman showed her the cloth; the wax had stuck to it, pulling out dozens of small hairs. 'That's much better,' the woman said. It should have been funny – someone trying to make her beautiful when for two weeks she'd been so depressed she could barely lift a toothbrush – but the strip of cloth, yellow sebum clinging to the hairs' root bulbs, had filled Angie with dread. After that day, she and Jess had drifted even farther apart.

K got her back into the wheelchair. Angie didn't have the energy to grab at the back of her hospital gown, so doubtless her fat white ass flashed the room. She didn't care; she cared horribly.

On the ward, she staggered to the social room. Two of the cata-tonics sat in the blue vinyl chairs; they weren't officially excused from groups, but no one expected them to go. Angie sank into a chair as far from them as possible and passed out.

She woke to find she'd slid half off the chair. She watched the light change on the ceiling, sharpening toward noon. She felt like she had a horrible flu, one that made her bones ache with fatigue, one that made the world flat, an unsteady platter whose edge she could slide off.

To herself, Angie whispered, 'What's your name?'

She whispered back, 'Angela Hedde Voorster.'

'Where were you born?'

'Presbyterian General, New York, New York.'

'What is your favorite movie?'

'*Chinatown* for good movies, *Valley Girl* for bad movies.'

'What did you do yesterday?'

She tried to think. She knew she must have spent time in this room and in the breakfast room. One of her parents had probably visited, and Trevor called every day. She hadn't seen or heard from Luke. She'd surely watched television, but she couldn't remember a single image. She couldn't remember what she'd eaten. Something, there must be something. She tried to imagine her plastic-wrapped tray; Natalie saying, 'Did I just go some-where?'; the *Cheers* theme song: a place where everybody knows your name ... But they belonged to every day.

In a just world, she'd have ECT on Drama Therapy day and be allowed to skip it. From the cacophony down the hall, though, this was Music Therapy day. A young guy from the community college – he wore lots of rope jewelry – brought drums and let the patients

210

whale on them. It was the only therapy group that didn't make her feel worse.

Angie got up and limped to the bathroom. There the ward's similarity to a hotel ended. The stalls had curtains, and the mirror was made not of glass but of polished metal: unbreakable, slightly dented in one place, so that if Angie stood at the second sink her forehead bulged, then shrank, bulged, shrank, as she moved. The Formica counter held a mermaid-shaped stain the color of milky coffee.

Back to the social room. Elsie had come in to sit on one of the couches, her head tipped forward so that her long graying hair covered her face. Rapidly, she raked her fingers through, not a combing motion – in fact, she was tangling it – but as though searching for something.

When Angie came into the room, Elsie looked up and froze. 'Are you an angel?'

'Yeah.'

Elsie continued to stare at her; then, quite suddenly, she ducked her head again and resumed her anxious sifting. The catatonics were still as the chairs they sat in, barely breathing. The television played a news program above their heads. It had closed captioning, black bars with white letters across the bottom of the screen. In movies the captions were edited down to the bare essentials, but the news was broadcast live, with no time for editing; the words came in fits and gushes. A woman wearing a turquoise power suit adjusted her face from sad to cheerful, while beneath her lagged

> >perished in the blaze.

Angie had checked the hall clock on her way back from the bathroom, but she realized she had no recollection of what time it was. No one knew why ECT worked, but the fact that she could speak, sleep a few hours a night, want a cigarette – want anything – meant that it was working. On the other hand, her short-term memory was shredded. The past was clearer than five minutes ago. She might lose a whole afternoon remembering something like the summer she was ten and had been tapped to swim with the thirteen-and-ups. That whole summer tasted of watermelon Now-and-Laters. Olivia Newton-John on the radio in the lifeguard office, a rabbit's foot of aluminum foil crumpled around the antenna for better reception. The older girls' coconut oil leaving a

211

rainbowed sheen on the water's surface when they dove in. Angie and Abe – the two younger kids singled out to swim big kids' practices – ran around fetching things for the lifeguards, showing off.

The social room had six wobbly ashtray stands, a plastic coffee table with no sharp edges, copies of *Family Circle* and *Newsweek* and *People*. Some of the magazines were semi-new, ones the nurses brought from home, first cutting off the small white subscriber labels that would have shown their addresses. The *Globe* wasn't left in the social room anymore, because Harriet had pica; she ripped pages out and ate them. If you wanted the paper, you had to get it from a nurse. Angie lit a cigarette. The smoke steadied her, as did the familiar movements, bringing the cigarette to her lips, pulling the harsh smoke into her lungs. She wandered to the window, surrounded by blinking green Christmas lights. Semis ground by on the highway. Old snow covered the cars in the lot, smudging their outlines. On the concrete apron of the emergency entrance, someone else – it was so overcast that they were smeared, indistinct – also smoked. Angie took a long drag and, six floors down, the other cigarette's tip flared orange, then faded.

Nighttime. The TV showed Whoopi Goldberg dressed as a nun. 'There she goes! She's taking the stairs!' shouted the gangster, and underneath, shortened to keep up:

> > She's gone!

Whoopi ran between pinball machines, and then another nun and another, the hit men turning each nun around, and it was never her, never the right one. Down the bright hall, a nurse said, 'Girl—' in a laughing voice that meant she was talking to another nurse, not the exasperated voice that would have meant a patient – and from the ward upstairs you could make out faintly someone screaming and screaming and screaming, and then the sudden silence of Isolation.

'Did I just go somewhere?' Natalie whispered, looking stricken. 'Did I just leave?'

'You've been right here.'

'Are you sure?'

Natalie had steel-rimmed glasses and a narrow uncertain face. In real life, she worked for a florist. Angie used to sometimes say *Nope, haven't seen you for hours,* but she'd learned not to joke.

212

Something terrible – Angie didn't know what – happened to Natalie in the fantasies she fell into. 'Yeah, I'm totally positive. You've definitely been right here.'

On the screen the nuns turned, a row of black bells, innocence and false innocence knocking against each other in their faces.

'Did I just disappear somewhere?' Natalie asked.

Angie shook her head. 'Did I?'

Natalie smiled a little. 'You know you didn't.'

The movie ended with a gospel song. Later a nurse came in to switch off the static. 'Night meds, ladies.'

It was weirdly calming, how the days were barely differentiated. Lights out at ten, movie at eight, ice cream at dinner Friday, Group every morning: the week turned slowly, a seven-toothed gear, Sunday night rising again and then falling slowly as Monday rose behind it. In her room's window, her face was less distorted than in the bathroom's tin mirror but fainter, as though she was fading. It was snowing outside. The flakes looked black as they whirled beneath the streetlamps.

A knock on the door. A nurse stuck in her head, swept a flashlight across the room; someone would check every fifteen minutes, all night. The door clicked shut behind her and Angie, alone again, turned back to the window. Through her reflection, she could see a thin moon hanging crooked over the empty softball field. She worked two fingers though the grating to touch the cold glass.

Chapter Twenty-Seven

It was more than a month after he found her that Luke finally forced himself to drive up to see Angie at Hayslip-Balsbrough after work. He knew from his parents that Angie was on the 'unlocked' floor. The 'unlocked' unit was actually locked, but some patients were allowed out for fifteen minuts or more, accompanied or unaccompanied, depending on doctors' orders.

Today, if he were in Madison, he'd be turning in his term paper for physical anthropology.

At the nursing station, he signed the register, surprised to see his hands shaking. He took his wallet and keys from his pockets. The nurse was young, about Angie's age. She checked for sharps, then handed back his things. 'Your sister's in the TV room.'

His heart began to beat faster. On a gurney beside the nursing counter slept a young woman. She must be sui-1, on constant watch. The first time he'd heard *sui* had been about his sister, after her overdose. The word had hung in his brain, hard and without meaning – suu-eee – before dissolving into the first syllables of *suicide*. Thinking of how much he'd had to learn since then, a wave of pride and self-pity moved through him, quickly followed by disgust. How could he congratulate himself about anything connected to Angie's illness?

Coming into the TV room, he said her name. His heart was beating painfully fast; he felt a little faint. 'Angie,' he said again, and she turned.

Her face was bloated, and her short hair stood up all over her head, like the hair of a child just woken from a nap. She wore a limp cardigan over her hospital gown.

She said, 'You have a beard.'

'It's not really a beard,' he said, stupidly. 'I just haven't shaved in a while.'

'Come closer.' She reached to touch it. 'It's *red.*'

'Yeah. It itches.'

She patted his beard. She usually wore silver rings on every finger; without them, her hand looked soft and vulnerable. Pat. Pat. Pat. 'I like it.'

'Wendy hates when I let it grow out,' he said. 'She thinks I look like an outlaw.'

'Very ... original.'

Without thinking he reached up and drew her hand down to his lips, kissing the back as he might have done with a girlfriend. Her knuckles still had a few scabs from where he'd ground his knees into them. He winced.

A commercial came on and Angie turned away from him, toward the television. The ad was for laundry soap, a woman grabbing her son as he ran past, stripping off his stained shirt and throwing it into the washing machine. 'I would've gotten dressed, if I knew you were coming.' She rubbed at her eye with the heel of her splayed hand. He watched until he couldn't stand it and had to pull her hand away. Her eyelid was chafed pink.

When he let go of her hand, she started grinding her palm against her eye again.

'Goddamn it, Angie.' He pulled her hand away from her face. More gently, he said, 'You're making your eye all – it's all red.' He ducked his head to make sure she was listening. After a moment, she nodded meekly. His mother had warned him that the ECT made Angie dopey, but he still hadn't been prepared. He wished that she *were* angry at him after all.

The TV wasn't caged; apparently this hospital wasn't worried that people would go to that particular bizarre length to kill themselves. Luke watched dogs bound toward a little boy, *tlck,* a woman scrubbing her counter, beaming, *tlck,* a man on a talk show saying, I just want a normal life, *tlck,* a soap-opera heroine in a bikini of leaves, kneeling on a desert-island beach, *tlck,* a fifties-era Clark Kent following a man, *tlck*—

'No, go back,' he said. 'That's the old Superman.' He knelt beside his sister. 'Remember this? Remember watching this?'

'When Mom was at work.'

He felt like cheering. 'Mom was at work and we used to get so

215

bored. We'd watch TV standing up, right up against the screen, so we could turn it off as soon as she got home.' Clark Kent sat at the restaurant counter next to the suspect, drinking water. Then he got up and pretended to make a phone call. Luke asked, 'Do you remember this one?'

Clark Kent shouted into the empty phone. Agitated, he asked the man who'd been sitting next to him, 'Could you hand me my water?'

'I remember old stuff,' Angie said, slow as a warped record.

Luke took her hand, lacing his fingers with hers. She was trembling slightly. They didn't look at each other but at the television screen, where Clark Kent slipped the water glass into his jacket pocket. Luke knew that later he'd check for fingerprints and find the man didn't have any.

Chapter Twenty-Eight

At the river at 6 A.M., after two hours of cello practice, the sky was a still, flat black. In winter, dawn didn't come until after seven. Pieter opened the car door and sat sideways on the seat to lace his skates, legs protruding from the car. He slid guards over the blades and made his awkward way down to the river. Above him, the sky prickled with stars.

Holding on to the back of a bench for support, he slipped the guards off his skates and into his pocket. He had to take a few wobbly steps from the bench to the river. As soon as his skate hit the ice, he felt his posture change.

On land his body often felt awkward to him, but on the ice his long limbs and sharp angles seemed to unlock and straighten. After the first mile he was warm enough to unfold his arms, then unbutton his coat. The Morrill ran twenty miles, starting in Cort, running south past Applefield, then through five miles of open country. Many days, he turned around at the covered bridge, but today he skated beneath it, ducking unnecessarily, and continued on.

He wished he thought about Jordana less – especially now, with Angie struggling. He saw Angie almost every evening, sad visits where his daughter slumped in a chair, listless but irritable, easily provoked to tears. He'd bought her a small portable stereo, and he brought CDs with him, Bach and Mozart. Sometimes they just sat together, listening to the music, and he held her hand.

But even on good nights when his daughter had seemed happy to see him, and even on bad nights when she sank into misery so deep she barely seemed to know he was there, on the car ride home he would find that – like a stylus dropping into the worn groove of a record – he'd moved back into thinking of his wife. If her love for him at first had been less overwhelming, he thought, marriage might ultimately have disappointed her less. But if her love for him had been less overwhelming, they would never have married.

Near Syria, the river became so shallow that boulders interrupted the ice's surface. He skated between them for another half mile, until the number of rocks, and the softness of ice surrounding them, forced him to turn around.

He'd met Em, the woman he'd lived with before Jordana, at Juilliard. This was the late sixties and modern dance was still relatively new, Greenwich Village still relatively cheap. They had an apartment there, two small rooms plus a tiny closet that held only a toilet; the bathtub was in the kitchen. It was fashionable to reject the institution of marriage, the drive to make money. Pieter had taken secret pride in the knowledge that he and Em had rejected those things not out of rebellion or fashion but out of genuine disinterest. For both of them, art eclipsed everything else. Their relationship had been one of friendship, of good sex. They had even looked something alike: pale, lanky. At moments, he was stirred by her, as when Em woke in the morning and stretched. Casually, she'd touch her forehead to her shin, cupping her long feet – veined and knotty as a hundred-year old woman's – with her hands.

When Pieter told her he was falling in love with the daughter of Jordan Cohen, he'd trusted Em to do what she did: stare at him out of those green-gray eyes, then cut him off mid-sentence with, 'Okay.'

In the middle of the night, though, he woke to find her shaking next to him. 'Em?' He reached to touch her shoulder and she jerked away. Then suddenly she turned and kissed him. If she'd been crying it had been without tears: her face was dry. She kissed him, groping for his penis, a knee on his hip. He was relieved.

When he was inside her, she asked him to hit her.

'Emily. Jesus.'

In the Grace Kelly voice, she said, 'I think you owe it to me to do what I want.'

'You want me to hit you?'

'I want you to hurt me.' She pushed back his hips so that he slid out of her, then turned onto her stomach. He moved back into her, trying to thrust as hard as he could, hoping that would be enough.

'Hurt me,' Em said, and he did the only thing he could imagine, taking hold of her hair, wrapping it around his hand, pulling her head back sharply so that her throat was bared. He didn't want to do it, and he didn't want it to excite him but it did, driving into Em without gentleness, jerking back her head. She was crying out, and then he realized she was crying, and he let go of her hair and tried to cover her body with his own, trying to push his face down into the space between her neck and shoulder, trying to kiss her, saying, 'Em, I'm sorry, I'm sorry, God, I'm so sorry.'

'Get off me.' She rolled from under him, stood, and crossed the room. The two rooms weren't separated by a door, only by the curtain they'd hung across the doorframe. It came to him that he wasn't sure he could afford to live here alone. There was the click of her lowering the toilet seat. He could hear her peeing, a noise that had delighted him when they first moved here.

Now he skated beneath the Park Street Bridge. Turning, he did the last quarter mile backward, neck twisted so he could look over his left shoulder. He skated as fast as he could, slowing after he passed the car. Coasting, he bent to catch his breath, gloved hands on knees.

At the riverbank he stumbled. Finding the rubber guards in his pocket, he slid them back onto the blades. Cumbrous again, he clumped to the car.

'Don't grip so hard,' he told his newest student, a bank teller. He adjusted her hand on the frog of the bow so that she held it in just her fingertips.

She complained, 'It feels all floppy.'

'You need to bow with the wrist, not with the fingers.' Together, they sawed again through the first eight bars of *Anna Magdalena Bach*. 'Your D is flat,' he said, moving her pinkie forward on the A string. 'Now play the note. Hear the difference?'

Lena nodded tentatively. She was a nice young woman who had told him that her dream was to learn to play the cello. He wasn't being patient enough with her; next week or the next she would call to quit, sounding determined and (this part would be painful for him) embarrassed. Students had been quitting for the first time in his teaching; in the past he'd often worried, in fact, that he was too supportive and understanding, to the detriment of the music. He needed students, but suddenly he couldn't find it in himself to be nicer.

219

Grasping Lena's pinkie, he moved it to D-sharp and said, 'Play.' Then he moved her finger to a correct D, then a D sharp, with his hand pressing her finger hard against the string. 'Now you try. Hear? Wait, stop. You're holding the bow too hard again.' Exasperated, he took the bow away and handed her a pencil. 'See how you hold this? The bow needs to be held the same way. If you try to choke it, the notes will come out choked as well.' He took the pencil away, thrust the bow at her. 'Try again.'

He usually loved teaching adults; their ambitions were small, they practiced dutifully, and they didn't expect unrealistic progress. They would frown as they played a difficult passage, one they'd struggled with for weeks maybe, then beam at his praise. In contrast, the younger students – he taught four high-schoolers who came to him from all over the state, and one fifth grader – each believed they would one day be famous, and this meant they took Pieter's corrections with faint skepticism. Two of the high-schoolers practiced fiendishly, but the other two got by mostly on talent. The most gifted, a chunky girl who wore thick glasses and reeked of cigarettes, often came to lessons and sight-read pieces she should have been practicing for a week. Her boyfriend lurked out at the curb, waiting for her to finish

Pieter said to Lena, 'Try one more time.'

'I can't play it anymore.'

He just looked at her. She ducked her head, breathed in, and played the first four bars. He interrupted her: 'Your D is still flat. Don't you hear that? Never mind.' He sank back into his chair. 'Enough for today.'

Lena packed her rented cello – orange-stained wood, fingerboard dyed black to look like ebony – into its canvas case. She wrote a check, not looking at Pieter, and held it out without meeting his eyes. Outside, the afternoon folded in upon itself, light fading.

Pieter said, 'I know that I'm pushing you very hard. But it's because—' Because his soul rattled in his body, dry and trapped? Because she filled one more hour that would otherwise have been spent knocking blindly around his house? 'You have talent,' he lied.

She looked at him. 'Really? I thought . . . I always sound so bad.'

If he said, *no, no, you truly have talent,* he'd inspire her for weeks. He wasn't able, though, to give her more than, 'These cheap rented instruments.' He pulled his lips back: a smile. 'Next week?'

220

Chapter Twenty-Nine

Nine at night. They ate dinner in the kitchen, a pizza Luke's parents had picked up on the way home from the hospital. Out the wide back window the moon hung low and heavy in the sky.

His mother had spent the afternoon on the phone with the insurance company. 'Plus they say she should be an outpatient, but they won't say they'd pay for treatment even if she *was*.'

'Have you explained to them—' his father started.

'Of course I've explained to them! I've spent the last two weeks fighting with them while you've fussed with Mahler.'

Shoving away from the table, his father crossed the kitchen and pushed through the door so that it swung noisily in his wake.

Luke's mother put her hand over her eyes and said, 'Shit.' She rubbed her temples. 'Now he's going to play Dvořák.'

'The last time I was home it was Elgar.'

'Now it's Dvořák. There.'

The first notes rose from the living room. His mother ate a couple of bites, then put the pizza down. 'I can't eat to this music. It's just too sad.' Jumping up, she pushed open the kitchen door, leaving Luke alone.

She would stand in the hall outside the living room now. She got the most reluctant expression on her face when she watched his father play the cello, like he was talking her into something.

Luke had bought cigarettes the other day on the way back from the hospital and he lit one now, ashing onto his greasy plate. He felt homesick for Madison. Even for being at the hospital with Angie. He wished Wendy were with him, and at the same time he felt strangely pissed at her, going on with her life when he'd had to put his on hold.

Loneliness won out. He crossed the kitchen and dialed her number.

'I feel awful,' Wendy whispered. 'I feel awful all the time.'

He'd never heard her cry before. He closed his eyes, pressing the phone so tightly to his ear it hurt. 'It's okay. It's okay.' There were other things he should say, but they felt remote and muffled, as though he had a head cold. 'What is it?'

'It's nothing, I just – I'm . . . I'm . . . It's nothing.'

'Are you *seeing* someone?'

Silence. Then, in a rush: 'You don't know when you're coming back. You won't even say you *are* coming back—'

'I'm coming back.' Anger swam through his chest, something heavy and slick.

'You disappeared. You didn't even say—'

'My sister almost *died*.'

'I shouldn't have told you.'

His anger finally caught and held. 'It hasn't even been two months. I can't believe you.'

'I can't talk about this anymore,' she said. The line went dead.

He threw the handset of the phone across the room; it hit the fridge, bounced on the floor, and skittered, spinning, underneath the table. He stomped across the dark kitchen. He tried sitting down again but jumped up at once. *Fuck!* He kicked a cabinet door, then kicked it again.

'Luke?' His mother stood in the kitchen doorway, dark hair frizzed around her face.

It seemed her fault, somehow, that his girlfriend was cheating. 'Leave me alone.'

'Was the call about Angie?'

'*No*.' He turned and kicked the cabinet again, hard enough for the wood to crack.

'Stop it!' His mother had her hands over her ears, and he turned and kicked again as hard as he could.

At the Y, he turned on lights briefly as they passed rooms – the weight machines flickered into view, dimmed, then flared into clear trued lines as the fluorescent tubes came on. The next room had a wall of mirrors, and for a moment they reflected Luke, Cole, Khamisa, and Warren, looking small, framed by the doorway.

222

Luke's status at the Y was made hazy by the fact that he'd worked two summers ago as Assistant Pool Manager; he stepped in automatically now when there was a problem, and he had privileges – a desk, keys – that most instructors wouldn't have. He flicked off the light in the weight room and continued down the hall. 'I'll show you my office.' He unlocked the office, flipped on the lights.

'This is nice, Voorster.'

'The Y palace.' His desk, one of four in the room, was the gray metal kind high school teachers had. Working there during the day, if he stood up suddenly and cracked his knee on the underside, the desk reverberated, an echoing rumble. On the walls hung faded pictures of famous swimmers holding up Olympic medals, some posters advertising swimsuits and goggles, and other posters with vague success slogans. There was even a grim black-on-white NO PAIN, NO GAIN.

Every time he thought of Wendy, it felt like taking a step and pitching down a staircase. He couldn't believe she'd cheated on him.

He and Cole sat on the desk, Khamisa and Warren on the floor. They passed a joint around. Even though the other three were all at UNH, they didn't hang out together, except when Luke came home.

Warren had stopped swimming and joined a frat; he'd gotten jowly. He asked Cole, 'Where'd you get this stuff?'

'Remember that guy, Hideo Fugimoro?'

'The Chinese guy?'

'Japanese,' Luke said. 'Hideo *Fugimoro*.'

'We didn't all go away to UW,' Warren said.

'Yeah, but it doesn't even sound Chinese.'

Khamisa lay back on the floor, looking at the pimply ceiling tiles. She said, 'He should use a nickname. I mean, every time you hear it, you think *hideous*. Not because *he's* hideous.'

'Well, it's his *name*,' Luke said. Taking the joint from Cole he inhaled, feeling the rasp of smoke in his throat. He sucked saliva from the inside of his cheeks and swallowed; for some reason that helped him hold the smoke down. He exhaled. 'Water?'

'It's here.' Khamisa handed him the cup she'd filled at the water fountain. Their breakup had been drawn out without being bitter. During his first year of college, they used to hook up over vaca-

223

tions, and there was still a pleasant tension when they were together.

Cole rolled another joint on the desk between his thighs, licking the edge delicately to seal it. 'You looked just like a cat doing that,' Luke said.

'Thanks, hippie boy.' Cole reached over and flicked Luke's ponytail.

He began to feel the pot in his cheeks and elbows, which hollowed out, becoming light and buzzy. Cole grinned at him and tilted his head, bringing the joint's tip down to the flame of his lighter. He still sometimes dressed like he lived in the fifties, but no longer like a greaser: he had heavy black-framed glasses and rayon shirts that he buttoned all the way up to his Adam's apple.

Luke announced, 'I knew a girl in Madison whose name was Dung.' He took a hit. Holding the smoke down in his lungs meant his voice came out a squawk. 'Vietnamese.'

Khamisa held the joint out to Warren, but Warren was laughing. 'Dung,' he said, waving the joint away. 'You go halfway across the country to meet girls named Dung.'

Luke hadn't actually known her; she was in two of Wendy's classes. Wendy. She was too much in control of herself to be the type of person to hang up. For that matter, he hadn't imagined she could cheat on him.

He jumped up and went into the pool room, turning on the underwater lights. The room was cavernous and smelled sharply of chlorine. Water cast squirming shadows on the ceiling. It smelled of all the winter mornings he'd come here with his sister. Before Angie got her license his mother drove them here in the morning, and by the end of high school Angie had had Abe's Galaxie. But it was those first months of Ange driving – borrowing his mom's car, the months before her first hospitalization – that he remembered most.

Driving, Angie had worn her letter jacket, red and black. She used to pull the bench seat forward as far as it would go, and she drove about ten miles below the speed limit. When he complained, she jammed the accelerator all the way down. The car jerked forward and she swerved into the other lane, then back into their own.

'Jesus, what are you doing?'

'I'm a drunk driver,' she said. She jerked the wheel left again,

224

so that they slid into the path of an oncoming Buick, then past, onto the shoulder. Gravel spit against the undercarriage of the car and she laughed, twisting the wheel back to the right. She stayed in the wrong lane this time, accelerating. A van had honked and swerved and Angie had screamed, *'Pussy!'* yanking the car right. She'd been manic, of course. But at the time: God, he'd hated and admired her.

Stripping to his boxers, Luke dove into the water, going down and down. He closed his eyes, and when he opened them again he didn't know which direction was up. The underwater lamps lit the pool yellow and green, his friends' bodies gliding black around him, sleek as sharks. With his hands he pushed himself around in a circle until he began to laugh in the turbulence of water and then choked. Choking, he rose up and broke the surface of the water with a sound like cracking glass.

He treaded water, tasting chlorine in his nose. Cole was doing somersaults down in the shallow end, rolling over and over. Next to Cole, Khamisa leaned weakly against the side of the pool, hiccuping with laughter. Luke let himself sink until his ears were submerged. He could hear the *shush, shush* of blood passing through his heart's valves. He lay back in the water. Through the skylight's thick plastic, the sky appeared murky. A star blinked, then reappeared: a plane, moving slowly across the square of sky. Still on his back, Luke used his arms to push himself through the water, staying beneath the plane. It disappeared for a long time and when it reappeared in the next skylight, he exhaled in relief, although in the time he'd been waiting he'd forgotten what he was waiting for.

'Hey,' Cole said. 'Hey.'

Luke startled and looked down to the shallow end, but Cole was next to him. Cole said, 'Let's play Marco Polo.'

Luke was laughing too much to swim well. He struck out for the middle of the pool and closed his eyes. He could hear the lap of the filters, the soft splashing of his friends as they treaded water. The pumps chugged softly.

'Hey, Voorster. You're supposed to try to find us.'

'Marco,' he called, and from three sides around him came responses. He struck out in the direction of Khamisa's voice; she shrieked and dove beneath him. Her hair brushed the sole of his foot, whispery.

225

Later, he thought about getting out of the pool, and then he lost some time, and then he found himself in one of the long chairs. His toes: really hairy. With a finger, he tried to make the hairs all go in the same direction. 'Luke?' Khamisa said, and he jumped.

She wore black cotton underpants and a blue cotton bra, nipples hard against the fabric. Her arms were crossed at the wrist, hands clasped. She asked, 'You okay?'

'I'm okay. I just got kind of freaked out.'

She dropped to the floor. Even wet, her hair was curly.

'Yeah.' She laughed. The laugh came out like a piece broken off from something larger.

'What?' he said.

'What what?'

He leaned toward Khamisa, put his hand to the side of her face. He felt its wetness, the sharp angle of her cheekbone. Closing his eyes, he leaned forward to kiss her.

She jerked back. 'What? Did you have a fight with your girl-friend?'

He opened his mouth but didn't know what to say.

Khamisa said, 'Fuck you.' Jumping up, she ran toward the pool and dove in.

On the day Angie got thirty-minute off-ward privileges, he took her down to the little lobby restaurant. It had almost the same food as the basement cafeteria, but the space was smaller and there was a waitress.

Angie had a new habit of carrying a small notebook everywhere. Periodically, she glanced at the clock and scribbled something down. Maybe she had to keep track of symptoms for her doctor.

'Do you want breakfast food?' he asked.

'You order.'

'But what do you want?'

She shrugged.

'My treat,' he said.

She shook her head, which didn't seem like a *no* to what he'd said so much as just helplessness.

'Okay, I'll order,' he said. He'd wanted this to feel like a cele-bration, her first time off-ward, but he felt so beaten up it was hard to keep his voice cheerful.

The waitress came over, a woman in her forties with red hair held back by child's barrettes: blue bunny on one side, yellow *Sunday* on the other. Her eyebrows had been plucked out and redrawn, a high, thin red pencil line.

When she'd taken their order and left, Luke said, 'Did you see her eyebrows?'

'Yeah.' Angie picked up a napkin and began shredding it. 'I can't tell anymore what's fashion and what's mental illness.'

He started to laugh, then worried that she hadn't been joking. Bloated with drugs, her eyes were almost invisible, her hair drab and unwashed. She looked at the clock, opened the notebook, and wrote something down.

When she put down the pen, he took her hand. 'This is nice, isn't it?'

He could see the effort she made to say, 'We haven't been here before, have we?'

'It's your first day of privileges.'

She nodded and withdrew her hand. Glancing at the clock – four-thirty – she opened the notebook again to write something.

'Hey look at this,' he said. He held out his winter parka to show her the label: *Bi-polar*. She just nodded. He said, 'Isn't that funny?'

Angie shredded another napkin. The restaurant was nearly empty. A sales rep at a table near theirs was taking the week's order of sausage and frozen hash browns. He was about Angie's age and overdressed in a suit.

She said, 'He's doing the most basic thing, and I couldn't even do it. I couldn't do what she's doing—' she nodded at the waitress, '—or what you're doing—'

'I'm probably still going to be at the Y when I'm thirty,' said Luke.

'Yeah, well I'll probably still be making picture frames out of popsicle sticks.' It was the first time she'd even kind of smiled. Then the corners of her mouth crumpled in. She put her hands up to her forehead.

'You won't, Angie. You're so much better already—'

'I don't have anything,' she said.

The words that rose to his mouth were platitudes. He was too depressed to try to reply.

The waitress came over, slid plates onto the table: buttered toast, fried eggs rimmed in greasy lace. Dipping a hand into her short

227

apron, she pulled out their check, slid it between the napkin holder and the sugar.

'This looks good, doesn't it?' Luke said with absurd cheer. He'd gotten a side order of bacon and he lifted a strip, stiff and maroon.

The overdressed salesman was standing up, closing his expensive briefcase. Angie picked up a piece of toast, tore off a corner. She lifted it toward her mouth, then put it down on the plate instead. She tore off another piece, then another, shredding the toast the way she had the napkin.

He said, 'Come on, this is good. Try the eggs.'

Pushing back from the table, she said, 'I've got to pee.' She walked like someone looking for a bathroom in a bar, unsteady and lost.

The way the waitress poured coffee without looking – decaf with her left hand and regular with her right – reminded him of Wendy. She carried the cups over to two doctors who were just sitting down. 'How've you been?' one asked her.

'Oh, honey.' She pulled the order pad from her apron, shaking her head. 'Honey, if I was any happier I'd be two people.'

Luke pulled Angie's notebook toward himself, opening it a crack and tilting his head to see her writing.

7:50	Eating room
8:02	Breakfast late
8:14	toast, eggs, banana
8:40	pills (o.j.)
	No seconds on eggs. Nurse says: kitchen's fault.
9:03	*A.M. Show*
	news
	Christian Slater
	Mosaic table
	Saving money
	(bathroom, 9:23, back 9:26)
	Senator Palmer (Rep., AZ): More prisons, America's schools for Americans.
	more news
	pets/ seniors
	tomorrow: Susan Lucci, homemade baby food
10:00	Group
10:06	Group hasn't started. Linda crying, needs shot.
11:02	Mom calls from work.

228

He flipped back a page, and then another: more lists. His scalp went cold. In one place, she'd made a list of facts he'd told her about his job; the notebook was her memory.

'What are you doing?'

He startled and yanked his hand back. Angie stood in front of him, arms hanging by her sides. He opened his mouth.

She was trying to control her face. The corners of her mouth jerked. 'You looked.'

'I just – it was—' He stopped, hating himself.

'I can't believe you.'

He put his head down on the table, which smelled of bleach. God, did he have to fuck *everything* up? 'I'm sorry.'

'I want to go back.'

He looked up at her. 'Please eat something. I barely read it. Really, I'm sorry.'

Angie wiped her eyes roughly with the palm of her hand. 'And really, I want to go back.' Her eggs, toast shredded like confetti across the top, were still warm, faint wisps of steam rising into the air above.

Chapter Thirty

The night before Angie's discharge from the hospital, Jordana was jarred awake by excitement and panic. Pieter wasn't in bed; she found him in the dark kitchen, eating a cold red potato over the sink. He turned and looked at her briefly, then sprinkled salt on his potato and ducked his head to eat. Jordana pressed her forehead to the back window, watching the snow.

The next morning, Luke went with them to Hayslip-Balsbrough, though discharges were lengthy and bureaucracy-filled events. Their insurance had finally agreed to pay; then, midway through Angie's course of ECT treatments, had declared that her status was no longer 'critical' and had halted payments. Parts of the bill – tens of thousands of dollars – were on Pieter and Jordana's credit cards; though she had no idea how they'd pay them off; other parts were covered; other parts were going through the appeals process.

The hospital lobby had a tall tree and an elementary-school chorus singing carols. On the ward, paper chains festooned the nurses' station. Drugstore Santa cutouts and one faded paper menorah covered the hallway walls. Visible through the glass of the nursing station stood a small fake tree, its lights flashing. Beneath it were boxes wrapped identically in red paper, decorative rather than actual presents.

'Christmas isn't tomorrow, is it?' Jordana asked her husband.

'Day after.'

Angie sat on her bed next to her packed suitcase, and this small detail – Angie had packed her own suitcase – made Jordana's heart fill with pity and gratitude.

After they'd helped Angie fill out all the discharge paperwork, she and Pieter met with Dr. Geary, who had a dark tan. He wore gold cuff links and said things like, 'Discontinuation of lithium means a potential decrease in effectiveness, even at an equivalent dose.'

Jordana asked, 'What does that mean?'

Dr. Geary said, 'If she goes off lithium again, she's screwed.'

Jordana had Angie's scrips: a higher dose of lithium, Inderal to control side effects, and a new antipsychotic. 'She'll need to have her blood levels tested weekly for both lithium and Clozaril.' Dr. Geary stood up and put out his hand to be shaken. 'Her memory should return to normal within six months.'

Walking down the hall toward the social room, she said to Pieter, 'My God, what a prick.' She looked at the scrips she still clutched. 'This is so much medicine.'

'Jordana,' Pieter said. 'Jordana, look at me.'

Unwillingly, she turned. Putting his hands on her upper arms, he said, 'If these meds don't work ... It's not all or nothing. You think it is, but it's not.'

'I just ... there will be side effects, and she hates antipsychotics so much, and this is barely even *tested*—'

'Whatever happens, we'll make it through.'

'Aren't you worried?'

He said, 'Of course I'm worried.'

There had been times she almost envied her daughter's hospitalization. She imagined letting go of self-possession, falling into the hands of people who would take care of her. With her new relief, though – Angie was coming home! – she realized how much she hated the psych ward. Angie would live at home for a while; then maybe she'd move out but stay in Cort, or near Cort. She might get a job cooking again, take a class at New Hampshire State. It sounded to Jordana like a good life, a sustainable one. She wanted so badly for it to work that she was scared to think about it.

The children's choir had moved up to this floor. They sang 'Joy to the World' in the mostly empty meetings room. As she and Pieter passed, she glanced in; most of the kids still had the earnest I-am-a-winsome-creature expressions she'd noticed earlier, in the lobby, but a few looked overwhelmed. Their audience consisted of one young woman who kept touching her face, and one woman who sat in the meetings room all day filling out her Day Runner. 'I can't see you at one o'clock,' she was saying, causing some of the children to falter. 'I might have a space open next week.'

At the end of the corridor, the social room was smoggy with cigarette smoke. Angie and Luke stood and came forward, shapes wavering in the haze. When they were close enough, their outlines steadied. Jordana caught her breath: Angie was a woman. Big breasts and wide hips, her heaviness no longer a stage but the person she'd settled into being. Pale, tentative, hand shaking as she stubbed out her cigarette, but sane. Herself.

'Let's get your bag,' Pieter said.

'I'll get it—' Jordana and Luke both said, then looked at each other.

Angie followed Pieter down the hall, leaving Jordana with Luke. As clearly as if it were happening, she saw Luke reaching out, putting his arm around her the way he did to Angie. Instead, he looked away, cracking his knuckles.

Angie reemerged from her room and Luke jumped forward to take her bag. As he took it, he pretended the weight was making him stagger. 'What's in here?'

'I'm smuggling out another patient.'

There. She was back.

Luke sat in the backseat, next to his sister. Being driven, able to see the road only at a distance, he felt small and uncomfortably submissive. In Angie's hand was a crumpled piece of paper; at her request, they'd stopped for coffee in Hanover. Leaving the shop, she'd frozen just past a kiosk, then turned back: a flyer, water-stained and faded, but her face still recognizable above MISSING – ILL – MAY BE DISORIENTED.

'You're fucking *kidding* me,' she'd muttered, yanking it down.

He'd almost said, 'One down, five thousand to go,' but thought better of it.

In front, his parents were silhouetted against December's snow-brilliant light. His mother leaned over the seat. 'What do you want for your first dinner home, Ange?'

'I don't know.'

'There must be something you missed on the ward. Steak?'

'She's vegetarian, Ma.'

'Still?'

'I was thinking maybe we should do Christmas shopping tomorrow,' his father said into the rearview mirror. 'I know I haven't done any of my shopping yet.'

232

Luke imagined Wendy walking to class, pale skin flushed, books held to her chest, long red hair flowing behind her. No, she'd be home for Christmas. His love for her seemed clearer now than it had been when they were together and happy. He imagined being with her somewhere, a room with a fireplace and dogs, imagined curling up on the floor with his head in her lap. And then, an image of her as he'd really seen her, resting one foot on the sink, bending her small strong body forward, using a cheap pink razor to shave her calf.

If Angie was better, he could go back to Wisconsin soon.

He loved Wendy. Sometimes he felt he loved Cole. He loved his parents. But Angie was the only person who sometimes, when he looked at her, made him feel a love that was like happiness and distress colliding in his chest. She'd called him selfish that time, and it *was* selfish, wanting her to get better for his sake, not her own. He would stay if she needed him to.

But maybe she wouldn't need him to?

In the front seat, his mother said, 'Look.' He opened his eyes: the nativity scene Christian high-schoolers staged in front of the clinic every year as a protest. Trees made blue shadows against the snow. Today had been warm, and in places the snow had melted back so that the earth showed through, cracked like old leather. The manger scene used real animals, a cow, a goat, two sheep.

At the house, Angie said, 'Oh, hey, is that your car?'

'Yeah.' Luke smiled goofily, despite himself; he loved his car.

'Nice.'

Luke said, 'I have something for you.'

She followed him upstairs, to his room. He pulled the package from his desk drawer. It was her Christmas present, but it suddenly seemed like a good idea to give it to her early.

'What is it?'

'Open it.'

He'd bought her a watch, a man's because she didn't like dainty things. He'd used almost all the money he'd earned at the Y. The jeweler had removed three of the wristband's heavy metal links and then slid the watch over his own small, clean hand. Scratchproof, waterproof to 500 feet, accurate to fifteen seconds a year. At the top of the face was a small window in which the sun, then the moon, rose and fell.

'*Luke,*' she said.

233

'If you don't like it you can return it.' It was an almost-logical reason for giving her the watch early, except that he hadn't thought of it until just now.

She touched the face, the size of a quarter.

'The moon goes through its real phases; it waxes and wanes.' She didn't say anything, lips pressed together. 'The jeweler kept pointing me toward the "young ladies' watches."' Still nothing. She hated it. 'Really, if something else would be better. You won't offend me.'

'This is the best present anyone has ever given me,' she said.

Pieter pulled down the narrow ladder that led to the attic. Climbing up, he tread gingerly through the beams and yellowed insulation the color of freezer rime to the boxes of Christmas tree ornaments. Dusty light, partially blocked by an old dresser, drifted from a low window. The attic smelled sweetly of mothballs and dry rot.

As Pieter turned with the first box in his arms, Luke was just coming up, emerging slowly: head, shoulders, torso, hips, feet. He and Pieter edged past each other, and then Pieter made his way back down the ladder, one-handed. His son followed him, more quickly. Luke had a box under his right arm; he jumped backward a few rungs from the bottom, to land – graceful, thudding – in the hallway.

The bare tree stood in the living room, already shedding its needles. Luke and Angie had made most of the ornaments in grade school: paper chains, the red and white links faded to the same pinky-beige; Styrofoam balls that, as they were lifted from their boxes, rained glitter and chips of yellowed glue onto the floor.

'Who wants something to drink?' Jordana asked. 'We have eggnog. Or beer?'

Luke said, 'Maybe eggnog.'

'It's virgin nog.'

'Sounds obscene,' said Angie.

Pieter laughed, too hard, and stopped when he heard that Jordana and Luke were also laughing too hard.

At the hospital, when he'd gone with Angie to get her suitcase, she'd stood for a moment frozen in her room. 'Daddy?'

'Yes?' He'd picked her suitcase up from the bed.

'I'm okay here.' She didn't look at him. 'I think I should maybe stay.'

234

Gently, he'd said, 'Your mother and Luke are waiting for us.'

The words came out severe, embarrassingly dry, when he'd meant them to sound simple and undramatic. He'd meant to acknowledge Angie's fear and also her courage; had meant to communicate that life could be almost unbearable, but you bore it.

Jordana, handing him a cup of eggnog, said, 'I wish you didn't have to play tonight.'

He wished he could stay too, though he wondered, if staying were a possibility, whether Jordana would still want him to.

Angie and Luke argued over which of them, in kindergarten, had made the better pipe-cleaner angel. His wife put her arm around his waist. He sipped the sweet eggnog, which came from a carton and tasted like melted ice cream. He would have to leave in twenty minutes, but for a moment he let himself relax; for once he let himself accept contentment without asking that it last.

Six P.M., long past dark. On the ward, they would be lining up for dinner, each picking up her tray from the rack and taking it into what was called the breakfast room, though it was also the lunch and dinner room. Despite being the focus of much of the afternoon ('What do you think's for dinner?'), the meal itself was usually over in ten minutes for all but catatonics. Half an hour from now, at six-thirty, the nurse would turn on *Jeopardy!* The windows had wire inside the glass, cross-sectioning the outside world into dozens of small octagons: manageable pieces. The same kind of glass fronted the nurses' station, making it seem like a fragment of outside world brought inside.

That the nursing station was glass on all sides made Angie think of a museum case. Exhibit 1: Nurses eating their wan salads, or an extra dinner tray someone didn't want. Exhibit 2: Nurses writing down everything you said in the log.

Stop it. She was thinking crazy. Going over to the couch, she sat down and sipped from her virgin nog, which had the consistency of Elmer's glue.

Cole came through the front door, his dark hair and the shearling collar of his coat glittering with snow. He shook his head, and tiny water droplets flew in every direction. He seemed more handsome every time Angie saw him. Raising the silver foil icicles he'd brought, he said, 'Ho, ho, ho.'

'I'm going to put on carols,' Angie's mother said, jumping up

235

to turn on the radio. As she fiddled with the knob, the room filled for a moment with music from the *Nutcracker*. Everyone but Cole groaned.

'Should we listen to this?' her mother asked, making her face serious.

'What is it?' asked Cole.

'"The guests depart – the children go to bed – the magic begins,"' said Pieter. 'Please change it, Jordie.'

Angie and Luke glanced at each other, brows raised; their father never used pet names.

Cole sat next to Angie on the couch. Beneath his unbuttoned coat he wore a plaid flannel shirt and jeans worn to white thread at the knees. As he bent to unlace his boots, his hair falling into his face, she smelled the tang of his soap. For a moment, longing – not exactly for Cole, she didn't know for what – stuck in her throat.

'So you're a logger now,' Angie said, about his clothes.

Cole shrugged. 'How are you?'

'Mental.'

Cole laughed. 'No, how are you really?'

Did he even remember that they'd fucked that time, in the shower room? 'Really mental.'

'I made that in second grade,' Luke was saying about an orna-ment Pieter held, Popsicle sticks in the shape of a listing star. 'It has to go on.'

Angie found the remote control between two cushions. Channel 8, 7, 6.

'Ange?' said her mother.

She turned her head. They were all standing very still, looking at her.

Angie said, 'It's time for *Jeopardy!*'

'It's your first night home,' her mother said, looking stricken. 'Here, come get more eggnog with me.'

'I'm tired.'

'Help me with the angel,' her father said.

Luke jumped to get the stepladder. 'I'll help with the angel.'

'I asked Angie.'

Luke was standing very still, a glass bulb in one hand. 'Why don't you leave her alone?'

'Never mind,' Angie said. 'Never mind. I'll get the fucking eggnog.'

When she came back into the room, someone – probably her mother – had turned the TV off. Cole had escaped to the other side of the room. Her father held the small ladder steady and Luke, on the last step, stretched toward the top of the tree. Jordana came over and hugged Angie, the cardboard eggnog carton awkward between them.

On *Jeopardy!* there was a rhythmic way the answers came first, the questions second:

This Baltic nation lies between Estonia and Lithuania.

Where is Latvia?

This part of the brain controls involuntary nervous functions such as breathing.

What is the medulla oblongata?

Her mother moved away, pouring eggnog. Angie put her hand around the new watch on her wrist, grounding herself.

This writer's actual name was Samuel Clemens.

Twain, Mark Twain.

Luke was struggling to make the angel fit. The tree was so high he had to bend the top branch.

Please rephrase that as a question.

Who is Twain?

Luke tried different angles: The top branch bent forward, so the angel seemed to be bowing; sideways, so the angel lay on her flank. Across the room, Jordana raised her mug to Angie. A toast, but one that contained wariness, warning, as though she meant, *Please be okay.* In return, Angie raised her own mug, wondering how to say *I will.*

Chapter Thirty-One

Wendy stayed at school during winter break, taking a bus home just for a couple of days around Christmas. Her younger sister, Julie, got engaged; her father's drinking seemed worse. She was back in Madison in time to work New Year's Eve, a good night for tips. Classes started mid-January. She avoided the guys she'd slept with last semester. She worked on Valentine's, which waiters called Amateur Night; the restaurant filled with couples who weren't used to going out to dinner. They had exaggerated visions of what the night would be and took out romantic disappointment on their servers. Still, Wendy made close to two hundred dollars.

She hadn't heard from Luke since mid-December. When he'd been here, her life had seemed full: boyfriend, studying, friends, work, dinners in her crowded kitchen, all the people on campus she knew by sight and greeted. If asked then, she would have said that she steadied Luke, not the other way around. She wouldn't have guessed that his leaving – like a log removed from the bottom of a pile – would make everything else fall over, showing wormy undersides.

Her best friend, Kim, said things like, 'You know, I'm totally here if you want to talk.' She had a deep raspy voice, at odds with her pert nose and neat brown ponytail. She sat cross-legged on her flowered bedspread, beneath the Doisneau poster of a man and woman kissing in the street. 'Freshman year, when John and I broke up, I was completely depressed.'

'I'm not depressed.' Wendy didn't turn from her Selectric, where she was typing a history paper about the Belgian Congo. She could have said that she and Luke hadn't exactly broken up, but she didn't want to open the conversation any wider. Loneliness vibrated inside her all the time, a motor in her chest. But to let her friends see how pathetically she longed to throw herself at them would be even worse than being lonely.

In the first two months after Luke left, she'd slept with seven people, most of whom she barely knew. Each time, she'd felt so dislodged the next day, so unlike herself, that the only way to feel better was to throw herself into a new flirtation. Over Thanksgiving in Iowa, she'd slept with her old boyfriend Steve, something she thought she'd never do; because Steve was still half in love with her, usually she kept interactions with him cheerfully casual.

After Luke guessed she was cheating, she'd stopped. She just hadn't wanted to anymore.

Kim pulled a loose thread from the comforter, wrapping it around her finger. 'Well, I'm here, if you want,' she said, sounding unhappy.

Wendy typed another line of her paper.

Luke finally called one afternoon in the last week of February and asked what she was doing. She'd been reading Kim's *Vogue,* but she said she'd been studying. 'How's your sister?'

Angie had been out of the hospital two months. She seemed stabilized. He named some new drugs she was taking that seemed to be working. Then he said, 'I'm not there, I'm here.'

He was at Cleveland's, and she walked down to meet him. Seeing him through the window, she felt – she couldn't help it – a surge of happiness. She didn't think *There he is* but *Oh.*
There you are.

She made her way past the tables of aging hippies and crew jocks. Standing, he crushed out a cigarette in the ashtray and shook back his hair. He wore a coat she didn't recognize, a high school letter jacket. Taking the edges of his jacket in both hands, she pulled herself tight against his warm, solid body. Behind her eyelids, and against her throat, she felt the pressure of tears.

'Oh, Wendy.' He stroked her hair with his big hand. 'I really missed you. It's okay. It's okay.'

She stepped back. Who was he to think he could soothe her? To cover up her annoyance, she did something cheerleadery, laughing as she flicked her hair back from her face. She slid into the chair opposite his. 'Since when have you smoked?'

'I don't know. A few months.'

239

'I've never eaten out here. When I waited, I ate in back.'

He was still puzzling out the smoking question. 'At the hospital, everyone smokes all the time. I guess I started to be social.'

She drank some water from her pebbled red plastic glass. 'So. How long have you been back? Have you seen anyone?'

He shook his head. 'I just got in. I called you as soon – all my stuff's still in the car.' He nodded toward the street outside the diner. 'I guess I'm going to get a job, see if they'll let me back in school for next fall.' He started to take another cigarette from the pack, then pushed it back in. 'Are you still . . . are you seeing—?'

If she'd been better at lying, she might have said yes, but she shook her head.

He reached across the table. 'I missed you.'

'You said that.' She pulled her hand back from his and studied the menu. When she looked up, he was looking hard at her. She smiled quickly and looked away.

'Where's our waitress?' she asked. 'I don't remember the service being this bad.'

'The service used to be great,' he said, reaching for her hand again.

She waved a waitress over. Luke ordered breakfast – besides smoking, he was drinking coffee now. Wendy shook her head and said, 'Nothing, thanks.'

'Being home was so . . . and my parents . . . At least Angie's better. There was a while when I didn't know. You've never been on a psych ward. God, Wendy, sometimes I'd think of you here, and I missed you so much, and this all seemed so unreal and pure.'

She couldn't stand him. Mildly, she said, 'I don't think it's particularly pure.'

He took her hand. 'I love you. I want to make things work.'

She pulled her hand away for a third time and stood up. 'You can't just reappear and expect I've been waiting for you.'

'Well, since you were *fucking* someone else, I know you weren't waiting for me.' Then, 'I'm sorry. Wen, I'm sorry. I don't know why I said that. Please sit down. *Please*.'

She'd wanted to hear this for months, but it didn't mean anything. She stayed standing. His eggs came and he stared at them. 'I haven't slept.'

She forced herself to be nice. 'Since when?'

'I don't know.' He put his face in his hands.

Suddenly, she couldn't stand the way she was acting. She dropped to her knees on the dirty floor next to him, putting her arms awkwardly around his body, burying her face in his stiff coat.

That afternoon, she rose from bed and looked down on Luke sleeping but couldn't summon any of the relieved tumult of the last two hours. Luke had followed her to her room and they'd made love, touching each other's faces and laughing. When Luke came, he'd cried, 'Oh, oh!' and then he'd pulled her down tight against him, his body shaking.

Sitting at her desk, she opened an anthropology textbook and tried to study. The last owner of the book had highlighted with an orange pen sections of text that seemed random to Wendy: *fluorine ... becoming common ... interglacial ... seasonally in some cases ...* Luke had cast off the blanket in his sleep; his long pale back was divided by the blue channel of his spine. Late winter afternoon; the sky was a dark, wet gray, with the streetlights haloed pale yellow against it. She copied information she needed onto index cards, got up to go to the bathroom, copied more information down. Her notes seemed messy; she hated looking at them. She threw down her pen in frustration and went into the kitchen to make toast.

When she came back in, Luke opened his eyes. 'Wen.'

She wanted to be alone. She could actually feel it in her muscles, as though she were holding them locked to keep from bolting. What was wrong with her? Luke reached out an arm from under the covers and she sat beside him. His body gave off heat. She put her nose down to his shoulder, which was round and smooth. Closing her eyes, she breathed him in, the familiar soap smell of his skin and the new burnt smell – coffee, cigarettes – of his breath.

'There's a rent party tonight,' she said, face buried in his neck. 'Do you want to go to a party?'

A dreadlocked white boy took their money. He was shirtless, fans of faint blond hair around his nipples. Behind him smirked a poster of Jerry Garcia. The boy danced as he counted back their change, head bent, bare feet stomping. A line of darker hair ran down his stomach and disappeared into his pants, which had slipped low on his slender hips. Something about the beauty of his narrow abdomen made Wendy obscurely angry – at him, at everyone there.

241

'I'll get us some beer,' Wendy said, and escaped Luke.

In the kitchen, people were sitting on countertops; one group passed a bulbous purple bong. The boy handing out beer stopped to pump the keg, then resumed filling the plastic cups held out toward him. He had long hair that he shook back from his eyes as he handed Wendy two cups of beer the color of urine and not very cold.

Out in the living room, Luke was talking to friends. She handed him his beer, standing just far enough from him that he couldn't put his arm around her.

How many parties had she spent smiling and taking sips of beer, Luke's arm over her shoulders? Luke talked easily, so that she'd felt like he covered them both; in groups with him, she didn't bother sticking to her say-something-at-least-once-every-twenty-minutes rule. He had the gift of seemingly effortless charm, a way of keeping his attention on other people without making them self-conscious. He was very social – he didn't like to be alone even to study – but he didn't show very much of himself to the people he surrounded himself with. They didn't notice because he came across just the opposite, open and up-front. People learned right away that his sister had a *serious mental illness*. They probably felt (as Wendy had) that he was revealing himself in a way that was unique and intimate, whereas Angie's illness was just such a fact of his life that he wouldn't have thought to withhold it. In return, people told him about themselves. Wendy used to see it back when he brought girls into Cleveland's for breakfast; the girls talked and talked.

Now she drank from her beer, disliking Luke. He was telling a story about teaching adults to swim, a German woman who kept panicking and throwing her arms around his neck, *Mein Gott,* nearly drowning him. People laughed. At other parties, Luke's stories had always been ones she'd heard first, which made the stories almost both of theirs. She knew what he was leaving out, what he embellished. This story was different; he'd probably told it, in an original and truer version, to Angie weeks ago.

The conversation moved on. Luke seemed happy, unhaunted by how long he'd been gone and where. He took a step toward her and she stepped back, saying, 'I'm going to the bathroom.'

In the hallway, a girl whose name she didn't remember said, 'I see Luke is back.'

242

Everyone knew Luke, thought he was great. Turning back toward the living room, Wendy could see him through the arched doorway. He was bent over with laughter.

I hate you.

The thought caught her off guard. But it also felt good, like throwing herself into bed after a night at work. *I hate you,* she said again in her head, testing the words.

Mark, one of the guys she'd slept with this fall, was at the edge of a group. She must have known he would be at this party. 'You're shitting me,' he cried. 'You're shitting me!' For a moment she wanted to duck away without his seeing her. Then she called his name. He looked up, smiled, trotted over.

At Mark's house, she lay on the futon looking up at the kitchen cabinets all around her. Mark lit candles with a plastic lighter, then rolled toward her. The apartment Mark lived in had been made out of two smaller ones, and this bedroom had once been the kitchen of the second apartment. The stove and refrigerator were gone, but a countertop ran along one wall with fake-wood cabinets above and below. One open cabinet showed Mark's folded T-shirts; the former sink held stacked issues of *Sports Illustrated* and *Rolling Stone* and the Victoria's Secret catalog. He was short and pale, cheeks bluish with five o'clock shadow. It exhausted her to think of Mark in the dank bathroom every morning, his small face canted anxiously toward his own reflection, that delicate, wary look men got when they lifted their chins, the careful scrape of razor around their Adam's apples, the vulnerability of their flat hips wrapped in a worn blue towel. Had Luke noticed yet that she'd left the party?

'You have the most beautiful hair,' Mark said.

'Why do all men love long hair?'

'I don't know. Because we don't have it?'

'Luke's hair is long.' She thought of Luke's hair in her fingers, its silkiness when it was just washed, the way that summer lightened it. Talking to boring, stupid Mark only made her feel the wrongness of being here. She wanted to leave. Instead, she lunged forward and kissed him.

And then there were all the motions. He kissed her throat, took her nipple gently in his teeth, flicking it with his tongue, until she felt herself growing wet and heavy and arched her back up toward him. Part of her mind was marveling at this, at how the body could express passion when she felt none, while at the same time she was slipping away, into an old fantasy. *Lean over the desk,* a man was saying, his hand pressing hard against her breasts. Mark moved his hand, slipping beneath the waistband of her jeans. She lifted her hips to him. *Open your legs now.* The man was lifting her skirt from behind. Mark pressed his hand against her, twisting to work his fingers beneath her underwear. *Pretty,* the man said, and she began to come, shallowly.

'Christ,' Mark said.

Through her closed lids, she saw a flash in the corner of her vision; she bucked toward Mark's hand. He stopped moving and she put her own hand over his, pressing down through her clothes.

There was a flat, metallic smell, and Mark said, 'Oh, *shit,*' and hit her, a glancing, indirect blow that just skimmed her cheek.

'What are you doing?' she screamed.

'Shit! *Shit!*' He was tugging beneath her head, pulling out the pillow and whumping it down against her face. For a moment it covered her mouth; she smelled cotton and detergent and smoke; she couldn't breathe and tried to roll away. The pillow lifted, and as he started to bring it down again he gasped, 'The candle—' and she realized her hair was on fire.

She walked through the dark streets – she'd left Mark over his dim protests about girls walking alone. Reaching up, she felt her hair, which crackled and broke off in her fingers. The charred hair was black and dry like cornsilk. She felt eerily calm. Here at last was something concrete, something to cope with.

At home, Luke was sitting on her bed. He squinted up at her, uncertain and unhappy. 'Where did you go? You just disappeared.'

Wendy turned her head.

'What *happened*?' He jumped up and put his arms around her. 'Wendy, God. Why didn't you come find me?'

He thought that her hair had gotten burnt at the party. For a moment, she was tempted to lie, to put her head on his shoulder. *I was embarrassed,* she could say.

She stepped back, raising her eyebrows. 'I was with someone else.' She wanted it to come out grand and contemptuous. Instead it sounded adolescent.

Luke said carefully, 'With.'

'Fucked,' she said. 'I was fucking someone else.'

'That guy you were seeing last fall? You were with that guy?'

'I wasn't seeing just one guy.' She took off her coat, throwing it over the back of her desk chair. 'Are you happy now? You get to be the saint again.' Luke didn't say anything. 'Aren't you even going to call me a bitch?'

He stared at her.

Shoulders back, posture carefully perfect, she stepped around him, going to the mirror over the dresser. Her hands shook. The hair looked even worse than she'd expected, with a patch of frizzled black on the right side, the left half the way it was supposed to look, a dark red curtain to her waist.

'Pass me the scissors,' she said. 'It was time for a change anyway.'

'What are you doing?' Luke said. 'I don't even know you.'

She said, 'Huh,' as if he'd said something mildly interesting. She was surprised by her own coolness. Why couldn't she be like this more often, instead of awkward and messy?

He picked up the scissors from her desk. Their eyes met in the mirror.

Suddenly her own falseness frightened her. 'Here,' she said more quietly, and held out her hand for the scissors.

'I'll do it.'

He took hold of the long side of her hair, wrapping it around one hand. Her head jerked back; she stifled a cry. He opened the blades as wide as they would go. The cold metal brushed her skin, higher than he needed to be cutting, but she didn't stop him.

The soft crunch of hair shifting against the blades, then the scissors snicked closed. Luke stepped back, hair bandaging his hand. He unwrapped the hair – it took a long time, there was so much of it – and let it fall to the floor.

She wanted to take it all back. 'Luke—'

'Shut up,' he said quietly, dropping the scissors on top of the hair.

Wendy sat on the bed, trying not to cry. If she started, she didn't think she could keep it soft, and all her housemates would hear. The swatch of hair lay over her knee; she realized she'd been stroking it like a cat.

A knock on the door; after a moment, Kim slipped in the room. 'I heard—' Her eyes went to Wendy's hair; she put her hand over her mouth. 'Oh, my heck.'

245

Kim usually spent the weekends at Ian's these days, and Wendy said, 'You're back early.'

'It wasn't such a good weekend. You?'

She'd cut off the burnt hair, which lay in a snarl on the dresser. The roomed smelled terrible, like when she had cavities drilled at the dentist. Wendy said, 'Yeah, not so good.'

It was the first time she'd admitted any unhappiness. When Kim laughed, it seemed like all Wendy had ever wanted from her.

Kim sat carefully next to Wendy on the bed. 'Your hair used to be so long.'

Sometimes on the street, strangers had come up to Wendy to tell her how beautiful her hair was. She reached up, touched the bare back of her neck. The vertebrae felt round as marbles. 'I know. I don't want to think about it.'

'I think I can straighten it out. If you want.'

Wendy nodded. She closed her eyes: Kim's hands on her hair, the tiny tug of scissors with each cut. It went on, it seemed, a long time. Kim's hands arranged her hair, then withdrew. Wendy opened her eyes.

Kim moved in front of her, checking that the hair was even. She said, 'Now people can see your face.'

Chapter Thirty-Two

Pieter sat on one of the molded plastic chairs of Cort's small airport, awaiting Gyongyi Horvath's flight from Hartford. On the runway, a man brought a stepladder out to a small plane. Under one arm he held a roll of paper towels, and the wind meant that he had to crouch over to climb, bracing himself as he sprayed the windshield with glass cleaner. He ripped paper towels off the roll and wadded them in his hand. He wore a torn blue jacket and moved with grace. As he stretched out across the windshield, Pieter thought: *Ben*.

After all this time, Pieter still didn't know how to stop being reminded of Jordana's lover. And of course it wasn't him, just a tall kid, jumping down to the pavement, shaking hair out of his face.

'Your flight's coming in,' said the woman behind the desk.

High against the hard blue sky, the nailhead plane dropped toward them. It took on features: wings, then nose cone. Pieter had met, over the last fifteen years, only a few of these flights, only when the visiting musician was a cellist, one Pieter was interested in. He didn't think Gyongyi Horvarth was a great cellist. Her playing did not quite stretch to pure euphoria or pure pain; she struck him as dramatic rather than passionate, gifted but not inspired. She was not, for example, as good as Jordan Cohen, Jordana's father, had been. She was very famous, though, and that was interesting in itself.

The boy was on the runway now, using plastic rods to guide the plane to the gate. His arms moved back, forward, back. In the landscape of black trees and sage-green hills, his orange signals were the only color.

247

Gyongyi Horvath was the second person off the plane. Pieter was holding up a piece of paper on which he'd written her name in ballpoint pen, but when he saw her he realized how unnecessary the sign was; even if he hadn't known her face from her CDs, she was carrying a cello case against her right hip. She wore a long camel-colored coat, and her short hair was cut to fall over one eye. She carried herself as though she were beautiful, shoulders back, hand extended for a sharp, almost fierce, handshake. Close up, she had three small moles on one cheek, something he didn't remember from pictures. The wings of her nostrils were chapped: a cold.

'How was your flight?'

'They barely had time to serve drinks. Up and then down again.' She used one hand to describe a quick spike in the air. She didn't thank him for picking her up. She must have been picked up from many airports. They made small talk, waiting for her luggage. Through the window, the boy was unloading baggage now, his jacket open, heaving suitcases onto the belt that brought them into the terminal. He used the back of his forearm to wipe sweat from his face.

Cort's airport had only one baggage claim. It would have been quicker, Pieter thought, to just wheel the cart into the room and let people pull their luggage off themselves, but the airport seemed to want to act out the conventions of a larger place. At least the boy wasn't also responsible for flying the planes and serving the drinks. When Gyongyi Horvath's black suitcases appeared, she pointed them out to Pieter and he stepped forward to lift them. She was carrying her cello, and he would have insisted on carrying the bags anyway, but he was struck by her assumption that he would.

They got into his car and began the drive to Cort, about twenty minutes away. He and Gyongyi talked about the orchestra, about Friday's concert. He said, 'We'll go to your hotel before dinner. Drop these things off.'

'I've been on the road for two months.' She sat forward in her seat again, turning the car's air vents with her hands. He felt cool air, then its absence. 'Hotel rooms are beginning to really depress me.'

'You could stay with us. Our son's room is empty.'

'Oh, that's nice, but I'll be fine,' she said instantly. 'I shouldn't complain. The hotel's fine.'

'Well, if you change your mind ...' He was relieved, though.

He'd made the offer without thinking about Angie; they couldn't possibly have a guest. These last three months – since Luke had gone back to school – Angie had barely left the house. She never went out on her own; if he or Jordana ran errands, she always wanted to come along but then trailed listlessly behind, complaining that it took too long.

Gyongyi said, 'I am looking forward to dinner Monday, though.'

She was still turning the vents – he thought at first she meant to adjust them, then realized she was fidgeting. Her hands were small for a cellist and strong, the nails lacquered a dark rose. He'd never understood women's painting their nails. To begin with, nails were such an odd feature, tiny bits of horn. How far down did they go, and what was the line between nail and non-nail? His own nails made him think of fish scales, flat and iridescent. His mother had used red polish, Revlon's Fatal Apple. He remembered her brushing it on slowly. Her hands had been old, with a silveriness beneath the skin. When she was alive, she had repelled him. She stole from restaurants, butter pats and sugar and jam. She emptied the bread basket into her purse and called for more – Pieter squirming in his seat, hissing, *Mother, I'll buy you bread.* She didn't steal ketchup, though: Ketchup hadn't come to Holland until the Canadian liberators brought it, and so she didn't associate it with scarcity. He'd hated the way fear kept her from leaving the block and then, increasingly, from leaving the apartment. Then from leaving even the bedroom.

His mother had never let him forget that he'd gotten out. She'd stayed and almost starved; his father had died in the bombing of a munitions factory in Germany where he'd done forced 'volunteer' labor. Only Pieter was unscathed. But he'd been six: It was hardly as though he'd chosen to desert, or as though his parents hadn't chosen to stay.

What enraged him most were his mother's stories of defiance: gluing the German stamps onto the wrong corner of the envelope, greeting acquaintances with a meaningful *O zo,* which with a heavily significant look came to stand for *oranje zal overwinnen.* Orange will triumph. Or *Hallo: hang alle landverrders op.* Hang all traitors. She presented these stories of petty resistance as evidence of courage, of what she'd endured, her face solemn and self-congratulatory beneath her flame-orange hair. When Germans came into a restaurant, the Dutch would stand and leave, until a law was passed that no one could leave a restaurant within ten minutes of a German's entrance. After that, if a German entered a restaurant, everyone would take off their watches and place them on the tables, counting off exactly ten minutes. Since her death he'd been able to pity her. During the Hunger Winter she'd eaten tulip bulbs and wallpaper paste: Of course she hoarded things, of course she wanted someone to recognize her valor. He couldn't believe pity hadn't surfaced earlier, while she was still alive. At the same time, he suspected that if she were to come back somehow, his pity would dissolve again.

Gyongyi Horvath had turned to look out the car window at the potato fields. It was June. In the rearview mirror, her suitcases filled the backseat. Day gave way to evening as fields gave way to town, to square lawns, the chink and hiss of sprinklers across the darkening grass. He imagined they were married. Gyongyi came into their kitchen in a silk concert dress, her arms around his waist, lips against the back of his neck. In this vision, simultaneously, he and Gyongyi were both who they were – Gyongyi a famous cellist, Pieter a supportive husband – and they were other people: Pieter the famous one, Gyongyi the supportive wife.

As he drove, they made conversation about the Brahms they'd play in concert the next two nights. The orchestra had been practicing with Pieter taking the solo part; Gyongyi had been playing the piece too, with different orchestras all over the East Coast. It turned out that they both loved Brahms. Of modernists, they loved Janácek and Webern, admired Schoenberg. 'You know who's severely underrated, though?' asked Gyongyi Horvath. 'Joaquín Rodrigo. A friend and I are working on transcribing the *Aranjuez* for cello.'

A brief silence fell. He tried to think what to say. The *Aranjuez* was written for the guitar. Pieter wished he'd thought first of transcribing it. Then he smiled wryly at his jealousy; he didn't even *like* the piece.

How incompatible his life was with art. He couldn't imagine Gyongyi Horvath sitting on a plastic chair at Jiffy Lube, flipping through a tattered *People* magazine while she waited for an oil change, or spending an afternoon on hold with insurance companies, or realizing the only bread in the house was starred with blue mold. He couldn't imagine her using a dull knife to scrape the

250

mold off before putting the bread into the toaster.

Jordana lay on the living room couch, reading in the near-dark,
Bean curled up by her hip. Pieter turned on the light.

'You're back.' She sat up, squinting. 'I didn't even notice it was
getting dark.' Beside her, the cat stretched, yawning so widely
Pieter could see the delicate ribbing of the roof of her mouth.

'How is she?' he asked, gesturing with his shoulder at the
ceiling, toward Angie's room.

'She's at her computer, playing that dungeon game.'

'Still?'

Jordana nodded. Leaving the book splayed face down on the couch
arm, she stood and stretched. Pieter had been wrapped up in Gyongyi
Horvath for the last five hours, and the deep familiarity of Jordana's
appearance startled him. Her body still moved him: her height, the
dungarees rolled up at the cuffs, the black cotton T-shirt so old it had
faded greenish. She had long bony feet. Pushing hair back from her
eyes, she asked, 'Have you already eaten?'

He held his wrist toward her so she could see the watch: it was
almost ten.

She said, 'Maybe I'll have some crackers and cheese. I don't
feel like cooking.'

'You never feel like cooking.'

She laughed. 'Sometimes I feel like cooking. You can't schedule flights of genius.'

'Oh, is that what they are?'

'That's what they are.' She came over and rested her head
against his chest.

He stroked her hair. 'If you could schedule a night of genius for
tomorrow ...'

'For Gonggi—'

'*Gyongyi.*'

'—*Gyongyi* Horvath. What's she like?'

What *was* she like? 'Very polished. Polite but distant. The whole
conversation was about Friday's program.'

'Was she nice?'

'Hard to say. She was playing a role.' Often, talking to Jordana
was how he knew what he thought. He spoke slowly. 'She's used
to being taken out to dinner, and used to downplaying that she's
famous and the people taking her out are not. I guess that makes

251

her nice. She was very pulled together, in a suit. She kept twisting her fingers under the table, though.' Before Jordana, he hadn't noticed details like that: the books on people's shelves, whether someone wore a wedding band (Gyongyi Horvath did not).

'Did Nita have on one of her ornate sequined things?'

'Of course.'

Jordana laughed. Her head was still resting against his chest; he lifted his hand to stroke her hair. She sighed. He imagined Gyongyi coming into the kitchen. The stiff black satin of her dress flared behind her like the wings of a skate. A small girl with dark straight-cut bangs raised her arms, asking to be lifted. It seemed to him that his whole life had gone by, elsewhere and without him.

He could feel his wife's sadness underneath their conversation, but he didn't ask about it: What more was there to say? He let go of her and stepped back. He went over to one of the bookcases that held his thousands of recordings, LPs, CDs, a few (well, less than three hundred) cassette tapes, mostly made for him by friends. He ran a finger quickly over the spines until he found the case he wanted: Gyongyi Horvath's recording of Bach's cello suites.

'I knew it.' Her moles didn't show in her pictures; they'd been covered up or airbrushed out.

Jordana didn't ask, Knew what? She cupped one elbow with the other hand.

Gyongyi Horvath's interpretation, as he remembered, was faster than the Casals recording. Pieter listened to her rendering of the fifth suite and then stopped the recording to play the suite himself. It had a mathematical precision, and yet, buried, there was incredible darkness and beauty. Standing to switch the CD, he realized Jordana had left the room. Sitting again, he played with Casals. He didn't think about what he was doing but let the music come through him, concentrating only on laying each note alongside Casals's. It was the first time in years he'd played sustainedly without self-consciousness, without awareness of time. In the final notes of the sixth suite's gigue, the bow nearly left the string with each note, and with the final note he did lift it off the string.

His elbow felt as if it were vibrating. The CD player spun down. He staggered to the kitchen and in the wan light of the refrigerator gulped water straight from its pitcher. It was ice-cold. His teeth ached.

*

252

His wife slept naked, but she'd pulled the covers up so that only one bare shoulder showed. In the faint light from the street, her shoulder was smooth and white as marble, and when he touched it its warmth surprised him. He moved his hand until the curve of her shoulder perfectly fit his palm. She didn't wake. Her dark hair fanned across the pillow.

Jordana seemed clear to him, vulnerable, her sadness something real and not just a way she kept him out. He lifted the covers and slid into bed, kissing her sleeping mouth. With his tongue, he gently circled her lips, then parted them. She grunted and burrowed into her pillow.

He ran his hand down the smooth plane of her breastbone. The smallness of her breasts meant that they hadn't sagged, despite pregnancy and breastfeeding. He pinched her nipple lightly, the way she liked.

'Sleeping,' she groaned.

He took her hand, guiding it to his hardening penis. He whispered her name.

She opened her eyes. 'I was *asleep.*' She gathered the covers to her and flopped onto her other side, facing away.

Snaking his hand into the sheets, he found her nipple again. She used to make fun of his fascination with her breasts; when the kids were infants and Pieter put his hands under her shirt, inside her nursing bra, she'd laugh and say, 'You're just like Luke.' He twisted his hand down her belly, fighting the tight sheet. He found her pubic hair, and as she started to roll away from him again he used his other hand to grip her hipbone, digging his fingers into her.

'You're hurting me,' she said. 'Pieter, stop.'

She was twisting away and he clawed his hand, holding on, middle finger searching. When he thrust his fingers into her, she was dry. She cried out in pain, and he put his hand over her mouth and shoved his fingers into her again.

Then he pulled out and away, flopping onto his back, covering his eyes with his hands.

'What was that?' his wife said. 'What the hell was that?'

He pressed down on his eyes, too heartsick for words.

Jordana put her hands on his; he was grateful. But no, she was trying to pull his hands away from his eyes. 'Look at me,' she said. He resisted, pressing tighter, and saw blue. Her fingernail scratched his forehead. Then the energy went out of her and she let go of him. After a moment, he opened his fingers a little, peering out between them. Jordana knelt beside him, hands limp in her lap. She was crying, or something like crying: without tears, soundless and yet deep, her mouth open as though she couldn't get enough air.

How had they come to this? He should take his wife in his arms. Her face – gasping, eyes clenched – reminded him, involuntarily, of the way she looked during orgasm, and hating himself, hating them both, he rolled out of bed, stumbling to the bathroom, locking the door behind him.

The orchestra practiced for two hours in the morning and four in the afternoon. They were having trouble adjusting from Pieter's phrasing to Gyongyi Horvath's. Her fame, it seemed to Pieter, was made up of a magical combination of factors. She played beautifully. She was young, striking. She liked to find pieces that weren't usually performed or that had been written for other instruments. She was ambitious. Her playing, Pieter thought, was accessible, unafflicted by genius.

He would have liked to say that to his wife: *unafflicted by genius*.

Jordana didn't come to the performance Saturday night. He didn't believe she was staying away to punish him but because she was too angry to sit through the concert. He admired her, grudgingly. He would have been just the opposite – when he had a grievance, he claimed to be fine, going through his regular motions but refusing to give more than one-word responses, refusing sometimes even to look at her. All at once, he despised his own stinginess. It felt nearly unbearable to be trapped with himself.

He didn't feel so different at fifty-eight from the person he'd been at thirty-four, when it had seemed he would be a soloist and his life had been filled with promise. He'd married a girl madly in love with him, a girl who was beautiful and intelligent, vital, as unscathed-seeming as anyone he'd ever met. He had wanted passion in his life, even if it wasn't his own.

Angie slumped at her desk playing a computer game. She was wearing the clothes she'd worn for three days: sweatpants from Yale, a sweatshirt from Brown. The overhead light wasn't on; the

254

room's only light came from the screen, where an animated figure moved down a gray stone corridor. He went to the window to check that Gyongyi was still in the car. She'd fallen asleep on the way to his house, where they were having dinner that night. 'Do you know where your mother is?'

She shook her head without turning around.

'She's supposed to be cooking for eight people!' The room was heaped with clothes, battered magazines, plates smeared with syrup and cigarette ash. Onscreen, the figure glanced around herself. She was elfin, with pointed ears, chain-mail armor pressed tight against round breasts. 'Could you please turn that off?'

Angie hit a key. The character on screen froze, crouching, sword raised. Angie half turned in her seat. *'What?'*

'There is a famous cellist in the car. People are due here for dinner in twenty minutes, and your mother isn't even back? Have you heard from her?'

Angie shook her head. In the still screen's trembling light her skin looked terrible, ashy and rashed. Without thinking, he took a step forward and touched her face. 'Your meds—'

She twisted away. 'I'm *taking* them.'

'I know, I know, that's not . . .' He looked around the room. On the floor by his foot was a bowl, its bottom crusted with milk. He bent down to pick it up.

Downstairs, the front door opened and closed. Gyongyi Horvath's voice, uncertain, called, 'Hello?'

He ran out to the head of the stairs. 'Hello!'

She twisted her head up. 'I was asleep,' she said, sounding baffled.

'Do you want a glass of wine? There's wine in the kitchen. No, wait. Never mind. I'll come down.' He poked his head back into Angie's room. Quietly, he said, 'Why don't you get dressed? Come meet Gyongyi Horvath. Have a glass of wine. Just for five minutes.'

'I can't have wine. In case you've forgotten.'

'Come down anyway.'

'Just because you hate being social and Mom's not here, it doesn't mean I have to – to do your . . .'

He waited to see if she could go on, then said, 'I didn't think that. It's just – it would be nice for you to leave this room.'

'It would be nice for you if I cleaned up. If I was a credit to

255

you, if I looked like a nice daughter and not a fat embarrassment.'

He walked to the closet. Most of the wire hangers were bare, but on one he found a blue skirt and blouse she used to wear. He carried them over to the bed. She held her hands over the keyboard, watching him, her eyebrows raised.

'Are we done?' she asked.

He spread his hands apart. Angie turned away and started the game. Onscreen, the sword slashed down. Trying to think what to say, he watched Angie's character battle a troll. No noise accompanied the blows, only quick, uneven bursts of typing.

Jordana got home forty minutes later. By then, their guests had arrived; Pieter had gotten them into the living room with wine and was in the kitchen, trying to figure out what the hell they were going to do for dinner.

She came in carrying paper grocery bags, kissed him quickly on the side of the mouth. She had on her work clothes, a brown shirt and black jeans: not elegant but not scandalously shabby. 'Protesters,' she said. 'Everything took twice as long all day. How's Angie?'

'The same.' She was acting so normally that he was caught off guard, having trouble focusing his anger, though he could feel it inside him, immense. 'We have guests in the living room.'

'You can go be with them. I'll make dinner.'

'It's already almost eight.'

'I got chicken,' she said, reaching down into one of the bags and pulling out, unbelievably, a plastic container holding a roast chicken.

'You bought *takeout*?'

'I'll make a salad. There's good bread. You go be with your guests.'

'Gyongyi Horvath is here. We have her CDs. We can't serve chicken from the IGA.'

Very slowly, his wife said, 'It's just a *chicken*. They *roast* it. It will taste like *roast chicken*.'

'There isn't the smell of cooking. It's going to be obvious we didn't cook it.'

'*I* didn't cook it, you mean. So what?'

He hit his fist twice lightly against the counter. Then he smiled. 'You were with someone.'

256

Immediately he was terrified. He had said the thing he was determined not to. Exposed to air, it would begin to rust, turn corrosive.

Jordana put her head down on her arms on the counter. When she straightened up again, she looked enormously tired. And something else: old.

'I worked twelve hours today,' she said. 'I spent my lunch hour arguing with the insurance company. Clozaril's only in their formulary for schizophrenics. Fifteen-year-old girls shouted at me that I'm a murderer. Now I'm putting together dinner for your friends.'

'I'm sorry. I know you—'

Jordana had a small, distant smile on her face. 'You know I what?'

'I know you're – that you're not going—'

She kept smiling. Falsely light, she said, 'Not going to leave?'

'Are you going to leave?'

She was still smiling, but the corner of her mouth began to tremble. She turned away and stepped to the counter, lifting the lid off one of the chickens. A cloud of steam rose into her face. The rich smell made his empty stomach contract painfully. Her back to him, his wife said, 'Go be with your important guests.'

In the living room, Pieter threw himself into the nearest conversation. They argued about people they all seemed to know, Deanna and Jean-Luc. No: they were talking about television characters, *Star Trek*.

Fidel, the conductor, said, 'Oh, crap.' He'd dropped a glass. It had bounced on the soft Oriental rug, but there was a dark, wet splotch.

'It's okay.' Pieter's voice came hearty and false. 'It's nothing.' Kneeling stiffly to blot the carpet, he remembered gathering the bits of coffee cup after Jordana threw it at him, the moment he had begun to love her back. Later he'd found a bruise, blue and tender, above his left nipple.

It was hard to stand; he had to grasp at the back of a chair. His hand was ridged with pale veins. He pulled himself up, then took his hand off the chair and turned it over. His heart was beating fast and the pale fingertips trembled, an almost imperceptible vibrato.

A dip in the conversations told him that someone had entered the

257

room. He turned, thinking, *Jordana*. Thinking she had softened toward him, at least this much.

But it was Angie who stood there. She wore the blue skirt and shirt that he'd laid out for her. He remembered now that these had been the clothes she'd worn when interviewing for college. The skirt was tight across her hips, and the shirt gaped between buttons, showing the pale skin of her stomach. On her face was an expression that shocked him: such embarrassment, such longing for acceptance, that he had to look away.

Part Three

Chapter Thirty-Three

Iowa. The hot night air carried the smell of mown grass and, fainter, of chemicals and manure on the invisible surrounding fields. He and Wendy had been driving since midafternoon, and when Luke got out of the car he found himself stiff and dizzy. Driving, Wendy didn't like to stop for anything – not to eat, not to shake off some of the road's hypnosis, not to look at scenery.

She released her seat belt, opened her door, started to pull things out of the backseat. They were on a short suburban street: Wendy's father wasn't a farmer but a bookkeeper for farms. It was nine o'clock, and a few shreds of orange light still clung to the horizon. Luke went to help her with their bags. From all around them came the swishing arc of sprinklers over square and vacant lawns.

'This is nice of you,' she said. The dimness made her face look white, floating, almost ghostly.

'I wanted to come.'

'I know. That's why it's nice of you.'

Her younger sister, Julie, was getting married in a few days. Wendy lifted her pink bridesmaid's dress out of the car, sweeping her other arm underneath so she carried it the way that bridegrooms carry brides, and started up to the house.

After she'd fucked that guy at the party, they'd broken up for more than a year. They hadn't even stayed friends during that time; if they saw each other on campus, they talked awkwardly, and then he was usually in a shitty mood the rest of the day. He knew that Wendy had dated a med student for a while; he'd started seeing a girl, Reina, who lived in one of the co-ops. She was easygoing and pretty and wore tinkling silver anklets from Nepal. He'd been excited about her, had even wondered if he loved her.

Then, six months ago, his mother had called to say she'd left his father and moved across town. He was surprised to find his eyes filling with tears. He missed Wendy so much, all of a sudden, that he'd had to sit down on the bed.

The day's sticky heat was only just now beginning to dissolve, and his T-shirt clung damply to his shoulder blades. Wendy shifted the dress so that she was holding it with her chin. Under the porch light, her freckles stood out, rusty against her pale skin. Fishing in her shorts pocket for the house key, she muttered, 'Who would get married in August?'

'Maybe she's pregnant.'

'Maybe,' Wendy said.

'Really?'

'No.' She found the key. Of course she would still own, and be able to find, the key to her old house.

The car was packed with his few things; he would drive home to New Hampshire after Julie's wedding. He wanted to be closer to Angie, and he wanted Wendy to go with him, but she insisted she couldn't leave Madison. She and Kim were planning to move into a smaller apartment together. She had a job as a research assistant for her ex-professor – finally, something besides waitressing – that would last into the winter, possibly beyond. He felt, though, that she was wavering; this weekend might help change her mind.

Wendy had the door open. Air-conditioning, with its peculiar Saran-wrap smell, enfolded him. Without looking, she dropped her keys into a bowl on the front hall table. 'We're here!' she called. 'We're home!'

'In the kitchen!'

Wendy's mother sat in the breakfast nook, pink satin puddled around her. She made a gesture of pushing back from the black horsehead of the sewing machine, but didn't actually get up. 'Guinevere. Lukas.'

Cammie said, 'Mom, it's Luke.' She half stood, giving Wendy and Luke quick one-armed hugs. 'Mom thinks the world is full of people shortening their rightful names.'

He'd almost forgotten that Wendy's full name was Guinevere. Julie, the bride, lifted her hands full of ribbon and paper in a gesture to show she couldn't hug. 'Sorry. Programs.' All three sisters had been cheerleaders, but to Luke only Julie – Juliet – looked the part: yellow hair, round breasts, easy smile. Cammie and Wendy were paler and smaller, with fine, slightly pinched features. Cammie had pale red hair, while Wendy's was much darker, almost maroon. When he'd first met Wendy, she'd looked like a small-town girl, but seeing her with her sisters he realized how she'd changed: hair unpouffed, eyes unlined, legs freckled in cut-off jeans and black fake-Teva sandals. Her sisters wore pleated khaki shorts and white Keds and tennis socks, the kind with a small pastel pom-pom behind the ankle. Mrs. Miles wore the same things. She was a thin woman with ropy tendons in her neck and arms. According to Wendy, she was never not on a diet. Once, for three months, she'd eaten only seafood and vitamin C tablets.

'Camelia, are the snaps by you?'

Cammie poked under the programs and magazines until she found a cardboard of snaps, which she handed to their mother.

Luke had been here once before, for Thanksgiving his junior year. At night, Wendy had come down to the basement den where he was staying. In the laundry room, the part of the house farthest from her parents, they made love against the dryer. Wendy bit his shoulder as she came, and the surprising pain had made him come too, so suddenly and so hard that he felt it all the way up his spine, down his arms, into the small, humming bones of his hands. The next morning, at breakfast, Wendy and her mother and sisters kept jumping up to get napkins or turn the bacon. Their bare feet all had the same square nails, the same high blue arch. The quick patter across the cool clean linoleum had pleased and vaguely aroused him.

The men were coming in from the backyard. Julie's fiancé Matt was handsome, with the beginnings of a belly and a jovial insincerity. He and Julie worked as tellers in the same bank, but he was management track and she wasn't. Wendy's father let the screen door bang behind him. A big man, red hair yellowing with age, wearing an expensive Polo shirt. He hugged Wendy, then held out his hand to Luke.

He asked Luke questions about graduating – Luke had managed to complete his requirements to graduate a year late – and about Madison. He didn't use Luke's name, and Luke wondered if he'd forgotten it.

'Honey, get me a drink,' Mr. Miles said to Wendy.

Wendy was standing at the microwave. The only indication that she'd heard was that the muscles at the back of her neck tensed.

Julie and Cammie stiffened also, looking down at their work. In high school, Luke knew, Wendy and her sisters had put clear tape on their father's bottles to track how fast the levels went down; they'd kept intricate charts. When Luke had asked why, Wendy gave him a confused look, as though she couldn't believe he didn't see. But then she'd laughed. 'I don't know,' she admitted. 'It made us feel more in control, I guess.'

'Gwennie?' said Mr. Miles.

'I'll get it,' said his wife, jumping up quickly.

Wendy continued to get forks and napkins from drawers. She folded the napkins in careful triangles. She took down glasses and asked Luke what he wanted to drink. He wanted a beer but he said, 'A Coke?'

When at last she turned back to the table, her face was perfectly composed to say *nothing's happened*. She put their plates down.

Matt asked Luke, 'When are you guys getting married?'

'We don't have any plans.'

'Good man.' Matt cuffed his shoulder. 'Stay free as long as you can.'

'*Matt,*' Julie said.

He laughed, hooking his arm around her waist. 'These girls make it hard.'

That night, Luke woke to Wendy whispering his name. He was sleeping in the basement den, on a pull-out sofa.

'Matt is awful. I don't want Julie to marry him.'

Half asleep, Luke said, 'Hi, Wendy.'

She whispered, 'I feel like I barely even know her all of a sudden. She told me this long story about someone who hasn't been paying his share of the coffee pool at the bank, and how annoyed she is.'

He opened his eyes wide, forcing himself to wake up. Rolling onto his side, he pushed some hair back out of her face. 'This is nice, isn't it?' He put his hand under her shirt, along her stomach. 'In New Hampshire we could sleep like this all the time.'

'Shh.' She pointed at the ceiling; she didn't want her parents to hear that she was down here. 'Are you going to miss me?'

Her inviting him to Iowa might not be a sign of wavering but its opposite: she wasn't afraid time together might change her mind. He felt sick of it, suddenly – that she didn't want to be together but wanted reassurance that he was unhappy about it. Unhappy, but of course not mad at her. She acted like his being near Angie was just a preference, not something he needed to do.

Wendy kissed him. He let her, keeping his mouth still, until she moved back and said, 'What?'

'What are you doing?' he said.

'What do you mean, what am I doing?' In the thin light from the hallway, he could see her flush to the roots of her hair. He'd often thought how much she must hate it that the fairness of her skin gave away when she was embarrassed or angry or tipsy. 'We still have two days. Just because I think we should break up doesn't mean I don't love you.'

He said, 'You tell me you don't want to be together—'

'I don't want to *move* to be together.'

'This is bullshit, then.'

'*Shush,*' she hissed, jabbing her finger toward the ceiling: he'd forgotten to whisper.

'God, listen to yourself.'

She was on top of the covers; she began to shiver. 'So why'd you come?'

'I don't know,' he said. Being cruel had a crazy energy to it, one that made him feel both jacked up and deeply calm. 'But I'm going to sleep now.'

He turned away. Wendy said, 'Luke,' putting her arm around him. 'Luke?' Then she rolled away from him and off the bed. Apparently not caring if she made noise, she ran up the basement stairs.

At the wedding rehearsal Saturday afternoon, Luke and Wendy sat in a middle pew of the church. All nine bridesmaids were there, dressed in cotton skirts or short white shorts; he and Wendy, in their T-shirts and cut-offs, were the only people in the church wearing dark colors. At the front of the hall, Wendy's sister and mother talked to the organist.

Wendy's hands were under her thighs. She looked tired and fragile, her pale skin blotchy. He'd hurt her last night. Realizing that made him want to hurt her again. Without saying anything, he got up and walked to the back of the church, where he made himself read the names of boys killed in World War II. One was Luke Palmer Tripp. He traced the engraved nameplate with his finger. Luke Palmer Tripp had been killed in 1943, when he was nineteen. Luke tried to feel some kind of tragedy or portent but didn't feel anything but the itchy need for a cigarette.

He walked outside, onto the front porch of the church. Across the street, a tractor was making slow circles in a field of green. People who didn't smoke missed this, just standing on porches and balconies, watching the world for seven minutes without moving. He pulled the smoke down into his lungs; it was abrasive yet soothing.

The second cigarette wasn't as good and he was beginning to feel awkward out here. Weddings didn't make any sense to him. You dressed to look totally unlike yourself and dressed your friends to look as much alike as possible – a girl team for the bride, a boy team for the groom. Then you read from the same script everyone else used, and it was supposed to be moving.

When he went back inside, the dimness made it hard to see, and he thought at first that Wendy was approaching the altar in Julie's place. He couldn't distinguish colors clearly in the half-light; the woman at the front of the church had Wendy's way of standing so straight she almost canted backward. Taped Pachelbel played on a small boom box. At the front of the church, Julie reached Matt, then shook her head. The shake of her head was like Wendy too, the same sharp certainty. She turned, and with a shock he realized it *was* Wendy, standing in for her sister.

Up until now, he hadn't really felt the loss of her. Now, for a moment, it gaped open in his chest.

She walked to the back of the church and gave him a dispassionate glance. The music started again, and Mrs. Miles said, 'Okay, first bridesmaid. Second bridesmaid. Third bridesmaid.'

Wendy took her father's arm.

'Ninth bridesmaid. Okay, bride.'

Mr. Miles had brush-cut hair and a military posture. He and Wendy moved down the aisle, backs straight as ironing boards.

'Luke?'

He turned. Julie was at his elbow. He asked, 'Why is Wendy pretending to be you?'

'What? Oh. It's bad luck for the bride to be in her own rehearsal.' She watched Wendy for a moment, then asked, 'Do you have a cigarette?'

He pulled the pack from his pocket and tilted it toward her but

266

she'd already started out to the porch. He didn't feel like hanging out with Julie, though her prettiness and ease charmed him, in the same way he'd been charmed at first by Iowa, its long furrowed fields and flat horizon; charmed by the Dairi Shoppe where Wendy had once waitressed, the high school football field where she'd led cheers.

Across the street, a thresher was making its way toward them, bringing down a long row of sunflowers. Julie lit one of his cigarettes, handed back his lighter.

'Your hair is longer,' she said.

'Yeah, that happens.'

She laughed. Then, looking up at him through her bangs, she asked, 'What about you guys? When *are* you going to get married?'

It was a little bizarre, the flirtatiousness of her manner contrasted with the seriousness of the question. Had Wendy not told her sisters they were breaking up? 'I don't know.'

'She's crazy about you.'

That all Wendy's seeming nonchalance about his move might be self-protection depressed him. They'd known each other four years, five if you counted the year she worked at Cleveland's.

'I don't know anyone who smokes Trues,' Julie said.

'My sister smokes Trues.'

Julie made a quick sympathetic face at the mention of Angie. She inhaled some smoke. Cigarettes had become so Pavlovian to him that just watching someone else smoke was pleasurable.

'I have a favor to ask,' Julie said.

'Shoot.'

'It's about the receiving line. Bridesmaids' boyfriends and husbands and ushers' girlfriends and wives are going to be in it.'

'Oh, sure. No big deal.'

Julie smiled and took a breath. So that hadn't been the favor.

'It's just, everyone's going to be dressed up.'

'I brought a suit.'

'Juliet, honey?' Mrs. Miles called from inside. 'We've got the timing figured out.'

'That's great,' Julie said to him quickly, though there was an undissolved tension in her shoulders. 'A suit's great. I'm glad you brought a suit.'

*

267

That night, they went to a bar called the Kennel. Wendy's old boyfriend, Steve, was there. Before Luke, Steve had been the only person Wendy had slept with. Luke had also gotten her to confess that they'd slept together during Angie's breakdown, which made Steve an asshole. His brown hair, still wet from the shower, showed comb marks, and his hands were large and knobby.

Luke found himself talking to a girl named Sherry, round-faced and pleasant. He drank too fast and flirted with Sherry, who flirted back until the strap of her tank top fell off her shoulder and he pushed it back up with his finger. She frowned and leaned away and a minute later excused herself to go talk to someone at the other end of the table.

Wendy looked over at him, smiling thinly, raising her glass in a sardonic toast.

He pushed back his chair and stumbled into the men's bathroom (labeled NEUTERED; the women's was SPAYED), where he splashed his face with cold water.

Later, Wendy took his car keys away. She acted annoyed, but he could tell she was self-righteously pleased. Back unnaturally straight, she drove them home, shifting hard when she changed gears. They were silent for a long time. He turned on the radio, finding a staticky song by Led Zeppelin.

Wendy said, 'I hate Led Zeppelin.'

'How can you hate Led Zeppelin?'

She said, 'Just because *you* like something doesn't make it good.' She snapped the radio off.

As falsely as he could, he said, 'You're right. You're always right.' He leaned his head back against the seat. They were on a long dark stretch of road; he couldn't see farms but he could smell the water on the fields. He felt the same precariousness, the same sickly pleasure, that he used to as a child when he fought with his sister.

They passed fast-food restaurants, a funeral home. Slipping lower in his seat, he could see stars through the windshield.

'You can turn on the radio if you want,' Wendy said. When he didn't, she clicked it on herself. All the stoplights blinked yellow. Slumped in his seat, he watched from beneath as they fell through the intersections.

Wendy pulled into her family's driveway. On the neighbor's lawn, a plaster gnome in a red hat beamed, rosy-cheeked, holding up a lantern. 'Nice gnome,' he said. Gnome, gnome, gnome. Who had come up with that word? *Gnome.*

Wendy turned off the car but didn't move to get out. 'Julie asked me to ask you a favor.' The gnome's smile was too merry, as though it knew wicked secrets. 'She wants you to cut your hair.'

'What?' He laughed, turning. She wasn't smiling. 'Are you serious?'

She pressed her lips together, shrugging.

He knew Wendy liked his hair long. She would run her fingers through it or sometimes, idly, make little braids. 'Is that what you want?'

'Julie's the one who's the bride.' She wore the haughty touch-me-not face that meant she was embarrassed.

'What do *you* want?'

Crickets chirped, insistent, all around them. She looked away. 'What Julie wants.'

'You know what?' he said. 'Fine. You're the boss. Whatever. Fine.'

In the morning, Luke drove to downtown Greenfield and found a barbershop. The barber pole was white tin, painted with red and blue stripes and the slogan LOOK BETTER ... FEEL BETTER! Hadn't he learned somewhere that barbers used to bleed people? With leeches. Or had they used razors? Or was he thinking of dentists?

Inside, he expected a kindly older barber, a crowd of newspaper-reading men waiting their turn. The shop was empty and cool, with a lone young woman in a pink smock talking on the phone. She had long permed hair that spilled around her head.

She said, 'I'll call you back. I've got a customer.'

After fastening a cape over him, she took out the elastic from his ponytail. His hair reached his shoulders. With her hands, she combed it out, long nails scritching gently against his scalp. Their eyes met in the mirror.

Her breasts were half an inch from his head. Stroking his hair, she asked, 'You want a pop?'

'What?'

'You want a pop? Pepsi, Seven-Up?'

'Oh. Sure. Thanks.'

She turned and bent from the waist, ass in the air as she reached into a low fridge. As she handed him the soda, she asked, 'How

269

about a nibble?'

'A nibble?'

'Fritos? Chips?'

It was eight in the morning. The absurdity of the situation began to break up his bad mood. 'I'm good with this,' he said, lifting the Pepsi can, silvered with frost.

'Okay, then.' Putting her hands in his hair again, she steadied his head. 'What do you want me to do?'

'I want it all off.'

'Are you sure?' she asked, then surprised him by saying, 'Your hair's so nice.'

It bolstered his anger at Wendy. 'I want, like, a buzz. As short as you can get it.'

She shrugged and reached for a comb. With each snick of the scissors – the sound so sharp he could almost taste metal – he thought, *Fuck you, Wendy, fuck you fuck you*. The woman switched to clippers. By the time she was done, he looked like a Marine. His forehead jutted forward, bony. Well, fuck that too.

When he got back to the house, he went straight to the basement and started to pack. Wendy came down after him. She looked tense, and there was something strange about her face: a thick layer of beige foundation that hid her freckles. The pink dress was a bad color on her.

'I was up all night,' she said. 'Your hair's so short.' She reached out to touch it, then stopped herself and fisted her hand and cried, 'Oh, fuck! This whole trip. I don't know how to fix anything. Everything's so bad. I love you so much. Do you believe I love you?'

'I guess,' he said.

'I do. I love you so much it's – I get all confused. I know I've been awful. I want to go to New Hampshire with you. Or something. I don't know. I just want to be with you.'

'I'm leaving now,' he said. 'If you want to come, you have to come now.'

'Now?'

'I'm not staying for this wedding. If you love me, you'll come.'

He wanted her to say no. The truth was he would wait.

Outside Cedar Rapids, they stopped for food at a convenience store. Luke sat on the curb, eating peanut butter crackers, while

270

Wendy changed in the bathroom. She came out wearing clothes of Luke's – a T-shirt, cut-offs. When they'd left, she'd grabbed only her purse.

'Where's your dress?' he asked.

'Trash.' She'd washed off the foundation makeup and was very pale. His clothes hung on her small frame. She looked terrible, or else very beautiful, he didn't know which. Sitting beside him, she twisted her arms together and pinned them between her knees.

She said, 'Once, in high school, the Rowes needed extra hands, so I was walking beans.' He knew she meant weeding soybean fields. 'We were near the east side of the farm, not far from the Millers', the next place over. The Millers were spraying their crops, and this flock of blackbirds, a huge flock, came toward us. They flew right through the pesticide and out the other side, and then they started falling to the ground around us, straight down. And they're pretty heavy, so there was this noise, like *thud, thud, thud thud thud—*'

Luke found his cigarettes, fished one out, and lit it.

Wendy was staring into space. Without breaking her stare, she said, 'They're married by now.'

'Uh-huh,' he said cautiously, waiting for her to go on.

She put her head down on her knees.

He touched her back. 'It's okay, Wen. It's fine.'

'I'm just tired.' She sounded choked. After a while, she said, 'Oh, God, I'm such a bitch.'

'You're not a bitch.'

She nodded into her lap. For a long time she was still. Then she straightened and stood, picking up the wrapper from the crackers he'd eaten. She walked to the gas pump island to throw the cellophane away. His white T-shirt was so big on her it looked like a dress.

They reached Cort at four in the morning. Wendy got out of the car, swaying a little with exhaustion.

'I thought it would look different,' she said.

'Different?'

'I don't know. Bigger?' She laughed. 'Maybe smaller?'

He looked at their brick Colonial, trying to see it as she might, but he was too tired. 'I don't want to wake them up.' Then remembering his mother was gone, corrected himself: 'I don't want to wake my dad.' He walked around to the side of the house, letting Wendy follow. 'They don't lock the upstairs windows. I'll boost you.' He knelt, interlacing his fingers.

'Won't I hurt you?'

He shook his head. She put her foot in his laced hands, trusting only part of her weight to him at first, checking his face. She asked, 'Does it hurt?'

He didn't answer, just lifted her. She grabbed a knobby branch, pulling herself into the tree. She climbed quickly, then ran crouched across the roof.

He followed her. 'It's this window.' Dogwood leaves stuck to her arms and hair. In the dim light from the streetlamp, she looked familiar and unfamiliar, the way a movie star was familiar and unfamiliar. He pushed open the window and they crawled inside. He turned on the overhead light, then turned it immediately off: too bright.

Wendy touched the prom photo tacked to his bulletin board: the tacky Polynesian sunset, Khamisa's green fuck-you dress, his arms around her. He'd had a crew cut then, too. Luke reached across, unpinned the picture, and dropped it in the trash.

He woke a few hours later. They'd slept in their clothes, pressed together in his narrow bed. It was hot now; he was sweating. He tried to get up, but Wendy was wrapped in the sheet, pinning him down.

Angie was here for breakfast; he could hear her voice rising from downstairs. The house smelled of syrup and coffee.

Wendy rolled toward him and opened her eyes. 'Good morning,' he said.

She sat up and looked around. 'Oh, God,' she said. 'Oh, my God.' She laughed once, then covered her eyes and drew a long, shaky breath.

'I wish it was yesterday,' she said.

'Wendy,' he said. He held her as tightly as he could, holding on with his arms and legs and torso, wanting to disappear into her.

He'd gotten what he'd wanted. Now they would walk downstairs and into the unsuspecting kitchen. He wanted them to have done it better, he wanted to feel happy, but it was already about to happen; and then it was happening.

272

Chapter Thirty-Four

Across the street from the house Angie shared with four housemates lived a family with a brindle mutt. Most of the time the puppy was left alone in the fenced yard, which was bad enough, but occasionally the men who lived in the house wrapped the puppy in chains and weights and made it run. One of the chains had been connected to a doormat that dragged along the ground. The east side of the yard had a small hill; the owner would squat at the top with a piece of meat. The puppy charged gallantly up, dragging its chains and padlocks and doormat behind it. At the top, sides heaving, it would gobble the meat, then try to burrow into its owner's hands to be petted, but the other man would hook a hand into the dog's harness of chains and drag it – yipping, feet scrabbling desperately – back down the hill. If the owner did pet it for a minute, the puppy would freeze, eyes closed, like a lizard in the sun.

Angie was glad she had a back room, because she couldn't stand seeing the puppy's misery. The woman who had last lived in her room (Alison; the housemates often talked about how great, how *funny,* Alison had been) had painted it periwinkle blue, with gloppy purple trim. Angie had a Victorian couch with claw feet, a desk that had once been a high school lab table, a beautiful old iron headboard. They were the first pieces of furniture she'd ever bought for herself, and she loved them, although they were crammed together in the small space – the desk right up against the bed, the couch keeping the door from opening all the way. Above the bed, a window looked out across their house's scraggly yard onto a motel whose sign flashed WELCOME, then VACANCY.

She hated weekends. They made her feel aimless and dull, unable to enjoy what regular people looked forward to all week. Her body ached with exhaustion, but she knew that if she lay down, she wouldn't be able to sleep any more than she already had.

She forced herself across the room – it felt like walking through chest-deep water – and into the bathroom across the hall, where she pulled down her pants and peed. She should shower, too, but she didn't feel ambitious enough. The bathroom had incense, seashells, driftwood. A claw-foot tub, its curved toenails painted with red nail polish.

Out in the hallway, she forced herself to turn right, toward the stairs, and not left toward her room. Their house, on Cort's western outskirts, was a ramshackle Victorian. The front staircase curved grandly; each time the front door opened, dustballs rose from the steps like startled moths. There was also a narrow, twisting back staircase, the wood worn to satin, which she made her way down now, shutting down her mind: she couldn't look at the steps, at the hallway she had to cross to reach the kitchen. If she thought of having to bend to the cabinet where the pots were kept, fill a pot with water, carry it to the stove, she would sit down on this stair, a fat girl in a sweatshirt, and be unable to stand again. *Good girl,* she found she was saying to herself with each step. Her legs ached to lie down on the stairs. She took a step. *Good girl. Good girl.*

For the last couple of weeks she'd been sleeping badly, waking at three or four, thoughts racing. The mood chart she kept for her therapist dipped from 4 to 3. She forced herself not to fall below a 3, going to her temp job even though she was so exhausted by the end of the afternoon that she came home and slept. Her housemates used the word *crash: I'm gonna go upstairs now and crash.* Coming into her room she literally crashed, falling onto the mattress. It was the only thing all day that felt okay, the moment between hitting the mattress and sleep, when her body seemed to dissolve.

She'd had six good months this spring and summer, doing the things people just did, the grocery store, movies, forty hours of work a week. Most of her housemates had graduated from college, but they worked the same kind of jobs as Angie's. Isobel waited tables, Jason temped out of the same agency – Temporary Solutions – that Angie did, and Bradley and Maureen both painted houses. They generally treated these jobs with casual good humor. They all had political causes or artistic projects that they considered their *real* work. Except for Bradley: he was apparently content painting houses and drinking wine and sharing a bed with Isobel.

274

When she'd lived at halfway houses, everyone had battled demons just to get breakfast or get dressed. Angie had usually been the most together person there, her functionality a source of wonder. These housemates were the first friends outside the System that Angie'd had since high school, and they stunned her a little, how easily they accepted the world. They probably would have said they didn't accept the world at all: they smoked pot, Bradley hadn't finished college, all of them were vegetarians, and Isobel belonged to about six environmental and animal-rights organizations. They knew each other from State or from the Art Institute and hadn't moved away from Cort after finishing. But they seemed to accept unquestioningly the world's inherent structure and logic, their own natural ascendancy. They didn't probe when Angie said she'd spent the last few years 'around New England.' She mentioned the year at Middlebury – scrunching her nose and saying, 'I wasn't really into college' – and her housemates nodded pleasantly, unconcerned.

Dishes were piled in the kitchen sink, the pot she needed at the bottom. It held water orange with grease, a few slimy pieces of spaghetti. She looked at the ratty sponge, the plastic bottle sticky with soap.

She couldn't wash out the pot.

Of course she could wash out the pot. She just needed to raise her hand to the soap bottle. Just reach down into the sink, lift the pot, pour out the greasy water.

She sat down at the table, which had newspapers and breakfast dishes piled on it. She hadn't eaten all day. On a saucer in front of her lay two toast crusts, one with a burnt black fringe. She made herself eat them – her mouth ached, chewing – and then drank from a cup of cold amber tea, a blond hair wrinkling its surface.

She woke to a grainy dusk. The front room where she'd fallen asleep had a red couch, the TV, and Maureen's artwork, abstract canvases with a lot of rips and slashes. In the dim light, the TV stand – an ugly sixties occasional table – seemed to float above the floor. The fish tank behind the couch held a small, circling nurse shark. It had a face like a catfish, flat and whiskered, its eye small and hard and blue, bisected by a slit of black pupil. Turning, muscles undulating beneath its gray suede side, it kept its eye fixed on Angie.

This depression didn't feel like ones she'd gone through before. Those had been so blank and terrible it had felt like being wrapped

275

in gray wool blankets, one after another, until she was choking on her own breath. This time was different. With her illness pushed back, she had to look at the full extent of her fucked-up life. She'd accomplished nothing in six years; she couldn't even lay claim to her own thoughts. Was she the thoughts she had on meds, when her brain was as it should be? Or was she the thoughts she had off meds, her brain as it really was? If she existed only when her brain was balanced on meds, she existed only on the *right* meds: she'd been on nineteen different combinations. Either way, she'd been herself only a tiny part of these last years. And the rest of the time, she'd been – who?

She swung her legs off the couch; it took her a long time to move from sitting to standing, but once she stood she walked to the kitchen, where Bradley sat at the table, drinking wine from a coffee mug and watching Isobel chop onions.

'Hey.'

'Hey.'

'Hey.'

Angie went to the sink. 'The big pot's gone.'

Isobel glanced at Bradley, then pointed with her knife toward the stove. 'I'm using it for pasta. You can have some if you want.'

Angie suspected she was supposed to say no, but she was too relieved at the idea of not having to cook. She sat at the table with Bradley, who lifted the wine bottle toward her. She shook her head. Everyone in the house liked Bradley, who was quiet and good-natured, with bushy hair and a long nose. 'I don't know what he's doing with *Isobel*,' both Jason and Maureen would say, as though being people who recycled and grew their own herbs meant they weren't susceptible to simple beauty. Isobel was very tall, taller even than Angie, and had modeled for a year and a half in Milan. She had long brown hair and slightly oversized front teeth. 'I hated modeling, though,' she'd told Angie once. Later, Angie had asked Maureen if she knew that Isobel had modeled.

'Of course I know that. She lets it drop the first time she can get you alone. Did she tell you about Spanish *Vogue* yet?' When Maureen talked about Isobel, her face took on the look of someone tearing a piece of stale bread with her teeth. 'She was in Italy a year and a half without learning ten words of Italian.'

Isobel moved lightly between the cutting board and the stove, onions held between the blade of the knife and her palm. She swept

276

them into the skillet, where they hissed in the heated oil. 'Should we eat up on the roof?'

'Sure,' said Bradley.

Angie asked, 'Do you want some help, Isobel?'

'No, thanks.'

'Does everyone call you Isobel?'

Isobel added a jar of sauce to the onions and mushrooms in the skillet. 'Well, it's my name.'

'I mean, your family? Like, my family calls me Ange sometimes.' Her voice pitched too high, coming too fast.

'That's very original.'

'Be nice,' Bradley said. He turned to Angie. 'Her family calls her Is.'

'Is. That's great.'

She needed to take her six o'clock meds, but she couldn't stand to be alone and the pills were hidden up in her bedroom. Isobel busied herself with finding a colander for the pasta. She wore a man's white tank top, a long Indian-print skirt, running shoes. Across the front of the tank top were small orange asterisks where the tomato sauce had spit. Bradley lifted the bottle questioningly toward Angie again and this time she said, 'Yeah, okay.' The pale yellow wine was warm and tasted of ash.

A song began on the radio, something so familiar she couldn't place it. Then Stevie Nicks's voice came in: It was 'Gold Dust Woman.' Without thinking, Angie jumped up and switched the radio off. When she turned, Bradley and Isobel were both looking at her.

'I don't like that song,' she said lamely.

They glanced at each other. Then Isobel shrugged, not looking at Angie, and began loading three plates with pasta and sauce. Not sure if she'd been invited, Angie took her plate and tagged upstairs after Isobel and Bradley.

They climbed out the attic window onto the roof. The sun had gone down already, but the sky still held streaks of light. They ate without talking much. The early fall air, loose around them, was cool. When Isobel stood and untied her sweater from around her waist, Angie realized both she and Bradley had paused to watch. Isobel slipped the sweater over her arms, then raised them so it fell down her body.

277

Chapter Thirty-Five

Jordana's house was tiny but two-storied and many-roomed, as though a larger house had shrunk in heavy rain. It was set far back from the road, next to a small pond rimmed with silvery-green weeds.

In the kitchen, Jordana cut a red onion in half, the two pieces rocking apart on the cutting board. The kids were coming for lunch, a picnic. Angie had been here before, but Luke had not. Luke *and Wendy* had not: Jordana wasn't used to thinking of Luke as part of a couple. She turned and tossed the onion skins into the trash. She'd never enjoyed cooking before. Now she found herself admiring her hands as she lifted apples from their bowl, as she sliced bread, as she lifted a glass of wine. She'd changed in other ways, too, these six months she'd lived alone. She slept better, and therefore less. Instead of rocketing to the clinic two hours before she needed to be at work, she spent mornings curled up in a blanket on her porch. From thrift stores she'd picked out rag rugs and old quilts, things Pieter would have called precious. She'd never thought of herself as a nature lover, but she loved the animal life around this house: grazing deer, skunks waddling toward the pond at twilight, a family of opossums filing into the trees that edged the property.

It had taken more than a year to leave Pieter. She'd begun to look surreptitiously at places for rent but had talked herself out of each apartment: too noisy, or Angie was going through a rough spot, or too close to home. Sometimes she'd thought it was just a game, that she wouldn't leave at all. But then she'd seen this place. The idea of someone else getting it had made her feel robbed.

Angie's car turned into the lane. She still drove Abe's ancient

Galaxie 500, pale green and finned. Jordana wiped her hands quickly on a napkin and went to open the front door. Cool, crisp air: it was September, the first leaves changing on the trees. The Galaxie rattled even after the ignition was turned off. The kids were getting out of the car, talking, slamming doors. Wendy was about half Luke and Angie's size, and her neatness made her seem even smaller next to their flapping shirttails, loose jeans, rolled-up cuffs. She and Luke had been in New Hampshire about a month; they were still staying with Pieter, which allowed them to save up some money. Jordana had mixed feelings about their living there. If Pieter wasn't alone, it made her desertion of him less stark. Other times – even though she'd been the one to leave – it made her feel rejected, the three of them together.

Jordana hugged her daughter; Luke didn't move in to be hugged. 'So this is it,' Jordana said. She opened the door and motioned them inside.

Luke glanced around, then picked up the newspaper from the table.

'It's very nice,' Wendy said.

Angie walked around without touching anything. 'It's still strange seeing your stuff here.'

Jordana stored pots and dish towels in the drawers of a bureau that had been in their basement, its legs warped by water damage. Her books were in the living room in three unmatched wooden bookcases, also from the old house. On the fireplace mantel roosted things she'd found on walks: a smooth black stone; a broken shard of blue and white pottery; a fragile nest, a spray of dark hair woven in with the twigs.

'Here, let me show you something,' she said to Luke, and led him into the kitchen. 'Put your hand here on the wall. No, to the right a little.' She didn't pick up his hand to show him: he'd shake her off. 'Do you feel it?'

'What am I supposed to be feeling?'

'There's a seam.' When downtown Cort had been 'revitalized,' some of the older houses were sold off. The woman who was now Jordana's landlord had paid a dollar for this place, with the agreement that she would haul it to a new plot of land. 'They sawed the house in half to transport it out here, then put it back together.'

'Huh. Cool.' He dropped his hand, turning as Angie and Wendy came into the kitchen.

279

Angie asked, 'Is she showing you where they cut up the house?'

Hurt, Jordana said, '*I* think it's interesting.'

'They cut up the house?' Wendy said, and so Jordana had to show her the seam under the wallpaper, explain about the Preservation Act. Luke and Angie were talking about Angie's housemates, Angie imitating someone and Luke laughing. Jordana wished she could hear better what they were saying, but Wendy was asking polite questions: 'How is the neighborhood?'

Jordana swept an arm toward the window. 'No neighbors.'

Despite the sun, it wasn't really warm enough for a picnic. Jordana tramped down a circle of grass, then spread the wool blanket. The grass beneath was bristly through the fabric. She pulled tomatoes and cheese and eggs from the basket. She wasn't a fan of Angie's vegetarianism – the faint air of self-righteousness to it, the rejection of sensual pleasure – but at least Angie wasn't proselytizing against meat to strangers anymore.

Luke picked up a plate. 'You made deviled eggs.'

She blushed a little: Pieter had always made deviled eggs. 'How is your dad?'

Angie stiffened and said, 'He's fine,' just as Luke said, 'Why do you care?'

'Luke. I care.'

Wendy stood abruptly. 'I think I'll get our coats.'

'You don't have to. It's warming up,' Jordana said.

'I'll just get them.' She took off across the yard.

Jordana picked up the bread and realized she'd forgotten to bring a knife for it. She thought of calling after Wendy, but instead tore the loaf into ragged pieces.

Passing one to Angie, she asked, 'How's Trevor?' trying to keep that she wished Angie weren't with him out of her voice. Luke rolled onto his stomach and picked at something in the grass.

Angie said, 'They started him on a new med. It just came on the market. They have to crush them up in applesauce so he doesn't cheek them.'

'You mean he doesn't know he's taking it.'

'Right. Twice a day they just say, "Time for your special snack, Trevor."' Angie reached for an egg. 'No, of course they've told him.'

Her hair fell forward into her face, silky, blond with sun.

280

Another tick on the getting-better side of the list: she wasn't too depressed or too medicated to shower. Angie was temping, she saw her therapist two mornings a week. Four or five would have been better, but even with a sliding scale they couldn't afford it. Just the lab bills for Angie's bloodwork were sixty dollars a week.

Wendy returned, her arms laden with coats. She handed them out, then sat, and they made awkward conversation. Wendy was waitressing at a fancy French restaurant called Temps Perdu.

'I loved that book,' Jordana said.

'Book?' said Wendy blankly.

'*À la recherche du temps perdu.* Proust.'

'Oh.'

Cutting himself more cheese, Luke raised his eyebrows without looking at Jordana, as though she'd deliberately tried to show Wendy up.

Why had Luke chosen her? Wendy was pretty, and apparently she was smart – Jordana knew she'd graduated summa cum laude – but she was so self-contained that no personality leaked through. Maybe she was different when they were alone. Luke's other girl-friends had been drastic and messy – sexy girls who got their clothes at thrift stores and called in the middle of the night, drunk and apologizing but could they talk to Luke *please*? With them, Luke had always seemed to be sitting back, lazy and contented as a cat, while with Wendy he was focused, touching her constantly: her hair, her knee.

'Do you miss Iowa?' Jordana asked. 'Or Madison?'

'I've lived out there all my life. The Midwest.'

Did that mean she missed it or didn't miss it? Luke stood abruptly, reaching his hand down to Wendy. 'Do you want to check out the pond?'

She glanced at Jordana, who said, 'Go ahead, it's fine.'

Hand in hand, Luke and Wendy made their way back across the weedy field.

'Does she make you feel about ten?' Angie whispered.

Relieved, Jordana said, 'More like five.'

She leaned back on her elbows and a grasshopper rose up, clack-ing, from the dry yellow grass. Luke and Wendy had taken off their shoes and were wading at the edge of the pond. Luke tripped, stumbling a few feet, and grabbed for Wendy. Their laughter floated across the high grass.

'He's going to marry her,' said Angie.

Jordana's heart seized for a second. 'Did he say something?'

Angie shook her head, still watching her brother. 'Just guessing.'

For the first time since moving into the house, Jordana felt lonely. A new moon had already risen, pale in the afternoon sky. An arrow of geese barked as they crossed overhead, chasing the last of summer south.

Chapter Thirty-Six

The business district of Cort had red brick office buildings from the 1930s – each window with its eyebrow of lighter brick – and two or three taller, newer buildings. For the last three weeks, Angie had temped in one of these buildings' management offices. The regular secretary was out on maternity leave, which people talked about as though she were doing something particularly indulgent and childish that they were being particularly generous in allowing. Cort's most hard-core businesses were in this building: branches of Dean Witter and Merrill Lynch, a publisher specializing in companies' year-end reports, a real-estate office that sold vacation homes to out-of-staters.

The job Angie inherited was mostly answering phone calls. If a toilet was stopped up on the sixth floor, she was supposed to say, 'I'll send an engineer right away'; then she went up with the plunger. A burnt-out lightbulb on the third floor? She'd send the engineer. Could someone run out for nondairy creamer? She'd send the engineer.

How did you meet people if you weren't in school, if you could have done your job with both eyes bandaged shut? She saw Trevor; she saw Luke and Wendy. Wendy only half counted as a friend, because she had to be nice to Angie. Wendy turned out to have a mode other than perfect composure; she had a tendency to blurt things out. Once she'd told Angie that she sometimes imagined meeting someone just like herself.

'"What's your name?"' Angie had said, then jumped left. '"Why, Wendy Miles, what's yours?"' Jumping right again: '"Hey! My name's Wendy Miles too!"'

Wendy had laughed. It made Angie like Wendy more, that she

could laugh at herself. And Angie liked that she and Luke always touched. At the same time, it made Angie need to tackle Luke, tickling him, messing up his hair.

The Xerox machine was out of toner. More had been ordered but hadn't yet arrived. When Angie copied documents, she could only do two pages before the copier stopped and complained in a halting voice that slurred, as if drunk, 'I am out of toe-nurr.' Then Angie had to open the front of the machine, remove the toner cartridge, and put it back in. She closed the copier and it hummed, warming up happily, thinking it had new toner. It would do two more pages, sometimes three, before realizing it had been tricked. She was copying a long memo for the building's tenants; it was going to take her all afternoon. Leaning her hips against the machine, she stared at its lid. *Flash. Flash.* A hesitation, then *flash.* Before the voice could begin, she bent down to undo the front latches.

After work – it wasn't one of her therapy days, and she didn't want to go home – she drove down to see Trevor, who still lived at the halfway house in Manchester. On his bureau was a pink slip; she asked, 'You got *another* write-up?'

'Like it matters. They call my mom, and all she wants to know is that I'm not being sent home. Anyway, I'm full-paying. They're not going to kick me out for being antisocial if being antisocial's the whole reason I'm in.'

'That and attempted self-immolation.'

'Right, and that.' Trevor laughed, and she felt a wave of affection for him. She could talk some to Luke about being sick, but Trevor was the only person who got that it could be funny.

They were lying side by side on his bed. Feeling the shift in her, he put his hand on her ribs, just below her breast. She stiffened, then slid away. Sex, the effort and nakedness of it, seemed impossible. Crossing the room, she pushed the window open farther, then lit a cigarette.

His roommate, Kurt – a slow-moving man of about forty with wide, cracked hands – wasn't home yet from his day-treatment job in a mayonnaise factory, where he checked the lids on jars. Kurt's side of the room was decorated like a high school locker with pictures neatly torn from magazines. A sports car, baseball players, a woman in a low-necked dress, ads for computers.

Trevor's walls were bare except for two photographs of Angie thumbtacked above the brown-painted dresser. Although he'd lived here more than two years, Trevor's things were still packed in cardboard boxes labeled SHIRTS, PANTS, TAPES, SHOES, PAPERS. The house rules required he do laundry once a week; afterward, he folded the clothes up and put them back in their boxes.

'You know what Kurt used to do? He used to cut himself with an electric carving knife. This is when he was a *kid*, like seven or eight.'

'Jesus.'

'I know.'

'What's he on?'

'Klonopin and Thorazine, I think.'

'Klonopin made me feel like I weighed about four hundred pounds.' She blew smoke at the ceiling light, watching the smoke tear as it rose. 'Isobel was in some kind of protest this weekend. She lay down in front of the hospital.'

'What was she protesting?'

'I don't know. Isobel probably doesn't know. Probably she saw people lying on the sidewalk and recognized her chance. She loves getting arrested.'

'She got arrested again?'

'Yeah. Bradley bailed her out. I think she's already using the experience to craft her essays for grad school.'

'When am I going to meet these famous housemates?'

She picked up the empty True package and peered inside, as though a cigarette might be hidden there. 'They're not around much.'

Trevor winced. 'What, I embarrass you?'

'It's not like they're so great or anything. They're just regular people.'

He shrugged and looked away. 'You're the only regular person I know.'

Chapter Thirty-Seven

Moving out, she'd left dozens of small things. Pieter threw out lists in her handwriting, a tin barrette in the shape of a fish. He threw out the dish soap she liked, Earth – the name was supposed to sound clean but didn't – and the green felt-tipped pens she used. He grimaced as he threw away sneakers shucked off on the basement stairs, a book forgotten on the kitchen windowsill, a Hank Williams tape left in the stereo. Like the other objects, the tape seemed stubbornly complete, something whose existence he couldn't erase even as he buried it deep in the trash among juice cartons and the gone-slimy remains of a tomato.

After a week or so, he came upon her things less and less frequently. Her mail continued to arrive: political newsletters, notes from friends who didn't know she was gone. Reaching for aspirin from the glove compartment as he drove home one afternoon from practice, his hand closed around her hairbrush. It was blue plastic, with black and gray hair tangled in the bristles. He pulled to the side of the road, rolled down the window, threw the brush out. It bounced down a small hill and came to rest.

He jerked the parking brake on, feeling his movements become stiff, his face going blank with injury, just as when he and Jordana fought. Leaving the car running, he picked his way down the hill. At the bottom, he bent with difficulty and then chucked the brush farther, into a copse of small ash trees.

Wendy was ironing her clothes for work when Pieter came in the back door. He'd forgotten to take aspirin, and his head pounded dully.

'Let me move this stuff.' She unplugged the iron, setting it on the counter.

286

'No, it's fine. It's fine.'

Ignoring him, she folded a pair of ironed black pants carefully over the back of a chair, then picked up the ironing board and resettled it in the corner. She lifted a wrinkled white shirt, snapped it in the air, and arranged it over the board.

Filling the kettle for tea, he asked if she'd like some, knowing she'd say no. She'd turned down every cup of tea he'd offered in the two months she and Luke had been here. Her consideration was so thorough it almost bent backward under its own weight into a form of rudeness.

So strange to live with a woman who wasn't Jordana. He didn't find Wendy particularly beautiful or alluring, but sometimes he caught himself looking at her body. The situation seemed to suggest it. How could he hear water in the pipes when she showered and not think of the fact that she was naked? He never heard the slightest noise of Wendy and Luke having sex, which forced him to imagine their being quiet so he *wouldn't* hear.

'How's work?' he asked.

'Last night, a woman ordered rosé and then dumped three Sweet 'n Lows into it. The sommelier almost had a fit.'

Pieter made himself chuckle. Jordana found Wendy uptight and controlling, which made him protective of the girl. He thought her abruptness came mostly from being shy. He poured water over the tea leaves and said, 'Well. Lessons.'

He carried the cup with him into the front room. He wouldn't start teaching for another twenty minutes, but making conversation was more than he could handle right now.

He taught two adults and then Adam, a twelve-year-old small for his age. Today Adam wore a T-shirt of consummate ugliness, a shaggy cartoon character thrusting forth its middle finger.

'Handsome shirt,' Pieter said, sitting in the chair opposite. He leaned forward, thumbs on temples, fingers across forehead, as though shading his eyes from the sun.

Adam was on Bach's unaccompanied working suites. His playing was fluent but one-dimensional. When Pieter stopped him, Adam flinched. He practiced three hours a day, at his parents' insistence. Pieter had no idea – he suspected the boy himself had no idea – whether he liked anything about the cello.

Pieter spent the last five minutes showing Adam how to tune his A string down to a G for the fifth suite. 'It takes awhile to get used to not having an open A. Play G on the D string, as normal; don't use open G.'

Adam nodded. At the end of each lesson, his sense of freedom was visible. Pieter felt the boy's relief so strongly that he almost experienced it as his own, at the same time that he knew Adam's liberation was from Pieter himself.

Adam's father, who waited for them out in the hall, was slight, dressed in khakis and round glasses. 'What happened in there?' he asked. With two fingers, he flicked his son on the temple, hard. 'You *know* that piece.'

Pieter put on a Brahms Mass to get the thin, ashy taste of lessons out of his mouth. In the kitchen, he ran the hottest water he could and washed the dishes. Bean wove around his ankles. He shoved her away with one foot; he had no patience for her these days. When the phone rang, he let the machine get it. Suddenly, his wife's voice filled the room.

Hello, she said. *You've reached the Voorsters. Neither of us is here right now . . .*

He felt weak with wanting her back. He opened the cabinets, but she'd taken her coffee mug, the black and red one that said KEEP YOUR LAWS OFF MY BODY. Without her, their kitchen was reduced to the shabbiness of its elements: the brown linoleum floor, the white metal cabinets scabbed with rust. Gone from the dark living room were her few CDs, all her books, the small needlepoint pillow she used to put behind her neck. (A patient at two-hospitals-ago had left the project behind, half-finished, and Angie had completed it in boredom and despair: *A HOUSE is made of brick and stone, a HOME is made of love.*) He needed to find a piece of her. He went upstairs to the bedroom, their bed a raft on the terrible green carpet. Spiny wire hangers jangled when he opened her closet door and reached for the light cord. The ill-fitting clothes he'd teased her about were gone, the boy's dungarees and sweaters unraveling at the hem, along with the two or three dark good dresses he'd chosen. Their absence shocked him every time. It was unfathomable that the clothes would continue on but not for him.

Finally he found a shoe under the bed. Lying on his side, he pulled it out from among the gray dustballs: a pump, black, something Jordana wore resentfully and only when she felt she had to. She would have kicked this shoe off at the end of the night, with enough force that it skipped across the green carpet before disappearing. Still on his side – shirtsleeve furred gray from reaching under the bed – he put his hand into the shoe, where sweat had left pale gray outlines of her sole and toes.

When Jordana wanted something, she went after it. The reason she had been able to convince him to move away from New York, to have a child and then another, was not because he loved her, though he did, but because her absolute surety so outweighed his flimsy indecision. He pressed his fingers against the shoe lining, the ghostly imprint of his wife's foot.

The house where Jordana was living turned out to be very small, a wooden place out in the middle of nowhere with a listing porch. The brown grass was so tall that at first the house appeared to be floating a few feet above the ground. It reminded him of something, and he closed his eyes until it came: a house half underwater that he'd seen the day he left Holland. In an attempt to hold back the invasion, the dikes had been opened, flooding the fields. Water pushed softly against the downstairs windows, so that the house had appeared to bob, unanchored.

All the lights in Jordana's house were on. They'd always been careful about electricity, and now he tried to think back to whether he'd been the one who'd started conserving. He couldn't remember; for so long they'd just done it.

He turned off the car and stared at the building. After a while, he realized how cold he was, a chill that reached his bones. He shivered. He stepped out of the car, shutting it quietly. He trod softly on the house's front steps – each had a low dip in the center, wood worn velvety soft – and looked in through the front window.

Jordana sat on the couch, legs outstretched. A glass of wine was next to her on the floor. She was reading a book, running the thumb of her other hand over her lips, over and over. It was a scene he had seen hundreds, thousands, of times in their own house. She'd left him for this? Country music wailed faintly.

He lowered to a squat, knees creaking. Being with a younger woman had somehow muted his awareness of his own aging, rather than heightening it. He'd almost used Jordana in place of a mirror: she had gray hair woven through the black, fine spiderwebs of lines at the corners of her mouth and eyes, definitely age but nothing alarming. But these last few months, without her, he'd become conscious of the way his shoulders stooped, of the thick

289

purple veins in his hands. His mind exaggerated his own frailty: He imagined his grip palsied though it was steady; saw himself shuffle forward, grinding slowness when his walk was still brisk.

He clamped his teeth together to stop their chattering. The phone rang, a faint burble through the glass. She put down the book, and in the first minute, while her back was toward him, he had time to imagine her lover. Had Jordana left him for someone after all, despite her insistences? She might now be arranging to meet, might be inviting someone to come over, to drive up and park behind Pieter's old Volvo. He would bound up the stairs, pass Pieter without seeing him, enter the house.

Then she turned, and on her face was a mixture of love and anxiety he recognized. Just Angie then, checking in. Pieter felt odd disappointment. It cleared his head enough to see himself, an aging man crouched in the cold. What if Jordana found him here? He backed down the porch steps. Then, abandoning caution, he ran to his car.

In the morning, he practiced for longer than usual but still he finished too early to go to rehearsal. He got into the car nonetheless and swung toward Applefield, instead of going straight to the rehearsal hall. He stopped at the general store, where he bought a carton of apple juice, not really wanting it but wanting something. Laura, who ran the store, had iron-gray hair, short except for a single braid, narrow as a shoelace, which reached down into the collar of her sweater. 'Nasty out there,' she said.

'Yes.' On another morning, it might have been he who commented on the weather and she who concurred. After more than twenty years in New Hampshire, he still wasn't considered a native, though he was no longer an out-of-towner, either. He didn't know if there was a word for what he was.

He stood near the woodstove, drinking his juice and looking out through the glass door. Across the street was the school bus parking lot: buses lined up neatly, a box of yellow pencils. It was a wet, gray morning, cold with fog. He wore a green sweater Angie had knit for him last Christmas. Though the wool's scratchiness irritated his neck and wrists, he'd begun wearing the sweater every day. It made him feel less solitary.

A man turned from the counter, paper bag in one hand, the other arm around the baby girl on his hip. Next to him, a small boy walked drunkenly, swinging his whole body with each step, and as they came close Pieter could see a metal bar, some kind of orthopedic device, holding the boy's feet apart. Sitting down, the man unscrewed the baby's bottle and carefully poured in orange soda.

Without Jordana, Pieter found himself imagining what she would notice or say. He couldn't turn it off, which meant he walked around flayed, open to all stimuli. He could be moved almost to tears by something like this family, the man gently pulling off his son's knit hat, smoothing down his hair. Pieter aimed his carton into the trash can's neat hole. Tenderness kept flooding him at odd moments like this one, dark water that could take him down as easily as it had once borne him along.

He let himself out into the cold drizzle of the parking lot – wet black leaves; a tabby cat crouched under a parked car, blinking unhappily – and drove to the empty rehearsal hall to wait out the rest of the hour there. He longed for the others to arrive; then he longed for rehearsal to begin; then he longed for it to be over.

Fidel had the other sections wait while the winds went over their part in the Shostakovich. Pieter thought of Jordana and felt his spirits lift a little, the way they might when he looked out the window and saw the mail being delivered. He realized he was imagining that he would see her again tonight, which of course he wouldn't. The hours ahead hollowed out.

Later, walking to his car, he was startled to see himself in the window of a store. He almost expected not to have a reflection.

Chapter Thirty-Eight

Wendy loved Sundays. When she woke, Mr. Voorster would be gone to quartet rehearsal and Luke would be sleeping against her in his old single bed. Sometimes she woke him, bracing herself on her arms and dragging the ends of her hair very lightly across his face and neck, laughing when he swatted at her sleepily. This morning, she just turned on her side and watched him sleep. Cut short, his hair looked darker than it had long.

They hadn't bothered rearranging Luke's bedroom, which was full of his old things: record albums in plastic milk crates, faded swim ribbons pinned above the desk. Early-morning sunlight streaked the ceiling. She wrapped her arm around his waist. His shoulder blade smelled of soap and chlorine. Running her hand down his stomach, she slipped it into the opening of his boxer shorts – in Iowa boxers were old-man underwear, and it had taken her awhile to adjust to Luke's wearing them – cupping her palm over him. It wasn't meant to be arousing; she just liked the feel of him in her hand.

When she woke again, Luke was propped up against his pillow, pen in hand, doing the crossword in *The White Mountain Times*. 'Hey,' he said, using the pen cap to lift a strand of her hair and tuck it behind her ear.

'What time is it?' She groped for his wrist: past ten. 'Wow.' She never slept so late. It took her aback and pleased her.

'When did you get in last night?'

'Late.' She yawned, saying through the yawn, 'I made more than a hundred bucks, though.'

'Ah mud muthahunnedbuhs,' he imitated, pretending to yawn and then overtaken by a real one.

She rolled over onto him, pummeling his shoulder. He laughed, catching her wrists in his hands. With one motion, he rolled them over, so she was on her back. He kissed her lips, then her neck, running his hand down her side.

The phone rang.

'No. Don't get it.'

He was already stretching his long arm across the bed. 'It could be Angie.'

The hostess showed them to a booth, dropping laminated menus in front of them. Angie wasn't there yet. 'Weekends are hard for her,' Luke said to Wendy for the third time.

She shrugged: What was there to say? She could hardly complain about missing one morning in bed together, when Angie had missed literally years of her life. What Wendy hated was that Luke seemed bewildered, even hurt, if she didn't feel just as enthusiastic about his sister as he did. He was always repeating some insight of Angie's, waiting for Wendy to say how amazing she, too, found it.

This restaurant wasn't Luke and Angie's kind of place. They liked diners with shabby remnants of fifties glitz – like Cleveland's, where Wendy had worked in Madison – or else cafés with community bulletin boards and homemade squash soup and hairy-legged waitresses. They'd chosen JP's only because it was near Angie's house; the Galaxie was in the shop. JP's had striped vinyl wallpaper, shiny floral upholstery in the booths, a wobbly gold-framed stand with ornate script that instructed customers to wait to be seated. The menu listed a scrumpdiddilicious banana split, nachos that would blow off the roof. Under the fried chicken with greens was *Mmmm-hmmm!! Dat's de GOOD stuff!!*

But Wendy liked this kind of restaurant. Families, still in their church clothes, sipped Cokes and cut into thick slices of ham steak topped with canned pineapple. Coffee cups, upside down on brown plastic trays, waited by one of the side-work stations. Senior year of high school, Wendy had worked at a place like this, a big step up from the Dairi Shoppe and McDonald's. She used to do homework during lulls, standing at the bread station. Steve picked her up every night; if she still had tables he sat at the counter eating pie the other waitresses brought and refused to charge him for. For years, her memories of Steve had been edged with contempt or embarrassment – she didn't know which – but now that she was far enough away, she could let herself miss him a little. His long legs wrapped around the stool's base. His big, tanned hands that smelled of soap.

'We need to move out of your dad's house,' she said.

'You said last week—'

'We're always with other people.' She felt fragile, jagged, like she might cry.

Luke said, 'It's just that every time I suggest we look for a place you say no, we're saving money, we should be patient.'

'I didn't mean indefinitely.'

Angie, out of breath, appeared by their booth, sliding in next to Luke. 'Sorry. Always late.' To Wendy, she said, 'Is this place okay? I know it's tacky.'

Wendy shrugged, trying to keep her face neutral. 'It's fine.'

'So, the funniest story.' Unwrapping an electric-blue scarf from around her neck, Angie launched into a narrative about her temp job, how she'd begun to answer her home phone *Hello, Regier Management*. She never seemed to be having a very hard time, though Luke always said she was; she chatted and laughed and called for more decaf.

Out the window, the trees blazed yellow and dark orange. In Cort, whose numbers swelled with tourists this time of year, everyone called this season Foliage. Apparently New Hampshire had a sixth season as well, Mud Season, between winter and spring.

'Why so glum, chum?' Angie asked Wendy.

'I'm not.'

Angie raised her eyebrows at Luke. 'Could've fooled me.'

Wendy shook her head and looked around for the waitress. She and Luke ordered hamburgers, Angie grilled cheese.

'Meat's like the worst thing for your body,' Angie said. 'We're not supposed to be meat eaters. We don't have the teeth for it.'

Luke groaned. 'Like I've never heard this before.'

'We can't even digest meat right. Sharks don't like to eat people because they taste rotten.'

'So you're more likely than I am to get eaten by a shark?' Luke asked.

The waitress brought their plates. 'I'm going to wash my hands,' Wendy announced. She hadn't spoken for a few minutes and her voice came out over-loud. She slid out of the booth.

She locked the bathroom door behind her. Her back ached from waitressing the night before. The floor didn't look too dirty; she sat, then lay down flat. Cloudy brown water stains drifted across the ceiling. She pulled her knees to her chest, unlatching the tightness in the small of her back.

She missed her sisters. God, she was alone.

She didn't want to get up from the floor, but of course she did. She held her hands, then her wrists, under the cold water. In the mirror, she looked very pale, freckles standing out like chicken pox.

She started back to the table. The waitress was just putting down their orders. Angie took one of Luke's French fries, and he slapped her wrist and she laughed, taking another. If Wendy didn't know them, she would think they were in love.

Luke looked up at her. He half frowned, half smiled – what are you *doing*? – and the moment for seeing him passed.

Chapter Thirty-Nine

Angie stepped off the porch of their rambling Victorian, crossed the street, and crouched by the fence. On the other side, the brindle puppy cringed and wriggled. She glanced around to make sure the owner's car was gone and pushed the cold scrambled eggs she'd brought under the fence. The puppy wolfed them down, and Angie worked three fingers through the fence to scratch its head. The puppy (in her head she called him Gibson) stilled, seemingly spellbound, though if she moved too suddenly he would yip and spring back.

Even though it meant getting to work too early, she took the eight o'clock bus instead of the eight-thirty; what if the bus was slow one day? The thought of being late to work was terrifying.

The bus drove east on Route 138, passing the bank building with her mother's clinic, a half mile of car lots with plastic flags, hanging limp and dripping in the rain. A new not-yet-grimy billboard advertised pork as 'the other white meat,' and across the street, The *Hard Times* marquee echoed:

EXXXPLOSIVE DANCERS

'SCHOOLGIRL SALLY' THE OTHER
OTH3R WHITE M3AT

This temp job had gone on two months now. As she was sorting the mail, one of the managers stopped by her desk. He was in his early thirties and WASP-handsome, with receding hair and watery blue eyes. 'How are you liking the job?'

'It's good,' she said.

'You're good at it.'

She was good at it because she still couldn't concentrate enough to read books, and because she didn't have people to whom she might make long personal calls, and because if she sat still too long, she thought too much. During the long afternoon lulls, she had reorganized the filing system, thrown out the outdated catalogs and phone books, and started a recycling system. She dusted the front office twice a day and made fresh coffee constantly.

The manager asked her, 'How much are you getting for this job?'

'Seven dollars an hour.'

'You know we pay the temp agency fifteen?'

She nodded.

'Anita's decided she's not coming back. You can quit the agency; we'll hire you and pay nine. Everyone wins.'

A real job: The idea was terrifying. When one of her house-mates' friends asked what she did and she said *I'm temping,* the very uncoolness of the job made it cool. The job at which you temped could not, by its very nature, be an identity – you shed it at the end of the day as surely as you would eventually shed it entirely after a few days or weeks. Her housemates' friends did things like temp for three weeks, then make silkscreens for two, or use office temp jobs to work secretly on their screenplays. Now Angie wouldn't be *temping,* she would be a *receptionist.*

Seeing her hesitation, the manager said, 'Nine-fifty.'

'Eleven,' she heard herself say. It was like a game.

'Ten.'

'Eleven. It still saves you more than six hundred dollars a month.' She'd always been good at doing simple math in her head, a mostly useless skill.

'Fine.' He didn't look as cheerful, and Angie realized as he walked away that she didn't care – and how rare it was for her not to care – that he liked her a little less than he had.

So. A receptionist.

Angie had heard that a house's actual matter would fit in a teaspoon; the rest was the space between atoms. In the same way, the day's actual work took maybe an hour: a few phones answered, lunch ordered from the Great Wall, some papers to be copied and sent off. She reorganized the filing system a second time, threw out old magazines in the waiting room. Always, she prodded

297

herself gingerly, like touching a bruise or a cavity. Did her restlessness mean her meds weren't working? But mania felt invincible and pure, and all she felt now was a need to keep moving. A faint dread always moved in her like a steel rasp, but if she kept busy enough she didn't have to pay attention to it.

She computerized the list of things to be ordered:

- ☐   Lightbulbs
- ☐   fluorescent tubes
- ☐   incandescent, 40 watts
- ☐   incandescent, 75 watts
- ☐   Toilet paper
- ☐   Cups

She found an insulated paper cup to order instead of environment-fucking Styrofoam. It was wonderful and awful, to succeed on such a small scale. To measure out days restocking the coffee station and unjamming paper from the Xerox machine, fingers blackening. The ink had a strange powdery texture, and when she turned her fingers they glittered a little, as though dusted with mica. She went into the bathroom, where the pink and frills made her want to touch things with her inky fingers and mar them. Instead, a good employee, she washed her hands, washed the black streaks from the basin, went back to her desk. She tried to channel Wendy, to be neat and efficient and give nothing away.

She saw Luke and Wendy Friday night, but then Saturday stretched, hot and terrible, toward Saturday night. Angie's room, at the back of the house, faced east. She'd hooked a wool blanket over the curtain rod to keep out morning light, shutting out the motel with its sign that seemed to command WELCOME VACANCY. She got up, took her lithium, and went back to bed. Faintly from downstairs she could hear the bird clock strike eleven with eleven white-breasted nuthatch calls. She wished she could work all weekend.

When finally she dragged down to the kitchen, Maureen said, 'Trevor called. He says he really needs to talk to you.'

Angie made a face and sat down at the kitchen table. Trevor called constantly, three times a day sometimes, always with something crucial.

298

Maureen washed brushes in the sink. Angie, watching her, tried to think how to ask if she could watch Maureen paint. She wanted it to sound like she was interested in painting, not just dreading the afternoon. Unfortunately, she didn't like Maureen's work much: too gooped and muddy.

Isobel wandered in. She wore an Indian sari, pale pink that made her skin look golden brown. 'I'm bored,' she said to Maureen.

'Where's Bradley?'

'I hate Saturdays.' She sat at the table. 'They make me feel like killing myself.'

'Me too,' Angie said.

'Not literally.'

'Oh, me neither.'

'Bradley's with his fucking band.' Isobel picked up a catalog from the table, flipped through it aimlessly, then threw it down. 'Maybe we should go for a drive.'

'I'm painting.' Maureen, her back still to them, held up brushes.

'*I'll* go with you,' Angie said.

'I don't know. I probably won't even do it.'

Above the sink, the bird clock ticked, then whirred into twelve owl hoots. The curtains lifted on a thin breeze. Outside, a car approached, stereo thumping.

With her thumbnail Isobel scraped some varnish up from the table. 'Oh, fuck it. Where should we go?'

They drove to Portsmouth. The whole town reminded Angie of Cort's historic district; like in Cort, the old brick warehouse buildings had been turned into shops selling candles and pottery and gourmet coffee.

Isobel picked up some shoes from the sale table outside a store. Turning them over, she frowned at the size. 'They're too small. They might fit you, though.'

The shoes were high heels, the upper part made of dozens of narrow silver straps. 'It's not really my look.' She didn't take the shoes: she hated Isobel to see how much her hands trembled. 'I haven't worn heels since – in a long time.' Manic, her skirts got shorter, makeup brighter, heels higher. But she knew that only from photographs and fleeting memories of feeling charming and irresistible, filled with wit and power. She'd felt more in touch, saner, than at any other time in her life.

299

'They'd look cool with jeans. No offense, but your clothes don't do as much for you as they could.'

Isobel was always saying *no offense* right before she was rude. Angie could never get away with wearing those shoes. You had to be, like Isobel, so cool you didn't think about coolness. You had to be someone resolutely sure of your own sanity to risk looking bizarre.

They bought ice cream and wandered down to the water, dark green and smelling of brine. Trash rocked listlessly against the docks' pilings. Isobel still wore the pink sari. People turned to look at her; she was six feet tall, only a few inches more than Angie, but her carriage made her seem even taller. Angie felt like Igor, rushing and scraping behind, saying *Yes, master.*

'Let me call home, see if Bradley's back.'

Angie watched her call from the pay phone. Isobel glanced at her through the glass and Angie quickly looked away. Nearby, a shipping company had dumped hills of dirty salt, of gleaming coal. Seagulls wheeled and cried.

Isobel came out of the booth. 'He's not there. But apparently Trevor called twice more.'

'I'll call when I get back.'

'Is he your boyfriend?'

'He'd like to be.'

Isobel nodded, accepting this.

It was the truth. Still, Angie felt like shit, having said it. The halfway house had recently gotten a new doctor, who had picked up Trevor with the enthusiasm new doctors always did, reexamining his files and giving him a new diagnosis.

Isobel had seemed not even to notice the casual cruelty of *He'd like to be.* She wrapped herself in a hairy sweater, olive green, that would have made any normal person look like Oscar the Grouch but somehow just made her look more ethereal. Her brown hair streamed behind her in the wind.

You are with your friend Isobel, Angie told herself. *You are with your friend Isobel.* Salty wind blew, and Angie had to hold back her hair with both hands to keep it from whipping her face. Maybe after today Isobel would invite Angie along the next time she went out with friends from State.

When Wendy had confessed the desire to meet someone just like herself, Angie had thought it was narcissistic. Now it just seemed

300

lonely. Angie wanted to be loved most by someone. She wanted to be held. She wanted to be happy her brother had found Wendy and not to wish for them to break up. She wanted her father to stop being sad, and she wanted it with a frustration and impatience belying the months she'd spent depressed and knowing there was no way to *just snap out of it*.

In the car home, she felt quiet and sun-stunned. Isobel was talking about the year she'd modeled in Italy. She said, 'I hated it.'

Angie kept almost knowing who Isobel reminded her of, but then the connection would slip away. She was getting bored with Isobel, though the boredom was still edged by a starstruck sense of luck. Forcing herself to make an effort, she asked, 'Which did you hate? Italy or modeling?'

'Both of them. All of it.'

Isobel had lived in a house owned by her modeling agency and had spent all her time going from go-see to go-see, dragging out her portfolio and mostly being rejected. 'They'd say things, to my face, like, 'You're too *pretty*' – except they said it like something disgusting, and then they'd say, 'Pretty's *old,* it's *boring.*' And then the rest of the time, when I wasn't going on calls, I was not eating. There were four of us in a room, in these fucking bunk beds, and all anyone ever talked about was how to lose more weight. It was like ninety-five percent of your brain got sheared away. You forget there's anyone in the world who's *not* fixated on clothes and being thin and learning to Walk.'

The resemblance finally clicked: Hannah, the college girl at the farm. She and Isobel were both tall with similar coloring and surprisingly deep voices. Angie let herself tune Isobel out, feeling an unlikely rush of nostalgia for the farm. At seventeen, she'd thought she'd hit bottom; there had been no farther down she could imagine.

Oh, she missed herself. It felt like the way she used to miss Abe, when he was at Harvard and then after they broke up. No, deeper than that: the way she'd sometimes missed her parents when she was a child and had slept over at a friend's. She was homesick for herself, a longing so deep and unanswerable that for a moment it took her breath away.

At the house, Maureen met them at the door. 'Trevor is here.'

Angie's scalp went cold. 'Here?'

301

'In the living room,' said Maureen.

'The *living* room?' She was talking like her shrink, repeating statements as questions. She and Isobel still stood on the porch, Maureen in the door. Maureen and Isobel exchanged a long look. Angie ducked into the house.

'He's been here, like, two hours,' said Maureen behind her.

Jason stood uncertainly near the living room's closed door. Jason was the roommate she'd had the least conversation with; easygoing and usually stoned, he listened to the Samples in his room and emerged to devour bags of chocolate-chip cookies at the kitchen counter. Now he looked spooked. 'I tried to go in and your friend, like, screamed at me.'

'Oh, God.'

'I had this really bad trip once—'

'It's not a trip.' She closed her eyes, forcing herself to breathe less shallowly. Then she called, 'Trevor? It's me. It's Angie.'

There was no answer. She made herself push open the door, closing it behind her on the curious faces of her housemates. The room was dark, curtains pulled, and she didn't see Trevor. Then he turned toward her.

He was panting. There was just enough light from around the edges of the drapes to see his face, high cheekbones and sharp chin, and the glint of a white shirt. In the dimness, his dark eyes appeared as hollows, as though they'd been gouged out.

She turned on the light.

Trevor cried out. He was naked. What she'd taken to be a white shirt was instead the smooth silvery gleam of scar tissue. Leaping up from the corner, he bounded across the room, face distorted. He smacked the light switch off and leaned into Angie's face. 'Don't you fucking do that.' Spit sprayed her cheek. 'Don't you fucking do that to me again.'

'Stop it. Keep your *voice* down. Don't pull that mental-patient stuff with me.'

Trevor wheeled away from her and began pacing, hands gripping his hair.

'What are you doing here?' She said it fiercely but quietly, so her housemates wouldn't hear. 'Who said you could come here?'

In the dark, his naked chest gleamed white; his legs were dark with hair, so that his torso almost seemed to float disembodied. She bent, patting the floor near where she thought she'd seen his clothes.

Finding his jeans, she thrust them toward him. 'Put these on.'

'Oh, Christ.' He backed away from her, eyes wide. His lips were moving.

'Put them on!' She threw the wadded pants toward him. They hit his thigh and slid to the floor.

Someone knocked, and Maureen said, 'Angie?'

'It's okay!'

'What's going on?'

She opened the door a crack. Isobel, frowning, said, 'Is everything under control?'

'Everything's fine.' Angie hoped her body blocked Trevor. 'He's upset,' she added lamely. 'Just go. It's better on my own.'

Trevor bounded up, crossing the room. He thrust his arm through the open door just as Angie slammed it, hitting him with a loud *crack*. Maureen cried out.

'Don't go,' he said. *'Don't go.'*

'Angie?' Maureen said uncertainly.

'It's okay,' Angie said to him, forcing her voice to be soothing. To her housemates: 'Go hang out somewhere else. Trev, I'm going to touch you now, okay? I'm about to touch your arm. Okay, I'm touching your arm now – *you guys can* go! – we're going to walk over to the couch.'

He was trembling all over. She wanted to hit him as hard as she could in his naked stomach.

'Do you think you can get dressed?' she asked.

'That girl hates me, she *hates* me.'

Ignore the specifics, address the emotion. 'You're safe.'

'Everyone's going to see what's inside me.'

Struggling to get his pants over his ankles she remembered, from a hundred years ago, making Lily dress. She told him to raise his arms. His new meds must not be working. How had he decompensated so fast? She hated herself for hating his vulnerability – her, of all people.

'I'm going to call Teresa.'

His lips were moving, but she didn't try to catch what he was mumbling.

She opened the door. Her housemates had followed her directions and moved off, into the kitchen. An old David Bowie song played softly, a pot clanked: the noise of an ordinary night. Someone laughed.

Lucidly, Trevor said, 'Don't leave me.'

'It's just for a moment—'

'Don't go!'

The phone was just upstairs; she could call the halfway house and be back in less than five minutes. Less than two. Nothing bad would happen to Trevor, but she couldn't leave him scared like this.

Her housemates would have to make the phone call. She didn't let herself balk. Closing her eyes, she yelled their names.

Chapter Forty

'Is Luke there?'

'Hi, *Angie,*' Wendy said, as pointedly as she dared; she didn't particularly feel like being called on it, but she was also tired of Angie acting like Wendy was Luke's receptionist. 'How are you?'

'I'm fine. Is Luke there?'

'He's at work already.'

'Shit.'

From the living room window, if she craned her neck, Wendy could see Cort's town square down the street, through the black trunks of trees. It was November and overcast, and the late-morning sky was the dull color of tin.

Wendy suppressed a sigh. 'Is there something I can do?'

'I need a ride to the hospital. The Galaxie's in the shop again.'

Wendy had Luke's car today because she planned to grocery-shop later. 'I don't have to be at the restaurant until five-thirty.'

'Oh.' Angie sounded taken aback; there was a long silence before she said she guessed that would be okay. So she hadn't been fishing for a ride from Wendy after all.

Annoyed at losing her morning, annoyed at Angie's tactlessness, annoyed at Trevor for being in the hospital, annoyed at the microwave for choosing just that moment to *ding* – she'd been baking a potato – Wendy stomped into the bedroom and changed out of her blue sweater and into one she liked better, a gray that matched her eyes. Mostly, she was annoyed with herself for wanting Angie to like her.

Wendy sat in the cooling car in the hospital parking lot, balancing her checkbook. She disliked her backward-slanting handwriting;

she could force it to be neat but not to be pleasing. She wrote out a check for her student loan, entering the amount in the register.

The passenger door whooshed open and Angie flung herself into the seat, bringing with her a gust of cold air. 'Trevor won't see me.'

'Oh.' It wasn't even that Wendy came up with platitudes and then rejected them; her mind was literally blank.

'Shit,' Angie said. 'Shit. Shit.'

The more Wendy tried to find words, the more words retreated back to the edges of her brain. Finally, she came up with, 'Have you ever stayed here?'

She couldn't believe she'd asked. Angie didn't seem to find it outrageous; she ducked to look up through the windshield at the hospital, a tall yellow rectangle with mauve curtains at each window. 'Once. It's super expensive, so depending on what kind of insurance ... Trevor's family is pretty rich.'

'So is yours.'

'No, we're not,' said Angie, sounding confused.

It began to rain, a few heavy drops plunking on the windshield and hood. Wendy's gray wool turtleneck, which had looked so nice when she put it on, felt tidy and dull next to Angie's ancient black fisherman's sweater and her waterstained workboots, her long legs akimbo in old Levi's.

'Why won't he see you?'

'I don't know,' Angie said. 'Maybe because he's crazy?'

Wendy laughed, then covered her mouth, stricken. Luke would never have said something so blunt. Straightening up, she asked, 'So. Is there someplace you'd like me to drop you off? Work?'

'It's my fault he's here.'

'I'm sure that's not true.'

'Well, but you don't really have any idea, do you?'

Wendy exhaled and rolled her eyes, looking straight ahead, as though there were a witness there. Preferably Luke.

'I called in sick at work,' Angie said.

There was by now a slow, loud, heavy rain, though the air wasn't dark. New Hampshire, like Iowa, had hundreds of kinds of rain. Wendy shivered, suddenly cold, missing home.

'I actually have sick days,' said Angie. 'I get paid even if I get sick. I've never had that before.'

'So where should I drop you then? Home?'

Angie turned toward her. She had on mascara and dark eyeliner, which Wendy hadn't seen her wear before. 'Thank you. For driving me here.'

'It's not a big deal. Where—'

'It *is* a big deal.'

Lonely as she was, she felt disappointment. Part of her wanted Angie to continue to act badly, wanted the clarity and the buffer of resenting her.

They drove back down along Route 64, with its package stores, houses with Big Wheels littering the mangy lawns, convenience stores advertising Budweiser and Broasted Chicken. When Wendy pulled up in front of the brown Victorian, Angie bit her cuticle, suddenly distracted and unhappy.

'My housemates are pissed at me,' she said. 'For the whole thing with Trevor. They say I should have told them.'

'Told them what?'

'Just Isobel, really. That I have a *history*. She says it wouldn't have changed anything if I'd told them, but now she's uncomfortable because I lied.'

Wendy had met the housemates. It was irritating that Angie thought bitchy Isobel was so beautiful and cool. They sat and watched people go by, Angie playing with the end of her bootlace. She must have just washed her hair; the air in the car smelled like orange and cloves. Wendy couldn't think of anything to say that didn't smack of false cheer.

'I've been thinking about moving,' Angie said. 'I mean, really moving. To San Francisco.'

'Who's in San Francisco?'

'No one. That's the point. It's just a city I like.' Angie jiggled her leg, staring out the window; then she turned and looked at Wendy. '*You* started over.'

It was nice, hearing her move to Cort described as courageous; it had felt so desperate and scattershot. 'I had Luke, though,' she said.

'Don't tell him, okay? He'd get all worried. It's just a fantasy.'

Wendy nodded.

'Well.' Angie gathered up her bag.

Suddenly, Wendy wanted her not to go yet. 'What kind of shampoo do you use?' she asked.

'Maybe there's something I could have said at the hospital? A message for them to give Trevor? Do you think?'

'I don't know.'

'Yeah, you're right,' Angie said, and got out of the car. Late afternoon; behind her, a dirty moon had risen. She seemed about to speak, then shrugged and bumped her hip into the car door. The noise of its shutting cracked across the cold purple air. The faint, spicy smell of her hair lingered in the car for blocks.

Chapter Forty-One

Twice a day, Angie called the psych ward. Whichever nurse answered would put her on hold, then come back to the phone and say they couldn't confirm or deny Trevor's residency but would take a message. He didn't return her calls.

She took a succession of cold buses to the hospital. In the front lobby she waited behind a troop of Girl Scouts who needed directions. They clutched lumpy teddy bears they must have sewn themselves. Painstakingly, the volunteer at the Information Desk traced a route on a Xeroxed map, showing the troop leader how to get to the children's ICU.

When Angie said she wanted to go to the sixth floor, the volunteer phoned. Because it was a locked unit, she couldn't just go up; without the key card, the elevator proceeded smoothly from five to seven as though there were no sixth floor.

The volunteer hung up. 'They can't confirm or deny his residency. I can't send you up.'

'I know he's there,' Angie said.

'They can't confirm or deny—'

'What are you, a recording? Brain-dead?'

He raised his hands like someone being held up, blinking rapidly. He had a tuffet of white hair in each ear. She realized she was leaning over the desk, her face close to his, and she made herself move back.

She recognized him. No: she recognized something *in* him. She had developed radar for mental illness, for the small awkwardnesses and hesitations, the sudden blurtings, things that to someone else might look like stupidity or shyness or misplaced enthusiasm. This guy was volunteering here because he couldn't hold a paid job; his case manager had probably worked hard to get him this position.

'Trevor's refusing to see me,' she said flatly. 'At least tell me the truth.'

'You're not on his list.'

She wondered if he'd recognized her also. 'Thank you.'

Outside, a bus slumbered, breathing heavy clouds of exhaust into the cold air. Angie knocked on the folding glass door; the driver opened her eyes and shook her head.

'What?' Angie shouted. 'You're not going to let me on?'

The driver said something.

'What?'

The woman used the lever to crack open the door. 'I'm on my break.'

'You can't let me on, just to sit?'

'Ten minutes, I'll pull up to that stop.' The driver nodded toward the bus shelter. 'Then you can get on.'

'It's really cold,' Angie said, but the driver had already pulled the door closed and shut her eyes. 'Petty fucking bureaucrats!' Angie shouted. She drew back her fist, about to pound on the door. She felt the desire – enormous, rising like a submarine – to lose control.

She imagined the relief of it, of letting go. Of screaming and beating against the fabric of the world until it ripped. Attendants in hospital whites would lift her, bear her to a bed. On the locked ward, she could be taken care of. The personality she'd jerry-built could collapse.

Crazy. It was crazy to think that way. She covered her face for a moment with her hands, whispering *keep it together, keep it together, keep it together*.

She looked up. Tree branches, encased in ice, clicked in the wind; a woman tethered to an IV smoked outside the hospital doors. Above them hovered a seagull that looked like a child's drawing of a seagull, a blunt V against the gray sky. Doing her best imitation of someone who knew how to live in the world as it was, she went to the bus stop to wait the driver out.

She took the bus to the hospital every few days until the Galaxie was finally fixed; then she drove, almost every day. She asked whoever was volunteering at the front desk to call up to the sixth

310

floor. One day, the volunteer (an older woman, with hair dyed the same beige as her cardigan) put down the phone. 'All right.'

'That's okay,' said Angie, starting to turn away. But the volunteer was opening a desk drawer that held elevator key cards.

Being on the other side of this process made her feel like an imposter as she took the elevator to the sixth floor, signed a visitor's book, emptied her pockets. A nurse checked for sharps and took Angie's cigarette lighter before buzzing her into the hall.

Trevor sat in the dayroom. Her hands began to sweat. He wore hospital clothes. The runneled scar tissue of his arms and neck gleamed. Above him, the TV showed a woman beaming as she cleaned her kitchen counter.

Trevor looked up at her and said in a spookily gentle tone, 'Angie. It's nice to see you.'

She dropped onto the couch next to him. The vinyl squeaked. His gaze drifted to the television.

'You look great,' she said.

A nurse walked into the room, counted heads, walked out. What Angie remembered from living on this ward was that there was nowhere to go for quiet or privacy, the dayroom filled with the blare of bad television, bathroom trips with an aide waiting restless outside your stall so you didn't hang yourself with the toilet seat. Every psych unit was different. At Beechman, they'd only let you use spoons to eat. At White Mountain General the lighter could only be used by a nurse; at Hillman-Stowe you could use the lighter yourself but it was leashed to the nursing counter like a pen at the DMV.

This ward wasn't segregated by gender. In an orange chair was a woman with paper napkins knotted around hanks of her hair. She said loudly, 'I've got so many boyfriends it's *pathetic*.'

'How are you doing?' Angie asked Trevor. She remembered him naked that night at her house; the contrast of heavy hair on his legs to the pale scar tissue of his chest had made him look like a satyr.

'No.' The woman addressed the spot that happened to contain Angie. 'I said, *no*. Because I've got too many *already,* that's why.'

'So. What have you been doing?' Angie asked Trevor.

Trevor glanced around the dayroom, then looked at Angie with the barest trace of his old irony.

'Are they treating you pretty well?' Angie sounded to herself like all the people who had visited her and not known what to say.

311

Sometimes, she had deliberately not made it easier for them. Let them be uncomfortable. Why shouldn't they be uncomfortable? Trevor was either employing the same logic or just too miserable to make an effort.

She asked how Group was, whether he knew people here from other places, and he gave brief, vague answers. Listening to him was like listening to a tape player with weak batteries, his voice slowed and a little slurred. His attention floated away; he laughed, and it took her a moment to realize he was laughing at something on the television, a commercial for bread. She scrubbed her sweating hands on the legs of her jeans.

'Up the ass,' said Napkin Woman.

'How's the food?'

His gaze was unsteady, like the flicker of a candle. 'Do you have cigarettes?'

She dug the pack from her jacket pocket and gave it to him. The nurse walked into the room, counted heads, walked out. Trevor leaned over to another patient, briefly bumming a cigarette to light his own. Then he handed his cigarette to Angie so she could light hers, a gesture so familiar she felt a moment of woozy disorientation.

She blurted, 'I might move to San Francisco.' Up until now, it hadn't been something she thought she'd actually ever do, only an image, something to hold onto: *I could always leave. I could go to San Francisco.* As she said the words, they felt possible. People left; she could leave.

'You what?'

'I might be moving—'

For the first time, he was looking right at her, stricken. 'You can't.'

'I—'

'You're not leaving me here!' His voice rose, and he took a deep breath. She could feel his struggle to keep steady by biting off each word: 'You. Are. Not. Leaving. Me. Here.'

'Trevor, please.'

Two orderlies jostled through the door, and for a moment, dislocated, she thought they'd come for her. One moved behind Trevor but didn't touch him. The other said, 'Calm down, man. C'mon. Calm down.'

The napkin woman said, 'Yeah, if the world was a giant *twat*. Which it's *not.*'

312

'Don't leave me,' Trevor said quietly.

She nodded. She did care about him: maybe not as a lover, but she did. And he needed her. She stood. Madness was as real a part of her as anything else. She had to embrace it, because to deny it would be annihilating – though she'd always thought the opposite.

She took a step toward him and then stopped, heart banging.

'Oh, God,' she said. 'I'm sorry.'

She bolted, passing the nurse without retrieving her things, saying loudly, 'Buzz me out, buzz me out.' The elevator came; inside she leaned against the wall. There was a roaring in her head and she sagged against the wall, flooded with shame, face breaking out in prickly sweat. What had she done?

The elevator bell dinged; the doors slid open. Half expecting someone to order her to halt, she walked through the lobby and out into the night, free. The tree branches glittered with ice. She gulped in air so cold she felt it might crack her open.

Chapter Forty-two

Wendy had noticed that Luke's male friends, if they danced, always danced *ironically*. They would assume looks of false seriousness and do disco moves, pretending to respond to their own brilliance with expressions of awe. Or they'd hunch up their shoulders and move like robots. Luke wasn't like that; he just jumped earnestly up and down.

The party was down in Syria, at the apartment of four guys, semi-friends of Luke's from high school. They'd decorated the place with stolen traffic signs: MEN WORKING § BE PREPARED TO STOP.

The room was small and hot. They took a break – a decision reached by hand signals and lip-reading, the music too loud for words. Pushing through the crowd, Luke opened the sliding glass door to the patio. He closed it behind them, the noise suddenly muffled to a buzz.

Wendy pushed sweaty tendrils of hair back from her forehead, gulping her drink. This was her third beer but, surprisingly, it didn't seem to be affecting her much.

'God,' Luke said. 'Too much high school at once.' His voice was too loud, as though they were still inside. She was hearing a persistent growl, like holding a seashell to her ear.

'Is, um, Khamisa here?'

Luke shook his head. 'I forget that you haven't met.'

She hoped she hadn't let jealousy slip into her voice. He asked her something. Shaking her head, she said, 'My ears are ringing.'

'Water?'

'Beer.'

He raised his eyebrows: she didn't usually drink so fast. 'Not even buzzed,' she said, probably too loud. Her eardrums felt achy and plugged, like she was at the bottom of a swimming pool.

Luke opening the sliding door released a quick burst of noise, cut off abruptly as he closed the door behind him. She might be a little drunk. Wendy turned and leaned over the balcony railing. She could see a little way over the town, but not very far. She wasn't entirely used to the hills and thick trees in New Hampshire that meant you never had a clear sight line.

The door opened behind her and she said, 'Hey,' and turned, smiling, to see a woman with dark magenta lipstick. 'Oh, sorry. I thought you were someone else.'

'You're Luke's wife.'

The woman wore gray wool pants and a shimmery top, the kind of outfit magazines advised for the office Christmas party, too fancy here. Wendy glanced inside for Luke. He wasn't looking at her; he had that expression he got around lots of people, anticipation and happiness. His mouth was a little open, his eyes bright.

'You're Luke's wife,' the woman said again.

Something about her intensity made Wendy not set her straight about being just Luke's girlfriend. 'Wendy. And you're—'

'Kristin Cannon. I knew Luke in high school.' Behind the casualness of her voice was a pressure that made the words come a little too fast. 'We weren't friends exactly. I just used to stand outside his house at night.' She laughed. 'I was madly in love with him. I thought I was.'

So this was the girl from the yard. After a moment, Wendy asked, 'What do you do, Kristin?'

Kristin laughed, as though she found the question absurdly square. 'What do *you* do?'

Wendy wished she had an answer other than the truth. 'I wait,' she said. Kristin frowned and she added, 'Tables.'

'You look like a teacher.' Kristin laughed again. Then silence. Kristin nodded to the faint beat of the music from indoors, her face distant. In slight increments, she turned her body toward the party, the way people did when they were bored with a conversation. Drunkenness hit Wendy all at once, like something she'd been falling towards. She held the rail, forcing the world steady.

Kristin turned back to her and said, quickly, 'I'll show you something. Here.'

She handed Wendy her drink, took a step back, and undid the

315

top button of her slacks. Pulling up her shirt a few inches, she bent to look at her own stomach. 'It's faded some,' she said, and then straightened, holding her waistband down with one hand and her shirt out of the way with the other.

'What?'

Kristin pinned the shirt to her side with her elbow, freeing her hand, and picked up a candle from the small table behind her. When she held the light near her belly, a crosshatching of white lines came into view. It took a moment for Wendy to put together that the lines were scars, that the scars were letters, that the letters made up the name luke voorster. They staggered across her skin, shrinking as they neared her side, the final ter so cramped it looked like a single letter.

'*God.*' Without thinking, Wendy reached out. Under her fingers the marks felt shiny, thin and polished as fishing line. She jerked her hand back.

'A letter a week. And then I'd pour vodka on it.' Kristin had her head tilted to the side, regarding the scars. 'You let the cut start to close up and then a few days later you go over it again so it won't heal over. I always thought I'd show them to Luke one day. I had this whole thing worked out where we finally got together, and when he saw them he started crying.' She pulled her pants up and took her drink back from Wendy. 'I'm pretty drunk.'

'I noticed.' She didn't want to be feeling empathy, but she could imagine perfectly the fantasy of Luke crying over the scars, head pressed to Kristin's thigh. It was odd, and oddly charming, that Kristin could tell the story.

'He was – you should have known him then. It was like he had this shield around him. Not a shield, a glow or something. He wasn't like other people. I didn't think he'd get soft.'

'He's not soft.'

'I don't mean physically.' Kristin shrugged, letting her shirt drop. 'I didn't think he'd turn out so – like everybody else.'

A ragged snow of heavy, slow flakes had begun. Luke steered down the slippery streets, glancing occasionally from the road to Wendy's profile, sharp against the dark window. He asked if she'd liked the party. *Sure.* Was she tired? *No.* Was she okay? *Yes.* Was she sure? *Yes!*

Just as he got onto the 91, which would take them back to Cort,

Wendy said, 'Pull over.'

'We're not near an exit—'

'Pull over!'

He steered them onto the shoulder. Wendy was already fumbling at the lock. She wrestled the door open before the car had completely stopped, stumbling out with her arm still caught in the seat belt. She leaned over and threw up, her arm held up behind her before she managed to jerk it free from the shoulder strap. She fell to her knees and threw up again in a series of long wrenching coughs. He got out of the car without looking and a tractor-trailer roared by, two feet from his body, a gust that blew his eyes closed.

When he reached Wendy, she was on all fours on the road's shoulder. He crouched and pulled her hair out of her face. The speeding headlights of cars slashed the patch of gravel where they knelt. Snow eddied around them. Wendy leaned forward, ratcheted with dry sobs.

'Oh, God, I'm sorry.'

'Don't be sorry. Don't be sorry.' He brushed the gravel off her hand and kissed the palm. He liked when Wendy let him take care of her.

She said, 'People don't get over things.'

He would never know what was going on inside her. A car passed. In the swell of headlights he could see her face for a moment, the careful features, a scattering of whiteheads up near her hairline. Snowflakes fell thickly, yellowish and greasy-looking.

When the headlights passed, he and Wendy were in darkness, the snow invisible again. 'I hate us. I hate how we are,' she said.

She was breaking up with him again. 'Wen, don't. Just – just don't.'

Still on her hands and knees, she said, 'We should get married.'

Chapter Forty-Three

Wind bent the treetops toward each other as Pieter parked at the river. Snow blew against the car. It would be too cold to skate for very long, but he didn't want to skip skating altogether.

As he finished lacing his skates, he put his shoes onto the passenger seat and closed the car door, stumping awkwardly to the river's edge, then bending cautiously to slip off his skate guards. River ice was lead gray close to the bank, then silver and, nearest the river's center, chalk white.

The blades hissed over the surface. Skating was the only part of the day when his thoughts didn't tilt and clash, past and future locking and unlocking horns in his head. How had he come to be so alone?

He had thought, because of the snow, that he'd skate to Lightstone, but when he got there he kept going. He felt faster than usual today. Skating under the bridge, he went all the way down into parkland. Firs lined both banks, dark spires against the porous gray of the sky.

When finally he turned to go back, he realized that he'd felt so energized and fast because the wind had gotten much stronger. At his back, it had pushed him forward. Now the sparse snow felt suddenly like a blizzard. The wind whipped into his face. He bent his head, skating into the wind, but the skates meant he was too easily moved; he kept being blown backward. In ten minutes, he gained perhaps two hundred yards. He stopped to rest. At this speed, the car – eight miles away – would take hours to reach.

He would have to zigzag, skating at a diagonal to the wind. Bowing again, he made for the river's south shore. The wind hit him now at an oblique angle, and he was able to move – not freely, but with less of a struggle. When the ice became dark underneath him, he turned and skated for a point northwest on the north shore. Because he was skating perpendicular to his direction, he was not progressing quickly, but at least he wasn't exhausting himself.

With less exertion, though, the sweat on his body began to cool. He'd dressed warmly for a brisk skate, but the layers – long underwear, sweater, long wool overcoat, two pairs of cotton socks – weren't enough in this kind of snow. Worse, his vision was narrowing, becoming rainbowed: his eyes were watering in the wind, freezing his eyelashes together.

Scared, he put his gloved hand over his right eye, pressing as hard as he could. The vision in his other eye was slowly darkening, like a movie fade-out. When he could see nothing, he lifted his hand away from the right eye. The ice had melted; he could see. He felt a flare of gratitude that pushed back his growing panic. He moved his hand to the other eye. By the time vision shrank in his right eye again, his left eyelashes had thawed.

His fingers in their glove were stiffening with cold. Switching hands, he put the right one under his clothes, into his left armpit. He wouldn't make the eight miles to the car, not at this speed; already his legs shook with strain. He could actually die out here.

In a little ways – a mile? – he'd reach Applefield. The general store wasn't far from the river. He began talking to himself. For some reason, he was saying *we*. *There, we're almost to shore. Now, turn around. Good. We're going to aim for the elm.* He sang bits of symphonies. At Applefield, he'd have to take off his skates, climb a small hill in his socks.

He went around a bend and the wind abated. He could skate more directly now, and he repeated this fact aloud to himself: *We're in good shape now. Another half mile. Another three-eighths.* Saying this helped him block out the fact that, when he'd come around the bend, he'd expected to see a red boathouse near the bank. Was that the next bend? Or was he picturing something in Lightstone, not Applefield at all? It had shingles, a wide metal door, a sagging dock. He could see it so clearly that as he came around the next bend, he actually did see it for a second, shimmering like a sunspot.

He tried to push up the sleeve of his coat to check his watch, but his hands were too clumsy. He didn't know how long he'd been skating. If he missed Applefield there wasn't another town for two

319

miles. On the other hand, if he stopped too early, still in parkland, there wasn't even the chance of a stray house. When he came around the next bend he would try hiking inland. He must have gone far enough.

A dark tree overhung the river. Avoiding spots of weak ice at the river's edge, he skated to shore. His body trembled from having pushed against the wind. He took a step on land, then fell. Too stiff with cold to push himself up, he rolled clumsily onto his back, then clutched at the branches of a scrubby bush, pulling himself up. Snow began to seep through the seat of his wool pants. He reached for the skate laces and found that they'd frozen.

He felt he would cry – with bewilderment, like a child.

He was very tired. It felt good to be sitting down. He closed his eyes.

And saw his family coming toward him. Jordana was there, her hair long and wild. Next to her, the children, barely to her hip, Luke's hair golden-brown and Angie's white-blond. The children were in bathing suits. He had wasted his life.

His wife saw him. Her face lit up in a smile. He raised his hand to her.

She said, We need to take off your glove.

Opening his eyes, he pulled it off reluctantly with his teeth. The fingers were white and noncompliant; he forced them to bend, pulling at the knot. At last the lace snapped. He stared at it dumbly for a moment before realizing he could pull the skate off. He broke the second knot as well and shimmied his other foot free.

His socks soaked through almost as soon as he stood. Sliding backward with each step, he struggled up the hill. Out loud, Pieter said, 'The pellet with the poison's in the vessel with the pestle, the chalice from the palace has the brew that is true.' His throat was raw, from cold and from talking to himself.

The snow's crust crackled beneath his feet. Another step and sliding back, another step and he stood on the spine of the small ridge. Two hundred yards to his left was the general store.

He shouted with triumph. His feet were so numb that he felt as though he were skating over the surface of the snow as he made his way down the bank and along the road. Clutching the rail, he clumped up the store's steps and across the porch.

As he stumbled through the door, the warmth of the room pushed against him like a hand. There was a ringing in his ears.

320

At the Formica tables, clustered near the roaring woodstove, a mixture of locals and New Yorkers drank coffee from paper cups and read the paper. A woman – an out-of-towner, with glossy gold jewelry and a beige turtleneck sweater – glanced up at Pieter as he stood on the threshold, and so it was to her he spoke.

'Something happened,' he said.

He was guided to a chair by the stove, given a mug of coffee, his wet socks stripped away for two pairs of wool socks that customers took off their own feet. He shook so violently he could hardly hold on to the coats they'd wrapped around him.

He'd been in here dozens of times without exchanging more than basic pleasantries with Laura, who ran the store. Now she pulled two pairs of mittens from the shelf, breaking off their tags with her teeth, and fit them over Pieter's stiff hands. One of the out-of-towners was a doctor; she looked at his hands and feet and said she didn't think he needed to go to the ER. 'You have hypothermia,' she said. 'Possibly mild frostbite. You need to get warm.'

'Look at this.' One of the telephone repairmen who'd given up his socks walked over, lifting his foot with his hand and hopping the last steps. His two smallest toes were glassy black, like obsidian. He showed the foot to Pieter first – as though he were the guest of honor – and then turned so that others could bend over, murmuring.

'Grouse hunting,' said the repairman. 'Crouching down in the snow. Eighteen years old, so drunk I didn't know I was cold.'

The doctor told a story about unwrapping a frostbite patient's bandages and seeing the dead tissue creep. 'Maggots. A fly found its way into the dressing to lay eggs.' She leaned forward to take a bite from her croissant. 'Maggots only eat dead flesh. It's actually better than surgery.'

Pieter was shaking too much to drink from his mug, though its warmth felt good. 'Here,' said the doctor, and took the cup from him and held it to his mouth.

People still stood loosely around him, not ready to return to their tables. He told them, 'I skate that way almost every day. I couldn't even feel the wind until I turned around.' He floated an inch above the chair.

The bell tinkled as the door opened, bringing in a momentary gust of cold and two teenage girls, who stood stomping snow off their boots. 'It's *cold* out there,' they called to Laura. Beautiful girls, in their parkas and boots and eyeliner, long hair stringy with damp, water droplets sparkling on the crowns of their heads.

The doctor tipped the cup to Pieter's lips again. He remembered feeding Beatrice de Groot on the ship. The coffee burned as it went down, at once painful and comforting. Through the window, the school buses in the lot across the street were white humps, obscured by snow. It felt good to be wrapped in coats, surrounded by people. For once his life didn't seem right or wrong, only true – like a high note, or the aim of a blow.

The girls were buying cocoa mix and a bag of marshmallows. Laura took their money but stayed on the wrong side of the counter, leaning back to thump the keys of the register and scoop out change.

'See that guy?' she asked.

The girls turned their lovely, incurious gaze on him. Laura said, 'He could of died out there.'

Chapter Forty-Four

Angie waited for her paycheck at work but didn't give notice. She didn't tell her parents she was leaving, or her housemates, or even Luke. It took less than an hour to pack her things and carry them to the Galaxie. Other than a few pieces of furniture, which she'd have to come back for sometime, she didn't own much.

During psych evals, after you counted backward from one hundred by sevens or whatever, they asked you to explain an aphorism, to prove you could understand abstract thought. One of the aphorisms she'd been given was *a rolling stone gathers no moss*. In other evaluations, she'd been given other aphorisms and had done okay with them – *glass houses* and *a stitch in time* – but she'd never been sure if moss was a good thing you lost by moving or a bad thing you avoided. Good or bad, the moss she'd gathered in twenty-five years barely filled half the backseat. Most of the things she'd once valued in her life she'd lost, or left behind, or destroyed, or given away. She had some clothes, a few recent photos, her Walkman. She had the two books she'd carried around for years – the Dickens novel and the mystery with the wedding cake and toppled plastic groom – waiting for the time her brain slowed and she could read again. She still wore the ring Abe had bought her when she visited Harvard, with its narrow hopeful band of blue-green stone set into the silver.

She and Abe talked occasionally. One odd residue of their relationship had been that, after the night Evan Johansson found Angie by the Charles River, he and Abe had become close. They'd ended up rooming together all four years and had both moved to New York after graduation. Abe worked at a brokerage company and dated a woman who worked at a different brokerage company; he said he was happy. Angie knew he couldn't have admitted it if he wasn't happy, and that comforted the part of her that hoped he felt the same nagging regret she did. She didn't know how much of her nostalgia for him was really nostalgia for being eighteen, when more things had seemed possible to her than they did now.

It was past midnight, shatteringly cold. Back inside the house, she wrote out a rent check: a lot of her money, but she needed to get out as cleanly as possible. Besides, she'd come back for her furniture once she had a place, so she couldn't leave her house-mates too pissed off.

They slept in the house around her. She scrambled two eggs and tipped them into a plastic bag, which immediately fogged with steam. Carefully, she washed the frying pan and set it in the rack to dry. With the rent check, she left a note against the sugar bowl as eloping daughters did in forties movies, the kind she'd watched on wards because they couldn't see anything that might be *disturbing*.

The girl, a small suitcase in one hand, stands with the other hand on the doorknob, looking over her shoulder. From the curb, the young man calls, 'Are you coming?' The girl blinks back tears. She runs a hand over the surface of the table. Pushing her voice into cheer, she calls, 'Yes, I'm ready.' Then, softly to herself, 'I'm ready.' Music swells. She walks out the door.

Angie smiled. There was nothing dramatic in her leaving, no one watching, no one waiting for her in California. If she could like herself enough to be amused, maybe she'd be okay. She might even one day come to love herself, the way people did in arranged marriages.

Outside, the motel sign blinked: WELCOME VACANCY. WELCOME VACANCY. WELCOME VACANCY. The air was so brittle with cold it felt breakable. She crossed the street and very slowly lifted the hook of the gate, opening it a few inches. She whistled softly, holding out a piece of scrambled egg.

'Gibson,' she whispered. 'Come on.'

The dog came toward her tentatively, dancing backward once before eating the eggs from her hands. Moving slowly, she reached out, unlatching the chain from his collar. The house lights were on, but she didn't see movement. She breathed in deeply, then put her arm behind his back legs and lifted.

He panicked in her grasp, twisting and whining. He nipped her upper arm before she managed to get her hand around his muzzle. Eyes wide with fear, he bucked and strained. Holding him tightly to her chest, duck-legged with effort, she staggered across the street to the car. The dog writhed in her arms, heavier than she'd expected; she feared she would drop him.

'It's okay,' she muttered into his fur. 'Everything's going to be fine.'

Part Four

Chapter Forty-Five

Behind the house where Jordana lived listed a tiny shed, its wood gone silver with age. Saturday morning, she wrestled the lawn mower out from the tangle of objects cluttering the dirt floor, croquet mallets and oil cans, a hand-painted sign advertising a garage sale, an ax handle without a head, a collapse of knotted yellow rope. The shed's corners were hung with cobwebs dense as the layers of a wedding veil.

The mower itself was relatively new. When she'd managed to pull it out into the yard, she checked the gas. One lever on the handle seemed to be for accelerating, another for adjusting the blade's height. She placed one foot on the casing, as she'd seen Pieter do, and yanked the starter cord. The motor caught on the second try, coughing a few times before settling into a low rumble.

She needed to occupy herself. Angie was flying in this morning from California, but Jordana wouldn't see her until late afternoon. Angie would stay the weekend, then drive a U-Haul truck back to California with the rest of her things. It had been four months now that she'd been out there. The first few weeks she'd been vague and cagey about what she was doing – she'd said she was staying with a friend, but the friend didn't have a landline, only a cell phone, so Angie couldn't be reached.

Jordana said, 'You're not sleeping in your car, are you?'

'Mom, I *told* you. She just doesn't have a phone.'

Angie sounded okay when she called, steady. She was talking to Luke more often, and Jordana trusted him to act if Angie was really in trouble. And then she'd found a job – in the benefits office at a community college in Oakland – and an apartment, also in Oakland.

Jordana wouldn't mow the whole property, only the quarter acre or so nearest the house. At the small pond, she edged as close as she could, then backed up, dragging the heavy machine, turned cumbrously, and made a rough circle around the water. When she finished the circuit a knee-high fringe remained, pleasantly feral, spiked here and there with tall blue cornflowers.

She wore an old tank top and cut-offs, April sun heating her shoulders and the backs of her legs. The grass threw out its deep green smell: part wood, part lemon, part sweet rot. It sometimes seemed to her that she'd lived her life backward. If only she and Pieter had found each other *after* she'd gone to college, lived alone, had lovers and jobs.

Fruitless to think of it now. Instead she focused on the warmth of the sun, the satisfying ache in her muscles as she pushed the mower up a small hill. Damp swatches of grass clung to her legs and forearms.

The mower lurched slightly. Glancing back to see if she'd hit a rock or stick, she saw a family of bunnies nibbling grass. They were pale brown, the size of her fist. She stopped and, moving carefully, reached to turn off the mower. The noise of the yard became audible again: insects, rustling breeze, leaves clicking overhead. Occasionally, without alarm, a rabbit glanced up at her and then bent its head again to the grass.

As slowly as she could, Jordana lowered herself into a squat. The rabbits were so close she could have reached out and stroked one. They nibbled, glancing up at her every so often. After a minute, legs already aching, she stood up again. As she gingerly shook out her leg she saw a sixth rabbit a little distance from the others. It was lying on its side, panting in fast, shallow breaths. Its legs paddled as though at swim.

Jordana took a step forward, then covered her mouth. Bits of soft gray, like shredded eraser, were scattered on the ground. A clump of bloody fur clung to a stalk of grass.

She ran to the edge of the driveway to find a rock. She expected the rabbits to scatter as she came back toward them but they didn't. She knelt by the injured animal. The back of its skull had been sheared away by the lawnmower's blade. Oh, God. Oh, God. With both hands, she raised the rock. She closed her eyes and brought the rock down hard, jerking to a stop somewhere before the rabbit's head.

She couldn't do it.

Breathing in deeply she raised the rock again, the insides of her elbows watery. She blew out her breath and crushed the rabbit's skull. A crackling noise, like fire. Its back legs jerked. Faintly, through the heated air, she could hear the buzz of a small plane overhead. Twice more she hammered the stone against the rabbit's head. Its siblings watched her, curious.

She got unsteadily to her feet. 'Get out of here! Get out!' She shook her arms and the bunnies leapt up, flashing into the tall grass.

At the house, she didn't know whether to ring the doorbell. It felt presumptuous to let herself in and ridiculous not to. Finally, she knocked on the doorframe, which seemed less formal than ringing the bell. The hallway was dark. She knocked again, then started to push open the door for herself just as the kitchen door opened. Quickly she pulled the door shut and waited to be let in.

It was Pieter, wiping his hands on a dish towel. 'Wasn't it open?'

She shook her head, shrugging. 'I don't know.'

Neither of them knew what to do. They saw each other sometimes, meeting at Papa Toby's to deal with bills or running into each other at the Igga, but this was the first time she'd seen him here at home.

Not *home*, she reminded herself.

She took a step forward to hug him, then stopped. Pieter still had his hands in the dish towel. She ended up patting his arm, above the elbow. An awkward silence – not quite silence, because Pieter was doing his nervous back-of-the-throat humming.

'Well,' he said. 'We're in the kitchen.'

She followed him, feeling meek. The first times they'd met at the diner he'd been angry and silent, refusing to order anything, giving one-word answers to her questions and then standing to say, 'Are we done here?' Then, sometime midwinter, without explanation, his hostility had suddenly slackened.

She expected Angie and Luke to be doing their usual thing, teasing and poking at each other, but when she came into the kitchen, she found Luke sitting at the table, Angie hovering in the center of the room. Wendy sliced red peppers at the counter, knife rocking neatly against the cutting board.

Jordana rushed to embrace Angie. She hadn't expected to feel overwhelmed in this way. She took a step back to look at Angie,

who wore a man's yellow oxford shirt untucked over paint-splattered jeans that were tight around her hips. She looked solid,
capable. Her shoulder-length hair had brightened, the way it used
to in summer, to the color of buttercups. 'Oh!' Jordana said, and
hugged her again, and Angie laughed and said, '*Mom.*'

'You look wonderful. Doesn't she look wonderful?'

She expected Luke to say something half mocking like *She's
ravishing, as always*, but it was Wendy who said, 'You do. You
look great.'

Angie smiled and rolled her eyes.

Pieter hadn't come all the way into the room but hung back,
leaning against the doorframe. Wendy gathered pepper scraps
between her hand and the knife blade, moving quickly to the trash
can to dump them in. Strange, seeing Wendy so comfortable in this
kitchen. But she'd lived here more than eight months.

Angie opened the fridge. 'Wendy fixed the thermostat,' she told
Jordana, pulling out a green apple and biting into it. 'Want one?
They're not frozen.'

'Aren't you going to wash that?' Luke asked.

Angie spun to face him. 'Why are you so on my back?'

'I just asked if you were going to wash it.'

'"Is that really all your luggage?" "Isn't it time for your meds?"
You've been on me ever since I got in.'

'Kids—' said Pieter.

'You always' – Angie wheeled around – 'you *always* want no
one to be mad. It's not a crime to be upset.'

'Leave him alone,' said Luke.

Stiffly, Pieter said, 'I don't need you to defend me, Luke.'

There was a silence, then Jordana said, 'I forgot the wine in the
car.'

She glanced at Pieter, giving the merest tilt of her head, and he
said, 'I'll help you carry it.'

Out in the driveway, she asked, 'What is going on with them?'

Pieter shook his head. 'It's been like this all day.'

'Christ.' She opened the driver's side and stretched across the
seats to pull out the wine, which she'd jammed down against the
opposite door. The day's warmth had drained away into cold lavender dusk. She handed the bottle to him. There was more to say,
but she couldn't think what, and the moment passed.

*

Wendy and Pieter had cooked chicken with peppers and onions. There were loaves of French bread, a salad. Jordana started to get up for butter, pausing halfway out of her seat when she realized the awkwardness of opening the refrigerator that was no longer hers. She sat partway down again, then stood. 'I'll get butter?' she said, and waited for Pieter's nod.

Wendy was already out of her seat. 'I'll get it.' She took the butter dish from the fridge and put it in front of Jordana. 'There you go.'

Angie told stories about her apartment hunt. 'San Francisco was so crazy. I went to this one open house – kind of a bad neighborhood, just a studio. The whole thing was, like, as big as this room. And people are showing up with the first year's rent in cash. This one couple had a résumé for their cat.'

'But you found something,' Jordana prompted. The thought of Angie without a place to live made her throat tight.

'Oakland's much easier. And especially with a dog.' Angie looked toward Luke. Normally, their banter would have filled the spaces. He concentrated on his plate, eating with one hand, the other hand holding Wendy's under the table. Angie hadn't once mentioned the friend she'd supposedly stayed with before finding a place; she must have lived in her car after all.

To break the silence, Jordana blurted the first thing that came to her. 'I did something awful today.' She told them about the rabbit.

'My God, Mom.' Angie put down her fork.

Pieter asked, 'Did you bury it?'

She shook her head. It hadn't occurred to her.

'I'll do it with you,' he said. 'If that would help.'

She shook her head. 'That's okay.' Why had she told that story, which made her look incompetent and cruel? She reached for the salad and busied herself with the tongs.

'So on that cheerful note—' Luke said.

Wendy broke in. 'Maybe later, Luke.' The two of them looked at each other.

Angie covered her lips with her hand. 'Oh, my God. You're getting married.'

Jordana's heart jumped unpleasantly. 'You're getting married?'

'Actually . . .' Wendy was blushing a deep red.

Luke put his arm around her shoulders and said, 'We got married. Last week. At City Hall.'

'Wow.' Angie looked stricken. 'Congratulations. I mean . . . well, just congratulations.'

Automatically, Jordana had started to reach for her husband's hand. Remembering, she pulled back.

Pieter went around the table to hug Wendy. He said, 'I think we have some champagne in the cellar. Just a moment.'

'Why didn't you tell us?' Jordana asked, as his steps receded down the basement steps. She tried to keep her voice light.

'We wanted it to just be us,' said Luke.

Angie seemed near tears. Feeling Jordana's gaze, she said, 'I'm fine, I'm fine, I'm just surprised.'

Pieter held a bottle of champagne by the bottom as he came back into the room. 'It's not chilled, but the basement's pretty cold.' He found glasses, tore off the foil.

Angie shoved back from the table and picked up a glass, holding it out toward Pieter.

'You're drinking now?' asked Luke.

'God, lay *off.*' Angie flushed. 'I'm behaving like a normal person. It's like you *want* me to be crazy.'

After dinner, Pieter said he'd found an old reel of film they'd taken.

'That's so TV,' Angie said, and, when they looked at her blankly, 'That's always in TV dramas. You know, a scratchy home movie of happier times.'

'We're happy,' Jordana said.

She and Pieter had only recorded part of one reel of film – a few minutes at most, if she remembered right, but it was good to have the distraction of figuring out how to set up the projector. They flipped switches until they found the right ones, and on the living room wall suddenly there Pieter was outside against the back of the house, tall and boyish in a way she'd never thought of him before; he'd always been so much older than she was. He crouched down as baby Luke – naked except for a diaper, his brow powerful even then – staggered toward him. Angie ran into the frame and stopped, legs planted wide, until Jordana appeared and swooped her up.

Several seconds of darkness and then a slightly older Angie leaned toward a lit cake. Pieter reached out to catch her hair back, holding it out of the way of the candles.

'God, look how little I am,' Angie said.

The old projector hummed and clicked. Onscreen, there was jiggling, a ragged swoop toward the ceiling, as Jordana handed Pieter the camera without remembering to turn it off. Then back to the party, children spooning up ice cream with wooden paddles from small paper cups.

Jordana's hands ached; she realized she'd been clenching them. She massaged one with the other. Now Angie, about nine, stood on the concrete apron of the pool. She used both hands to smooth her hair into a ponytail, pulling a rubber band from her wrist with her teeth. When she looked toward the person filming, she waved. Then, still waving, raised her eyebrows, signaling *enough already*.

The starter must have told the swimmers to take their marks, because the line of little girls quieted and bent forward, toward an invisible water. They dove, and the camera followed the twenty-five meters of butterfly. Even then, in Angie's awkward, galloping stroke, you could see the sureness underlying it. She touched the opposite wall with both hands, looked around, and saw she'd won.

The screen went black and stayed black.

'We didn't film much,' Jordana said. 'We don't have a lot of pictures, either.'

Wendy moved to the projector. She turned the knob to *stop* and then to *reverse*. Onscreen, the girls swam backwards, wake disappearing behind them. Angie was absorbed back into the group. Together, they sprang backward onto the blocks, the churning water gone magically still. Children took pieces of cake out of their mouths; Angie blew her candles alight. Jordana and Pieter kissed, then Jordana said something, put Angie down and walked out of the shot – rather she hadn't yet walked into it. Luke in his diaper was staggering back, his grin dissolving into furious concentration, and only Pieter remained, talking to an invisible Jordana, his hands gesturing elegantly. He turned and walked backward toward the camera. He became larger, enormous, filling the whole screen, and then he disappeared and only the back of the house was left, brick and stone.

Jordana hadn't eaten much, and when she got back to her house, she put water on to boil in the kitchen. Cream of Wheat with sliced bananas and heavy cream was one of her favorite dinners. Now that she no longer had to accommodate Pieter and his insistence on 'real meals,' she usually ate on the porch swing, sometimes with a book or the radio for company, sometimes just looking out across the fields.

She was upset, somewhere inside herself, upset by the strangeness of the whole night, but she couldn't close her fingers on what she felt. Maybe it was because she'd cried already today, after killing the rabbit: she'd sat next to the lawn mower and wept, stopping when she couldn't breathe, wiping her face and nose with the flats of her hands. She'd cried without thinking about anything. Crying had just felt necessary, the way it felt necessary to throw up when she was sick. It had left her feeling scoured out, limp, weirdly virtuous.

With the Cream of Wheat and a glass of red wine, she made her way to the front door, pausing there and moving the wineglass to the crook of her other arm so she could flip on the porch light.

'Hello.'

She startled; there was a man sitting in the old wooden porch swing. The light from inside the window reflected off his pale hair. For a long second, she didn't even think his name. 'What are you doing here?'

'I don't know,' Pieter said. 'I wanted to see you.'

'You made me spill my wine.' She heard how childish she sounded. 'Did you follow me?'

He shook his head. His pant cuff had ridden up, showing a pale swath of shin. Behind him, across the road, a nearly full moon was rising between the tines of the trees. She drank more wine. Pieter used his foot to gently rock the porch swing.

'So, married,' she said. 'I can't believe he didn't at least tell Angie.'

'Maybe it's good. I mean, getting married. They seem good for each other.'

'Maybe.' She didn't want to argue.

A silence. Pieter looked out over the yard. 'This is a nice place.'

They had filled hours, years, with talk. Even when things had been bad between them, she'd never felt they weren't talking because they had nothing to say. But everything she could think of now seemed too minute or too huge.

Pieter's long, slender hands rested on his knee. She stood and walked to the porch rail. It was too disquieting, those hands that had touched her so many times. It wasn't even sex that seemed

336

most impossible and intimate to her now, but the touch of his hand on her shoulder as he pointed out something through the car window, or his fingers unthreading an earring from her earlobe.

A sharp breeze rifled through the grass. Pieter crossed his arms across his chest. 'You're cold,' she said. 'Let me get you something.'

'I'm fine.'

'I'll get a sweater or something.' Glad to have something to do, she put down her glass and went into the house. Upstairs, she grabbed the largest things she could find: a sweatshirt from a clinic fund-raiser (it said NEVER AGAIN under a picture of a wire hanger), a wool hat that had once been Luke's, a pilled red sweater, the letter jacket had been Angie's. Halfway down the stairs, she remembered the sweater had belonged to Ben. Like the hat and letter jacket, she'd had it so long she just thought of it as hers. Furtively, she put her nose to the sweater's shoulder but smelled only her own detergent.

As she held out her offerings, she realized she didn't expect Pieter to accept any of them. He reached out for the jacket, though, awkwardly poking his arms back through the sleeves. 'I'll help you with the rabbit,' he said.

She led the way to where she'd left the lawn mower. The rabbit wasn't where she'd thought. Pieter went to get a flashlight from his car, jogging down the lawn. Returning, he began to make increasing circles around the mower. She wanted to grab the flashlight from his hands – she hated following – but swallowed her irritation.

'Are you sure it was around here?'

'Of course I'm sure.'

He shrugged, which made the beam of light bob. 'Something must have carried it off. A hawk?'

Taking the light from him, she trained it on the spot she thought she'd left the body. No smear of blood or wisp of fur. There wasn't even a depression in the grass to show where it had been.

She clicked the flashlight off and the fields leapt back in focus. Clouds scudded across the moon. The hair on her arm prickled with the closeness of Pieter's body. For the first time she understood that she would never kiss him again. Never put her palm flat against his stomach, never lie pressed against his naked back, never watch his familiar, beautiful face wrench, as though with pain, when he came.

She could take it all back. She could turn to him, as she had years ago in her father's study, and put her arms around his neck.

Taking a step away, she said, 'I'll walk you to your car.'

If he noticed the tremor in her voice, he didn't comment. They walked in silence down the long driveway. The moon cast its unsteady blue light across their path.

They reached Pieter's old Volvo. 'Well.' He reached out and took her hand. He turned it over, looking at the palm, and then let go.

Opening the car door, he bent to fit his long body behind the wheel and shut the door. He rolled down the window.

'Twenty-six years,' he said. 'You'd think . . .'

'I know. I—'

'Don't tell me.'

'It's nothing bad.'

He shrugged, smiling crookedly. 'Still. I'd rather not know.'

He could still do it, make her feel messy and immature. She wrapped her arms around herself.

He started the car and turned it around. When he reached the foot of the driveway, she thought he would do something – honk, put his arm out the still-open window and wave. But he just pulled into the road and drove away.

She remembered standing next to him in their bathroom, wrapped in towels, waiting for the shower to get warm. Pieter knew the second the temperature changed: there was a change in pitch. He'd tried to show her, humming the two tones. 'You can't hear it?' he asked. 'You really can't hear it?'

She stood there for a long time after his taillights disappeared, so long she forgot where she was. When she finally turned, she was surprised not to see their old brick house but the small one, her own. Its lights shone across the dark grass.

Chapter Forty-Six

Luke followed the U-Haul in his car. It was six in the morning, still dark out, and for a moment he thought of driving with Angie to swim team practice one morning before she got sick. Angie had quizzed him for a biology test; she balanced his study sheet on the steering wheel, glancing between it and the road.

At the house where she used to live, Angie parked – the truck continued to shudder for a minute after the engine was off – and climbed down. Silver clouds of their breath rose in the cold air.

'Do they know you're coming?' he asked.

'No, I'm an idiot. I thought I'd surprise them.'

'I'm just asking.'

She sighed. 'They know. They'll be asleep anyway.'

He shrugged, looking away from her and up at the house. On the porch, three or four bikes leaned together; behind them sagged a water-stained beige armchair.

Angie unlocked the front door and they walked quietly upstairs. He followed her down the long dark hallway, up two small steps, and into her old room.

'They haven't rented it out,' he observed.

'Obviously.'

'You don't have to be a bitch.' They'd come for her iron bedstead, the big wooden table she used as a desk, and her couch – Victorian, covered in olive green velvet, with lion-claw feet. 'I don't understand why you need this stuff.'

'God, Luke! Would you just stop?'

He shrugged, stiffly. Talking as little as possible, they disassembled the bedframe and lifted the headboard between them. As he backed out into the hallway, headboard awkwardly clasped between his arms, a girl in a pink kimono came out of one of the bedrooms. Isobel, her brown hair knitted with sleep.

'We're here for my stuff,' said Angie.

Isobel yawned, raising her arm and curling it over her head to pull her hair behind her ear. Her breasts pressed against the kimono silk. She looked at Luke. 'Who are you?'

They'd met several times. He said, 'I'm Angie's brother.'

'Hi, Angie's brother.' She yawned again, this time fighting it, keeping her mouth closed. Her eyes narrowed and the wings of her nostrils trembled. Raking her hand through her hair again, she turned away, groping sleepily for the doorknob of her room.

'God, she hates me,' Angie said, when the door closed behind Isobel.

'Why do you let her get to you?'

She just shook her head, not looking at him.

The U-Haul was parked behind the house so they used the back staircase. They stowed the headboard in the truck and came back for the rails. Then they carried down the wood table. The couch wasn't big but it was surprisingly heavy: Luke hefted his end then staggered back a few steps. 'Jesus.'

They backed and feinted to maneuver the couch into the hallway. Velvet on the arms had worn away in patches, and the bald fabric glimmered. 'They don't have a Salvation Army in Oakland?'

'This is *mine,* though.'

Luke felt carefully behind him for each step. The weight of the couch made his arms shake; his face flushed. The couch had big springs underneath, hard to grip. Halfway down, where the narrow staircase turned, they got stuck.

'Back up!' The couch pressed against Luke's breastbone; he couldn't breathe all the way in. 'Back up!'

Angie took hold of the legs and yanked, taking a step up. The pressure eased from Luke's chest. They struggled the couch onto its back. He went down a step, then was jerked as the sofa leg caught the wall, ripping a stuttering gash in the paper.

'*Shit,*' said Angie.

'We're not going to get this down.'

'They got it up. Bradley and Jason.'

'Maybe it's different going backward.'

His sister's forehead, sheened with sweat, shone dully in the dim hall light. Her hair was slipping out of its ponytail. 'How could it be different? Going backward?'

'Parallel parking is different going backward.'

She stuck out her lower lip to blow hair out of her eyes. 'Listen,' she said. 'I'll take a step up and we can roll it onto its side.'

'Ange, it's not going to go.'

'Why won't you even try?'

'It's not going to go! How many ways can I say it? It's not going to go!'

She shook her head, not looking at him.

Trying to speak more gently, he said, 'We have to take it back up. We can try the front stairs.'

Angie didn't say anything, head turned, looking at the wall. Finally, still not looking at him, she nodded.

He pushed and she pulled. The couch didn't budge. Luke crouched to set his shoulder against the arm, throwing his weight against it, but the sofa was wedged between the two walls.

Angie crawled awkwardly under the couch, emerging with the crown of her hair standing up. They both wrenched at it together. Nothing. He kept his arm from touching hers.

It was Angie who finally straightened and said, 'Just leave it.'

'*Leave* it?'

She turned and started down the stairs. After a minute, he let go of the couch – even though he knew it was jammed, he let go carefully, half expecting the thing to come crashing down – and followed.

A thin sleeve of light was beginning to line the yard. They tromped across the frosty grass to where the back of the U-Haul stood open and mostly empty. Besides the two pieces of furniture, Angie had about a half-dozen boxes of things she'd packed up from her old room.

'It's hardly worth it,' Angie said.

It had been completely not worth it, but his anger was slipping away, out of reach.

Angie said, 'Everything . . .'

He waited for her to finish the sentence, but that was all. Reaching over tentatively, he smoothed down her hair, still standing up from when she'd crawled under the couch.

'Cobwebs?' she asked.

'Just static.' His fingers brushed against sticky threads. 'No, cobwebs.'

His sister bowed her head under his hand. Her crooked part shone white. From her hair he slid a small ball of silk: not cobwebs but the delicate egg sac of a spider. He showed it to her on the tip of his finger, tiny black dots stirring in the center of the gauzy thread.

Next to them was an ancient swing set, its sky-blue metal freckled with rust. Gently, he pulled his finger along the side rail until the sac stuck. Angie shut the back door of the U-Haul and shot the bolt. 'God. You're married. My baby brother.'

'Yeah.' He didn't know why he hadn't told her before they married; somehow it had seemed cleaner this way.

She kicked a tire. 'Why do people kick tires anyway?' She kicked it again. 'I can't believe we fought so much. I ruined the whole weekend.'

'No, it was still nice.' She looked at him and he amended, 'Okay. Not so nice.'

'I wish we could do it over.'

There was nothing to say to that. Angie toyed with her keys.

'Can you imagine when they find it?' she asked. 'The couch?'

He began laughing. 'Maybe they'll get used to just ducking underneath it whenever they go up or down.'

'Or maybe they'll use it. They'll move the TV onto the landing.'

He heard himself whoop with laughter, something that only happened with Angie. 'Can you see them, all lined up on the couch?'

'Isobel—' She was laughing too hard to get the words out. She tried again: 'Isobel—'

'I have to say, I don't think this is going to improve her feelings toward you.'

They were laughing so hard his stomach ached. Angie leaned against the U-Haul.

Finally they wore down to an occasional giggle. He looked at her. 'Don't go. Stay here.'

'I can't. I just . . . I can't.'

They didn't hug. He reached for her hand, clasping it, then bringing it to his lips. She smiled. Pulling herself up into the cab of the truck, she started the engine. He took a step back. Foot still on the brake, she put the U-Haul in gear, then rolled down the window. 'Luke?'

'Yeah?'

'You're my best friend,' she said. 'You're really my only friend.'

He nodded, throat closing. He'd always thought of *heartache* as just a term but now he felt it: an ache in his chest.

He followed her for a few blocks in his car. Each time she turned a corner, the U-Haul listed and then swayed, righting itself. There was a sign for Route 91. She went right and he stayed straight. The truck curved up, around the entrance ramp. Glancing over his shoulder, Luke could still see the orange of the truck, could still see it, still see it – and then it was gone.

His breath made a silvery cloud in the air of the car. He turned onto Route 121, passing the old vinyl banner – GUYS: GIRLS DIG CLEAN CARS! – of the detailing place. He saw, for an instant, Isobel, back arched as she yawned, nipples pressing against the fabric of her robe. It might be awhile before they even discovered the couch. Or they might have found it already. He imagined them looking down at the sofa, wedged against the walls so that it floated three feet above the stairs, and began to laugh again. He pulled over to the side of the road and put his head against the steering wheel, laughing until he could barely breathe.

He stayed like that, head against the wheel. His face was wet.

For as long as he could remember he'd wanted Angie to get better. And when he'd driven Wendy away, the only other thing he'd wanted was to have Wendy back. Now Angie was making a life for herself, and he'd married Wendy. He'd had those two desires for so long that, without them, he didn't know who he was.

Blowing out a hard breath, he shifted the car into first and pulled back onto the road.

He felt half outside himself. The feeling persisted as he passed his mother's clinic, then the car dealerships and the Hard Times Café. Here and there on the ground were patches of old snow, bruised green with shadows. He turned onto the familiar streets that narrowed and narrowed to his house.

As he walked up the lawn, he could see his father in the kitchen, lifting the kettle. Wendy came to an upstairs window. Her presence startled him, something so clearly in the present and not the past. She was watching for his return. She wore a white nightgown, and her hair, not yet brushed and tied back, tumbled around her face. She raised her hand. He started to raise his own in response, then realized she couldn't see him. She wasn't waving

343

but putting her hand to the glass, shielding her eyes to look out.

He stood motionless under the oak, trying to see his house as a stranger might: solid and unremarkable, small squares of light where a man and a woman separately began the day. He wanted to hold on to the feeling of suspension; there was something he almost understood, seeing his life from outside like this. The neighbor's sprinkler whirred; *The White Mountain Times* lay in its yellow plastic wrapper in the driveway.

In a moment, he would make himself move. He would walk up and unlock the door, and daily life would reclaim him. The smell of toast, the radio playing classical music. He would step into the front hall. Close the door behind him. From the bedroom he'd had since childhood, Wendy would call down, *Luke? Is that you?*

Acknowledgments

I am incredibly grateful to the Wallace Stegner program at Stanford University, and to my teachers Elizabeth Tallent, Tobias Wolff, and John L'Heureux. Thanks also to Elizabeth Evans, the Creative Writing program at the University of Arizona, the Rona Jaffe Foundation, the Barbara Deming Memorial Fund, Kim Witherspoon, Eleanor Jackson, and my wonderful editor, Elisabeth Schmitz.

Molly Breen, Judy Breen, Julie Orringer, Malena Watrous, Angela Pneuman, Lysley Tenorio, Tamara Guirado, Otis Haschemeyer, Jack Livings, ZZ Packer, Adam Johnson, Ed Schwarzchild, Tom Kealey, and Tom McNeely read versions of this novel and provided astute criticism and encouragement. I want also to thank Gould Farm, where I had the luck and privilege of working and living for two years.

Thanks to my parents, Margaret Wilkins Noel and Gordon Noel, for their unflagging love and support, and my amazing sisters, Margaret Lea Noel and Jennifer Noel, who read drafts of the novel and were there for me through every step. And thanks most of all to Eric Puchner, first and last reader, love of my life.